Men in Books Aren't Better

by

Amanda Nelson
Lisa-Marie Potter

Plus One Series

Men in Books Aren't Better

Contact Information: info@thewildrosepress.com

Cover Art by *The Wild Rose Press, Inc.*

The Wild Rose Press, Inc.
PO Box 708
Adams Basin, NY 14410-0708
Visit us at www.thewildrosepress.com

Publishing History
First Edition, 2024
Trade Paperback ISBN 978-1-5092-5878-9
Digital ISBN 978-1-5092-5879-6

Plus One Series
Published in the United States of America

Dedication

To the Screaming Peens, without whose help and encouragement this book may not have been possible; and to Nicole Payne, for believing in us when no one else did.

Enjoy your new book boyfriend!

Praise for Amanda and Lisa-Marie

"Love the build between Molly and Jared."
~MN Bennet, YA and adult LGBTQ+ paranormal author

~*~

"I loved this book."
~Lindsay Maple, rom-com author

~*~

"Love the voice and great dialogue."
~Jackie Khalilieh, YA author

~*~

"I love this story!!! It's so damn fun."
~Crystal Hill, aspiring author

~*~

"The banter is fantastic."
~GS Bower, aspiring author

Chapter 1

Molly

Searching for an escort was not the same as searching for porn.

At least, that's what I kept telling myself as I hit *enter* on my keyboard. Holding my breath, I waited as the list of results—*Elite Males, Premium Gigolos, Stags R Us*—populated my laptop screen. I perched on the edge of my black leather desk chair in my home office overlooking the Seattle harbor. All the entries sounded like adult films. Each one screamed precisely what to expect, which made choosing any one in particular impossible.

With one eye shut and a tentative finger, I clicked on the top entry, *Elite Males*. An obscene amount of oiled flesh filled most of my monitor—a close-up photo of a smooth-chested guy flexing his defined muscles while lying on his back. The shot highlighted his torso and prominent tattoos, capturing only his lips and chin; he was clean-shaven, and his jaw was also, for some reason, shiny. *Ugh! Too much!* The home page wasn't quite as bad as I'd expected but still cringe-worthy: almost laughable. The guy in the image provided what was supposed to be an enticing, yet exaggerated, display, which I assumed—combined with his other "talents" listed in the reviews that read like porn—must have earned him his five-star rating. To each his own.

The parts of the man I could see on my screen were considered conventionally hot. However, after reading the list of customers' erotic comments, I swallowed back the bitter tang filling my mouth. I felt dirty just looking at his image—and desperate. But I guess, for all intents and purposes, I was. My deadline from my publisher loomed overhead, and I had no manuscript to submit. My stomach rolled.

"It's been a year, Molly," Renee had said last week after huffing into the phone. "The editors expect *something* after that advance. Your reputation will only buy you so much time. Can you at least give me the first fifty pages so I can appease them? Try to barter an extension?"

Picturing Renee's scowl was easy—an otherwise non-existent crinkle above the bridge of her button nose, with her perpetual bold lips in full pout mode.

A cold sweat broke out across my forehead. "I'll get you something soon. I promise." My hollow words sounded more like a question as I brushed off the brittle ends of hair that flaked onto my sweatshirt, an inevitable consequence of straightening my Jamaican locks with my flat iron. However, my hair wouldn't have done that if I hadn't fallen asleep at the computer the night before, attempting to muscle out some words that never came. I should have just gone to bed at a decent hour with my silk hair wrap.

"Look, Molly, you've been a real trouper since breaking off the engagement with Enrique. But I think gifting your cousin your non-refundable venue for her wedding was…a mistake. Admirable, but a mistake nonetheless."

As I recalled how all my beautiful, handpicked wedding decorations had come together for Jenny in the end, I wrapped an arm around myself, fighting the thickness forming in my throat. The bride should have been me.

"All this selflessness and courage has really done a number on you. It's got you in a funk. I get your love for Enrique inspired you to try your hand at writing a romance. Unfortunately, and I know this will sound harsh, but business is business, and it doesn't care that your ex cheated. Your publisher's contract still requires you to produce a manuscript."

I sighed, leaning back in my chair. "I know. But nothing I'm doing is helping. I've read loads of rom-coms and watched every chick flick I could find, but I can't get into the plots."

"Maybe that's the problem. You're just watching; you need to be involved. Have you considered getting back out there? Going on a few dates? Finding a new man?"

I straightened as a half-gag choking noise came out of my mouth.

"Look." Renee sighed.

She ignored my dramatic response.

"The guy doesn't have to be anything serious—just someone to clear your mind and rile your senses. Hell, you can even go as far as hiring an escort; I don't care. You just need to find someone who can get you back into the right headspace."

Renee wasn't wrong. As my agent through my last ten thriller novels, she understood what I needed to make this change in genre work, and I was glad she hadn't held back. I trusted her. Although she probably hadn't meant for me to take her offhanded suggestion of an escort seriously, either. But with so little time left and no desire to fall in love, hiring a man seemed like my best option. Desperate times and all…

Besides, commissioning a professional as my muse fit right along with my history of unorthodox research methods, like when I wrote to a serial killer on death row—a suggestion made by my biggest supporter, my father. Everyone I was close to was used to my weird processes; however, I believed my taking Renee's suggestion would have even pushed my dad's comfort limits. My chest loosened.

A wave of guilt passed over me, and I widened my eyes. I couldn't believe I was relieved he wasn't with us anymore to convince me otherwise. I was a terrible daughter. Rubbing my forehead, I sucked in a breath, and the tightening of my ribcage returned tenfold.

Now, with only a two-month deadline to produce *something*, I was desperate, staring at naked torsos and movie knock-off-named websites. The shirtless, flesh-filled, playboy homepages were a common theme for each company, which convinced me each site's primary focus was on their sensual aesthetic. I wrinkled my nose and sighed, resting an elbow on my desk and leaning my forehead on my palm. A sleazy-one-night-stand-kind of guy wouldn't work for my novel. I needed someone who offered different kinds of stimulation, like those of the romantic or intellectual varieties.

I returned to the original search page and glanced at the following few entries. Judging by the play-on-words titles, the websites were all sex-focused. I tapped my lips. My story wasn't supposed to be about sex. If I'd wanted inspiration about that, I could have just gone to a bar. The idea I'd pitched was supposed to be about, well, romance. Love.

Is there another word for an escort who didn't have sex? Like the kind I expect to see in a Hallmark movie?

Clicking at the top of the page, I typed *escort synonyms* into the search bar. A whole list of alternative words populated the screen—*bodyguard, attendant, chaperone, custodian*, and…

Companion.

Yes! That was it. Someone who would talk and spend time with me, show me some romance, and pretend to sweep me off my feet. I gave a little clap before clearing the search bar and trying again with my newfound keyword.

The Plus One Companion Agency was the top entry. With a steady hand, I clicked on the link. The home page presented itself as understated and classy, with a gray background and a close-up of a companion in the forefront. The guy, who appeared to be in his early twenties, looked attractive, dressed in a black sweater—thank heavens—lying stomach-down on a white surface with his arms folded and resting his chin on his wrists. *This is more like it.* As I scrolled down the rest of the screen, the stand-out white lettering across the bottom of the page caught my eye—their *code of ethics*.

Plus One does not provide any form of sexual service. Our gentlemen offer companionship only. Please do not make lewd requests. Any contact of this nature will not receive a response. Furthermore, all personal information from the client and the companion will be held strictly confidential within the guidelines of the Plus One contract.

A no-sex policy and a non-disclosure—*perfect*. I smiled with a sigh—risk-free research.

Opening the tab labeled *companions,* I browsed their gallery of gentlemen. By the fourth page, with seven more to go, I gave up. Drumming my fingers on my desk, I thought hard. *Was there a way to narrow down my search?*

Under their *FAQs* tab, I spotted an entry for *companions willing to travel*. My heart sped. *Bingo!* Because although I hadn't planned on hiding the fact I was going to extremes for research, I also didn't want to bump into whomever I hired at the Seattle Fish Market or a pro football game sometime in the future.

I scrolled through the first page of the twenty remaining companions, making note of a few of the more handsome men. Was I being shallow? Yes, but I reasoned he needed to be more attractive and the complete opposite of Enrique for this whole thing to work. Not because I was looking for a rebound or any kind of relationship. I wasn't. But if the companion reminded me of my ex, this excursion would be a waste of my money. The idea was to stop wallowing over what could have been with my ex and remember the butterflies and excitement that accompanied romantic attraction. I clicked on the next companion.

My throat dried.

Deep-blue eyes jumped off the screen, demanding my attention. Jared Washington was beyond gorgeous with his strong jawline, light scruff, and tan skin. The way his fitted shirt accentuated his lean body clenched my stomach. Even his chic messy, medium-brown hair was a turn-on—a far cry from Enrique's tidy short black curls. But none of those were even Jared's best feature. That title belonged to the sexy dimple on his left cheek that complemented his succulent, full lips.

I was surprised by my sudden flush of warmth and the desire to keep scrolling through his other photos. The urge to picture Jared as the hero of my future love story was too hard to resist. The swarm of butterflies assaulting my stomach was a feeling I hadn't experienced in quite a while. I bit the inside of my cheek to repress a smile. *Yeah, he would do.*

My phone buzzed beside me. I clenched my jaw without taking my gaze off Jared and put the caller on speaker. "This is Molly."

"Hey, girl. It's Renee. I'm checking to see how your research is going."

I sat a little straighter. *Good thing I answered.*

"Have you made any progress? I know only a week has passed."

Her tone sounded strained. I was happy I had some good news. "Actually, Renee, yes. I've decided to do what you suggested and hire a male companion."

"Wait, what? You're doing that? You mean like an escort where you can bang out your frustrations?"

"No." I cringed. I wasn't into one-night stands. "A companion. It's different. Plus One contracts explicitly contain a no-sex policy."

"Yeah. Whatever."

Picturing Renee rolling her eyes as she dismissed my explanation, I had to bite back my retort.

"I guess I should have expected this from the writer who stays in haunted houses and voluntarily sits in on murder trials. Of course, you took me seriously when I said to hire a man."

Her sarcasm was obvious, but *I* liked the idea and did my best to keep the edge out of my tone. “My methods haven’t failed me in the past.”

“Well, let’s hope they don’t this time, either.”

You and me, both. I gusted a breath and rubbed my forehead. “I’ll make my deadline. You have my word. I’m booking Jared now.” I typed my info into the Plus One website.

“Good. Have fun with your new boy toy.”

I froze, my hands hovering over the keyboard, as my breath whooshed from my lungs. “Renee!”

She laughed and ended the call. And while her comment made me blush, a small part of my brain hoped she was right.

I stared at Jared’s face on my screen, and a familiar sensation ran through me—the adrenaline from doing hands-on research. The nitty gritty was what I was good at. If Renee was right, Jared *could* be just the man to get my creative juices flowing again.

With a flutter in my chest, I clicked the *billing information* button on the Plus One website and filled in my account details as I booked the Platinum Getaway. This package included a security deposit, a premium hotel fee, and a travel allowance. Past that, the page menu listed options for all kinds of extras. The list had my head spinning.

The majority of the add-on choices listed were self-explanatory, and I skipped past most. Knowing I was doing this for research, my gaze snagged at an entry labeled *romantic advantage* and I checked the box. Before the rendezvous, this extra perk allowed an hour’s worth of interaction, either in person or via videochat. All other expenses worked as if I was checking into a hotel. The agency would keep my credit card on file and charge me at the end of my experience. But, while Jared and I were together, he would use his business card to pay for anything in conjunction with our contract. The illusion of his independence would appear as though Jared was the one paying for the date, regardless of the truth of the situation.

The growing subtotal near the bottom of my screen burned my eyes, and I took several rapid blinks. While this was turning out to be one of my most expensive fact-finding adventures, I was stuck between a rock and a hard place. Besides, I could justify the cost because I might also learn something I could use in other future novels; perhaps a romantic suspense? I wasn't throwing away my money. Hiring Jared was a solid investment. Keeping that rationale in mind, I readjusted in my chair and typed out my request.

Hello,

I've already booked the companionship of Mr. Jared Washington for three days and three nights the week of September twentieth in a location yet to be determined. I have completed the necessary forms and made the initial deposit.

I look forward to hearing from Mr. Washington.

Sincerely,

Molly Covington

Double-checking my info on the application, I stared at the screen for a moment longer wringing my hands, before setting my jaw and tapping *submit.* The website said Jared would contact me directly. All I had to do was wait.

Then it hit me—in all my other previous research excursions, I'd been an observer; this investigation was the first time I would be a participant. My stomach quivered, and my legs twitched at the idea of spending all that time alone with a complete stranger. *Perhaps, I would feel better knowing more about him.*

I typed his name into FriendBook. Four Jared Washington profiles populated my screen, but as I studied each picture, none matched him. I tried the same on Instapic with similar results. Then a switch flipped in my brain, forming an idea that should have been obvious considering I was hiring a companion and I was a thriller writer—odds were Jared Washington wasn't his real name. Oh well, I guess I'd have to get to know him the old-fashioned way—by talking.

A *ding* indicated I received a new email. Wiping my clammy palm on my sweats, I clicked on the icon. A payment confirmation sat at the top of my inbox, attached to a letter stating Jared would be in touch. Since I wasn't having any luck on social media, I returned to the Plus One website and reviewed Jared's extended profile—

Age: 36.

I'd already verified he was only five years older.

Height: 5'11".

Average for a guy, yet tall enough.

Tattoos: none.

Eh, with a face like that, Jared could have gotten away with it either way.

Piercings: None.

Good. That was one of my personal preferences.

Smoker: no.

Thank goodness.

Hobbies: mountain biking, hiking, traveling, white water rafting, cooking.

No wonder he was in such good shape. And the mental picture of him in an apron...Bonus!

Education: math degree from ASU.

Oh man, my worst subject.

Residence: New York.

Requirement number one previously confirmed.

The site even mentioned every companion had an annual background check. *Perfect. Now, I didn't need to call any of my contacts at the police station.*

Going back to his photos, I tapped my lips and inspected them through my writer's lens. The way his hair flopped over his forehead, the full pout of his lips, his strong hands as they gripped the handlebars of his mountain bike in his action shots, and the way his shirts stretched across his back. *What do you think, Molly? Could your future rom-com heroine fall for this guy?*

Hell, yes!

Chapter 2

Jared

I wish I'd known the bride or groom before they'd booked this reception hall. If I had, I'd have warned them marriages that celebrate at this venue were doomed. This tidbit of knowledge stemmed from my past. Because not only had my parents used the Plaza, but my father revisited the establishment with his three subsequent weddings. His latest one had stuck so far, but I wasn't holding my breath, especially considering I'd stumbled upon him in a compromising position with one of his new wife's bridesmaids in the bathroom during his wedding reception. I wasn't familiar with the "happy" couple this time; I was here as the contracted date for a different bitter woman. This one was named Jacqueline. She used to date the best man. When she'd gone to the restroom a few minutes before, giving me a momentary reprieve from her snide comments about the bridesmaids, I was relieved.

"Look at you, thinking you're all that, you whore!"

A woman's slurred, top-volume shrill cut through the murmured conversations around me, piercing my ears.

I winced. *Tell me that wasn't my contract.* Sure enough, I swiveled in my chair and spotted Jacqueline in her bright-pink dress. I deflated.

She stumbled behind a brunette bridesmaid exiting the bathroom, drawing attention from the other wedding guests. "At least my boobs are real!" Jacqueline swayed, almost tipping over as she shimmied her shoulders, forcing her breasts to jiggle in the other woman's face—the same woman who'd been the target of the majority of Jacqueline's rage over the past hour.

The bridesmaid raised her hands and backed up, her dark, thin lips moving.

Unfortunately, I couldn't hear her from where I sat at our assigned table. But I didn't need to; Jacqueline was loud enough for the both of them.

"*I'll* say when I've had enough to drink, not you!" My date waved her glass around, her gold bracelets clinking as her Long Island Iced Tea sloshed onto the tile floor.

Time to intervene. With a heavy sigh, I heaved myself from my chair and sprinted across the reception room to my date, grabbed her wrist to steady the drink she held, and placed my other hand on her back. "Hey, sweetheart, don't waste your time on this woman. She's not worth it." I averted my gaze from the bridesmaid in question, gritting my teeth as I half-carried a stumbling Jacqueline back toward our table, the entire reception hall glowering with looks of morbid curiosity.

Blaring through the windows, the setting sun bathed the room in varying hues of gold. Judging from Jacqueline's heavy-lidded expression, she wouldn't be conscious much longer.

The bride's mother weaved around the chairs in her light-green, matronly dress, and her squinty eyes looked as though she wanted to ward off the commotion.

I set my date's drink on our table before wiping the

alcoholic concoction off her hand so it wouldn't get on my best suit. "Let me take you home so you can forget all about this." *And I could be done with you.* I wrapped Jacqueline's glittery shawl around her shoulders and picked up her purse, making a production of leaving for our audience. "He doesn't deserve you, anyway."

With pursed, bright-pink lips, the bride's mother nodded, and the tension left her posture as she stared down Jacqueline.

The drunk woman leaned into my side, with tears streaking black mascara down her face. "You think I'm pretty, don't you?"

I resisted rolling my eyes as I escorted Jacqueline toward the exit, with a plastered-on smile, lying through my teeth. "Of course, I do. Who wouldn't find you gorgeous?" In all honesty, my date was a pretty woman—blonde hair, blue eyes, nice body, but her behavior tonight was very unattractive-yet-typical for many of my clients. Tucking Jacqueline into the back seat of the rideshare, I buckled her seatbelt, brushed a curl out of her face, and wrapped my arm around her to keep her steady. I prayed she wouldn't get sick.

She cried into my shoulder for a few minutes before her breathing became deep and even.

The car arrived at her brownstone, and I thrusted my shoulder to rouse Jacqueline. No way could I carry her dead weight out of the car and up the steps to her front door.

When Jacqueline and I reached the stoop of her building, she fumbled with her keys.

"Here, let me." I struggled not to snatch them and held out a hand instead.

She smashed the keyring into my palm.

Pain bit my skin. Locating the correct key, I unlocked Jacqueline's door, steadying her so she wouldn't faceplant onto the entry's mosaic tile floor. With my arm cinched around her waist, I held her up as the elevator ascended to the third floor. I couldn't understand how someone so petite could feel like a million pounds as I half-dragged Jacqueline to her apartment, and opened the door, guiding her into the foyer.

Jacqueline swayed in my arms.

To keep her from hitting the floor, I scooped her up and carried her limp body into the living room. Her home screamed signs of a heartbroken woman—torn photos, melted half-eaten ice cream cartons, empty bottles of wine, and wadded-up tissues scattered across every surface of the retro wooden furniture. Even though Jacqueline hadn't acted like a lady tonight, for propriety's sake, I laid her on the brown linen couch in the middle of the room. "Can I get you anything?"

She belched and murmured something incoherent, maneuvering onto her side, facing the back cushions.

Shaking my head, I pulled a blanket off the nearby chair and placed the soft fabric over her with a sigh. Searching around the sparse furniture in the room, I spotted a trash can in the corner. Grabbing the plastic container, I set it next to the couch in case Jacqueline got sick during the night, doing my due diligence and all. Then, after tossing her keys onto the glass coffee table, I took out my phone, snapped a few discreet pictures to prove I'd returned my client to the relative safety of her living room, and flipped the lock on the doorknob. I couldn't wait to get home.

When I returned to my tiny, cluttered apartment

just off Central Park West, I ripped off my tie, folded it in half, and laid it on the entertainment stand before heading straight to the kitchen. I needed a Scotch. Then, I grabbed my laptop with my double in hand, flopped onto my lumpy, secondhand couch, and put my feet on the beat-up leather ottoman masquerading as my coffee table. I rested my head back on the cushions to catch my breath.

The evening had been a nightmare. I ran a hand over my face. Predicting how a date would turn out when a client hired me to make someone jealous was a gamble, but often, it didn't go well. Tonight was just par for the course and confirmed my cynical beliefs about love.

I uploaded the two photos I took at Jacqueline's, cataloged the evening's events on my Plus One portal, then marked the contract as complete, sagging into the cushions.

At least Jacqueline's fight with the other woman tonight hadn't gotten physical, like with some of my other clients. Despite the stereotype, a drunken catfight wasn't as sexy to watch in person as I imagined. Entertaining, yes, but never sexy. Just one more reason I was itching to get out of the companioning business and not have to put up with contracts like that anymore. They were exhausting.

Opening my banking app, I hoped my savings account would lift my spirits. The balance glared from the bottom right of my screen. I dropped my head. The total still wasn't enough. At this rate, I'd be stuck at Plus One for at least another year before I had enough to invest in the Sky's the Limit franchise. The slow process of saving money made me want to punch my screen, but I wasn't a violent person, and at least now, I could see the light at the end of the tunnel.

I scrubbed at my hair. Between the high cost of living in New York, unfair obligations I couldn't avoid, and having been reckless with my money in college, I'd screwed myself. But I was determined to do this on my own and not be indebted to my arrogant father. I hated how one missed payment and high balances affected credit scores which carried way too much weight in my opinion; otherwise, I would have taken out a loan and been done with the companioning business already.

My phone vibrated in my pocket. *What now?* Pulling out the device, I saw an automated text from Plus One illuminated my screen, alerting me I had a new client and to contact my boss, Erica Haversack. My shoulders relaxed a fraction. *One step closer.* I brought up my boss's number and checked the time. The clock read just after nine thirty p.m., not too late to call. Maybe a chat with Erica would lighten my mood.

"Jared, why are you calling me now?"

Her gruff opening made me smile. "Hello to you, too, Madame Erica."

She grunted. "You know I hate that name."

I chuckled. Riling her up was one of my favorite things to do, and it made Erica's Brooklyn accent even more pronounced. "I'm aware. And yet, considering your profession, the nickname suits you."

"Shut up. If you weren't so good at your job, I'd fire your sardonic backside."

"Oh, Erica. You wouldn't fire my tight backside; you like it too much."

She harrumphed. "Don't be so cocky."

I shook my head, the innuendo was too hard to

resist. "Now, Madame Erica, you know that part of me is off-limits."

"Ugh! I'm old enough to be your mother."

With all her plastic surgery and dyed hair, I had no way to tell her real age. The flint of a lighter sounded from the other end of the line, followed by two hard sucks and a long exhale. Cigarettes were her equivalent to my double Scotch.

"Weren't you supposed to be working tonight?"

"Yes, I did. She was a jealous ex. Lots of drinks. Tearful breakdown. All the information is in the file."

"That explains your early evening. Well, for your next contract, I've got something a little different. I'm emailing you the details as we speak. This one's a celebrity of sorts. She's prepaid but hasn't picked a location—she's open to your availability the week of the twentieth."

"Of sorts?" What did Erica mean by that? The big celebrities didn't hire companions, because they didn't want to get caught by the paparazzi and start a scandal. But if she booked a getaway, she had to have money.

"She's an author."

Ahh, my client was that kind of famous—probably known by her name and not her face. I know I couldn't pick Tom Clancy out of a lineup.

Silence stretched across the call for a beat. "She's one of my favorite writers."

Her admission was clipped, and a smile crept over my face. *Madame was a reader?* "Ooh, what's this client's name?"

Erica breathed hard into the phone.

The sound was as if she was reluctant to give me this tidbit of information she'd already forwarded to my email. Why was she being so coy?

"Molly Covington."

"Hmm, I haven't heard of her. What does she write?" I glanced at my modest bookcase against the far wall, wondering if I'd be interested in any of her work.

"Psychological thrillers."

I raised my brows, surprised by her answer. "Should I be impressed or worried?"

"What? Why?"

"Those aren't light reads, Erica. But I guess as long as you're not using them as textbooks or how-to manuals…" I shrugged and took a swig of my Scotch, letting the malty liquid burn my throat.

"If you keep this up, Jared. I will."

"You're such a tease," I chuckled. Keyboard clicks sounded from the other end of the call. While Erica's tone might have seemed mad, I was positive from being her employee for over a decade that she loved my banter. That was why she insisted on our phone conversations instead of emailing like most of the other companions. Plus, the conversations kept my flirting skills sharp.

"Did you get the email?"

I switched her to speaker and tapped on the correspondence. "Yep, reading it right now."

"Get on it."

"Yes, ma'am." I saluted the typical sign-off, even though she couldn't see me, and checked my calendar. A weight lifted from my shoulders. Any day during the week of the twentieth worked. I was grateful the client hadn't picked the following weekend. An extreme adventure at my other job occupied that date.

With a tilt of my head, I opened the attachment to

Erica's email. *Well, helllooo!* I shifted to the edge of the couch, ogling the image on my screen.

Molly Covington was a thirty-one-year-old author from Washington State with long, dark, wavy hair, beautiful light-brown skin, and sexy, heavy-lidded eyes. Her file had two pictures attached—one professional headshot, the other a candid photo. The difference between the two images was her smile; the expression transformed her whole face from serious in the first to playful in the latter. Between the two photos, I was both captivated and intrigued.

This, of course, made my job easier. Romancing someone I was physically attracted to was always a bonus, rather than faking interest in someone I'd had no chemistry with—like Jacqueline. Not that being a companion was the most challenging job I'd had. The money was good, after all, despite having to be "on" all the time. But the contracts drained me emotionally.

My college roommate, Lucas, was the one who had introduced me to the job. He worked as a companion and insisted the extra income from Plus One was a guaranteed way of supplementing my hobbies.

"Dude, if you go on just two dates every weekend, you could have your own top-of-the-line mountain bike by the end of the month and not have to rent one from your boss."

That was what sold me on the gig—affording my own bike. After joining the campus outdoor clubs, I discovered a passion for extreme sports. The biggest problem was the expense. Equipment was extortionate. While I'd found a job as an adventure guide at a place called Sky's the Limit, earning me free excursions, that income was just enough to pay for my education and necessities, not hobbies. I needed to find another way to make money if I wanted my own gear.

My father wasn't any help. He'd already cut me off when I'd chosen math as my major instead of his beloved business and engineering degrees—squelching his desires of me taking over the family business. Of course, I didn't even bother asking Heather—my selfish mother—because she could never bear to part with money she could spend on herself now that she was no longer with my dad. So, Lucas's suggestion seemed like my best solution.

As a Plus One employee, I would offer clients my company to any number of events, from a casual date, to a work function, a wedding, or a weekend adventure. Their strict, no-sex policy in their contracts was both a surprise and a bonus. Kissing or holding hands was permissible; contracts forbid anything more, and those actions would be grounds for dismissal from the agency. Since my intention wasn't to be a gigolo, the policy checked all the boxes. While I assumed the gig would be fun, money was still my first priority. However, I quickly discovered the drawback to the job—it confirmed my beliefs about relationships.

My first contract was my huge wake-up call. I'd been naive in the beginning, thinking my clients' motives were pure and they'd hired me for a good time. That was why, when that first woman booked me for a night on the town, I was excited. However, over dinner, I discovered the ugly truth.

"He's cheating." The woman closed her eyes, a single tear escaping down her cheek. "It's been going on for years."

A sense of déjà vu from my childhood swept over

me, and my stomach plummeted. I wasn't sure what to say and blurted the first thing that popped into my mind. "Does he know you know?"

She shook her blonde curls. "I don't think so. But it doesn't matter. I would never confront him. I've got too much to lose. We've got kids, and I haven't worked in years. I just"—she dabbed her eyes with her napkin—"needed to feel desirable, you know?"

The whole night continued like that—her droning on about her sob story while I listened and feigned sympathy, but instead of seeing her side, the entire evening had made me more bitter about love. The longer I was in the business, the more calloused I became with each monotonous contract; they were variations of the same scenarios. Train wreck after train wreck of relationships, accompanied by bitterness, and heartache. Like with Jacqueline tonight. Numb, I explored Molly's profile again, wondering what *her* deal was.

Erica's favorite author booked me for three days, the Platinum Getaway. My heart stopped, then picked up in overtime. This one contract was a substantial step forward, putting me within arm's reach of buying out my other boss's shares in the company, which would make me the proud owner of a Sky's the Limit adventure franchise.

I allowed myself to dream for just a moment, then switched tabs on my browser and typed my client's name to see what information I could glean online. As I read the top search link headline, I gawked, my eyes almost falling out of their sockets. *Molly Covington, best-selling psychological thriller writer*. The entire page contained an extensive list of entries about her—

interviews, conferences, and awards Molly had won throughout her career.

Running a hand through my hair, I switched windows to study her picture again. Molly didn't look like someone who'd written ten thrillers. She appeared, well, normal. Shaking my head, I scolded myself. "Way to stereotype, Jared. What did you expect? Ted Bundy looked like a normal guy, too. Hopefully, she's not as deranged as he was."

Feeling a little intimidated by her success and chagrined at my lack of knowledge about this world-renowned author, I browsed Molly's various social media accounts to ensure I devoted her the attention Erica was expecting—going above and beyond.

Molly engaged actively with her fans on her Bird app account by responding to their comments on her posts with inspiring words and hilarious GIFs. She had a great sense of humor.

On Instapic, Molly was a Bookstablogger. Almost all her posts had pictures of both her books and other authors', all alongside varying mugs of hot chocolate or some delicious-looking side dish. Each shot was strategic, with the book and cup or plate matching in either theme or color with a short synopsis. My favorite was a brown ceramic mug dotted with small, green fern leaves next to a novel covered in a silhouetted emerald forest against a white background. The photo screamed outdoorsy and called to my inner nature lover.

I switched over to FriendBook, but her profile was private, so I gave up and returned to Instapic, jotting down the names of some of Molly's titles. I'd have to read at least one. I heaved a sigh. Something about this contract didn't add up. Molly was hot, plus she had notoriety. I couldn't make sense of why she'd hired me, not that I was complaining, but I was curious.

"Let's see if Molly's email has any clues." I toggled between screens, tapping on the folder attached to her paperwork. Her letter was short and sweet but had no other requests, no agenda, and no expectations. She'd left the reason for acquiring my services on the application blank.

Scratching my head, I checked my calendar again, noting the days that worked best, and mused over where Molly would want to go. Something quiet and subdued or louder and more adventurous? *Erica would know.*

I leaned forward and rested my elbows on my knees as I browsed through my company's list of destination partners, places where Madame Erica had contracts for client getaways. Scrolling through, I weighed the pros and cons of several locations, pausing on the photo link displaying the twinkling skyline of one of the most popular travel destinations in the U.S.—Las Vegas. Where else could you see the New York skyline, the pyramids of Egypt, a look-alike Space Needle, and a mini version of the Eiffel Tower all in one place? Not to mention, what happened in Vegas stayed in Vegas. So, whatever her motive for hiring me, she was safe. The city checked all the boxes.

Content I had a solid plan, I opened my email, entered her contact info, and typed my message, switching on the professional charm:

Ms. Covington,

Thank you for choosing me to be your Plus One. I've sifted through your profile, and I'm intrigued. A writer can have quite the imagination, and I'm looking forward to how that will translate into our time together. Although thinking of your success as a suspense author, I might sleep with one eye open. Wink emoji

Since you haven't chosen a destination for our date, I'd like to suggest Las Vegas. We'll have plenty of activities to choose from while still allowing the anonymity I'm sure you'd prefer.

I can meet you at the Las Vegas International Airport on the morning of Monday the twenty-first and stay through Wednesday the twenty-third, leaving early in the morning on the twenty-fourth.

If this schedule works for you, let me know, and I will make arrangements for the hotel. My company has contracts with many of the casinos on the strip. However, if you would feel more comfortable making alternative accommodations yourself at your additional expense, I am open to that, too.

One more thing, considering we are on opposite sides of the country and both traveling for this arrangement, I suggest a videochat as our best option for your additional hour of interaction and we can also hash out the Vegas details—like the purpose of your contract and your expectations regarding our interactions. With the twenty-first right around the corner, we only have two days to squeeze in our chat, so how does tomorrow at one p.m. Pacific Daylight Time work?

Anxiously awaiting your reply,
Jared
PLUS ONE COMPANION AGENCY
Cell: 646-555-6975
jwashington@plus1.com
www.PlusOneComps.com

Sent at 10:22 p.m. Eastern Daylight Time

I closed out my email, but Molly's profile was still open on my screen. Raising my glass with a smirk, I toasted her picture on the monitor. "May our rendezvous go better than tonight."

Chapter 3

Molly

My home was perched high above the Seattle skyline—my little piece of heaven watching the ferries crisscross the Puget Sound. The apartment used to be an oversized caretaker's space at the top of a historic skyscraper. During the mid-1990s, the past owners converted the top floors into a whimsical, one-of-a-kind home with hardwood floors, diamond lead-patterned arched windows, a bedroom loft, and a room off the main floor I'd transformed into my office.

After setting my morning cocoa on the desk, I tied my hair into a messy bun. The nice thing about being a writer was I didn't need to worry about appearing professional. A pair of sweatpants, a baggy T-shirt, and a cardigan were more than sufficient for my day of writing.

I pulled one leg up under the other, relaxed back into my chair, and sipped my chocolate concoction, enjoying the scent of ozone and the sound of the rain as the drops cascaded down the windowpanes. I never tired of the reassuring patter. I found the melodic sound of raindrops inspirational. It often sparked my creativity…that was until the raindrops mirrored my tears from Enrique's betrayal. *Jerk!*

In my original manuscript outline, the one that had

earned me my rom-com contract, I'd based the plot on my relationship with Enrique, but I couldn't bear to finish the story once I'd ended things. After a week of self-pity and tears, I discussed my options with Renee, and she and I decided my best course of action would be to scrap everything I'd written so far. Now, I was starting from scratch and based the new meet-cute on my younger brother—the only decent guy I still knew—and his wife, who'd met online. My characters would begin their relationship with flirty texts as they got to know each other, which I'd angle to forge an instant connection between them when they met in person. With any luck, if I mimicked this experience with Jared, I'd channel my own reactions into my characters' correspondence. As long as I didn't force a script and he was good at what he does, the pretense wouldn't squash the authenticity, and Renee would get her manuscript.

I glanced at the whiteboard sporting my character bios. Pinching my lips together, I grimaced. Since scrubbing Enrique from the novel, I'd given my new male main character the name Sam, but I hadn't written down any physical features. Yet, ever since I'd decided to hire Jared, whenever I pictured the love interest in my manuscript, I envisioned his face. With a bounce in my step, I picked up the marker and filled in Sam's description with the brown hair and blue eyes of Mr. Washington. I tilted my head to the side and tapped my lips—the words alone weren't doing him justice.

Heading over to my laptop, I pulled up Jared's Plus One profile. With a sigh, I bit my lip and printed out my favorite of his pictures—not that I should have one—him in a black cable-knit sweater with a brooding expression. His sleeves were pulled up to his elbows, showing off beautiful muscles and cording veins on his forearms. *Yum!*

I taped the photo onto the whiteboard and took a step back. "Yeah, that's better." As for my female main character, I was still debating if I should revert the generic female back to myself, at least for the time being, since I would be participating in the research. Because even though *I* wasn't the one who would be dating Jared—I mean Sam—I would be channeling *my* emotions and reactions from the exchange into the female character.

For fun, I printed my author headshot and taped the image onto the whiteboard next to Jared's photo. Adrenaline pumped through my veins. I couldn't deny it…Jared and I made a handsome couple, and the daydreams about the two of us together were coming hard and fast.

"Stop it, Molly!" I chided myself out loud. Getting caught up in my imagination would get me into trouble. The real-life Jared couldn't live up to my rom-com expectations, no one could, so I needed to stay grounded and let whatever happened play out and give the research experiment a fair chance.

Taking a dark-chocolatey sip from my mug, I sat and opened my email. After deleting the spam from every store I'd ever entered, I stared, my breath catching. I had a message from Jared Washington. An unexpected lightness bubbled from my stomach, through my chest, and emerged as a smile at seeing his name in my inbox.

Sitting straight, I shook myself, putting my thoughts back in order. This was for research. But damn, even the mental picture of him fake romancing me sent a shiver up my spine. I chewed on my thumbnail. Maybe I should have chosen someone less attractive… *Nah!*

I glanced at Jared's picture on the whiteboard again. Reading his email, I sucked in a breath, my pulse racing, and my mouth went dry. "Vegas, huh?" The city had always been on my bucket list, but whenever I had spare time, I often spent those hours in my kayak or forging new trails in a national park. However, Las Vegas did have the Crime Scene Experience. That investigation-solving simulation was the main reason Sin City called my name. I would love to see that.

Halfway through Jared's email, I paused to search for hotels on the strip, wondering which ones Plus One had contracts with, starting with the south end. But after checking out several, my head began to spin. They were all so beautiful, and having never visited there before, I would have been happy with anyone.

Picking a hotel at random, I clicked on the photo galleries of the rooms. I stared as a double queen bed picture popped on my screen, my stomach dropping to the floor. What would the sleeping accommodations be for our time together? While I was no prude, and despite Plus One's code of ethics, the idea of sleeping in the same room with the sinfully delicious Jared had my lungs constricting, and I couldn't get enough air.

I clicked on a new tab with shaky fingers, searching for the agency's fine print on the subject, surprised Jared's sex appeal had overridden my "he could kill me in my sleep" overactive writer's imagination, and I hadn't thought to question the sleeping arrangements sooner. Oxygen filled my chest.

I didn't even have to squint to see the words, and I wasn't sure how I'd missed the requirement the first time.

COMPANIONS ARE FORBIDDEN FROM SHARING BEDS OR INDIVIDUAL ROOMS—AS OPPOSED TO SEPARATE ROOMS IN SUITES—WITH CLIENTS. SEPARATE SLEEPING QUARTERS ARE REQUIRED.

The remaining tension left my shoulders. *One less thing to worry about.* With that out of the way, I returned to Jared's email. Damn it! He wanted to videochat today at one p.m.—forty-five minutes away. After shooting back a quick confirmation for both Vegas and the videochat, I jumped out of my chair and scuttled to my room, angry at myself for not checking my messages sooner.

I ran to my closet and threw on a fresh blouse, a drapey, deep-teal number my sister said complimented my brown skin but opted to keep on my sweatpants. The camera would be focused on my upper body, so wearing business on top and a party on the bottom wouldn't be an issue. This chat would be stressful enough without fighting a tight jean waistband cutting into my stomach. Next, I worked on straightening my hair and perfecting my makeup. Lastly, I spritzed my chest with my perfume. Even though he couldn't smell me through the screen, the fresh, orange-jasmine scent gave me the boost of confidence I desperately needed.

With just minutes to spare, I sat at my computer. A new email containing a videochat invitation waited at the top of my inbox. I wiped my palms on my thighs, double-checked the time—I didn't want to appear too eager—and prepared to click on the link, putting my thoughts in order.

Jared would need to know the purpose of our contract. I sat back, tapping my fingers against my lips. But the origin behind my motivation wasn't something I wanted to divulge, at least not the whole story—I would feel too vulnerable. If possible, I wanted to keep Enrique out of this. Somehow, just the thought of dumping the details from my disastrous previous love life on Jared seemed utterly pathetic, but I also didn't want to lie. Perhaps I could just tell him I was struggling? I shrugged. The excuse seemed reasonable. Authors complained about writer's block all the time. Going into the gory details of how my issues originated wasn't necessary. After all, my relationship with Jared wasn't real life; he and I were just pretending.

Chapter 4

Jared

As I strolled up to the bookstore, a prominent poster of Molly's latest novel, *Dark Side of the Rose,* hung proudly in the store's front window. I shook my head, I'd been living in a hole. She was famous, and I didn't even know. In my opinion, any woman with that level of success was a force to be reckoned with. I was impressed.

Although despite being a renowned writer who I'd bet was on her computer most of the day, she'd taken all morning to email me back the confirmation about our videochat. However, Molly could have been one of those creative types who got absorbed in their projects and forgot about the rest of the world. Not that hyperfocus was bad because, according to my Internet searches, it'd worked well for Molly, but the habit would say a lot about her personality if she were.

I still had some time to kill before I met her online, and my mother—or Heather as I liked to call her—texted me, letting me know she was in New York with her newest boyfriend. Heather had been hoping she could stop by so I could meet him. While guilt weighed on me, experience told me I'd be better off not seeing her this time around. The last thing I wanted was to meet another temporary "father figure."

When I realized Heather's visit coincided with Molly's call, I felt the tension in my neck loosening. The coincidence gave me the perfect excuse to turn her down. So, after I'd told my mother I was busy, I'd made myself scarce by using the interim time to head to the bookstore and pick up one of Molly's books. I wouldn't have put it past Heather to pop by on the pretense of not receiving my message and forcing herself and her new man into my life, regardless of my desires. She had no respect for me, my feelings, or my boundaries. So, why risk it? Besides, she'd be in touch when she needed something—she always did. This surprise visit was just a formality to keep up the pretense of a mother who cared.

The thriller section was on the second floor. As I strolled between the tables, I noted several other displays promising, *If you like Molly Covington novels, you will love these books*. I couldn't help thinking I had my work cut out for me. Homemakers and executives were one thing, but a renowned celebrity? That was a whole other ballgame.

Scanning the Molly Covington endcap display, I noted a book with an image of a woman drowning—a definite no, another with a snapshot of a firing gun—a possibility, but ultimately, I decided on *Stern Shadows.* Madame Erica recommended the novel as one of her favorites. And if the title and cover—a black jacket with a huge silver meat hook dripping with blood were any indications of the text, I'd be reading some gruesome murders in my future. After nabbing a copy, I bought the book and headed home.

Sitting on my couch, I put my feet up, ready to begin Molly's novel, and spotted a missed call alert from the Plus One office. I tapped on the voicemail from Madame Erica and rolled my eyes. No doubt she was panicking since I hadn't logged any progress on the client portal about her favorite author.

"Jared, tell me you've contacted Molly Covington. She's a big deal, and I don't want you ruining my reputation. Call me—STAT!"

I smiled and shook my head. How do you ruin the reputation of a woman who contracted companions? She was a step away from being a female pimp, hence her nickname. But she was acting like an irrational fangirl; Erica had no reason to worry. I'd always come through.

Shooting off a quick email to the Plus One travel department, I booked the two-bedroom apartment atop the Euphoria Tower. The penthouse suite had everything—views of the strip, a small kitchen, a living room, a bar, and two separate bedrooms complete with private bathrooms and walk-in closets. I'd only ever stayed in the Euphoria Tower one other time for a different contract. Unfortunately for them, but lucky for me, the client's husband found the Plus One email confirmation, and the woman canceled at the last minute. So, I still got paid, but I was fortunate enough to have the whole apartment to myself for the entire weekend. The suite blew my mind and solidified the Euphoria as the best place I'd ever stayed in Vegas.

After noting my contact with the client in the Plus One portal to appease Erica, setting up a videochat link, and emailing it to Molly, I cracked open *Stern Shadows*. Only three chapters in, and I'd already drawn several conclusions about Molly. First, she was an excellent writer. The descriptions and emotions that went into her prose were engaging. Second, the tension in her book was pretty much instantaneous. The opening scene had the main character hiding in a closet from someone or something. The intense moment turned out to be harmless, but the whole scenario tensed my muscles.

I kept reading, despite the main character boarding a cruise ship in chapter three, which caused all my hair to stand on end. But when, in chapter six, one of the crew members went overboard, visions of shark attacks flashed through my mind, and I had to put the book down.

Getting up to grab something to drink, I checked my notifications—another missed call from Madame Erica. Molly's book had sucked me in so much I hadn't heard my phone ringing. I had to fight the urge to ignore my boss until after my videochat with Molly, so I'd have more to report. But Erica was impatient, and if I didn't call her soon, she would put a bounty on my head. I grabbed a water bottle from the fridge and took a swig of the cold liquid as I tapped Erica's number.

"Jared! It's about time."

Her thick New York accent made her words sound more menacing than they were. "Hello to you, too, Madame Erica."

"Stop it with that name. Did you contact Molly Covington?"

"What do you think?" I took another drink of water and flopped back onto the couch.

"Good. Give her your best work."

I laughed. "My best work isn't allowed, according to company policy."

"Don't be a butt!"

"You've mentioned my backside two days in a row. Somebody's got an obsession."

Erica scoffed. "Whatever. Just behave."

Her supposed offense sounded half-hearted. "Or what?" I smiled, taking advantage of the opportunity. "You'll spank me?"

"Don't start with that again."

I could hear the smile in her tone. "Yes, ma'am."

"Good. Get on it." She ended the call.

I glanced at the clock. My chat with Molly was in ten minutes, giving me time to clean up a bit. Throwing on my favorite song, I sang along at top volume to psych myself up for what I had no doubt would be yet another soul-sucking conversation.

Being given commands instead of requests was always one of my pet peeves about this job. Most people didn't care if they treated others like instruments for revenge rather than actual people. A fact that held true for my clients. My purpose always centered around whatever I could do for them.

Hold my hand.

Take me over there so he can see us.

Pretend I said something funny.

Look at me like you want me.

I had no doubt Molly would be the same. As the song ended, I ran a hand through my hair and poured myself some Scotch, letting the smoky, caramel aroma soothe my nerves as I wandered around my apartment, turning on the lights and angling my laptop so the one brick wall of my living room would serve as the background for our call. The red stones looked nicer than the three remaining, grayish plaster ones.

With the burn of the alcohol in my stomach, I

clicked on the video link. Molly was already waiting in the virtual lobby. Toasting the screen, I tossed back the rest of my Scotch. “Here we go again.”

Chapter 5

Molly

Before Jared's face appeared, the window on my laptop screen flickered black. Butterflies fluttered through my whole body, and I fought to keep a squeal of delight from erupting out of my mouth. His photos hadn't done him justice.

"Hello? Molly? Can you hear me okay?" Jared's gaze darted around the screen.

His tone was flat. Still unable to speak, I nodded.

"Good." He ran a hand over his mouth. "So, this is what a world-renowned thriller writer looks like." A hint of a smile crossed his lips.

Shockwaves rippled through my body. I lifted my shoulder in a half-shrug, downplaying my excitement. "Well, I'm hoping to be a romance writer, if everything goes well with us."

Jared's eyebrows shot up. "Romance, huh? So, I won't have to be on my guard?"

My thoughts froze for a moment before I made sense of his comment and laughed, a tremor in my tone. "No. While I have written about murderers, I'm not one of them."

He exaggerated the wiping of his brow. "That's a relief. So, how do I fit into all of this?"

"Well." Heat burned my cheeks. "I'm struggling

with this new genre. Therefore, I decided to seek the help of another professional, aka—you." I gestured at his exquisite face. "Because even though my stories are fiction, I like to portray as much accuracy as possible in my work. Like any method actor, I immerse myself in my plots so I can think like my characters."

As he frowned, a crease formed in Jared's brow, and he nodded along.

"That's why I'm genuinely looking forward to our time together."

He smirked.

I stiffened. The expression was so sexy, my stomach clenched, causing me to stammer out the rest of my explanation. "I just assumed, considering your occupation, you must have romance down to a science. I'm hoping to pour that wisdom into my characters."

"Okay. What do you mean when you say you're immersing yourself in your plot?"

I was glad he didn't balk at my request, but the adrenaline kept pumping. "I guess I'd like to both pick your brain and experience your expertise firsthand." I clenched the smooth, foam stress ball sitting next to my laptop, releasing the sphere a bit at a time as I worked to slow my hammering heartbeat.

"Sounds interesting." He slowly rubbed his palms together. "So, how do you see this going, exactly?"

"Well, I've got a plan." I paused, biting my lip.

"Which is?" He cocked an eyebrow.

I swallowed to relieve the dryness in my throat and prayed he'd play along. "I'd like us to mirror the meet-cute I've outlined for my fictional couple—two people who've met online and agreed to meet face-to-face."

"Not too far off base so far. Go on."

I studied the fraying drawstring on my sweatpants, fighting the blush crawling up my neck. "To do that, I wondered if it would be possible to text in the lead-up to our date?"

Jared's head tilted to the side. "You're the boss; that's up to you."

This man was at my disposal. I gasped, my toes curling at the rush of power, and I had to clear my throat before I could speak. "Okay, for starters, I'd like the two of us to do the get-to-know-you thing over our future correspondence. That way, I can observe your responses to our beginning-of-a-relationship scenario. Then, once we are together in person, we can continue the charade."

Jared's cheek hitched up, and he leaned forward. "Our first order of business should be to stop thinking of us as a charade."

My stomach flipped. "Fair enough. But I might have to occasionally break character for clarification or follow-up questions about our interactions."

"Not a problem." He winked.

Desire engulfed my whole body, setting me on fire. I had no idea how I would cope in Vegas when I was already struggling just to keep my composure on our videochat.

"Since you agreed to Vegas, I've taken the liberty of booking us the two-bedroom suite at the Euphoria." Jared's hands tapped against the keyboard "I'm sending you the details."

"I'm excited to see Vegas. I've never been there."

Jared's eyebrow drew up again.

Have mercy; that was sexy.

"You're a Vegas virgin?"

I let out a nervous giggle. "I guess you could say that."

"Good to know. Do you want me to be gentle, or do you want to take the lead?"

I dropped my jaw, my heart racing. "I'm sorry?"

"With the itinerary. Do you want me to schedule our activities, or you?"

"You, please." I did my best to hide my exhale but was sure he'd seen it.

"Then I should ask, what do you enjoy?"

His seductive smile had my mind in the gutter, and I had to dig myself out before I could answer. "Well, I love to hike and kayak."

Jared's expression lit up. "You love the outdoors?"

I gave an emphatic nod. "Absolutely. Last week, Fin and I kayaked after my cousin's wedding on Orca's Island. It was brilliant."

His eyebrows squished together. "You hauled a kayak to your cousin's wedding? And who's Fin?"

"Oh, Fin is my younger cousin slash best friend. And yes, of course, I took my kayak. She might as well have put it on the invitation. The ceremony was held on an island, surrounded by water; how could I not?"

Jared barked out a laugh. "I guess I have no room to talk. I take my workout gear to most places, too, if there might be a chance to run. How was it?"

I raised a hand to my chest, my heart warming. "You should have been there; the water was so calm. Letting the kayak rise and fall with the waves was freeing."

Jared was shaking his head before I finished talking. "I'll take your word for it."

My spine straightened. "What? Why? Don't you

like kayaking?"

"I do, but not on the ocean." Jared ducked his head. "I was kind of traumatized by that seventies great white shark movie."

He had to be joking. "The President Channel is nothing to be scared of. Kayaking is so peaceful, with the salty air, the open waters, and the breeze through my hair…" I closed my eyes, shaking out my locks and reliving the memory in my mind.

Jared pursed his lips. "Nope. You still lost me at open waters."

"You make no sense." I squinted and smiled. "How is kayaking in the President Channel any different from your white-water rafting, like in that picture used in your profile?"

"Because that white-water rafting was on a river. There are no sharks in rivers."

I grabbed my phone and opened the browser.

"Molly, what are you doing?" Jared leaned forward again.

His tone was cautious, and as if he could see over my phone through the screen, I pulled my cell toward my chest, hiding it from his view. "I'm searching the Internet to see if there are sharks in rivers."

With a twinkle in his eyes, Jared threw his hands up "Really? Are you trying to get on my bad side already? We haven't even had our first date."

"Okay"—I gaped at the results on my phone, unable to hide my smile—"I won't tell you what I found."

"Great. Just by your response, I'll never go in a river again." His gaze slid to the side as he shook his head. "And here I was, already hesitant, thanks to that piranha movie." Jared ran a hand through his hair.

The motion created a sexy, messy look I adored.

"I better let Chris know."

Cocking my head to the side, I shifted in my chair. "Who's Chris?"

"He's my boss at my second job. I also work at an adventure franchise called Sky's the Limit. I was leading the excursion in the picture." His gaze shifted off-camera. "Speaking of dangerous waters…I picked up a copy of *Stern Shadows*." He wagged the paperback at the camera.

"Wow, I'm impressed." My chest warmed. I hadn't expected Jared to buy one of my books for our simple contract. Although, I wasn't surprised Jared searched me on the Internet because who doesn't check out potential dates online these days—even fake ones. I'd imagine the policy was standard practice or even a requirement for his job.

"If I had known sharks were in your novel, I'd have bought a different one. Honestly, I'm not even sure I can finish it, and I'm no quitter." His lips twitched.

Sensing his teasing tone, I played along and folded my arms across my chest. "There are no sharks in my book."

"It takes place on a cruise ship in the ocean. And the first murder is a bludgeoned guy being thrown overboard. Into the ocean. Where there are sharks. That's my worst nightmare!"

Shaking my head, I smiled. "Okay, you win."

Jared leaned toward his screen. "Speaking of irrational fears, what's yours?"

"Easy, zombies." I suppressed a shudder.

"You mean like the living dead, brain-eating, slow-moving kind of zombies? What about the Romeo and Juliet remake zombie movie? Have you seen that one? The male main character isn't a bad zombie. Only the skeletal ones in that movie are bad."

He wore a smug smile. Little did he know how much I'd thought this through. "First of all"—I held up a finger—"a zombie is a zombie, and none of them should exist. Second"—I held up another finger—"I take a particular dislike to those zombies that walk slower than molasses and yet still manage to catch you. And what's with the noises they make? Ew!" This time, I couldn't stop the shiver that ran down my spine at the memories of Enrique guilting me into watching those kinds of horror movies.

Jared let out a deep chuckle. "Have you ever tried running? I'm pretty sure those slow zombies could never catch up if you ran from them. As far as their noises—they're undead. Did you really expect them to talk in coherent sentences?"

I reared my head and scoffed. "Are you defending zombies now? Whose side are you on?" I sat a little straighter, my gestures becoming animated. "And while running was my option once upon a time, the newer zombie movies have them all scurrying around like human-sized cockroaches."

He held up his hands. "You're right."

I gave a curt nod. "That's right, I'm right. Get used to it."

This time, Jared and I were both struggling not to smile.

"Besides, I'm sure I'd trip, fall, break my leg, and the zombies would eat my brains anyway." I made a gagging motion with my finger in my mouth.

"What makes you so sure that would happen?"

Oh, that's right; he didn't know me. If he had, the answer would have been obvious. "Because I'm super clumsy."

"You can't be that bad."

Jared's expression mirrored the doubt in his tone. "Well, let's see." I tapped my chin. "I broke my ankle while playing soccer with my brother and"—I held up a hand—"despite his protests, he had pulled an illegal move, making my injury all his fault." I glared at Jared, a warning not to challenge me.

He mimed zipping his mouth closed.

Satisfied he believed my side of the story, I gave a sharp nod. "The medical bills for that one helped me put my orthopedic surgeon's kids through college. I've also fractured my skull while hiking rocky terrain with my sister, but that one was on me."

"You broke your skull hiking?" Jared's eyes were wide. "How? Did you fall off a cliff?"

"I wish the story was that interesting. No, we were hiking along a beach, and I slipped on wet rocks. For some stupid reason, I cared more about saving my phone screen than breaking my fall." I smirked as I scrolled through my photos, selecting the image of me with a giant knot on my forehead, and rotated the screen toward my laptop camera. "I fractured my skull in three places."

Jared winced. "Ouch! That looks so painful. Why would you use your head instead of your hands to break your fall?"

"You do know how much a phone costs, right?"

"Yeah, but hospital bills usually trump a phone

screen."

"Ha!" I barked. "Hospitals are for the weak!"

Jared's mouth fell open. "Hold on. You didn't go to the hospital?"

I shrugged. "Not right away, but after we got back to Seattle, I called and made an appointment with my general practitioner, who then sent me for some X-rays."

"Wow, Molly. You're one tough woman."

My cheeks were so hot they could have melted a polar ice cap. "Tough, clumsy…tom-a-toe, tom-ah-toe. Anyway…" I waved a hand in the air, dismissing his compliment. "Have you broken any bones?"

Jared shook his head. "Nope. Despite my interests, I've never broken any bones." He held up a finger. "Wait, I lied. A few years back, I broke my pinkie toe, but that's more of a rite of passage into adulthood rather than an injury. Everybody does it. Otherwise, I've only had a few bad sprains."

I grimaced and leaned away from my computer. "Injuring your baby toe is a rite of passage?"

"Yeah, haven't you broken yours?"

I pinched my lips. "No. But I guess now I'll be on my guard." I glanced at my feet. "I can't believe that's the only bone you've broken, considering the hobbies you enjoy are pretty dangerous."

"Well, unlike you, I wear safety gear." He fought to keep the corners of his mouth from turning up.

"Ha-ha. Someone's a comedian."

Jared tilted his head.

I flipped my hair over my shoulder, eager to take the attention away from myself. "There are pictures of you biking on the Plus One website. Was that a one-off photo, or do you *really* cycle?"

He scoffed. "No, the picture's real. I love both street and mountain biking."

"Have you ever competed in any competitions or races?"

"I've only done mountain bike races." Jared took a sip from his tumbler. "I participated in the Kevinton Competition in West Virginia, where I placed thirteenth for my age group. Then I did the Wisp Mountain Bike Marathon in Pennsylvania. I took eighth." He flashed a proud smile. "And I'm ashamed to admit, last year, I participated in the Michigan Iceman Viking Challenge, because the race kicked my butt, so we don't talk about that."

He shot me the same challenging glare I'd given him when I told him my broken ankle was my brother's fault, but I couldn't stop the comeback that found its way to my lips. "Ahh, now it all makes sense."

Jared's brow scrunched.

"I guess I should have expected someone who'd gotten his butt handed to him in a little race would be too much of a wuss to finish my book."

Jared poked his cheek with his tongue to hide his smile. "I said, we don't talk about that." He squinted. "In fact, why don't we make that a forbidden subject."

"And when you say, '*we* can't talk about it', you mean everyone? That's a lot of control, Jared." I bit my lip. He was fun to tease.

"I'm declaring the rule specifically applies to you." He folded his arms and leaned toward the camera. "And sometimes, having all the control can be fun."

My stomach somersaulted at his sultry voice and innuendo, but I brushed his words aside, smothering my reaction. *Stay professional, Molly.* "And what about being too scared to finish my book? Can I still tease you about that?"

"Let's make that forbidden subject number two." He held up two fingers and winked.

His expression told me if he'd had a mustache, he'd be twirling it. Damn, he was sexy, and he was good at banter. Sparks lit up my insides; he was playing along. Picking up my now-cold hot cocoa, I ran a finger around the rim, unable to help myself. "You're pushing your control now, aren't you?"

Jared's eyes twinkled. "Ooh, okay. Are we setting forbidden boundaries? Like safe words?"

My whole body clenched. Our conversation was getting close to being off-limits. This was dangerous. But if Jared wasn't stopping, neither was I. "Yes, safe words are good. Mine will be 'sandwiches.'"

"Okay, no delis for lunch in Vegas. Got it." He winked again.

Bubbles rose in my chest, and I let out another giggle. I loved how Jared diffused the tension. When I booked my excursion, I didn't think he'd be this fun to play with—a surprising bonus. I'd have a real feel for Jared when I met him.

Ducking his head, Jared peered at his camera from under his thick, dark lashes. "If you don't mind me saying, your accent is ridiculously sexy."

Chapter 6

Jared

Through my laptop screen, I watched Molly wobble in her chair, clutching her desk, and I struggled not to laugh. I couldn't remember the last time a client had that kind of reaction to one of my moves, and I hadn't even left my apartment. I was just videochatting with her before our meetup.

Although, technically, what I'd said was true and not a move. Molly's slight British accent did a number on my male impulses. Either way, our allotted hour of video time was almost up. The call hadn't been the excruciating experience I'd expected. I was enjoying myself. However, per our contract, I was still obligated to wrap up on time or charge her for another hour. Oddly, I resented the fact our online time was strictly monitored. "Sorry, I didn't mean to embarrass you. Let's get back to business."

Molly sat straighter, brushing dark waves out of her face. "Yes, let's."

"Are there any specific activities you wanted me to schedule?"

"No, usually I'm the planner. It'd be nice to hand over the reins for once. So, why don't we do this the old-fashioned way and have you plan activities you think we'd both enjoy?" Molly perked up. "In fact, don't overthink it. Just have fun. The more organic our interactions, the better my writing will be."

I pulled the corner of my mouth up in a smile. Molly's request to play out a fake romance for her novel was intriguing. Something about being part of her research had my blood pumping. *This was gonna be fun.*

"But first and foremost"—Molly held up her index finger—"I want us to be *completely* transparent in our communications. If something makes either of us uncomfortable, we should speak up. Because, like I said before, I don't mind breaking character."

Already, this wasn't like any contract I'd had before. Not to put on a show scripted by someone else and to romance a woman the way I wanted would be refreshing.

Molly recognized I had a unique perspective on relationships working as a companion and valued my accumulated knowledge. She was interested in what I'd learned over my years at Plus One—my best moves, best lines, what worked with a woman, and what didn't. And according to Molly, after our time together, she planned on using that firsthand material in her next book. I straightened my shoulders.

Just thinking about being Molly's muse made me want to step up my game and give her something memorable to write about. This would be my first time having any say in a contract. Excitement washed over me, knowing with this client, I wouldn't be a selfish rebound or used to fan the flames of another failed relationship. Molly's request validated me as a person; yet for some reason, the knot in my stomach wouldn't let up. Probably because I was still helping her sell a lie—using my accumulated knowledge to romance her, despite my lack of faith in the subject. But that's what she was paying me for, so that's what she would get. "Okay, so do you want me to meet you at the airport in Las Vegas? We could share a cab to the hotel?"

Molly shrugged, dipping her head and glancing away from the camera. "Actually, if you don't mind, I'd prefer to freshen up at the hotel before meeting you in person."

"Sure. We can do that."

"Perfect. I'll forward my flight details as soon as I've got them, and we can go from there. In the meantime, texting is okay, right? I know that might add an additional fee to my contract, but I'd like to continue getting to know each other. I don't want to be nervous meeting you."

A rush of adrenaline flooded my body. "You'll be nervous meeting me?"

Molly bit her lip and stared anywhere but at the screen. "Well, if I don't get to know you better—yes. I'm not in the habit of going away with strangers."

I cocked my head to the side. My gut said Molly was keeping something from me, and it was rarely wrong. "Is that the only reason?"

"Of course." She smoothed her hair. "Plus, getting to know you will also help me with your background as a character."

"Then do you want me to answer your questions as myself or make something up?" I wasn't sure I was creative enough to falsify a background story, but telling her the truth might be dangerous, considering my profession.

"The truth is easier to remember, so why don't we

stick with that? Because I would be happy to mention you in my acknowledgments if you'd like, or not if you'd prefer to remain anonymous."

I mulled over her question and figured since I wasn't planning on being a companion for too much longer, I could just ask her not to use my name in the book, and I would be safe. "Okay, I can do that. But I'll ask you to keep my name anonymous. I don't tend to share personal information with my clients. Your contract is the exception." I winked again.

She covered her smile with her hand.

Her reaction was one I wouldn't mind seeing again. "Anyway, our time is up, so let me give you my cell number."

Molly picked up her phone. "Hold on, let me create a contact for you." She scrunched her lips in time with her fingers as she typed. "Okay, go ahead."

I rattled off the number.

She sent a text providing hers.

"Got it."

"Okay then." She rubbed her hands on her legs. "Right. Well. Think of some good things to tell me, and I'll chat with you soon?"

"Sounds like a plan. Just don't forget we have a time difference."

Molly's laugh trembled. "Noted."

I signed off, and I sat back on the couch. My phone dinged. Molly was texting me now.

—This whole thing is probably out of the ordinary for you, but I hope you'll enjoy playing along—

—I like the idea of this getting-to-know-you thing. It's different—

Sitting forward, I rested my elbows on my knees.

Molly'd said to be honest, and adding some Plus One charm into my responses couldn't hurt, right? That's what she was asking for, after all. I quickly added to my text.

—I'm looking forward to igniting your creativity, which shouldn't be hard, considering you already radiate plenty of heat—

An analogy popped into my head. I texted one-handed, and I poured myself another Scotch from the bottle on my coffee table.

—In my opinion, the beginning of a relationship is like opening a beautiful gift—there's a thrill that comes from unwrapping the outside and discovering what's underneath—

I bounced my knee while I waited as the three dots appeared and then disappeared on my screen, long enough that I worried I'd crossed a line. But then I received Molly's response.

—Until now, I never understood the appeal of those unboxing videos, but now I do. I'm excited to open your package. Winky face emoji—

I pinched my lips so I didn't spit out my drink. I hadn't expected comments like that from a thriller writer, but I liked how this was going. *How was she having trouble writing romance?* My phone vibrated in my hand, drawing my attention back to my screen, and I set down my glass.

—Since you mentioned this would be a new role for you, do you want me to give you a baseline for getting to know each other and the tenor of how I see this proceeding?—

I was pretty sure from our videochat I could predict how this would go—fun and easy. But since she was running the show, I complied.

—Go for it—

—We can exchange fun facts like how I told you I enjoy kayaking or how I think raw tomatoes taste disgusting—

The subsequent few texts from Molly came in quick succession after the first.

—They only belong in sauces or ketchup. Don't put them in my salads. Or on my burgers. I'll send them back, LOL!—

Her comments literally made me laugh out loud, jostling the ottoman coffee table and nearly knocking over the bottle of Scotch.

—I want us to share stuff like that—

Molly fired off another message before I could respond.

—Or we can tell each other stupid things like how I have the unique ability to move one eye independently of the other—

I furrowed my brow. She couldn't be serious.

—Really?—

I'd have to see that one for myself.

—Oh yes! I'm dead serious. It makes me quite the catch—

—LOL! Okay, the pressure's on. Now I have *to come up with some interesting things to share—*

—You're welcome. Smiley face emoji *TTYL—*

I read over Molly's texts again and couldn't help smiling. She was right; tomatoes only belonged in sauces and ketchup. I also liked how she mentioned loving kayaking. Sure, white-water rafting down the Hudson River Gorge would have been more interesting, but kayaking was better than what most of my clients did for fun—shopping. Plus, the eye trick comment was hilarious. Overall, after talking with Molly, I wasn't experiencing the indifference typical with my contracts. My pulse raced envisioning how this fake date would play out. I stood and paced the room.

About ten minutes later, I got another text from Molly telling me she'd sent her flight details. For some reason, with that one little message, the excitement over my role in her manuscript multiplied.

I strode into my bedroom, flopped onto my bed, and stared at the ceiling, picking at the fuzzy pills on my cotton comforter. I needed to calm down. Already, I could feel myself getting sucked in, caring too much when I shouldn't. Molly was just another job. A stepping-stone on the way to my goal. So, why could I feel the adrenaline pulsing through my veins? The only conclusion I could make was that her contract was something different.

Molly said our arrangement was for research because she was struggling and needed my help, and by pretending to be a couple, our experiences would unblock her writing. Most people would feel a sense of pride knowing they would be the sole muse for her novel, right? Why should I be any different?

But what if I was getting ahead of myself? Sure, she'd been chill and down to earth on the screen, but what if that attitude was all a show? What if, in person, Molly was no different from all the rest and ordered me around?

I guess she could have lied when she explained her circumstances. Perhaps I was wrong in thinking Molly valued my opinions and that I could trust her. I would have to stay on my guard, because even though Molly sounded as if she understood there was a man behind my face, I would hate to be wrong.

The idea that I might have misunderstood my role with Molly mirrored the same hollow feeling I got when I checked my bank account or talked to my parents. Because the terms Molly had laid out in this contract implied I wouldn't just be proving my worth as a companion, they would also be about the freedom and control she'd alluded I'd have during our time together.

Over the past few years, I'd almost forgotten the joy and satisfaction of having genuine interactions. For the most part, who I was with filtered my whole persona. Ninety percent of my life, I was paid to be someone else. Only my friends Rachael and Lorraine understood the real me.

Then again, why should I care if Molly was lying? Playing a role was part of the job, so whether or not she was being honest shouldn't bother me, first-world problems and all. I was getting paid either way. But I had to admit, I liked the novelty of the situation Molly presented rather than having to pick up the pieces of someone else's broken relationship. Doing my own thing and having fun would be freeing. I just hoped I wouldn't end up making a fool of myself. Pulling at my hair, I withdrew my phone from my pocket to book my flight, my heartbeat picking up speed again.

I toggled between screens. Molly's email was at the top of my inbox. I checked her itinerary, and as I made the connection between Molly's contract and my amped-up feelings, an involuntary smile spread across my face. Despite all my doubts, pleasing a woman elicited a high no extreme sport could replicate—not jumping into a void with nothing more than a bungee cord around my ankles or threading the needle of cars through midtown traffic. Nothing compared to the rush of a woman's true gratification. Although I'd never used my skills on an intellectual level, I looked forward to the challenge.

Chapter 7

Molly

I folded my clothes and organized my case, angry at myself for leaving packing until the last minute.

Fin sat on the edge of the bed, tapping the toe of his red-checkered, slip-on sneakers. “What’s his name? What does he look like? What’s he do? How’d you find him?”

I shook my head. “Fin, the situation isn’t like what you’re thinking.”

“You’re telling me you’re not interested in this random guy you’re meeting in Vegas to help with your research? Because that’s not what your face says.”

My ears burned. “No, no, no. Jared’s a funny guy, but I’m not *dating* him.” I was just pretending. “Not technically.”

Fin’s head reared back with his eyes wide. “What does that even mean?”

I took a deep breath, counting to four as I exhaled. How could I explain my situation to Fin? Because “meeting a research buddy” was too vague for him to wrap his head around. “Remember how I use method acting as a form of research?”

Seeing Fin nod, I elaborated on how that process had previously translated into helping me get into my characters’ heads. Then I reminded him how my breakup with Enrique resulted in writer's block and how when Renee suggested I hire some inspiration, i.e., Jared, the idea, although far-fetched, seemed like the perfect solution—combining my previous research tactics with my current problem. I finished by outlining the agreement between Jared and me, his tie-in to my story, and my deadline.

"Research, huh? Is that what you kids are calling it nowadays?" Fin waggled his eyebrows.

"Shut up!" I slapped his shoulder and my brain glitched at the thought. "It's not like that."

"It sounds *exactly* like that."

I huffed, although the mental picture was enticing. "Even if I wanted to, the Plus One contract has a strict no-sex policy."

"So you want to?"

"Stop putting words in my mouth." I placed my shoes in a packing cube.

"He's not hot?" Fin took the tie from his wrist and pulled his shoulder-length hair into a man-bun.

"Oh, he's hot." I recalled Jared's text about a new relationship being a gift—*there's a thrill that comes from unwrapping the outside and discovering what's underneath*—and had to fight the urge to fan my face. Fin wouldn't have let me live that down. The remark sounded like Jared had been talking dirty, but not. I'd been surprised at how much I'd liked it—still liked it, one hundred percent more than I should have, and the image his words conjured sent my imagination into overdrive.

Before I knew it, I was picturing Jared and I in different scenarios—walking hand in hand, snuggling on a couch, eating dinner, nibbling other things.... No, I couldn't go there. Jared was the perfect muse; that was all. Well, almost. I recalled his fear of the sea. I sagged my shoulders knowing Jared hated open waters, considering the ocean was my second home. Not that his phobias mattered, this being research and all, but he was still missing out.

"Yeah," Fin spoke up, his words bringing me out of my reverie. "That's what I thought. Got a picture of this man who's not pushing your buttons right now?"

I rolled my eyes and pulled up a profile shot I'd saved to my phone, the one I'd printed out for my character board downstairs. "Here." I passed him my phone.

"OMG! You've saved this to your photos? How professional."

Fin's voice was heavy with sarcasm. I was about to explain myself when my phone pinged, alerting me I'd gotten a text. As Jared's message flashed across the top of my screen, I knew Fin read it.

—Did Fin agree to take you to the airport?—

Fin's eyebrows shot up. "He knows about *me*? By name? I feel so violated." Fin's hand slapped against his chest.

I attempted to rip the phone from Fin's hand.

But he pulled it out of reach.

Lying my way out of this would be impossible. "Fine. Yes. We're being honest with each other. Now, give me back my phone."

Fin tilted his head, his gaze boring into mine, passing my cell over. "Cuz, be careful."

I rolled my eyes again. "The trip is just a fact-finding mission for my manuscript. Plus, I made sure the company was legit and aboveboard. I think I'll be safe."

Fin shook his head. "That's not what I meant. You already seem smitten. I don't want to see you get hurt again."

Aww, bless him. Despite being three years younger Fin always had my back. Not that he had anything to worry about anyway. *I was not smitten.*

My phone buzzed again, alerting me I hadn't opened Jared's text, and my heart fluttered. *Calm down, Molly.*

"That's a little fancy for research." Fin jutted his chin at the lacey dress I'd pulled out of my closet.

"We're pretending to be dating, remember? Not an old married couple who've been together fifty years." I threw back my shoulders. "I still want to look good." I laid the dress on top of the matching heels. "He was absolute perfection in his picture, remember?"

Fin blew air through his full lips, making them vibrate. "I've seen better."

I put a hand on my hip. "I don't even know why I asked you to drive me to the airport. I should have asked my mother."

"Oh yeah," he scoffed. "That would've been a lot better." Fin laughed. "I can see it now, 'He's probably a murderer' "—he mimicked with a high, haughty tone—" 'my daughter's dating a gigolo.'" Fin stood. "You know what? That option is sounding better and better. Let me call her; I'm sure she'd be willing." He made to leave.

But I shoved him back toward the bed. "Okay, fine. I wouldn't have dreamed of calling my mother."

Fin flopped onto my comforter, crossed his ankles, put his hands behind his head, and closed his eyes. "I know. However, your mum would make some valid points." He lifted one eyelid. "How well do you know this guy?" In one swift movement, Fin sat up and cradled his phone, fingers flying across his keyboard.

As I threw my straightener into my bag, I heard my cell chime. I gave him a flat stare. "What did you just send me?" The preview on my screen showed a link to a self-defense video. "Very funny, Fin."

"I'm dead serious. I'm worried about you."

Leaning over, I zipped my case. "I appreciate that, but you're fretting over nothing. Jared's company performs annual background checks."

Fin crossed his arms. "That just means he's never been caught."

I shook my head, digging through my black leather purse, double-checking for my license and keys. "Are you taking me or not?"

He sighed and rose from the bed. "Fine. Let's go."

Out at the curb, the crisp autumn air bit at my cheeks, and I was relieved to get into the warm car.

Fin shut the driver's side door. "So, what things are you doing?"

He wasn't letting up. As the car moved south on Interstate 5, I studied the football stadium next to the harbor, with its new sponsored logo, out my window. "I told him to plan everything, and when I asked, he said he didn't want to give me any spoilers."

Fin shot a sideways glare, his brows knitting together. "So, you're going into this blind? I can't believe you. What are you thinking?"

"Not completely blind." Being my best friend, Fin should know me better than that. "I'm more informed than you think. He said he'd spoil me with fine dining, casual outings, and his favorite show." I shrugged; they were harmless activities.

Fin's hands gripped the steering wheel. "That's code for, 'cutting you up into fine pieces, sautéing you in garlic, and serving you to his best friends,' who'll say you taste like chicken."

I laughed. "Wow, maybe you should be the one writing thrillers. You have quite the imagination." I patted his shoulder. "Stop worrying. I know what I'm doing. You were less paranoid when I sat in that cell with the serial killer."

"Because they have armed guards in prisons."

"And Vegas is a densely populated city. I won't be alone."

"Except in your hotel room." Fin brandished the stink eye before glancing over his shoulder to change lanes.

"Well, if worse comes to worst, I'd like you to sing at my funeral."

"Not funny."

Just then, my phone pinged again. Jared's name appeared on my screen, and I smiled.

—I stayed up last night finishing your book—

Sucking in a sharp breath, I could almost taste the pine from the air freshener dangling from the rearview mirror.

Fin jutted his chin in the direction of the cell. "Is that him, again?"

"It is." I let arrogance lace my tone. "And I'll have you know he's reading one of my books. Which is more than Enrique did—thank you very much." I waggled my head and responded to Jared.

—Wow, I didn't think you would. Good for you!

Did you like the plot twist?—

—Yeah! I didn't even see it coming!—

—Really? You should have expected that with a thriller—

—You got me, Molly. Can you tell I don't usually read thrillers?—

—Then I'm flattered you read mine—

"Is he asking for recipes to cook you with?" Fin flipped on the blinker to exit the freeway.

As my cousin veered to take the two-hundred-seventy-degree off-ramp toward the airport, I held onto the door. "No, we're talking about my book."

"What? That your story is giving him ideas?"

I punched Fin's shoulder—hard.

With a hand, he massaged his there's-no-way-I'd-hurt-him muscle. "Didn't your mother ever tell you not to hit the driver?"

I huffed and rolled my eyes. "Fin!"

He held up a hand as he approached the departure curb. "Okay. Okay. Fine. I'll stop." Fin exited the car, removed my bag from the trunk, and placed the suitcase on the curb, leaving the car running. "If I'm right, which I usually am, just know I'll be on the first plane out, if you need me."

I stepped forward and squeezed Fin. "I know, and I love you for it." Releasing a pent-up breath, I grabbed my overstuffed case, praying my cousin's concerns were unwarranted and Jared bore no resemblance to the antagonists in my thrillers.

****

After checking my bag, I pulled out my phone while waiting in the security line to find another text from Jared, continuing our conversation.

—Do you read thrillers when you aren't writing them?—

I grimaced, knowing how bad my response would sound.

—Sadly, I don't read for fun. Lately, every book I've bought has been for work. Gotta stay on top of the trends. I know, I'm the worst—

—Come on, you're not the worst. I would never say that about you. So far, you seem great—

My stomach fluttered. I couldn't remember the last time I'd been this antsy about a guy since, well, Enrique. Or at least, in the beginning, when I still believed my ex was a nice guy. But when your fiancé's mistress goes into early labor, and the hospital calls your house to locate the father—or in other words, Enrique—the situation makes you rethink how you feel about love. At the time, I couldn't even process the whirlwind of emotions caused by his infidelity, knowing that poor woman was struggling to keep her baby—Enrique's baby. After an experience like that, I'd given up on men, but my emotional reactions indicated my fake boyfriend would challenge that notion.

Chapter 8

Jared

Last night, I had stayed up reading the rest of *Stern Shadows*. Once I got past the whole "on the ocean" thing, I enjoyed it, except when Molly texted me at the high point in the novel. My buzzing phone had my heart leaping out of my chest. She was a damn good writer. Her book had me hyper-paranoid and second-guessing every sound in my apartment. Seeing her name on my screen pushed the fear away.

—Are you still awake?—

—Getting ready for bed. Just about to get in the shower—

—Sandwiches—

When she used her safe word, my heart warmed. Did that mean she was picturing me naked? I liked the thought, but I played off her comment anyway.

—Smiley face emoji *LOL! Sorry. Should I have said I'm at the kitchen table in a baggy turtleneck and oversized sweats? Is that better?—*

—Turtleneck? Like stuffy older men wear? LOL!—

—No. Ha-ha! I don't even own a turtleneck—

My father, on the other hand, owned plenty.

—Somehow, Jared, I don't believe you—

—I'll prove it—

I transferred the call to videochat and ran a hand

through my hair while waiting for her to answer.

Molly let it ring a few times before her image lit my screen.

My breathing hitched at seeing her face again, which surprised me. "I hope you don't mind; I wanted to videochat just to prove I'm not wearing a turtleneck." I'd dipped the camera to show her my retro NASA T-shirt.

Molly's eyes were wide, and her bottom lip was tugged between her teeth. "Mmm, yes. Definitely not a turtleneck."

Her voice became sultry and sounded downright sexy with the accent. I readjusted on my couch so it wouldn't be obvious I was flexing before turning the camera back to my face. "What can I do for you?"

Turned out, she needed tips on what to pack, and after I gave her some general suggestions, I returned to finishing her book.

My night had been restless, but when my alarm rang this morning, I popped up eager to get on my way, instead of having to drag myself out of bed like I did for my other contracts. I checked my phone. One missed text alert. Seeing the name on the contact handle made all my energy drain out of me—a message from my mother. Before noon was early for her to text, but I recognized this was her last-ditch effort to say she tried.

—Hey, Jared, I know you said you were busy, but would you have time to meet for lunch?—

I was relieved that, again, Molly was a built-in excuse, keeping me from having to lie. Why I still cared and tried not to hurt my mother's feelings by admitting I didn't want to meet her boyfriend was beyond me. Besides, she'd always been vocal about her distaste for my previous girlfriends. If she didn't care enough, why should I? Taking a deep breath, I gave in to my "son guilt" and answered her text.

—Sorry, Mom, but I won't be available until next week. Work, you know how busy it gets—

At least, I was easing my conscience by putting forth *some* effort and telling her part of the truth.

—Shoot! My boyfriend and I will be back in LA by tomorrow. Maybe next time! kissy face emoji—

—Next time—

Running a hand over my face, I tossed my phone onto the bed and headed into the bathroom to gather my things. There wouldn't be a next time. At least not with this guy, if Heather's track record held up.

I threw my clothes into a carry-on before perching on the edge of the bed to put on my shoes. I'd almost sat on Molly's book; I forgot I'd left it there last night. Picking up the paperback, I shifted to place it on the shelf when my phone chimed, startling me. My nerves were on edge. But the notification was only from my friend, Rachael. She was my ride to the airport.

—Lorraine and I are waiting outside. Hurry up. We're double-parked—

I rubbed my clammy hands on my dark jeans, then grabbed my bag. Feeling anxious was stupid. Molly's would be like any other contract.

Except, it wasn't.

****

I spent the drive to the airport in the back seat, my conversation split between swapping job-related horror stories with Rachael and discussing what could go on my list of get-to-know-you things to tell Molly.

"You could tell her your favorite color." Lorraine

swiped her white-blonde hair into a ponytail, making her thick charcoal-lined, blue eyes stand out. "Isn't it red like those panties that one client slipped you that time?"

I cringed. "First of all, I can't believe Rachael told you about that, plus they were maroon. And second, what am I, twelve?" I wanted my fun facts to sound clever, like Molly's. "Should I put my favorite color in a note and pass it to her in gym class?"

Rachael shot me a glare over her light bronze shoulder. "Hey, lay off."

The hint of her Italian accent lilted her words as she defended her spouse.

"She was trying to be helpful."

Lorraine smiled, reaching over the center console and squeezing Rachael's thigh. "Thanks, babe."

I rolled my eyes. "Fine. I'm sorry. But seriously, what's something good I can share?"

"Why don't you tell her your stepmom is the same age as you?" Lorraine smiled with a glint in her eyes.

Rachael's lips twitched, ruining her poker face as she waited for the pedestrians to cross before turning the corner and heading toward John F. Kennedy Airport.

"I'm not gonna tell her that." My tone must have sounded harsher than I intended because both women flinched, and pain seared the back of my throat. "Sorry, I didn't mean it to come across that way—knee-jerk reaction. Because"—I gestured at my friend behind the wheel—"as Rachael can tell you, our company policy suggests we shouldn't share familial information."

"Yeah, but didn't this client hire you for research?" Lorraine shrugged.

I regretted my outburst, especially since I did agree with Lorraine's point; this wasn't just any old regular client. Molly was different; she'd even said she wanted the truth to assist her in constructing my character's backstory during our videochat. Although I'd already decided if Molly asked about my family, I would tell her I wasn't prepared to offer that kind of personal information as "fun facts." I ran a hand through my hair. "It is fair game, but parental baggage is not the angle I'm going for. I want to come up with something more flirty and exciting than my dysfunctional family."

"Rachael has a crush on Portia de Rossi. Who's your celebrity crush, Jared?"

"Gal Gadot."

"Good choice." Lorraine nodded, licking her lips. "You could tell her that."

"Nah, then I might sound like I have a type, which could make things awkward."

"Fine." Lorraine huffed and pulled out her phone. "Here, since you don't seem to like my suggestions, I'm sending you a link for conversation starters. Maybe that will spark some ideas."

My phone vibrated in my lap, and I perused the list, not even the least bit sorry I'd annoyed Lorraine. "Thanks." I was aware I was being stubborn, but if the context of this contract was part of something bigger, I wanted to get it right.

Lorraine peeked over her shoulder. "What's the name of this client?"

"You know better than to ask me that."

"*Pffi*," Rachael chimed in, her gaze still fixed on the road. "Lorraine won't say anything." She leaned closer to her wife. "Besides, when I spoke with Erica earlier this morning, she couldn't keep her mouth shut. It's Molly Covington."

I dropped my head, my heart sinking. "You've got to be kidding me."

Lorraine's eyes widened as she rotated to face the back seat as much as possible from the passenger position. "You're meeting Molly Covington?"

She was even more of a fangirl than Erica, her enthusiasm making me hesitate to answer. Did she know something I didn't? "Yeah?"

"Oh. My. Gosh. I'm soo jealous. We've attended a few of her book signings." Lorraine gestured between her and her wife. "She's my favorite. Have you read any of her books?"

I nodded. "I just finished *Stern Shadows* late last night."

Lorraine barked out a laugh. "Did you know that story took place on the ocean when you bought it?"

I rolled my eyes. "No, but the book was fiction. I was fine."

Rachael scoffed, glancing over her shoulder before having a wordless conversation with her wife, then turning her gaze back to the road. "Really, Jared? You can't even handle watching *Captain Blackbeard's Pirate Capers* with my niece."

That was an exaggeration. "What? Taking my job seriously is a crime now? Besides, this is Erica's favorite author, and reading this book is just part of the gig. I don't want to let our boss down. She's been good to me over the years."

Rachael shook her head. "I hear what you're saying. But something's different." She squinted in the rearview mirror. "Erica's favorite author aside, you're putting in a lot of unnecessary effort. That's rare for you these days."

I turned away, crossing my arms as I gazed out the window, avoiding eye contact with the passenger in the taxi in the next lane. I shouldn't have to explain myself to Rachael. "I'll make a lot of money."

She tsked and waved a hand. "You've had big contracts like this before and didn't put in this much effort."

Staring into the rearview mirror, I met Rachael's gaze, willing her to accept my answer. "Yes, but none of those were putting me within arm's reach of my goal."

Rachael pulled alongside the airport's curb, her eyebrows raised as she threw the car in Park and held up her hands. "Okay, Jared. If you say so."

I nodded, hoping to convince her as much as myself. "I do." I grabbed my bag and opened the car door.

She turned, putting a hand on my forearm. "Lie to me if you want, Jared, but you can't lie to yourself. This client is different. She's making you act all"—Rachael released her hold and waved in an all-encompassing gesture—"I don't know, weird or something. Please, just be careful."

Giving a salute, I stepped out of the car. I spent the time going through security texting Molly about her book. She seemed pleased and surprised I'd finished *Stern Shadows*, and I couldn't tell if her response was because she'd doubted her abilities, which was absurd considering her accolades, or if it stemmed from her knowing about my galeophobia.

After shoving my shoes and belt back on, I was

ready to respond to her latest text, where she'd asked me if my morning had been drama-free. The response I'd prepared would spark some follow-up questions, and I'd waited because I needed my hands free.

—Yes, the morning's going great so far! I've even successfully evaded my mother!—

—Evaded? Like, you didn't want to see her?—

I stepped into one of the stores on the way to my gate, keeping out of the way of other travelers so I could answer.

—No, I didn't. She wanted me to meet her new man. Naturally, like the good son I am, I left town—

I perused the book section, waiting for Molly's response. Her answer would be a good litmus test on how she and I would get along.

—LOL! You don't like your mom's boyfriend?—

The fact she laughed was a good sign, and I felt my shoulders loosen.

—I don't even know who her latest man is; I've never met him—

—Shouldn't you at least meet the guy?—

—Why? Getting to know him would be pointless. He won't be around long—

—Oh, that's how it is. I'm really sorry. I can't even imagine—

Molly must be one of those lucky people with married parents who'd had a good childhood.

—I'm glad you didn't share my same fate—

My earlier conversation with Racheal and Lorraine popped into my head.

—Also, just so you know, I don't usually share familial information with clients. But because this is for research, I'm making an exception—

—Of course! In that case, thank you for trusting me with the stories about your family. I promise to keep everything confidential, but I'm sorry you've had to go through so much—

—It's fine. There's not much I can do about it, and everyone's got their own stuff. I try to keep mine at least an hour away. Laughing face emoji—

—Both of your parents live in New York, too?—

—Just my dad. He lives in Tuxedo Park. My mother lived there for a while after she moved out, but not anymore. She usually lives wherever her latest fling resides. For now, that's in Los Angeles—

—May I ask how old you were when your parents divorced?—

—Yeah. My parents split when I was two, officially divorcing when I was eight—

—Did either remarry?—

—Yes. They both individually remarried several more times, treating the institution like used tissues and throwing their subsequent spouses away at the first sign of a problem—

I sounded bitter, but I couldn't help it. My family dynamics were, in essence, my backstory, and since Molly was asking now, I figured I might as well get everything out. Besides, I wouldn't have to see the pity on her face over text, so I rounded out the details as I waited for the cashier to ring up my purchase.

—Despite having already cheated, my father is still on his fourth wife. She's the same age as me. Eye roll emoji—

—Yikes! Awkward!—

—It doesn't matter, though. Judging from how my stepmother spends my dad's money, she isn't with him

for his riveting personality. I doubt they will last too much longer—

—Do you have any siblings?—

—I've got a half-sister on my mom's side from her second marriage—

I ran a hand through my hair, deciding how best to describe Willow. Maybe I'd share just the facts without my warped opinion.

—She's seventeen years younger. I was in my last year of school by the time she was born. We're not close—

I gritted my teeth, angry at myself for sharing that last tidbit. I didn't need Molly to think I was a jerk, so I asked her the same question and headed to my gate.

—What about you? Siblings?—

—I have a brother and a sister, but I'm the oldest of the three. I'm also the proud aunt of two crazy nephews—

When Molly described her family, I envisioned a Norman Rockwell painting. Whereas I was scraping my tongue, desperate to get the bad taste out of my mouth from sharing all the gory details and complexities of my divorced childhood—time for a change of subject.

—On a lighter note, what's the craziest food you've ever eaten? Mine would be cactus, and the spiky plant was delicious. Who knew?—

—I don't know if I'd want to risk the spikes to try that one!—

Dropping my head to my chest, I gave a half-laugh.

—You know they serve it at restaurants. I didn't harvest it myself—

—I didn't realize it was a popular menu item. If they have it in Vegas, I'll have to give it a try. For my

answer, it would be frog legs on a cruise—

My boarding group was called, and I grabbed my bag and joined the line as I responded.

—I've had those too—tastes like chicken, right?—

Molly didn't reply, which was good since I was stowing my bag in the overhead and settling into my seat. Not until the announcement came to place our devices into airplane mode did her next text arrive.

—Seeing as I'm a newbie at hiring companions, and I don't know how this works, if we're pretending to be a couple, how does PDA fit into all of this?—

Chapter 9

Molly

Because I was one of *those* people, I had over two hours to sit and wait at my gate. Jared and I texted all morning, right up until I asked the question about PDA-public displays of affection. The anticipation over our meeting and my unanswered message bubbled in my stomach, causing me to fidget in my seat. I could only assume since his flight was almost six hours, and mine was less than three, that he hadn't answered because he was mid-flight.

Up until that moment, as my fake boyfriend, Jared had earned himself the title of "best texter." He was better in the past twenty-four hours than all my previous boyfriends combined, Enrique in particular. My heart sank. I couldn't think about my ex. Not now. That stupid breakup was why I was struggling with this genre in the first place. Enrique didn't deserve the headspace. Until the end of my contract, that slot belonged to my Plus One.

I glanced back over my conversation with Jared, regretting I'd asked about PDA. But now the question was out there, unanswered, floating in the ether. To distract myself, I switched to my browser to research Tuxedo Park since he had mentioned that was where his father lived. "Holy bats!" The houses on my screen were more like estates. "Someone's family has money." The guy in the chair beside me glanced my way, and I swiveled in my seat, hiding my screen. What did Jared's family think about him being a companion? His job had to be a scandal. Then again, from what he'd said, they didn't talk much. Maybe his parents didn't even know.

An announcement sounded over the speakers, declaring a gate change for my flight. *Are you freaking kidding me?* Gritting my teeth, I gathered my things and headed over to the new destination. Once seated, I pulled up the hotel information Jared sent yesterday. Between texting him, choosing my wardrobe, dealing with Fin, and fretting over my stupid text, I'd been so preoccupied that I hadn't checked. I assumed I'd be more than happy with the accommodation, but I was still eager to see if Jared's preference and the price tag for the Euphoria suite were warranted.

I tapped on the link from the hotel's website. "Shut the front door!" I let my mouth go slack as I swiped through the images of the Euphoria apartment. Jared was right. The suite was stunning—floor-to-ceiling walls of windows with panoramic views of the strip, lush cream furniture, and ornate trim accents. Every penny I'd paid was worth this venue.

For the next few minutes, I toggled between pictures of Jared and the hotel, letting the daydreams flow again—Jared lounging shirtless on the couch, me touching his dimple with one hand while the other traced his pecs. My whole body shivered. Although my thoughts were just a delicious fantasy that would probably get my contract canceled, I knew the truth would be a lot less salacious. Still, even with the reality check, this would be the best immersive research I've ever done.

A text from Jared popped on my screen, and heat ignited my ears.

—Sorry for the delay. They finally fixed the plane's Wi-Fi. Are you at the airport yet?—

Jared didn't need to know I'd already been at the Seattle-Tacoma International Airport for one of my two hours fantasizing about him. Not to mention, he'd ignored the massive elephant I'd left in our chat. But if he was ignoring it, so was I.

—Yes, just arrived at my gate—

Well, my answer wasn't a complete lie. I had just reached my *new* gate. Bouncing my knee, and taunted by the now-glowing elephant in the room, I decided asking now would be easier than in person. I grimaced briefly before steeling my nerves and typing.

—Did you get my last text before you went radio silent for three hours?—

Warmth and tingles spread throughout my body. I couldn't tell if I was nervous or excited. If I was being honest, the odd reaction was probably a little bit of both. I tapped my lips, waiting for the three dots to translate into Jared's response.

—You're asking about public displays of affection, right? That's not some writer acronym I'm not aware of?—

—Ha-ha. No, PDA does not stand for some writer thing. Smiley face emoji—

—Hmm, let me see how to put this...—

Another set of dots appeared under his last text, but then they disappeared, only to reappear a moment later and disappear again. Finally, after what seemed like forever, his response came through.

—I'll use an analogy: we can cherish everything about a wine except finish off the bottle—

My breath choked out of my lungs, and my face burned. But before I could overthink what Jared meant, he texted again.

—Hold on, that example was insufficient. Let me expand—

The dots came and went again as I caught sight of a woman reading *Picket Fences* near the gate and eating a breakfast burrito. The spicy scent of the chorizo made my mouth water. I'd been too nervous to eat anything before I left, and now, I was paying for it. However, I couldn't help but smile seeing she was reading one of *my* books. Half of me wished I could read minds to know what she thought, but another part realized perhaps I didn't. My phone vibrated in my hands, bringing my attention back to my screen, where a series of subsequent texts awaited as Jared elaborated on his analogy.

—We can enjoy the bouquet—the variances in flavors and depths—

—We can decide if the wine is heady or sweet—

—We can also appreciate the label and the packaging, savoring everything but never pouring the last glass—

I put a hand on my scorching hot face, hoping no one could tell I was about to burst into flames.

—Does that answer your question, Molly?—

No, not even close. In fact, what he'd described spurred a whole bunch more. But Jared didn't need to know my inappropriate fantasies were now part of my to-do list. I suppressed my giggle.

—*Fluidly*. Winky face emoji—

—LOL! Cute, very cute. No pun intended, right? I can see why you're a renowned writer. You're great with words—

—Thank you. You're pretty good yourself—

—Flirting, I'm good at. Creativity, however, is not my strong suit. You'll laugh at me, but English was my worst subject—

I highly doubted he was terrible at any subject. But I had to see if he was lying on his bio. I glanced at the screen behind the counter, double-checking my flight status hadn't changed again before I got lost in my conversation with Jared.

—What was your best?—

—I majored and have a degree in math but have never used it—

He hadn't been lying to beef-up his profile.

—Math. Really? Of course you like the one subject where I'm completely inept. However, the math degree accompanied by that face, I dare say you are quite the package!—

He was sexy and intellectual—a dangerous combo. That we hadn't met under different circumstances was a shame. Regardless, I couldn't handle him working as a companion outside of our arrangement.

—Your profile said your degree was from ASU. Did you grow up in Arizona? Or was that just a college thing?—

—Just a college thing; I didn't grow up there. I moved back to New York right after I graduated. I could never stay in AZ with their hell-hot summers, especially being an East Coast kid—

I understood what Jared meant about the heat. If

the temperatures reached over eighty in Seattle like this past summer, I melted. Even the morning sun blaring through the windows of the terminal was making me sweat.

—Technically, I was born in Albany, but I grew up in Tuxedo Park, where my dad is. While snow's a pain, I'd take the cold over the baking heat of the desert any day—

I disagreed with Jared about the snow and cold, though. Thankfully, Seattle didn't get much of the white stuff.

—Your accent is British, right? Were you born in England?—

I straightened, surprised he noticed from our short videochat. All of my British relatives said I sounded like an American.

—Yes, I was born in England, but I've spent the majority of my life in and around Seattle. I also attended the University of Washington—

—I won't hold that against you. In the spirit of getting to know you, how do you relax after a hard day of writing?—

The mental image of my thick, fluffy socks and sweatpants popped into my head.

—I curl up with a cup of hot cocoa and a blanket and watch a good British chick flick. Otherwise, if time permits, I will book a massage—

—What's your preference...deep tissue or just a light touch?—

Heat rose up my neck. I was surprised Jared's inconspicuous question elicited such a reaction from me. But he was so smooth it was ridiculous. While I expected Jared to flirt, I hadn't expected I would be a natural in return, considering my current views on love. Then again, perhaps the banter was easier because the situation *wasn't* real.

Jared's competency must be from his time at Plus One, considering what he'd said about his childhood home life. I was confident I'd chosen the right guy, and I hoped the chemistry between us would continue when we met face-to-face because I was very much enjoying myself.

The boarding call for my flight sounded over the speakers.

—Hey, they called for my flight. If they have Wi-Fi on the plane, I'll text you. Otherwise, I'll see you in Vegas!—

—Have a safe flight—

Collecting my things, I stepped over to the queue with a smile on my face. In less than two and a half hours, I would no longer be Molly Covington. Instead, I would be the fictional girlfriend of Sam Ellis, AKA Jared Washington, AKA—yum!

Chapter 10

Jared

I still had fifty-nine minutes left of my flight, and since Molly hadn't texted again, she must not have had in-flight Wi-Fi. Knowing that, I put on my noise-canceling headphones. I wasn't listening to anything, but wearing them deterred conversations and excess sounds and allowed me to focus on the book I'd picked up at the newsstand in the terminal—just one of many Molly Covington bestsellers. Her last mystery was excellent. So, after pretending to listen to the flight attendants announcing they were coming to collect our trash, I settled into the leather seat, eager to spend the remainder of my flight inside Molly's imagination.

By the time my red-eye flight landed at ten twenty-five a.m., I had just read about the fictional murder of the main character's husband. I was torn between my initial impressions of the wife being the killer or the mistress now I'd found out she was with child. Again, I was a few chapters into her novel and Molly had me hooked. I couldn't fathom how such vengeful, twisted stories originated from the same compelling, kind woman with the wholesome background I'd been talking to over the last few days.

Molly was nothing like her characters, and after reading some of her stories, I better understood why she was nervous about our situation. This was new territory for her, too. But I was a pro at fake dating, and I planned to give Molly my A-game so she'd be at ease and, therefore, get what she needed for her romance manuscript.

Deboarding the plane took forever, considering my seat was in row twenty-seven. As I strode off the ramp, I pulled down the brim of my cap with a huff, weaving past the slower passengers and watching for the signs to direct me to baggage claim. As I passed the slot machines in the terminal, I smirked. Only in Las Vegas would somebody waste their money waiting for their plane. I'd learned years ago that an easy way to get rich quick didn't exist. For the most part, I found that if something seemed too good to be true, it usually was.

After locating carousel three, I flopped into one of the stiff, black, faux-leather bench chairs, my knee bouncing impatiently, waiting for the bags to appear. Considering how long everyone took to deplane, I'd expected the luggage would have beaten me, but I was wrong.

Ten minutes later, the bags arrived, and after retrieving mine, I headed out to the curb to grab a cab. Being early in the day, I appreciated the pleasant fall temperatures. Later the forecast said it should reach the high eighties, but I relished the sixty-three degrees for now. I was running later than expected, and the cooler air would help keep any nervous sweating at bay. The speeding clock wouldn't allow time for a shower.

The circuitous route to the hotel had about a million turns before the driver dropped me at the front doors, and I entered the ornate lobby of the Euphoria with its red carpets and white walls. The atmosphere was calm and the floral scent was inviting, easing some of the tension in my pent-up muscles. With my company's established reputation as a valued guest, I beelined toward the tall, salt-and-pepper-haired concierge and handed him my card.

"Mr. Washington." He leaned forward, clicking his heels and inclining his head. "Right this way, sir."

Within minutes, I had my keycard, and a middle-aged guy with olive skin escorted me to the apartment.

I opened the door, cold from the air-conditioning enveloping me. I followed the bellhop who strode into the foyer and placed my bag on the living room couch that backed to the window overlooking the strip. I shook the man's hand and slipped him a ten. While the room was on retainer and included tips, my conscience wouldn't allow me to watch a bellhop leave without giving them some gratuity. I knew firsthand how inconsiderate some people could be toward a person in a trade they viewed as beneath them.

The door clicked closed, and I took in the space. The living room had been upgraded since my last stay. The dining table and wet bar now had light-tan granite countertops, and the seating area had a flat-screen TV disguised as a floral painting on a side wall. Past that room to my left and right were the separate luxurious bedrooms, with their private tiled bathrooms and walk-in closets. Back toward the front door was the butler's pantry that acted as a small kitchen with a full-size fridge, range, and microwave. Nothing had changed there.

Deciding to take the north room, I grabbed my bag and headed in. I chose the room because of its smaller size and the position of the bed. Here, the mattress was parallel to the wall of glass overlooking the strip, but in the south room, the bed was perpendicular to the window, giving a more impressive, awe-inspiring view. That's the room I'd previously stayed in when I was by myself, and considering Molly was the one paying the bill, she needed to experience the full effect.

Tossing my baseball cap onto the bathroom counter along with Molly's freakishly trauma-inducing book, I turned on the faucet to wet my hair. I didn't want to have hat-head meeting her in person for the first time. Not only was my job to impress, but I found that for Molly, I wanted to.

I finger-combed the front of my hair to the side. *Nope, too stuffy*. I shook the style loose. *Nope, now I look homeless.* Retrieving my toiletry bag from my case, I returned to the mirror. With another dab of gel, I achieved the look I was aiming for—casual and messy.

Glancing at the clock, I didn't have a lot of time to prepare everything before Molly arrived. As I sprinted to her side of the apartment, a knock sounded at the door—right on time. I detoured to answer.

The gift I ordered was one of many surprises I had in store for Molly. Since this charade was for a romance, I'd decided to show Molly all the best moves I'd accumulated over my years at Plus One, as well as many of the tried-and-true clichés found in every movie. This particular gesture—a rose bouquet—was always appreciated in both scenarios. The token effort was a complete waste of money, in my opinion. Sure, the flowers were beautiful and smelled nice when fresh, but they only lasted a day or two, maybe a week. After that, the blooms wilted, died, and the whole bouquet was thrown away. In fact, the cycle was a pretty good analogy for how my clients often spoke about their failing relationships.

The delivery man extended two vases and two small envelopes.

I headed into Molly's room. I set my first vase and envelope in her bathroom, dashing back to my room for the extra surprises I'd purchased before I came. After situating everything just how I wanted, I returned to the living area and arranged the second bouquet on the dining table alongside the rest of the gifts. I stepped back to admire my handiwork. *Perfect.*

Grabbing my keycard, I headed to the hotel's gift shop for my final purchase. I searched Molly's Instapic for inspiration and wandered the store.

I didn't take long to find what I was searching for, and upon purchasing the souvenir, a lightness filled my chest. I had no doubt Molly would love what I chose, and the gift was something she could keep that wouldn't die right away. Plus, being one of my few single clients, she could take the reminder home without getting into trouble.

With the box in hand, I headed to the casino bar to wait for Molly, double-checking her flight status, and smiled. I hadn't been this optimistic about a contract in years. *T-minus fourteen minutes and counting.*

Chapter 11

Molly

I took a deep, cleansing breath and ignored the knots in my stomach as I opened the door to the apartment suite. I shouldn't be this nervous; Jared told me he wouldn't be here when I arrived, but I couldn't stop chewing on my bottom lip. Had I given him enough time to leave? The last thing I wanted was for him to see me before I looked my best. Research or no research, I dared any woman not to care about their looks in front of someone like Jared. While I had woken early to make sure my hair and makeup were on point, I slept during the flight, flattening my hair in random places and rubbing off most of my makeup.

"Hello?" I called out.

No one answered, only silence. The coast was clear. The tension in my shoulder muscles evaporated.

Leaving my bags inside the door, I made my way like a moth to a flame toward the panoramic window. Downtown Las Vegas was so much more beautiful than I expected. As I gaped at the dozens of hotels and shopping areas on the street below, I struggled not to plaster my face against the smooth clear surface. From the pirate ships, to gondolas, to a modern, glass-front mall, this place was freaking amazing. "I could get used to this."

I stood in the middle of the room and took a slow spin, taking everything in. The décor was a mixture of varying golds, terracotta, and creams blended with effortless sophistication. The ornate ceiling, with its circular molding around a mirrored center, added to the room's charm and spacious feel. The suite's online pictures hadn't done the place justice. I felt so fancy.

A wet bar sat to my left, with a dining area near the window. I let my mind wander for a second, picturing Jared and I sitting at the table, eating breakfast and enjoying the view. Although I was pretty sure any view would pale in comparison when competing with Jared.

I strolled toward the dining table, noticing a bouquet of red roses, and I buried my nose in the buds, inhaling deeply. They smelled strong and sweet. Beside the vase was a forest-green, square tin embossed with a white fern leaf pattern tied with twine. A smile broke across my face. The packaging of my favorite hot chocolate was unmistakable, and hanging from the woven thread was a fern leaf-shaped tag that read,

HERE'S A TASTE OF HOME.

—JARED

PS—I TOOK THE ROOM ON THE NORTH SIDE.

While I had no idea which direction was north, I appreciated the handwriting on the card in neat capital letters, and the words made my stomach flip. I perched myself against the table, cradling the precious tin of hot chocolate. "Nice touch, Jared." His attention to detail was impeccable.

The cocoa he purchased originated in a small boutique-style café in Pioneer Square but was sold in specialty grocery stores nationwide. He must have seen the brand on my Instapic, and I loved he'd gone to so much trouble to get me some, like right off a rom-com script. *Good start, Jared!*

I retrieved my phone and opened my compass app. After determining which room was mine, I grabbed my bags and headed to the south side of the apartment. The view across the back wall of my room made me pause, but it'd have to wait. Dropping my things, I headed to the north side. The sleuth in me was curious about how a male companion presented himself in private.

Opening his door, I inhaled, the gentle scent of cologne fanning my face. I tilted my head back and moaned—it smelled so good. *Too good.* The aroma was woodsy with notes of mint and something citrusy. For a brief moment, I closed my eyes, wishing I was a fly on the wall when Jared was here.

My actions were invasive, and I was aware I should leave and go back to my own room. I was foolish to think I could justify my curious snooping as research, but I'd already crossed the threshold. In for a penny, in for a pound.

The room appeared untouched. The only clues Jared had been here were a baseball cap on the bathroom vanity, his toiletries lined up beside a bottle of his cologne, and another of my novels, *Summer of Silence*.

Hmm, another of my titles? That's interesting. More research? He should have started with this book instead of Stern Shadows. Summer of Silence *is set in the Midwest. No sharks!* I gave it an affectionate pat on the cover, impressed by how much time Jared was putting into our contract.

A damp towel was folded on the rack instead of cast on the floor like I would have done in my room. As

I ran my fingers down the fluffy, white terry cloth fabric, I pictured how amazing Jared would look coming out of the shower wearing nothing but this, his hard chest glistening. I tugged at my lower lip. *Stop. Not professional, Molly.*

I hurried back into the bedroom with hot cheeks and peeked inside his closet—a designer suit. *I bet he'd be damn sexy in that thing, too.* Shaking my head, I chided myself. I needed to pull it together.

Before leaving his room, I checked his drawers and desk, kidding myself that I was searching for an itinerary of what he had planned and not just snooping. But how a person organized their private space said a lot about them. Because even though not knowing was one of my biggest weaknesses, it wasn't why I was taking note of how he'd folded his boxer briefs and slept in a pair of navy pajama bottoms. My stomach clenched.

With zero luck finding a "schedule," I closed the drawer and ensured everything was the same as I'd found it, before returning to my room. Jared would be here if I wasted any more time, catch me red-handed, and I wouldn't even be ready.

Back in my bedroom, I eyed the floor-to-ceiling windows that wrapped around three sides of my room. I wasn't sure such a view would allow me to sleep. Although I had to admit, the king-sized bed with its overstuffed shams and luxurious bedding was more than enticing. I ran a hand along the soft white duvet.

Two remotes rested on the bedside table. Like a kid, I jabbed random buttons to see what happened. The lighting dimmed, and the curtains closed—I was so spoiled. Even an excessive forty-six-inch HDTV rose out of the footboard of the bed. *I wonder how much that gets used, considering the view?*

As I entered the bathroom, I couldn't hold back a whispered "wow" from escaping my lips. The space was twice the size of mine back home, with a spa tub, a walk-in shower, and a long, backlit mirror. The walls and floors were decorated in assorted golds and creams, with leather panels on the drawers. To my surprise, Jared had placed a second rose bouquet on the wide bathroom vanity. *Why didn't any of the guys I'd dated do stuff like this? Oh yeah, because I wasn't paying them.*

Sitting beside the glass vase were two tickets to the hotel's signature show, *Les Mysteres des Reves*, an oversized bar of English chocolate, and a note that read,

EXCITED FOR TONIGHT.

—JARED

Oh, be still my heart. I laid a hand on my chest; he was *actually* sweeping me off my feet.

The chocolate was my favorite British treat. If any of my family were planning a visit from England, the one thing I asked them to bring me was candy. When I traveled over there, I took an empty carry-on and filled the case with chocolate to take back home.

After the quickest touch-up job ever on my makeup, I re-straightened the flat parts of my hair, and sprayed myself with my citrus-patchouli perfume hitting my wrists, chest, back of my knees, and ankles. According to my sister, fragrance on these pressure points lingered the longest and drove men wild. While most of the spots seemed logical, no one had ever sniffed my ankle, but I wasn't taking any chances. I wanted to put in the same amount of effort I would if this were an actual date. Not to mention, Jared was setting the bar high.

I chose a pair of dark-blue skinny jeans, a fitted gray shirt, and black, heeled ankle boots. The outfit was classy casual because I wanted to look put together, but not like I was trying too hard.

As I checked myself over for the fiftieth time, I heard my phone buzz on the vanity, making me jump, my agent's name on the screen.

—Good luck with the research. Keep the deadline in mind—

My stomach twisted.

—I haven't forgotten, Renee—

—Of course, I knew you wouldn't. I have complete faith in you—

—Thank you. I'll get the manuscript done—

Great. I sighed and stared at the ceiling, letting my arms drop to my sides. Why did she have to remind me of this now, right before I met with Jared? My phone buzzed again, vibrating my hand. I groaned. *Oh, Renee. I got it. Please leave me alone.*

My heart leaped into my throat. Jared was here.

—Ready?—

I squared my shoulders.

—Am I ever!—

A knock sounded from the apartment door, sending my pulse into double time. Skipping to the foyer, I smoothed my hair in the entryway mirror one last time before sliding back the metal security lock—a habit I'd developed while researching my thrillers—and opened the door.

Jared stood in the hallway in black jeans and a navy, long-sleeved shirt, pulled up on his muscular forearms and molded to his well-defined chest.

I swallowed hard. He was even more delicious in person. When I found the strength to rip my gaze away from his pecs, I zeroed in on the dimple on his left cheek, enhanced by the sexy smirk that sent a quiver through my insides.

“Molly.”

His tone was deeper than it sounded over the call, rougher, almost sultry. “Jared.” My stupid, high voice sounded breathy. *Why couldn’t I sound more confident? We’d been texting for days and even videochatted.* I stood there, frozen in his gaze.

He stepped forward.

Panic seized my brain, and I jutted out a hand to shake.

His gaze followed the gesture.

My cheeks heated. His bemused smile told me a mere handshake hadn’t been his intention.

He nabbed my wrist and led my hand behind him before placing a soft kiss on my cheek.

I pressed my fingers against his hard back. I tried not to tremble as tingles traveled through my body.

Jared stepped away.

I let out a half sigh, half giggle. *What was wrong with me?*

His eyebrow twitched.

But Jared didn’t comment on my absurd teenage-girl reaction.

Jared flashed a broad smile. “It’s nice to finally meet you in person.” His gaze swept head to toe. “You look beautiful.”

I studied the entry tile, hoping to hide my blush and not sweat from the fire his attention ignited in my core.

Come on, Molly. You aren't usually this awkward. Why did the lack of a screen between us make me an idiot? I looked up, shaking back my hair.

Jared cocked his head to the side. "How was your flight?"

"Fine, thanks. I slept for part of the trip, so the time sped by fast. Of course, that meant I had to redo my hair when I arrived…" I chewed on the inside of my cheek. *Shut. Up. Molly.*

Jared pinched his lips together. "I bought you something." He held out a white box with a black bow.

I took the present gingerly, covering my mouth with my other hand. Illicit visions of "unwrapping his package" swept through my dirty mind, filling me with desire. "Another gift?"

"A small memento to take home." He nodded his chin at the box, a glint in his eyes. "Go ahead, untie the bow." He winked.

Fresh waves of adrenaline washed through me, as I untied the ribbon and peeled back the lid, trying and failing to keep my mind out of the gutter. "A Las Vegas mug!" I pulled the gift out and marveled at the small panoramic picture depicting the strip at night. I wasn't sure what I'd expected, but nothing as thoughtful as this. I cradled the cup to my chest. "Thank you."

"Now you can check 'get souvenir' off your to-do list. I wasn't sure what to get you, but I figured a mug was a safe bet since you like hot chocolate. Thank you, Instapic." Jared nudged my arm.

Electricity sparked from his touch, and I fought back a gasp, reminding myself the contact was just platonic. "Have you always checked your clients' online profiles?" I toyed with my new cup, anxious to know if my instincts were correct.

"Yes, but I would have researched you even if this were an official date, too."

My pulse pounded in my ears. "Good to know." I admired the design one more time before tucking the cup into the safety of the box. "You did well; the mug is perfect." Glancing up, I cleared my head with a shake. My nerves had gotten the better of me, and I hadn't even invited Jared in. *Where are my manners?* "I'm sorry." I hurried and stumbled to one side. "Come in. You shouldn't need to stand in the doorway. You're staying here, too, after all." I couldn't stop my mind from running wild again with the possibilities that presented.

His cheek pulled in a half-smile. "Actually, I hoped we could grab a bite to eat and talk? You must be hungry; it's past lunchtime."

He was right. I was starving, but he was referring to food. "That would be nice. Let me go put this with my things." I rushed into my bedroom, placed the mug on my bedside table, and grabbed my purse. Slinging the bag over my head, the leather crossing over my body, I walked over to Jared and hoped he couldn't hear my hammering heartbeat.

His gaze followed the strap from my shoulder to my hip.

The attention left a trail of tingles in its wake.

"Very smart. Lots of pickpockets here in Vegas." Jared stepped closer and looped his finger over the part of the strap that rested on my hip. He tugged at the leather, pulling me closer.

My breathing hitched.

Jared's eyes smoldered. "I'd hate for our time

together to be spent in a police station filing reports. I've got other plans." He winked again and captured my hand. "You ready?"

I glanced at our entwined fingers, filled my lungs, hoping my legs wouldn't give out, and smiled with a nod.

"Then let's go." Jared led the way to the door.

But my phone rang from my bag. Pulling out the device, I widened my eyes at the name of my credit card company on the screen. "Excuse me. I need to take this."

Chapter 12

Jared

Molly angled her back toward me and took a few steps farther into the foyer of our apartment, whispering into her phone.

But I could still hear her side of the conversation.

"Hello…? That's me… No, I did authorize that charge… Yeah, I can see why the amount raised a flag, but no, I made the payment. I'm doing research… Ha-ha, I know…Of course, my verification code is 1203…Umm-hmm." She flipped her hair over her shoulder. "Okay, thank you. Bye." Molly shook her head and squared her shoulders before turning around and returning her phone to her purse. "Sorry about that."

I tilted my head and raised my eyebrows. "Fraud alert?"

She nodded.

The scenario wasn't out of the ordinary. Several of my previous clients had these types of calls, but considering the circumstances were different with Molly, the situational reminder killed the moment.

Shaking the tremors from my fingers, I took her hand. "Let's try this again." I held the door open, but my limbs were still uncooperative, and I wasn't feeling as smooth as I'd intended, as if I'd lost my mojo. An awkwardness arose between us that wasn't there before Molly's phone call. I needed to get my rhythm back. No, I *wanted* to get my rhythm back.

Reminding myself to just be me, I steered Molly out the back entrance of the hotel and attempted a normal conversation. "I know this probably isn't the most romantic way to travel, but I planned on using the monorail. I hope you don't mind. Otherwise, the walk is kind of long." I nodded in the direction of Las Vegas Boulevard. "The passes are also cheaper and usually faster than taking cabs all the time. I'm sure you noticed the horrendous gridlock on the strip. Why anyone tries to drive through that boulevard is beyond me." As we ascended the gray metal steps to the train level, I kept pace with her. "Don't worry, we won't take the monorail every day; we'll use cabs or rideshares, too, when appropriate. But a pass is a convenient thing to have." *Great.* I was rambling. I shouldn't be so nervous. This was just a different role, right?

Stopping in front of the ticket machine, I purchased two three-day monorail passes before following Molly to the platform.

"Do you travel here a lot?" She stood on the edge of the cement that bordered the track, checking north for the train and fidgeting with her bag.

The redirection in our conversation told me Molly had also sensed the awkwardness between us, which, for some reason, untied the knot in my stomach. "Not too often."

"Business or pleasure?"

I dropped my chin and looked her in the eye. "Do you want the truth?"

Molly nodded. "Always."

I cocked an eyebrow at her solemn answer. "So, you don't want me to pretend this is a real relationship? As if no other women existed in my past?" A smile tugged at my lips. If my experience at Plus One taught me anything, it was that.

Molly barked out a laugh. "Good point." She gave me a gentle slap on my shoulder. "A real girlfriend wouldn't want to know about that. But this is just us. Tell me the truth."

The tightness in my chest loosened. My confidence had returned, and I'd earned a genuine smile. "Then, both. But I've only been here twice with clients. Once as a date for a convention attendee and another time as the boy toy designed to infuriate an unaffectionate husband, but she canceled at the last minute. Usually, my contracts are closer to the residences of my clients, not destinations. However, plenty of my co-workers have been here numerous times. That's why Madame Erica gets special treatment at the Euphoria. Our two-bedroom suite is on permanent reserve for Plus One contracts."

Molly stepped closer and pressed a hand on my forearm. "Madame Erica?"

"Yeah, the name infuriates her." I smiled, picturing Erica's bright pink face whenever I used the term of endearment.

"But you're not an escort."

I shrugged. "I know, but you have to admit, the nickname is hilarious."

Molly shook her head. "I'm sure she loves you," she deadpanned. "Anyway, continue. You said you also come here for pleasure?"

"Yes, every March, I come here with my buddies

for March Madness." But we stay four to a room in a dump of a motel off the strip.

Molly's forehead creased between her eyebrows.

She appeared confused, so I clarified. "The college basketball tournament?"

Molly nodded.

But I wasn't fooled. Her glazed eyes told me she still had no idea what I was talking about. I opened my mouth, prepared to launch into the logistics, but a gush of wind accompanied the arrival of the monorail, interrupting the conversation. Which was for the best, though, since her blank expression conveyed she didn't follow college basketball, and I didn't want to bore her. I could get carried away talking about sports.

Molly entered the sliding doors and stood by the opposite wall, holding onto a support pole.

I followed, placing one hand on the small of her back with the other above us on the railing hanging from the ceiling facing her, knowing most women enjoyed my proximity.

A slight tremor ran through Molly.

The motion reverberated along my hand. *Bingo.* I smiled.

She stared out the window.

Dammit! Had I misinterpreted her reaction? Was she uncomfortable? Embarrassed? "Is this okay?" I raised a brow, prepared to step away if I needed to.

"Mmm-hmm." Molly pinched her lips in a tight line and held her breath.

With any luck, that meant the physical attraction I was experiencing was mutual. I increased the pressure of my hand on Molly's back.

She swallowed.

Molly had to be a good nine inches shorter than my five foot eleven. The height difference, combined with her petite frame, caused a protective urge to wash over me. I stepped closer.

She continued to gaze out the window and pinched her lips together.

A warmth spread through my body, accompanying the unrelenting energy flowing between our bodies. Taking a step, I eradicated the space between us.

Molly gasped.

Unexpected bolts of desire shot through me, and I gripped the ceiling support tighter. The doors closed, lurching the train into motion.

Molly stumbled.

I braced a hand on her back and, on instinct, pulled her back against my chest to steady her balance.

As her head tilted, she stared, her lips parted and eyes wide.

I dropped my gaze to Molly's mouth, and I had the sudden urge to kiss her, but I resisted. This arrangement wasn't about what my body wanted; her book was what mattered. So, instead, I leaned down, nuzzling into her hair, close to her ear. "I've got you."

Molly choked out a laugh. Placing a hand on my chest, curling her fingers against my sternum, she nodded. "Yeah, you do."

I pulled back, chuckling low and deep, and cocked an eyebrow.

She smacked my pec and averted her gaze. "Stop. You can't make me combust on the first date."

I flashed her a devilish smile, lightning coursing through my veins. She *was* attracted to me. "Challenge accepted." This could be fun.

Molly leaned in and rested her forehead against my chest. "You're good."

"I try." She had no idea what was coming.

As the monorail approached the next terminal, it slowed, and with all the enthusiasm of a kid who'd been asked to give up his favorite toy, I loosened my grip on Molly's waist, curbing my impulses.

"Is this us?" She shook her hair back.

"No, not yet. We have a reservation for lunch at The French Corner."

Her face lit up.

"You've been there, I take it?"

She nodded.

"Excellent. The one here is at the Paris Hotel, so we have a few more stops." The train rolled forward, and I kept her close in case she lost her balance again, and part of me hoped she did.

Molly held onto the handrail.

Damn. No such luck. "Do you travel much for your books?"

"Whenever my schedule allows. It makes for great research. People-watching is priceless." Molly surveyed the compartment. "Like here, for instance, I'd observe the passengers around us and try to guess their motivation for travel and destination."

Nodding, I was eager to play along. I jutted my chin at a tired-looking man in a worn suit slumped in a chair at the end of our compartment. "Okay," I leaned toward Molly's ear, holding my breath so I couldn't smell her seductive citrusy-floral scent. "That guy looks like he's gambled away his last dime and is dreading going home to tell his wife." My buddy Derek had that same look last March when North Carolina lost, leaving him without rent money.

She shook her head.

The movement flooded my nostrils with her perfume anyway and put my senses on high alert.

"He looks more like a discouraged detective fresh from the scene of yet another murder in his serial killer case heading back to the precinct."

I pulled back and drew in some clean air before giving her a playful grimace. "Kind of bleak for a romance writer, don't you think?"

Molly scrunched her nose. "You're right. Let me try again." She tapped her lips, squinting at the fellow passengers, her gaze falling on a tall blonde in a silver sequin cocktail dress that showed off her long, tan legs who boarded at the last stop. "She's an informant who poses as a stripper for the mob."

Unable to hold it in, I burst out laughing. "How is that scenario an improvement?" While the woman's chest screamed stripper, Molly's motive was just as bleak as the last.

She screwed her lips together. "Fine. Then she's just finished her shift at St. Mary's Food Bank. Is that better?"

I was laughing so hard, my stomach hurt and my eyes watered. "Ya nailed it."

She blew on her fingernails, then buffed them on her shirt. "Of course, I did."

A young couple boarded at the next stop. They were all over each other like they were on the verge of clumsy, drunken sex—hands roaming, lips and tongues everywhere—typical hook-up for somewhere like Vegas. I'd be surprised if they even knew each other's names.

Molly peered at me, waving a hand in the direction of the couple. "Your turn."

With my best poker face, I said the opposite of what was obvious. "Newlyweds."

"Sure." She snorted. "The kind that will get an annulment in the morning."

"Ah, ah, ah." I wagged a finger, unsurprised she'd come to the same conclusion. "Think like a romance writer."

Molly huffed, staring at the couple. "Okay. They're young lovers who are in a forbidden relationship and ran off to Vegas to get married because 'to hell with their parents.' As twenty-somethings, They. Know. Everything."

I scrunched my brows together. "Wow, you need me more than I thought."

Her shoulders dropped. "Sorry. The default setting in my brain is murder mode." Molly's lips angled in a pout.

"What made you decide to write thrillers anyway? From what you've told me, you didn't have a traumatic childhood or anything. Not to mention, you don't have a mean bone in your body, either." She made no sense.

Molly snarked out a laugh. "You're hilarious. But I was a simple kid, and the story isn't as violent as all that. I was a Nancy Drew fan, is all."

"The mystery book series?"

"Yep. I read them as a child."

"Really?" I readjusted my hand on the rail above my head. Reading wasn't my thing as a kid.

"I loved them and found I had a knack for guessing the endings." She smiled, jutting out her chin. "By the time I was in high school, I was a mystery aficionado.

There wasn't a movie or book I couldn't guess the ending to. My obsession got to the point where my family refused to watch movies with me."

Something about the idea of Molly watching movies by herself put my nerves on edge. "That seems harsh."

She squeezed my bicep. "The ban was warranted, believe me." Molly released her grip.

My arm felt cold without her touch.

"Anyway, in high school, I also found I loved writing. I had the best English teacher for all four years. She was a doll." Molly beamed, looking off in the distance. "She was very encouraging of my creativity. So, with my uncanny detective abilities, combined with my love of writing, the progression to a suspense and thriller writer was natural." She raised one shoulder. "Piece of cake." Molly's lips transitioned into a frown. "So, why is romance so hard?"

I resisted the urge to push her cheek back into a smile. Running a hand down her arm, I laced our fingers together. "It doesn't have to be. Just be you."

"*Pfft*. That's easier said than done." Molly's lips ascended as she squeezed my hand. "How did *you* get so good?"

She had me all wrong. Thanks to my divorced parents and over a decade as a client in the middle of plenty of jaded relationships, I didn't want any kind of love—not the one she was selling or the kind that lasted. However, that didn't mean I hadn't mastered the art of romance—the adoration and affection that led to a woman being putty in my hands. But telling Molly that information right now wouldn't help her get into the right headspace for her novel, so I kept that detail to myself.

I shrugged one shoulder, rocking back on my heels. "I'm gifted like that."

A glint flashed in her eyes, but she didn't push the subject.

The next stop was ours, and we exited into the Paris Hotel. However, The French Corner was on the opposite side of the building, with seating on the strip. We had to pass through one of the promenade shopping areas toward the casino in the front.

Pulling Molly by the hand, I followed the signs through the cream-colored hallway, the stale scent of cigarette smoke growing denser the farther we ventured into the hotel.

Molly took everything in, her eyes alight with an awed smile. On the cobblestones of their main shopping area, Molly yanked me to a stop and stared at the sky-painted ceiling. "Wow." She gave a slow blink with her mouth ajar. "It looks so real." Her head jerked in my direction. "I mean, I assume Paris looks like this since I've never been." Her gaze returned to the ceiling. "But this is incredible. I thought the opulence of the Euphoria was beautiful, but this…"

I admired the pillowy white clouds overhead. "They do go all out here in Vegas." Turning back, I was curious to know more. "You haven't been to Paris?"

Molly's smile faded, and she focused on her feet, shaking her head. "No."

"Not even for a book tour?"

Molly bit her lip. "Uh-uh. Have you?"

I studied her face, wanting to understand what had caused her excitement to fade but found nothing. Maybe she was sad she hadn't had the chance to visit

France? Because according to my Internet search, they sold her books overseas, so I didn't understand why she'd never been to the French city. "Yes, I've been. I led a bouldering excursion in Paris a few years back." The actual city wasn't like this, though. While the hotel was beautiful, the recreation paled compared to the original—a cheap imitation of a masterpiece. However, Molly seemed so hopeful. I didn't want to burst her bubble. "They do a good job of making all this"—I gestured around the hotel lobby—"appear as authentic as possible." I tugged her along. "Come on, just wait until you see the Eiffel Tower."

As Molly and I stepped out onto the cool open-air patio of The French Corner, Molly's eyes almost fell out of her head. Across the street was the Bellagio Hotel with its famous dancing fountains. A loud boom reverberated through my chest and eardrums as Molly and I approached our table next to the wrought iron fence, which stood a few feet higher than the adjacent sidewalk. The jets rocketed the water high into the air as the soundtrack blasted through the speakers across the street.

Molly was so engrossed in the display she almost missed her chair.

"Whoa there," I yelled over the show's music as I stretched forward, grasping her hip and maneuvering her into her seat. "You'd better watch where you're sitting."

"But I might miss something," she said, her gaze glued to the spiraling water.

"Don't worry. You won't. The show replays every thirty minutes. We'll see it again."

Molly nodded, still not looking away.

Four minutes later, the show ended, and Molly angled her black-wicker chair toward the table. "That. Was. Brilliant."

I smiled at the use of her British lingo.

The server arrived to take our drink orders. The stout gray-haired gentleman glanced at the two of us. "Can I start you all with anything from the bar?"

I deferred to Molly.

She scanned the menu. "Um, could I maybe just have a strawberry lemonade for now?"

Following her lead, I opted for sparkling water.

The server left.

I watched Molly marvel at the Eiffel Tower overhead like a child seeing their stack of presents on Christmas morning.

"This city is so extravagant. I can't believe they put that much detail into everything."

"Well, considering Vegas is known as one of the 'most popular and iconic tourist destinations in the world.'" I made quotation marks with my hands. "It has to live up to its reputation."

"It does."

"After lunch, do you want to go to the top of the tower, or would you like to hit the casinos before the show tonight?" I laid a hand open on the table, reaching for hers. A standard move if she and I were to act like a couple.

Molly stared at my palm briefly before smiling and placing her hand in mine.

I rubbed a thumb over her silky brown skin, enjoying the smooth texture.

She glanced at her phone to check the time. The screen read one p.m. Molly shrugged. "I would love to go to the top, if that's okay?"

In another of my best moves, I guided her wrist to my lips. "Anything for you." My reward was a shaky breath and a smile, just as I'd anticipated.

The server arrived with our drinks.

I released her hand.

Molly exhaled and shook out her hair before giving her order to the server.

I added my sandwich and two tickets for the tower elevator to the check before he left.

"It's so tall. I can't wait to go up to the top." She glanced again at the dark steel structure. "I bet the view is amazing."

"Wait until you see the strip lit up at night. That's the real magic."

Molly's smile widened. "I can imagine."

Her contagious enthusiasm, along with the sparkle in her eyes, made me excited to see her reaction tonight. The bar I had in mind for later was a favorite among my fellow companions. "Just wait." I waggled my eyebrows and took a sip of my water. Time to prove I was a good listener—a must from every client I'd ever had. "Although something I *can't* imagine is how you can move one eye independently of the other?"

Molly sat straighter and tucked her hair behind her left ear. "Okay. Are you ready for this?"

I also sat forward, eager to see her put her money where her mouth was. "Ready as I'll ever be."

Crossing her eyes, Molly swiveled her right eye away from the bridge of her nose to the outside corner and back again while her left eye stayed in its original crossed position.

I clapped. "Well done."

She beamed. "Now, you try."

Molly looked like a proud two-year-old showing off her silly face. "Uh, okay." I focused on my nose, straining my muscles in discomfort. "Nope. Can't do it. Not happening." I blinked rapidly a few times, bowing my head.

"You hardly even tried."

"I did, but trying hurt." I squeezed my eyes shut a few more times to relieve the tired muscles.

Molly grimaced. "Not a quitter, huh?"

My heart felt like it shrank a whole size at seeing the disappointment on her face. "Fine." I tried again, but my eyes didn't work that way. "Ahh, that hurts." I pinched my thumb and forefinger over my sockets, vowing never to try that again.

Molly's mouth opened, then closed.

Watching the server place our meals on the table loosened my chest. The interruption of whatever Molly wanted to say provided me the opportunity not to let her down again, and I seized it with both hands. "I have a question for you."

"Mmm-hmm." Molly squinted over her mushroom and goat cheese triangles.

Her choice of meal was disgusting and sidetracked my original question. I wrinkled my nose. "Is that any good?"

"The mushrooms are delicious; you want some?" She held out her fork.

Leaning away, I shook my head. I preferred my mushrooms to stay in the forest. "No, thanks. I'll trust you."

She shrugged and threw the bite into her mouth.

I shook off my shiver of disgust for the slimy

fungi, ate a bite of my ham and brie sandwich, and tried again. "Even though you've never been to France for a book tour, why haven't you traveled as part of your research as a romance writer? They call Paris the city of love, after all."

Molly paused. Again, a fleeting shadow passed over her features as she cut another corner off her mushroom toast. But after a moment, the expression was gone, and she just shrugged. "France is on my bucket list."

I nodded, but she didn't elaborate. The tense set of her shoulders and her terse response indicated more to the story must exist, but if she wasn't offering any further details, I wouldn't pry. She was the one doing the research. "What else is on your bucket list?"

Molly swallowed her last bite as she stared up. "Let's see; I want to swim with sharks, visit—"

"Really?" I threw my napkin on the table dramatically. "You're starting with that?" I kept my expression lighthearted so she'd recognize I was joking.

She raised an eyebrow. "Not all of us are scaredy-cats."

Squinting my eyes, I scoffed. "I'm no scaredy-cat." I pulled out my phone and scrolled to the picture my boss, Chris, took of me free climbing El Capitan last year, shirtless and hanging on by one hand—a feat that had terrified me at the time but was now one of my proudest moments. I turned the screen toward Molly. "Would a scaredy-cat do this?"

She took my phone and zoomed in. Biting her lip, a smile tugged at the corners of her mouth.

I'd have killed to know what she was thinking but didn't have a chance to ask.

Molly returned my phone with a shrug. "Meh. I suppose that's brave."

I smirked. *Liar.*

Chapter 13

Molly

The temptation to swipe to the side and see Jared's other pictures was overwhelming, and I struggled to give him back his phone. Jared shirtless was a dessert in itself, and the image sent a whole swarm of butterflies into my stomach. If I didn't need to be in a swimsuit myself, I'd have suggested swimming as one of our activities after lunch, just to see his bare chest again.

Jared shook his head and studied his photo one last time before putting his phone on the table. "Don't lie, you're impressed." He smiled and leaned back in his chair, pushing away his plate.

"Maybe a smidge." I pinched my index finger and thumb a millimeter apart, willing the blush from my cheeks.

Jared smirked. "Anyway"—he reached for his water and took a sip—"you mentioned you were born in England but grew up in Seattle?"

"That's right. I lived in England until I was twelve, when my father got a job in Seattle. Well, technically, my adopted father."

"Oh?"

Concern laced his tone, and I rushed to clarify. "My biological dad died in a car crash when I was only six months old."

Jared's brow puckered. "I'm so sorry."

What is wrong with me? The more I clarified, the worse my childhood sounded. "It's fine. What I should have said is Kevin was the only dad I've ever known. He met my mum when I was eighteen months, and they were married by the time I was two. That's when he adopted me. And with him being an American, when he was offered the job in Washington, he jumped at the chance to be closer to family."

"If you moved when you were so young, how do you still have an English accent?"

I laughed. "My English family doesn't think I have an accent anymore. However, my mother made sure we traveled back every summer to visit family, and of course, she still has her accent. I guess some of the British lingo stuck."

Jared ran a hand through his hair. "And you've lived in Seattle ever since?"

I watched a group of twenty-something women on a hen-do, taking selfies with a man dressed as a gladiator on the sidewalk in front of our restaurant. "Yes, I love the city's diversity, but when I want to commune with nature, a short drive is all it takes."

"You mean kayaking?" Jared's gaze veered to the same group of people.

His attention didn't linger on the scantily dressed women. I repressed my delight from his reaction. "Yes, and hiking." Sighing, I reveled in his full attention and pictured the tall trees and majestic sea stacks of the Washington shoreline. "The coast is so peaceful. The Olympic National Park is my favorite place in all the world."

"I know what you mean. I love when the trees are

so tall, they make you feel insignificant."

His comment caught my attention, and I sat a little straighter. "You've been to the Pacific Northwest?"

"Unfortunately, no. But I've been in the state parks around Manhattan."

"Please tell me you aren't referring to Central Park," I teased, taking a sip of lemonade.

"Hey, those trees can reach one hundred and sixty-five feet."

His tone was flat, without even a hint of sarcasm. I stared, dumbfounded. Jared couldn't be serious. The trees in the Olympic National Park averaged over two hundred feet, not to mention the redwoods in Northern California.

The corners of his mouth twitched, and a moment later, he broke out in a laugh. "I'm just kidding. New York has several forest parks upstate with huge trees, but probably not even close to the Pacific Northwest."

With a hand on my chest, I gusted out a breath. "For a moment there, I thought you weren't joking."

"I could tell." The crease in his cheek deepened. "The expression on your face said it all, and I couldn't hold in my laugh any longer."

"Well, ya got me." My cheeks heated, even though I enjoyed his sense of humor.

Jared placed his napkin next to his plate. "Speaking of forest parks, the end of *Stern Shadows* goes into great detail about the Olympic National Park. Is it really like you described?"

A warmth exploded within my chest. *My favorite subject.* "It's better. I don't even think my writing did the scenery justice." I was positive. Even pictures paled next to the real thing.

"Care to elaborate?"

"Well…" I stared at the cloudless, white-blue sky, searching for the right words to encompass the splendor that was inseparable from my emotions. "The park is so beautiful, and you can't help but believe in God when you're there. The forest is a masterpiece. Blankets of ferns cover its floor, and you can smell the green." I inhaled, remembering the damp, earthy scent, and coughed. My lungs ridding themselves of the skunky smell of weed wafting from the sidewalk below.

Jared raised one eyebrow. "You okay?"

Damn, that was a sexy look. "Yeah, I'm fine. And I know what I said sounded weird, but I'm not lying. Green has a smell—the spruce, the hemlock trees, the ferns, the wet soil. Everything combined." I was talking with my hands now. "Then there are different shades of green, too. The trees are deep, while the moss covering their branches is almost neon. Oh, and the waterfalls. Have I mentioned those?"

He shook his head, leaning forward and resting his arms on the table with a smile.

"They're everywhere. The first time I visited the park, I pulled over every twenty feet to take a picture." As I confessed, I laughed. "And don't get me started on the coastline." I rested a hand on my chest, images of the sea stacks and driftwood-covered beaches running through my head. "My heart literally aches, wanting to be back there so badly."

Jared's smile grew. "Wow, I thought I wanted to go after reading your book. But just watching you talk about the park has me convinced."

I grabbed his forearm. "Oh, you should go. You really should. Everyone should experience the Pacific

Northwest at least once in their lifetime."

"Consider it on my bucket list."

"When you do go, you need to tell me what you think." Realizing my faux pas, I removed my hand from his arm, but I kept the smile on my face with effort. Reporting back wasn't really an option considering our arrangement. I'd gotten so engaged in our conversation; I'd forgotten none of this was real.

"Do you hike by yourself or take your cousin with you? What's his name again? Fin?"

I smoothed the napkin on my lap, grateful he hadn't acknowledged my invitation. "Yes, I always take someone along with me." I'd seen too many National Geographic specials not to.

"Don't you ever just want to be alone?" Jared pushed the sleeves of his shirt farther up his forearms.

"Yeah, of course I do." But hiking by myself in the woods, alone, wasn't an option. Being attacked or eaten was my biggest fear.

"Then why don't you?"

I hung my head; I was loathe to admit my reason because I would never live this down. "I'm too scared of bears."

Jared burst out laughing, slapping a hand on his thigh. "Okay, that settles it. You can *never* tease me about sharks again."

"Fine, I won't tease you, but I do have to point out bears don't stop me from hiking." Smugly, I jutted my chin.

"Are bears a problem in the Olympic National Park?" Jared cocked an eyebrow and folded his arms.

I pursed my lips. "No, I've never actually seen one on a trail"—I held up a finger—"but I know they're out there."

"As are sharks."

Jared waved a hand in a ta-dah movement. I hung my head. He had a point. "Touché."

Continuing, Jared asked about my adventures with Fin.

My stories transitioned into tales about my parents and family on camping trips.

"Man, Molly, you talk about your family like they're straight out of a cozy Christmas movie."

I scoffed. "Not really; they can get on my nerves from time to time, just like everybody's. I'm sure yours do." I gestured in his direction.

His brows nearly touched his hairline. "That would be putting it mildly. My family get-togethers are more like an episode of a reality show."

I cringed, wishing I could kick myself. "I'm sorry. I didn't mean to pry."

"Curiosity isn't prying if my parents put their business on display." Jared's eyes darted around our table as he ran a hand through his hair.

The gesture gave him a sexy-messy look I found hot as hell, leaving me tongue-tied.

After arriving with our check, the server gathered our empty plates.

I rifled through my purse, grateful for the interruption. His family dynamics seemed like a land mine I didn't want to trigger. Taking out my brown leather journal to retrieve my compact, I set the book on the table before reapplying my lipstick.

Jared handed over his company credit card to the server and jutted his chin at my notebook. "Any secrets in there?"

"Ha! No. I only use the notebook for jotting down impressions and feelings to be more descriptive in my writing. That high school teacher I told you about earlier gifted me one at my graduation and impressed upon me the importance of always having a notebook. I've kept one with me ever since. However, I did make a note of some questions to ask you about women and dating if things weren't going as well as I'd hoped or if our conversations became awkward and quiet."

Jared's gaze darted between me and the book, his eyes twinkling.

A stifling heat rose up my neck. "But obviously, the questions aren't necessary. We're getting along just fine." I grabbed the journal to put it back in my bag.

Jared grasped my hand.

His touch sent tingles along my arm.

"Whoa, whoa, whoa. You can't just tease me like that and not ask me the questions."

I ducked my chin and shook my head. "I don't think I'll need them; our interactions will be sufficient." He leveled me with a flat stare.

"Isn't that why you hired me? For my knowledge of those exact subjects?"

That, and so I could feel something again.

"Come on." He beckoned at the notebook. "Let's have a look."

I opened the journal and retrieved my pen, my shoulders slumping. "Fine. But you have to be honest."

Jared crossed his heart and held up his right hand. "Promise."

With a nod, I read off my first question. "Thinking back over your clients, what's something every woman enjoys?"

His head reared back. "That's easy." He shrugged a shoulder. "Compliments."

I tilted my head to the side. "Are you sincere when you give them?" To hell with my manuscript, I wanted to know for myself.

Jared curled the corner of his napkin with a finger. "Just because my job is to play a part doesn't mean I like to lie."

His body language screamed of vulnerability. "So, that's a *yes*?"

"Yes. I stick as close to the truth as I can." Jared held a steady gaze.

His expression was intense, leading me to believe he'd meant the compliments he'd given me thus far, but his words said otherwise. So, which was it?

"Usually, I can find something about a date I can compliment honestly, even if I'm only saying I like the color of their shirt." He tugged at the hem of my top, his fingers lingering.

I nodded; my mind jumbled, and I needed a moment to snap out of his hypnotic presence. I was even more confused but skipped to the next question. "What—"

Jared held up a hand. "No, no. You should answer these, too. It'll help get your creativity going. The interview can't just be one-sided." As he relaxed back into his chair, it creaked. He raised his eyebrow again. "What is something every woman enjoys?"

Was I mistaken? Or had his comment sounded like an innuendo—especially combined with his sexy expression? With a shake of my head, I decided I was reading too much into his words. "That's an easy one for me, too, then." Fidelity was on the tip of my tongue, but saying that would prompt a whole other round of questions, and I didn't want to talk about my failed engagement right now when things were going so well. Instead, I came up with a different, but still valid, answer. "Listening to them. Nothing's more annoying than when a man says he's listening, but he's really not."

Jared leaned forward, his gaze down, locked on his water. "A common complaint I've heard among many of my clients."

"Is that why you're so good at listening? Your years at Plus One?" Stupidly, a tinge of jealousy pulled at my heart.

"For the most part."

Ugh! I didn't want to be right.

Jared ran his fingers across the condensation on his glass. "I've always been pretty observant, but the truth is, in a business where the other side is only interested in themselves, listening is basically my only option."

I swallowed my guilt. "Well, that sucks. I'd hate to spend time with someone so self-centered. That has to get old. Why do you still do this?" I clenched my fists just thinking about his previous clients' pious behavior.

He didn't hesitate. "Money."

"But is the job worth it?" Even after a year, I hadn't entertained the notion of dating again after what Enrique did to me, so I couldn't imagine putting myself in belittling situations like Jared's repeatedly.

"It will be. I'm saving up." He took a deep breath. "Ultimately, I'd like to buy out the extreme sports adventure company where I work, Sky's the Limit."

Jared's sexy, smoldering gaze met mine. My breath caught.

"Not that this"—he gestured between the two of us—"isn't enjoyable." Jared folded his arms on the table. "But not all of my clients are as captivating as you."

Heat flooded my face as I shifted in my chair and took a gulp of lemonade. "I know that was a line, but I could totally eat it up like chocolate." And savor every bite.

With a smirk, he squeezed my hand. "You should. It's true." He relaxed in his chair and reached for his water. "Okay, next question."

He was ready to move on, but my thoughts were still stuck on how he'd admitted he found me captivating. I cleared my throat and forced myself to focus on my notebook. "What is a definite 'no-no' on a date?"

The side of Jared's mouth pulled up, enhancing his dimple. "Pretty sure that answer is spelled out in my contract."

I pinched my lips together, afraid I'd drool staring at his cheek with my imagination going places it shouldn't.

"What? Isn't that what you meant? Something off-limits?"

I ducked my head, embarrassed my thoughts had strayed. Even worse, from his playful tone, he knew it. "Your answer wasn't wrong, but I was actually admiring your dimple." Along with the sculpted chest I knew hid under his tight shirt.

He traced the crease. "It's not a real dimple; it's a scar."

My chest tightened at his distant expression. "Oh my gosh, what happened?"

"Back when I was nine, I was dirt biking with a friend. Being young and stupid, I attempted a jump I wasn't skilled enough to do. When I descended, I crashed in the brush and"—he mimed a scraping action over the scar—"caught my face on a stick."

I winced. "Wow, you were lucky. Just a few inches up, and it would have taken out your eye."

"Yeah, ten stitches." Jared ran a finger around the lip of his glass. "Despite my father having money, he refused to let me have plastic surgery."

I let my mouth fall open. "Are you kidding?" What kind of parent would do such a thing to their child?

"Nope, not kidding. My father said the punishment fit my stupidity."

His tone was bitter, and I understood why. During my ankle surgery, my parents insisted on a plastic surgeon—and that was on my leg, not my face. "Well, the joke's on him."

Jared stared; his head cocked to the side.

I raised my glass in a toast, leveling my gaze at him. "Because it's damn sexy."

Chapter 14

Jared

Heat pulsed between Molly and me.

The server returned.

Like a cold shower, his appearance interrupted the moment. Hearing Molly talk about my scar as if it turned her on wreaked chaos on my emotions. She'd been the first of my clients to even mention my cheek or pay me a compliment. Molly's attention dissolved my contempt for my disfigurement but didn't lessen my resentment toward my father and his twisted view of a punishment. But more than that, she made me feel seen.

I shook my head and swallowed hard, forcing down the increasing sense of vulnerability growing inside me, and signed the check.

Molly put her notebook back in her bag and closed her purse.

I waited until she looked up and met her gaze. "Thank you." My tone was sincere.

She paused. "You're welcome. I meant it, too. And I'm not gonna lie," Molly placed her napkin on the table next to her plate, stealing small glances but not holding my gaze. "Ever since meeting you at the apartment, I've wanted to touch your face."

Adrenaline coursed through my veins, abrupt and intense. I wanted her to touch my scar, too. I stood and pulled Molly to her feet. With my body inches away, I placed her right hand on my scarred cheek. The warmth of her palm radiated through me. Her gaze met mine and made a slow circuit to my lips, then over to my imperfection. I dropped my hand, leaving Molly's on my face.

She took a slow, ragged breath, running a thumb over my scar as she sunk her teeth into her bottom lip.

Her gaze was intense when it returned to mine, and I couldn't break away.

Molly shivered.

Her reaction was so primal; my head spun and echoed a desire that racked my torso. Most times, my clients' responses gave the impression they were putting on a show—smiles with too many teeth, cuddling me while scanning the crowd—all done as a performance for the audience for whom they hired me. Molly's radiating quiver felt completely uninhibited and instinctual—like the kind I invoked on actual dates. But this wasn't a real date.

"I should probably stop touching your face now."

Even though Molly's words were clear, her expression appeared torn, as were my emotions. She was right, though, so I helped her by taking a reluctant step back, allowing for some distance between us.

She withdrew her hand.

My cheek felt cold without her touch. "Was it everything you expected?" I cleared my throat, hoping to erase the roughness edging my tone.

"Better." As she looped her bag across her body, her reply was breathy, and her smile was tentative.

Grabbing the tower tickets from the check cover, I held my breath, hoping to slow my heartbeat. I extended my arm. "Shall we?"

She nodded.

I led Molly toward the Eiffel Tower elevators in silence, the memory of her hand on my cheek still fresh in my mind. I pulled her to a stop in front of a metal lattice covered in padlocks.

Her eyes sparkled. "Is this supposed to be like the locks on the *Pont des Arts* Bridge?"

I held my chin high. "That it is." Of course, Molly recognized its resemblance to the panels on the Parisian lovers' bridge. After all, Molly mentioned she'd been researching romance, and the Love Lock Bridge was considered one of the world's most iconic romantic tourist attractions.

Molly stepped closer to the display. "Legend has it, after a couple attaches their padlock to the bridge, they're supposed to throw the key into the Seine River, symbolizing their love is secure forever." She studied some of the locks, reading the couples' names out loud. "Thomas and Gina, Sam and Jade, Emily and Andrew, Lisa and Mandy."

I repressed my scoff, doubting any of those couples were still together. Since I was supposed to show Molly my moves, I'd done my research and came prepared. Pulling a small lock with each of our initials written in black sharpie from my pocket, I placed it in her hand. "Want to do the honors?"

Molly's whole face brightened. "Oh my gosh, you *really* planned for everything." She took the lock from my hand, attached it to the trellis, and spun. "Now, we need to kiss the key." She held it out, her gaze landing on my mouth.

I tensed. How could I both set her on fire while

keeping my own smoldering desires under control? Moistening my lips with my tongue, I leaned forward, closed my hand on top of hers, and pressed my mouth to the cold metal.

Molly's lips parted.

My gut clenched, and I had to restrain myself. With effort, I pushed our hands toward her. "Your turn."

Molly's throat bobbed once before she closed her eyes and kissed the key.

I ignored my rapid heartbeat and released her hand.

Molly's lids flashed open as if our lack of contact broke some sort of spell between her and me. "Toss it in." I nodded at the fountain next to the trellis.

"Um, yeah, sure."

I watched as Molly glanced around briefly before appearing to notice the key was still in her hand. I wasn't the only one unsettled by the moment.

She turned to the "Seine" water feature—a cement structure meant to resemble a hewn rock with cascading water into a half-octagon basin attached to the wall on the right of the trellis. Molly tossed the key into the water. She stared, as it sank to the bottom, her gaze following gleaming metal.

I stood back, letting Molly have the moment to herself. Not knowing what she was thinking gnawed at me. An intensity had been building between us since she'd complimented my scar. If I didn't lighten this mood, the physical aspect of this date would escalate to a point of no return. I was supposed to romance her, not seduce her.

Lacing my fingers with hers, I strolled with Molly to the elevator at the base of the tower. Several other couples and one, four-person family were crammed in the metal compartment with us, adding a much-needed atmospheric buffer.

I stood in a corner with my arms draped around her waist. With Molly's back against my chest, I could feel her frantic heartbeat. Or maybe I was just feeling my own. I'd never had this kind of reaction to a woman during a contract, and I couldn't understand why the palpitations happened now. Even past clients I'd found sexy hadn't affected me like Molly. Was this what being respected by a client felt like? Did Molly respect me? Or was this part of her research to hone her craft?

The elevator doors pinged open. Leaning down, close to Molly's ear, I forced myself to ignore the exotic scent of the coconut fragrance lingering in her hair and the urge to bury myself in it. "You'll have to tell me how this view compares to Seattle." I begrudged unwrapping her from my arms. "After you."

With a smile, she led the way onto the observation deck.

The rushing air cleared my mind, allowing me to get my head back in the game. The wind had been still on the street level, but it whipped Molly's hair into her face from all directions here, forty-six stories in the air.

With skilled precision, she tamed her locks into a low ponytail using a hair tie from her bag within seconds. She shrugged with her hands up.

I nodded my approval, wanting to compliment her, but refraining because it would be too genuine.

Molly twirled and took in the view beyond the cage surrounding the platform.

I stepped behind her, resting a hand on her hip.

She threw a shy smile over her shoulder.

My rush of joy had me floating on air instead of

sure-footed on the Paris Hotel Eiffel Tower.

The Las Vegas imitation was about half the size of the original, but the view was still remarkable. Beside me, Molly had retrieved her phone and took a few pictures of the strip. I couldn't get a read on her reactions concerning the sparks I felt—if she was as aware of the tension as I was. But my ignorance was probably because I was so overwhelmed by my own nonsensical emotions, I was having trouble reading hers. I needed to get back into my role and leave out my feelings. I snatched Molly's phone. "Smile." I snapped a picture.

"Hey, I wasn't even ready!"

Her eyes danced with sexy mischief. "Okay, I'll count down." I focused the camera again, centering her with a partial view of the street below. "One, two, three."

With mock exaggeration, Molly flung herself back against the metal cage, lacing her fingers through the wires with the "duck face" expression.

I burst out laughing.

"What?" She'd regained composure.

I smirked at her feigned innocent expression. "You know what." I stepped closer to Molly and scrunched down until my cheek pressed against hers, tapping the viewscreen to selfie mode. "Now, one of us together." This time, right before I hit the button, Molly and I both turned to kiss each other on the cheek, resulting in a spontaneous, awkward peck on the lips. I sputtered a laugh.

Molly covered her mouth with her hands and backed away, her shoulders shaking.

Pinching my lips together, I attempted to stifle the

consecutive bursts. Gathering Molly in for a hug, I rested my chin on the top of her head. "I promise I'm usually smoother than that."

She giggled against my chest and wrapped her arms around me. "I don't doubt that. But don't worry; I've had worse first kisses."

I erupted in laughter again. "Wow, the bar's pretty low then?" How could it be worse than missing each other's mouths?

Molly nodded.

A part of me wanted the details, but the rest of me balked at the image of her kissing someone else. "Thank goodness I can only go up from here." And I thoroughly planned to.

Molly pulled back, peeking over her shoulder at her phone. "What are you waiting for? Let's see the picture."

I released her, feeling extra cold when the wind whipped between us. Glancing at Molly's phone, I noted the screen had gone dark. I handed it back.

Molly unlocked the device and tapped to enlarge the photo. "Oh my gosh! I don't even know if I can keep it." She cradled the phone against her chest.

I didn't get more than a cursory glance. "Don't delete it!" I reached for the cell.

Molly pulled away.

I pouted my lips and batted my eyelids—my best puppy dog look. "Please, let me see?"

Her shoulders dropped, and her head lolled back as she passed me her phone, groaning.

Warmth flared in my chest. The photo wasn't as bad as I'd expected. Sure, we'd all but missed each other's lips—hers were too high, and mine half-covered

Molly's chin. But she and I were both wide-eyed with our cheeks pulled in happy smiles. "You might not want this, but I do." Tapping on the share icon, I woke my personal phone and wirelessly dropped the image to myself. Sharing the photo wasn't technically against the rules since a wireless drop wouldn't allow Molly to access my private phone number, but I was having fun and wanted a memento.

Molly ripped her phone from my hand and stared at the screen. "Did you…?"

"I did." I waggled my eyebrows, my chest expanding. "Want to head to the other side? The dancing fountains at the Bellagio should be starting again soon." Not giving her a chance to answer, I wrapped a hand around her waist and steered her to the west side of the observation deck.

A couple stopped Molly midway, asking her to take their picture.

"Sure." Molly took the guy's phone.

The two men in matching Hawaiian shirts stood against the cage, stepping in and out of different positions.

"You know"—Molly turned her head, whispering over her shoulder—"in my book, *Shadow Minded*, the killer put a tracker on the phone in this exact situation, found out where the couple lived, and killed them." Molly took several photos, then handed the cell back to the blond guy who'd asked.

The two men inspected the pictures.

"Thank you." The redhead with freckles beamed. "These are great."

"You're welcome." Molly nodded with a smile before turning back. "People are too trusting. Do you know how easy putting the tracker on would have been?"

I shook my head. "If they only knew they'd asked Murder Plot Molly to take their photo."

Molly laughed, and her gaze narrowed. "I like that name. I'm putting it on my blog."

"You're missing the point. You should be aiming for something more romantic, like Moonstruck Molly." Eagerly, I grasped her waist, stopping her when the Bellagio was just below.

She hung her head. "I screwed up again, didn't I? I'm stuck on thrillers."

Tilting her chin with my finger, I forced her to meet my gaze. "It's okay." I traced her lips with a thumb. "That's why *I'm* here." I'd used this move many times, but never with this much electricity. Without thinking, I leaned into her. I was aware of every inch of where my body touched hers.

The fountains sprang to life with a resounding boom, and Molly shifted her gaze away, breaking the tension.

Disappointment dropped like a boulder in the pit of my stomach. I loosened my hold on her waist so Molly could turn to watch the water display. *Stupid fountains*.

Again, she appeared mesmerized, and I spent the performance torn between watching the show and Molly. I had forgotten the wonder of seeing the Bellagio's sidewalk attraction for the first few times. Although only snippets of the accompanying music could be heard because of the wind and the height, the show was still spectacular.

I studied Molly's profile. How did someone as beautiful and happy as her have such a dark mind? She made no sense. I pushed a windswept tendril of escaped hair behind her ear.

She took a brief reprieve from watching the show to smile at me.

A lightness expanded in my chest. Seeing that spark of joy on Molly's lips, I couldn't get enough. Her grin appeared instantaneous and unscripted—genuine. She wasn't acting for someone else, because no one was around to perform for—no ex, no family, no audience. That smile was for *me*. I was eager for her attention again but didn't want to disturb her focus. Out of respect, I waited for the show to end before starting a conversation. "So, how does the view compare?" I turned to face her with my arms folded and hip against the railing.

Molly had both hands on the banister, continuing her inspection of the street below. "To Seattle?"

"Uh-huh."

"I don't know if you can even compare. Both skylines are so different but beautiful in their own unique ways." She pointed at the Colosseum attached to Caesar's. "What's that building?"

"Do you want an overview tour of the hotels?" I reveled at the excuse to touch her again.

"Yes, please." She scanned Las Vegas Boulevard and shrugged with a smirk. "I know a few of the more famous ones, but not all."

Satisfying my hunger, I stood behind Molly and placed a hand on her hip. Pointing at the farthest hotel to our right, I rattled off their names. "That's the top of the Stratosphere. As you can see, the architecture is supposed to mimic the Space Needle."

"It pales in comparison."

Molly's tone was flat. "I'm sure it does. Then our hotel is just a few blocks down from there, and the Venetian—Italian-themed, of course. Next is Treasure Island, they used to have an awesome pirate show, but then it changed to Sirens, which was…"

"Lots of boobs?"

I peeked at Molly out of the corner of my eye and smirked. "And then some. But they closed that, too. The front of the hotel only has some shops, a bar, and the ships in front now. Then the Flamingo Hilton, Caesar's Palace—"

Molly touched my arm and pointed at the hotel in question. "Are all of those buildings part of Caesar's? Including that colosseum?"

I nodded, ignoring the goose bumps from her fingers. "I know, it takes up a big chunk of the strip, but most of those buildings aren't the casino or hotel. Some are shops, too. Then the Bellagio, the Cosmo, Aria, Planet Hollywood, The MGM, New York-New York, Excalibur—they have a cool jousting show in the basement. You even get to eat one of those huge turkey legs." Even though I wasn't hungry, my mouth watered.

Molly's nose wrinkled. "Ew, no."

"What? You don't like those?" *Who doesn't like turkey legs?*

"No, I don't like watching people scarf back their food like barbarians." She shivered. "It's gross."

I bobbed my head, frowning. I loved them. "Good thing I didn't book that." I pointed back along Las Vegas Boulevard. "From there, you can see The Luxor, Tropicana, and last, but not least, the Mandalay Bay."

"Wow." Molly took a few more pictures of the strip. "They're all so unique."

"That's one way of putting it." I took her left hand, tapping my thumb on her ring finger ready to share another romantic detail I'd learned while preparing for Molly's contract. "Did you know every year over one hundred thousand marriages are performed here in Vegas?"

Molly pursed her lips.

"I know, I know. You're thinking tacky."

She shook her head, with a smile. "Actually, I was thinking how my mum would love to see an Elvis impersonator officiate my wedding."

I reared my head back. A mom who didn't want a traditional ceremony was a new one. "Big Elvis fan?"

"Huge. She even made our dad take the whole family to Graceland when I was in high school. I was mortified." She covered her eyes with her hand.

Hearing Molly describe her mother's obsession with The King, I was only half-listening, too distracted by the way her eyes gleamed with pride. Her love for her family was obvious; a foreign concept to me. She was glowing, and as she continued talking about them, her hand gestures became more and more animated. While I didn't understand where she was coming from, I couldn't deny her excitement was captivating. Molly's gorgeous smile was so big I was afraid the apples of her cheeks would explode.

After another moment, she paused and tilted her head to the side, staring off into the distance.

I returned my full attention to the conversation.

"Seriously, this place is insane; my mother would love Vegas. Not just the Elvis impersonators, but everything—the architecture, the costumes, the shows. I can't believe everything is fake."

My jaw tightened, her words hitting a nerve. "Oh, I don't know. Not everything in Vegas is fake."

Molly put a hand on her hip, cocking it to the side. "Name one thing that's real."

Her tone was challenging, and I paused to take a breath before answering. Because even though Molly was paying me to *pretend* to romance her, I found it easier by just being myself. But telling her what I was thinking would be wrong. On the other hand, she'd asked me to be honest. Tugging my ear, I met her gaze from under my lashes. "Me around you."

Chapter 15

Molly

I applied the final coat of satiny lipstick preparing for our show that evening, and I couldn't get Jared's "me around you" comment out of my head. Like a carousel, the words rotated up and down, round and round through my mind, toying with my emotions. I had asked him to be authentic during all of this, but now I wasn't entirely sure authenticity was possible, considering he was also doing his job. So, I had to wonder, despite his saying he didn't like to lie, had he?

My feelings were split on the matter. I wasn't ready for or pursuing a relationship, but being the recipient of Jared's attention made me feel more desirable than I'd felt in the past who knew how long. While bantering via text and even on our videochat had been easy, I had no idea flirting would be so effortless when I met him in person—and staring into his dreamy eyes while he flirted…yum. The way he touched me was almost instinctive, making my body react on its own volition. *What did that say about me? Had I gotten lost in this?*

No. I wasn't. Was Jared hot? Yes, definitely. Did he affect me? Absolutely. But even he'd admitted he was good at his job, so our chemistry had to be an act. My goal was to get back into a romantic mindset.

Research was the only thing happening here. I had to stop overthinking this situation.

Clicking on the back of my earring, I squared my shoulders and checked over myself once more before meeting Jared in the front room. When I rounded the corner, I found him dressed in his formal wear, sitting on the couch.

Jared's eyes were wide, and his lips parted.

The way he gawked ignited every nerve in my body. I'd never received such an intense stare. As if Jared found me… No. I was being stupid. But if I didn't know better…I mean…I could swear his expression held desire. At least, I hoped.

I smoothed my dress. The nude, black-lace-covered fabric hugged my every curve with sophistication and highlighted my slender legs. In my peripheral, I noted Jared was still staring while he crossed the room toward me. I smiled.

"Molly…" Jared paused a couple of feet away.

His stare slowly caressed my figure, jumbling my thoughts.

"Just, wow." He blinked a few times, his gaze darting between my body and face.

"Oh, this old thing." I infused a teasing lilt to my words, and as I picked some imaginary lint off my dress, my heart raced.

"Don't be modest." His finger traced a lace pattern on my hip. "You have to know I'm focusing on sandwiches right now."

My stomach dropped through my thighs, and I laughed as I shoved him, thinking of my own tuna on rye. "Shut up." Jared looked just as delicious in his dark-blue, slim-fitted suit with a white, button-down shirt open at the collar. As warmth exploded in my veins, I struggled to keep my focus clear. "I have the tickets." I waved them, simultaneously fanning my heated face.

He smiled, entwining his fingers with my free hand. "Then, let's go."

Thank goodness we were going out, because if I stayed in the suite with Jared any longer, I'd combust.

****

A few minutes later, I took my seat at the lobby bar, and Jared assisted me with my chair.

He pulled his leather stool forward.

I relished the warmth of his thighs pinned against mine, and the way his muscles tensed when he squeezed them. *Have mercy!*

Jared pushed the menu away, his lips at my ear. "Let me guess…margaritas and fried macaroni and cheese?"

His close proximity made it so I could hear him over the slot machines, music, and laughter filling the bar. The act was so sexy and intimate, my whole body clenched, and the warmth of his breath rattled my nerves. *This guy is killing me.* I was hardly a stranger to the dating world. I'd had several boyfriends before Enrique, but even then, this instant attraction and mental connection I had with Jared hadn't been there. This man both riled me up and put me at ease at the same time. And none of this was even real. I cleared my throat. "How did you know I love fried macaroni and cheese and margaritas?"

Jared's dimple deepened. "Well, for the macaroni and cheese, that was easy. You have a lot of pictures of hot cocoa and food with your books on your Instapic."

Jared blessed me with one of his sexy winks, and I couldn't help but laugh because he wasn't wrong.

"As for the margaritas, I found a picture online of you and your agent at a convention where you held one." Jared shrugged. "I took a shot."

The bartender approached, wiping the counter with a cloth. "What can I get you?"

Jared ordered the appetizer and drinks.

"Wow. Thank you. Your order was spot-on. I can't believe you found that picture. The writers' conference in Spokane was eons ago. That was a deep dive into my social media." Usually, I would mind the intrusion, but for some reason I didn't.

He waggled his eyebrows. "I can go deep if I need to."

I widened my eyes to the point they might fall out of my head. This guy pushed all my buttons.

Jared smirked. "Too much?"

I bit my lip. If he wanted to shock, I could play that game. "From my experience, you can never go too deep." OMG! I couldn't believe I said that.

His eyebrows shot up. "Is that so?"

Jared's tone was sexy as hell, turning me into putty in his hands. Time for misdirection. "Well, if you want to solve a case, you have to get all the facts."

"Ahh." Jared nodded slowly. "You're talking about research."

I threw a hand against my chest and gawked, trying not to laugh. "Of course, Mr. Washington. What were you talking about?" I was sure both our minds were on the same subject.

Jared lifted one shoulder in a shrug. "Sex."

Laughter bubbled in my chest, and heat flooded my

body. I was right. "You got me." How could such a teasing conversation with this man have such an effect on me?

"Yeah, I did." Jared's cheek pulled up at the corner. "I love your accent, Molly. I know this probably sounds cliché, but you could read the phone book and make it sound sexy."

It was my turn. I cupped a hand over Jared's cheek and guided his ear to my mouth. "Jenny, 8675"—in my silkiest voice, I whispered, my eager lips grazing his warm skin as I paused for effect—"309."

Jared roared with laughter, and it took him a moment to compose himself. Wiping his eyes, he shook his head. "I was right. That was way sexier than Tommy Tutone could have ever imagined."

When the bartender slid our drinks and appetizer in front of us, Jared scooped the macaroni and cheese serving me first, then some for himself. Swallowing a bite, Jared chuckled, pointing at his temple. "Now, Jenny's playing on loop in my head."

"I'm so sorry." I worked to keep my lips from smiling but failed. "My cousin, you know, the one who just got married, her name is Jenny, too. She's had to tolerate hearing that song her whole life. All of us cousins sang the chorus relentlessly at any family gathering." Even at her reception. While most of the cousins agreed to give her a pass on her special day, Fin commandeered the microphone and sang a solo. I twisted my lips in amusement at the memory.

"Tell me more about the wedding." Jared chewed a bite of pasta. "All you've told me is you kayaked after. Was the reception fun?"

More like depressing. "It was good." I sighed. "I

liked the venue." The refurbished barn was supposed to be where I had my wedding reception. I'd first spotted the coastal location while kayaking around Orca's Island and fell in love with the area promising myself to book a date at the quaint venue the moment I had the opportunity. However, when everything fell apart with Enrique, gifting the non-refundable reception hall and all my accompanying decorations to Jenny was my best option.

Jared tilted his head to the side. "Your expression isn't screaming you enjoyed it."

"No, I did. I had a good time." I pushed the last piece of macaroni and cheese around my plate with my fork, unwilling to share about my failed engagement.

Jared squeezed my leg.

With a heavy heart, I met his gaze.

"You seem upset. Why?"

Even his pout was attractive. "I'm not upset; just worried." At least, what I said was somewhat true as I channeled my grief into concern for my cousin. "Jenny's barely known her new husband six months, and the wedding was the first time any of my family met him." My heart was pumping. "He's a taxidermist, and his name is Ted Ridgeway—Ted Ridgeway!"

Jared stared.

His expression was blank. "You know, like Ted Bundy and Gary Ridgeway? That's two serial killer names smashed together." The link wasn't a concern for me—I only knew the names because of my writing background and research on murderers, but the connection made a good excuse.

As he traced a swirl of lace just over my knee, a smile tugged at the corner of Jared's mouth.

Goose bumps erupted along my thigh.

"So, you think he's a serial killer"—he squinted with creases in his forehead—"and he's planning to murder and stuff your cousin for display?"

I deflated like a popped balloon. "Well, my theory sounds stupid when you put it like that." How could I accuse Jenny's new husband of being a murderer? What was wrong with me? Ted seemed like a great guy who was madly in love with my cousin. I simply needed to be happy for them and stop sulking about my ex. Just because I'd gotten burned didn't mean she would.

"Is that why you're not married? You're afraid your new husband might stab you in your sleep?"

Jared's eyes were dancing, and he appeared to be struggling to keep a straight face. I dropped my gaze to my hands with a lump lodged in my throat.

"That's none of my business." He squeezed my knee. "I was teasing and that was wrong of me. I'm sorry."

"I was engaged once." After I let the words spill out, silence stretched between Jared and me for a beat.

Jared rubbed his chin.

I wasn't sure from his reaction he'd grasped what I'd said.

Jared released his breath. "You don't have to talk about it if you don't want to."

His tone was soft and full of remorse, diffusing my defensiveness. "No, it's fine. Our breakup isn't a secret. Talking about what happened is getting easier with every passing day." After a moment, I met his gaze and smiled, willing my lip not to tremble. "I dumped him over a year ago now."

"What happened?"

"He cheated." I flared my nostrils, my stomach roiling.

Jared hung his head for a second before meeting my gaze again. "Ahh. That's a one-and-done for you? You didn't want to try and work it out?"

I clenched my jaw, letting indignation lace my tone. "Not when a baby is involved. She gave birth a week before we were supposed to get married. He's also the reason I've never been to Paris. That was supposed to be our honeymoon destination."

"Oh, man." Jared winced. "Yeah, that would be tough. I'm so sorry." He placed a hand over his heart.

"That's okay. I just know now if I was to get serious about a guy, I'm researching him up, down, left, and right." As well as reaching out to my police contacts to run background checks.

Jared's cheek pulled up, and he shook his head. "That's not very romantic."

"Yeah, but knowing all the details provides a sense of safety." Even then, I'd still worry.

A glint sparked in Jared's eye. "But mystery can provide its own allure, too." He ran a hand up my thigh. "What about the spontaneity?" He leaned forward.

My heart leapt to my throat.

His lips grazed my jaw. "The passion?" Jared slid off his chair and stood over me, cupping my face. "Can research compensate for that?"

He kissed me under my ear, one hand brushing my collarbone. I couldn't breathe. My whole body was on fire, tingles shooting out every nerve where Jared touched. I didn't want him to stop. All memories of my broken engagement were burned from my mind by the flames of desire engulfing my insides. Jared's lips were millimeters from mine.

"You haven't answered."

"What was the question again?" My voice sounded breathy to my own ears.

He released me and sat in his chair again, his pupils dilated. "I know he was a jerk, Molly, but you need to remember not all of us are bad."

"I'll keep that in mind." *Are you different?* Jared's face brightened as if something just occurred to him.

"If you want to, my other job organizes adventures for singles—like group kayaking and hiking. I could get you the information and sign you up?"

Not the response I wanted, but I nodded anyway; the heat of the moment squelched. "That sounds great."

Chapter 16

Jared

Molly stared off across the slot machines boarding the bar, a distant expression on her face. I was so stupid. She still wasn't over her ex. So, why did I suggest the singles adventures and seeing her outside this agreement? She'd hired me for a specific reason and made her intentions clear; Molly didn't want anything past Thursday. Her ex-fiancé's infidelity had skewed Molly's views on romance, and I was here to put them back in line. I needed to wrap my brain around her motivation and keep my focus on my role.

I took a swig of my whiskey, savoring the burn as it warmed my throat. "Speaking of kayaking, you talked passionately about the coast, so I have to ask, why do you live in Seattle?"

"Family," she said the word without breathing.

I leaned away, but experience told me women liked when I kept contact, so I took her hand in mine. "And your family lives there, too?"

Molly shook her head. "In the suburbs. I love living near my siblings. Plus, I like being close enough to help my mum since my dad passed."

I knitted my brows together and squeezed her hand at the evident pain in her tone. "You're a good daughter." I laughed to myself. "And here I was fleeing the city when my mother came into town." I couldn't imagine wanting to live near either of my parents. Sometimes, even the hour and a half between my father and me felt too claustrophobic.

Molly nodded, the corners of her mouth angling up. "Right, to avoid the new boyfriend."

I sighed. My departure wasn't just because of the new man. "And Heather." My selfish mother who'd never taken to parenting.

"Is that your mum?"

"Yeah, she's my mother. I can only handle her in very small doses, preferably by text." And when her messages weren't about what I could do for her.

Molly cocked her head to the side. "She must have some redeeming features."

I scoffed. "Well, Willow and I made it to adulthood without dying. So, there's that." Even though she had very little to do with our upbringing and my sister and I basically raised ourselves.

"Willow's your sister, right?" Molly put her fork on her empty plate and pushed it away.

"Yes, from my mom's second marriage." I took the last swallow of my whiskey and signaled the bartender for another. If I was getting into the logistics of my family again, I needed a buzz. "We don't talk much." The last time was two years ago at Christmas. My mother wanted to have the whole family for dinner to impress her boyfriend at the time and give off the pretense of a doting mother. Had Heather not been drunk, she might have pulled it off.

Molly laced her fingers through mine. "I'm sorry you're not close with your sister. That must be hard."

Most days, I ignored my family and hadn't

considered the strained relationships a trial, but as Molly said those words, a weight dropped in the pit of my stomach. I shrugged a shoulder. "If you met them, you'd understand." Not that I'd ever want Molly to meet my family.

A lifetime of passive-aggressive manipulation and neglect were easier to ignore when the other side wasn't interested in bettering themselves. Besides, my previous clients who'd hired me to "talk" only wanted me to listen. Every time I'd opened my mouth to contribute something to the conversation or say anything about myself, they'd give me a not-so-subtle reminder they'd paid for my service and my job was to make *them* happy.

While Molly's interest seemed genuine, and the situation wasn't the same, I couldn't see how whining about my dysfunctional family could help with her romance novel. My broken past would make a better psyche background for a character in one of her previous thrillers, but not this one. "My family and I have all silently agreed periodic check-ins with each other are more than sufficient." Usually initiated by a want or a need.

A wrinkle formed between Molly's eyebrows.

I was sure she still had questions, but I didn't want to talk about myself anymore. "Whereabouts in Seattle do you live?"

She sat a little straighter, and the light returned to her eyes. "My apartment's downtown."

"Can you see the Sound from your place?" I didn't know much about her city, but I did know it was surrounded by a lot of water.

"I have an uninterrupted view of the Seattle

harbor." Molly sighed, sinking into her high-backed stool, and closed her eyes.

"Wow, I'd imagine the apartments with a view are hard to come by. Your place had to be in high demand." Like some of the apartments overlooking Central Park.

"Oh, you're not wrong." Molly beamed. "But *I* had an in." Her eyes danced.

I took a quick swig from my whiskey. Leaning in, I squeezed her thigh again, encouraging her to elaborate.

Molly tensed under my touch.

I repressed my smile. Apparently, I needed to jumpstart her brain. "Sounds like you've got a story there?"

She swallowed hard. "The story's not as juicy as it sounds—my agent, Renee, works in the building."

I cocked an eyebrow. "Your agent found you a place to live? Is she also a realtor?"

Molly shook her head.

"Was this some sort of signing bonus?"

She scoffed and swatted at my shoulder. "No. But Renee works in the same building as the apartment. I was in her office when the property manager offered Renee the living space. He told her the penthouse was coming available and"—she leaned in—"I think he secretly hoped she'd rent the unit." Molly wiggled her eyebrows.

I laughed. The gesture appeared so contrived and ridiculous it came off as cute. "The manager likes Renee, huh?"

"You said it, not me." She raised her hands, palms out.

"Hey, I'm only making assumptions about the information *you* provided." As I teased her, I couldn't help but smile. I enjoyed Molly's reactions—she was very expressive, and I couldn't decide if the trait was because she was a writer or something unique to her. Either way, I liked it.

Molly pressed her lips together, but a smile broke through. "Anyway, Renee said she didn't want to live in the same building where she works, so I jumped at the opportunity—it was fate!"

"Wow, lucky you." I toasted her with my glass.

Molly's smile widened. "Yeah, just one more reason having Renee as my agent has paid off."

She was practically glowing, lighting up the entire room, and I wanted to keep her on a subject she clearly enjoyed. "How did you and she meet? Is getting an agent easy as a writer?" I had no idea how the publishing world worked.

Molly grimaced. "No. It's a bloody nightmare."

Did I hit a sore spot? Regardless, my curiosity was piqued. "Really? How so?"

"Well, getting an agent is kind of like applying for your dream job. First, you write a query letter, which acts as your resume. But the process is not that straightforward—there are about a million hoops to jump through and rules to follow for the agents, but no two agents ever have the same guidelines. Then if the agent likes what they see, they call you in for an interview, or in my case, they request pages or the complete manuscript. From there, the agent has to find an editor or publisher who also likes your work, kind of like having a second interview where you have to put on the whole song and dance again. If all those people agree, you have to juggle flaming swords for the acquisitions board to show your book will be marketable. Only then will they finally give you a book deal, or in other words, you get the job. Although, in the writing industry, this process can take years. And when you finally tell your family and friends"—she gulped her margarita—"they just shrug and ask when the book will be made into a movie." She rolled her eyes and blew out a breath, shoulders slumping.

I had no idea. "That sounds exhausting. How long did the process take you?" I stabbed another bite of the fried cheesy pasta. The fact Molly went through all of that and came out on top was impressive.

"Umm…" Molly shrugged one shoulder and screwed her lips to the side. "I met Renee at a writers' conference. She was there representing the agency she used to work for, and I was just there to learn more of my craft and make connections."

"So, you approached her there at the conference? Slipped her a flash drive with your manuscript to see if she liked it?"

Molly giggled. "No. We found ourselves next to each other in the buffet line they'd arranged for lunch. I didn't even know who she was. I assumed she was a fellow writer." She traced the veins on the back of my hand with a slight smile.

Her touch sent tingles along my skin.

"I remember glancing over, and Renee had barely anything on her plate while mine overflowed." Molly laughed. "When she explained she suffered from a gluten intolerance and forgot to inform the conference coordinators, my heart hurt so bad for her, so I insisted we ditch the conference to find a place where she could eat."

"That was very nice." Molly wasn't only genuine;

she was also kind.

She shrugged. "It's what any normal person would do."

I scoffed and shook my head. "If that's true, then in my experience, most people aren't normal." At least, no one I knew.

Molly studied the grimace on my face, the corners of her eyes tightening. "You have such a negative take on society."

I couldn't argue. She wasn't wrong. "Considering Heather never even accommodated for her own son's cinnamon allergy"—I indicated to myself with a hand—"the notion of someone giving up something for a friend or total stranger just to be nice seems unfathomable."

Molly's forehead wrinkled. "You have a cinnamon allergy?"

I nodded. "Had it my whole life."

"That seems easy enough to stay away from. What did your mother do to exacerbate it"—Molly's hand shot forward and touched my knee—"if you don't mind my asking?"

Her hand sent a warm current up my leg. "Heather would buy holiday candles with names like Pumpkin Spice and keep them lit from October until January. Just thinking about them makes my mouth itch." I scraped my tongue against my teeth. Holidays were miserable growing up. At times, when Heather felt domesticated and made a meal, the recipes tended to have the offending spice, and I always suspected she left the cinnamon in on purpose.

Molly's mouth set in a hard line. "Nice parenting." She closed her eyes and inhaled slowly through her nose. "Sorry. I shouldn't say things like that."

As I realized Molly was not only upset on my behalf, but also worried about offending me, I felt warmth filling my heart. "Don't be sorry. I feel the same way. But enough about Heather, get back to lunch with Renee."

Molly straightened her skirt. "Right. Renee and I left the conference center and bought Berry Blast Acai bowls instead." She paused for a moment, closing her eyes and licking her lips. "Mmm, those were divine."

My mouth went dry, and all my blood headed south. She was sexy even when she wasn't trying.

Molly waved a dismissive hand. "Anyway…."

Her gesture cleared away my improper thoughts.

"Renee and I discussed what we liked and didn't like about the industry, and at the end of the lunch, she admitted she was an agent—I felt intimidated. But since I hadn't booked any one-on-one agent sessions at the conference, I didn't want to take advantage of the situation, so I said nothing." Molly motioned locking her lips and throwing away the key. "Renee surprised me, though, and asked for a sample of my manuscript.

"In the end, she loved the plot and offered to be my agent. I was relieved I'd finally be out of the query trenches after years of trying. I'd been lucky. The timing for thrillers was at a peak, and I only had minor burns from the flaming sword show in acquisitions before I landed a publisher—and the rest is history." She shrugged one shoulder with a smile.

I studied the upturned curve of Molly's alluring red lips and the sparkle in her eyes. She was a kind, genuine person, and her personality was magnetic. I couldn't imagine those qualities didn't have more to do with her landing Renee than just luck and talent. Molly was a lot more modest than most people. "You're fortunate." I pulled Molly's hand to my lips and kissed her fingers, watching for her reaction. "Like me, tonight. I consider myself extremely lucky to be here with you." The compliment wasn't a lie. Lowering her hand, I wet my lips teasingly with my tongue only half playing my role.

Molly's pupils dilated; her gaze still glued to my mouth.

An ache gnawed through my stomach. I pushed it back, unwilling to let my attraction rewire my brain. Glancing at my watch, I noted the time. Molly and I needed to leave, or we'd be late. "Are you ready to head to the show?" Standing, I pulled Molly to her feet, reminding myself of my role and ignoring the fire in my gut. "This much beauty needs to be shown off."

She gazed at my mouth, her lips parted.

I was close enough I could feel her breath on my face. Sparks ignited the air, and I had to restrain myself from closing the gap.

Molly swallowed, and her complexion deepened. "Um…thank you…yes…" She glanced around her until she spotted and grabbed her phone.

I suppressed the delight from seeing her flustered appearance. "Shall we?" I extended my elbow, keeping a fair amount of distance between us in order to keep my head straight.

Molly looped a hand under my arm, then withdrew it, her forehead creased. "I need to run to toilet first."

I choked out an unintentional laugh.

She ducked her head. "I mean, I need to use the ladies' room." Molly hurried off in the direction of the bathroom.

Had she said, “run to toilet?” That was the funniest phrase I’d ever heard. The saying must have been something left over from her English heritage. Although, when Molly returned, I’d need to apologize for my reaction. I was sure she assumed I’d laughed at her when, in reality, I found her use of the phrase adorable. Molly had nothing to be embarrassed about, but I was sure I’d have to convince her. Surprisingly, I looked forward to the challenge.

Chapter 17

Molly

Despite Jared apologizing as if he'd committed a cardinal sin for laughing at my "run to toilet" comment when I returned, I still wanted to kick myself the whole way to the theater. *Ugh!* I couldn't believe I'd let the phrase slip, but if I'd been with Renee, the term wouldn't have been an issue. She'd gotten to the stage where she no longer noticed my weird expressions. Or at least, she pretended not to. I made a mental note to watch my British slang.

Entering the theater, I gaped in awe, biting back the *bloody hell* threatening to escape my lips. Without taking my gaze off my surroundings, I handed the tickets to the maroon-uniformed usher.

The auditorium was incredible, with its circular ceiling draped in elegant red and gold fabric appearing like fire above us. Below was the water-filled stage with a fog-like mist hovering inches above the surface.

Hyperaware of his hand on the small of my back, I walked beside Jared to our seats located in the Indulgence section. According to him, they were some of the finest seats in the house—complete with chocolate truffles and champagne.

"Here we are." He pointed to a pair of plush, gold reclining loveseats, each with a small TV embedded in the pony wall dividing us from the row in front.

I squinted at the screens, unsure of their purpose.

Jared smirked. "They're for the underwater scenes, so we don't miss anything."

"Wow! There're underwater scenes in the show? That's fantastic!" I shrugged to remove my cardigan, and pent-up adrenaline surged through my veins, causing my hands to shake.

"Allow me." He extended his arms.

Jared's voice was soft, but his touch was softer still. As he slid the sweater off, his fingers grazed my skin. Goose bumps erupted along the length of my arms.

As he placed the cardigan on the back of my chair and sat, Jared never took his gaze off me.

I got comfortable in the seat. "This is beautiful." I swiveled my head, but the décor was too much, and feeling dizzy, I had to stop. "You chose well." If this was just the theater, what would the performance be like?

"Wait until the lights go down." He raised an eyebrow. "It gets even better."

As the lights shimmered off the tempting curves of Jared's mouth, I couldn't help thinking he was wrong—I couldn't see him as well in the dark. But in the amber glow of the theater overhead, his lips appeared perfect and plump, and I had the urge to bite into them, they looked so delicious. My stomach fluttered—again. My reactions were like a ridiculous teen in a YA novel, and I finally understood what the characters meant when they said they couldn't control their emotions. Jared was sex on legs and good at his job. I needed to divert my focus. "So, Jared, what makes this your favorite show?"

"The premise."

His delicious dimple sank into his cheek.

"The whole show is a dream where a woman chooses between two lovers—dark passion and true love." He stared at his hands. "In my experience, relationships aren't usually things of beauty; they're spiteful. Vengeful. But here"—Jared gestured toward the stage—"the performers portray love with elegance and emotion, completely opposite my typical clients. Watching this show is an escape where, for a few hours, I can forget the realities of my job."

My heart ached. Jared's profession, and the relationship between his parents, had tainted his view on love, making him see the show's portrayal as an escape rather than something attainable in real life. The combo of these two things drew me to one conclusion—since Jared was good at romance, he'd mastered the art of being a great actor.

"Come on, I know that look, Molly. Don't you go feeling sorry for me. I'm a big boy."

"I'm sure you are." He appeared to have his life together, with goals and a future.

Jared's eyes widened.

A few moments passed before the insinuation clicked. "Oh, no. I didn't mean…I wasn't…" Heat crawled up my neck. I couldn't believe I'd said a double entendre.

Jared settled into his chair. "You're hilarious." A smug smile sat on his lips.

I grasped his forearm. "No, what I meant was—"

"Stop. I'm just teasing you, Molly." Jared placed a hand over mine.

Noting the soft expression in his eyes, I exhaled and dropped my head. *I was such an idiot.*

"But you're not wrong."

At his admission, I inhaled sharply, and I was grateful the lights dimmed, shrouding me in temporary darkness so he couldn't see my wide-eyed expression. I darted for my champagne, downing the drink in three gulps. I chased the alcohol with a truffle, hoping the liquid courage would help me chill the hell out.

Jared faced the stage.

If he'd noticed my reaction, he pretended not to. Instead, he focused his attention on the acrobatic fantasy world erupting on stage. The light illuminated his face, and the shadows emphasized his scruff and strong jaw. He was beautiful. *He's research, Molly.*

As an array of colors flooded the theater, dancing fountains sprang to life. I let go of my embarrassment and leaned into Jared to enjoy the show. The ever-revolving costume changes, moving platforms, and intricate aerial work were intoxicating. The stage was an engineering marvel—transforming from shallow enough to dance on one moment to expanding into a deep pool for synchronized swimmers the next.

Seeing a high diver flip and twirl, end over end, into the pool below, I squeezed Jared's bicep.

He placed his hand over mine, with a smile.

Shivers ran along my arm. I'd forgotten how nice enjoying a show with someone could be. And man, Jared's woodsy cologne smelled good. His scent intoxicated me.

The lights came up, and the performers took their final bow. I lifted my head off Jared's shoulder, and I rose from my seat, clapping furiously.

Jared stood, too. When the applause died down, he raised his brows. "What did you think?"

He looked so hopeful, I put a hand over my aching heart. "The story was so tragic. Why did the protagonist have to choose? What's love if you don't have passion? But passion is so hollow without love?"

As he brushed the back of his fingers along my cheek, Jared's Adam's apple bobbed. "I'm glad you liked *Les Mysteres*. The *only* other time I've seen the show was when I bought tickets for Heather last Mother's Day, but she canceled last minute."

The back of my neck prickled. "Are you kidding?" I shook my head, clenching my teeth. With every story, his mother sounded worse.

"Well, she'd had her lips filled and wanted the swelling to go down and the bruising to fade before going out in public." He'd kept his gaze locked on the stage "So, I attended alone."

My chest tightened. "I'm sorry. It's none of my business, but hearing that breaks my heart." Without overthinking, I wrapped my hands around his waist and squeezed, resting my cheek against his chest. "You're a good son."

Despite Jared's exposure to volatile relationships on top of how Heather treated him, the fact he hadn't given up hoping for more with his mother was impressive. Perhaps Jared's walls were just a defense mechanism, and behind his sexy façade was simply a vulnerable man waiting to be loved. Or was I just fabricating what I wanted to see? A low rumble of laughter resonated through Jared's ribs against my ear.

"Well, at least somebody thinks so."

I pulled back to meet his gaze. "If your parents

don't see that, they're idiots." This man was something special. Jared laughed with real humor this time.

He kissed my forehead. "You're cute."

Cute? Not the response I'd expected after calling his parents idiots, but perhaps his dismissiveness meant he didn't want to talk about his family's opinion of him. I cocked an eyebrow. "Really? I was 'wow' earlier. Now I'm just 'cute?' "

"You're right." As he ran a finger up my spine, Jared's pupils dilated.

The gesture left tingles in its wake.

"My words aren't sufficient to describe how radiant you look tonight."

Holy bats, that was hot! Although, I wasn't going to tell him. However, I did make a mental note for my research. "Better." I shook my hair back and looked away, but the action didn't stop my ears from burning. Even my knees were shaky. Good thing his arms were around my waist.

Jared placed a soft kiss on my temple.

I shuddered.

"What about stunning?" He brushed his lips against my cheek. "Or irresistible?" His mouth was on my jaw. "Sexy?" Jared kissed along my neck.

I arched back, offering him access, giddy with anticipation. His ragged breath warmed my skin.

"How about desirable?"

Jared had used this move on me earlier at the bar, and I'd loved it then. I had no idea if the sexy advance was from his personal repertoire or something he'd devised from being at Plus One. But either way, I enjoyed my body's response, and dug my nails into the soft fabric of his jacket with only one thought in my head—*kiss me. Please, kiss me*.

"Excuse me."

I jumped, opening my eyes.

Jared shifted his gaze over my shoulder, his jaw tight.

I spun to see the dark-haired man with the strong Slavic accent who'd interrupted us, holding a broom and dustpan.

"We need to clean for the next show."

I smoothed my dress, regulating my breathing.

Jared raised a hand palm out and inclined his head at the gentleman. "Of course. We'll get out of your way." Reaching over, Jared grabbed the cardigan.

I had long since forgotten it.

"Would you like me to hold this for you, or are you chilly?" He grazed his finger along the goose bumps on my arm.

While I shivered, the temperature of the theater wasn't the issue. "I'm a little chilly." The lie was just an excuse to get him to touch me again.

Jared cocked a half-smile and held out my cardigan. He slid the knitted fabric over my arms and placed a gentle kiss between my neck and shoulder.

I gasped, my heart hammering against my ribcage.

Jared's grip tightened, and his nose skimmed my earlobe. He pulled my back against his chest.

If he didn't stop, I'd throw him on the recliner and have my way with him.

The usher cleared his throat.

With a curt exhale, Jared released me and took my hand. "Ready?"

To explode? Yes.

Chapter 18

Jared

The flashing billboards and strobing neon signs lining Las Vegas Boulevard assaulted my vision. Despite the night sky, I squinted.

"Holy bats!" Molly's eyes widened, and she pulled me to an abrupt halt. "This is incredible—what are their electric bills?"

I chuckled; that exact question crossed my mind the first time I was here. Having taken a class on renewable energy in college, I remembered Las Vegas had been referenced numerous times in the lectures, and I'd memorized a few fun facts. "The electricity used on the strip alone accounts for twenty percent of the city's energy consumption."

She gaped.

I smiled, then pointed toward the Luxor at the south end of the street and the casino's bright beacon. "You see the beam coming from the top of the pyramid?"

Her gaze followed the direction of my finger and she nodded.

"That beam is considered the most powerful light in the world and costs about fifty-one dollars per hour to illuminate."

Molly gasped, a hand flying over her open mouth.

"That's more than a thousand dollars per month for that one light alone."

I held in a laugh. Math really was her worst subject. "More like twelve thousand dollars."

She grimaced and shrugged before taking in the rest of the strip with a slow turn. "Forget my previous statement." She waved a hand. "I don't want to know how much they pay to keep all this running."

I squeezed Molly's hand and towed her to the taxi line at the entrance of the hotel. "Maybe not, but you have to admit the city lives up to its reputation. Vegas is about as flashy and obnoxious as most of the people who love it."

"Vegas aficionados are obnoxious?"

That was an understatement. "At least half the population contains as much plastic as the casinos." Just like my mother.

Molly laughed. "That's hilarious. Where are we off to now?"

Honestly, I wanted to go back to the theater and pick up where I'd left off, but that plan wasn't possible or professional. Over the last few hours, I realized my time with Molly would be more about restraint rather than effort. The last thing I should do was stray from my original plan. "You think the lights are beautiful from the street? This is nothing. I've got a better view in mind." *The one from your bedroom window.* The thought came unbidden, and denying its truth, I shoved it aside.

As Molly bit her lip, her cheeks flinched in a smile.

I followed the gesture with my gaze. I had the strongest impulse to free her mouth. To my surprise, I gave into my subconscious, and I raised a hand, tugging her lip free with my thumb on her chin, before the rational part of my brain could catch up and stop me.

Molly moaned a sigh.

My gut clenched. If I didn't remove my hand, I would end up kissing her, like *really* kissing her, and the taxi line was *not* the right time for that kind of kiss. Hell, I wasn't sure I should ever kiss her again with the way things were going. I wouldn't be able to stop. Lust wasn't what she wanted. I wasn't surprised by my innate physical attraction to Molly. After all, I clicked with her back on the videochat. Texting was effortless. But my desire was intense. Afraid of what I might do next, I forced my hand back to my side.

The short, jolty cab ride to the Mandalay Bay was just the cold shower I needed to get my head back in the game. Molly hired me for research. I shouldn't be pining this hard. I needed to be more vigilant with my thoughts and emotions.

As the elevator ascended to the rooftop bar, Molly eyed me before the doors opened. Looking back over her shoulder, she licked her lips and exited.

My throat dried. What was she playing at? The gesture taunted me and did weird things to my insides, but I ignored them. I remained professional.

The plan was to surprise Molly with a view of the strip from Mandalay Bay's rooftop. The packed bar prevented her from seeing the twinkling lights from the balcony when she and I arrived. Eagerly, I covered her eyes with a hand and pulled her into the nightclub lobby with its distinctive scent of sweat and alcohol mixed with desert air.

"What are you doing?"

Her tone sounded reproachful, but the smile on her

face revealed her true feelings. "Trust me." Feeling smug, I wrapped an arm around Molly's waist and pinned her to my side. Her form melted into my chest perfectly, screwing with my insides again.

"Okay." She slipped a hand around my back and braced herself.

I trampled the quivering in my stomach and maneuvered her through the crowd onto the balcony opposite the elevators. Worming past other onlookers, I guided Molly with one hand on her left hip and secured a spot against the railing. I stood behind her, a hand still covering her eyes, fighting to ignore the heat between Molly's back and my chest. "Okay, you ready?"

Her fingers curled against my hand. "Ready."

Uncovering Molly's eyes, I stepped beside her.

She took in the view. "Oh, Jared." Her hands grasped the railing. "This…"

"I know, right?" I pulled her snugly against my side, admiring what could only be described as a fairground for grown-ups.

Silent, Molly stared at the twinkling lights of Las Vegas Boulevard with a small smile. The rhythm of the music blared from the speakers, and she swayed her hips, syncing them with the beat.

I nodded at the tiled dance floor crowded with undulating bodies and pulsating lights. "Do you dance?"

Her eyes widened as they darted from me to the dance floor. "Do I dance? *Pffft.*" Taking my hand, she hauled me into the sea of people.

Gripping her hips, I swayed with her in tandem to the music. From the purse of Molly's lips to the sultry glint in her eyes, her love for dancing was evident, and she was good.

She wrapped her cardigan around her waist.

Molly moved as if letting the music dictate her actions—a captivating seductress on the dance floor. She appeared wholly in the moment—no agenda, not caring who or what was around her, just dancing for pure pleasure—her pleasure. A new concept for one of my clients.

I raked my gaze over Molly's curves, and the beat thumped in my ears, reverberating through my chest.

Her hips swayed to the beat, and her arms moved and twisted above her head. She stepped forward, inches away, and placed a hand on my chest. Molly traced the line of buttons on the front of my shirt with heavy-lidded eyes, stopping just before my belt.

The suggestive motion hitched my breathing. *Was Molly for real or just dancing? Either way, this woman had me undone.*

I spun Molly around to distract myself, thinking the closeness would be easier if I wasn't staring at her exquisite face. I was wrong. I pulled her backside against me, and her body gyrated with mine, and the blood in my head worked its way south. This position was anything but distracting.

She raised an arm and held the back of my neck.

Losing my focus, I ran a hand along the length of Molly's side and gripped her hips again. Sweat trickled down my back from more than just the dancing. I fought a losing battle to keep my head straight. *Sandwiches, sandwiches, sandwiches.*

Molly stepped away and fanned her face.

I shook my head, mad at myself for having such little control.

"Do you want to get a drink?" she shouted over the music.

I nodded, grateful for the distraction, and led her off the dance floor. Pushing through the crowd to the bar, I forced my way to the counter, never letting go of Molly's hand, and pulled her to a spot next to me. I leaned in, my lips to her ear. "What would you like?" Her pheromones teased my senses.

Molly grabbed a napkin from behind the bar and dabbed her forehead. "Gin and tonic, please."

I placed the orders. Noting the occupant behind me returning into the fray, I nabbed their stool. "Here." I pulled Molly toward the seat. "Sit down."

She put a hand on her chest and smiled before perching on the barstool. Using the tip of her shoe, she slipped off one heel, then the other, letting them drop to the floor.

"How are your feet?" I trailed a hand from her knee to her ankle, massaging along the way.

"Better now. Just never stop."

I barked out a laugh. Longing to please her, I kneaded my fingers into her silky calves.

Molly closed her eyes and relaxed in her seat.

Leaning over, I worked my way along her leg to her foot, caressing the arch.

She jumped.

"Sorry." I threw my hands up, worried I'd done something wrong.

Molly shook her head. "I'm ticklish," she yelled over the din of the crowd.

I made a mental note for any future massages—and there *would* be more.

The bartender set the drinks on the granite counter.

I nodded my thanks. The bar was too loud for conversation, so after Molly and I finished our drinks, I towed her out for several more rounds on the dance floor. By song three, restraining myself had become difficult. I suggested heading back to the hotel to put some space between Molly and me. Hopefully. the fresh air would clear my head before I reached the apartment.

She agreed, following me out of the crowd.

Molly and I found ourselves alone on the elevator. The small space and lack of audience intensified my desires tenfold. Clenching my jaw, I nearly pulverized my teeth as I fought my instincts. I stood as far away as possible in the confined area. As we descended to street level, the music was quiet enough for a conversation. I needed to focus on something other than how Molly's skin glinted with sweat—a tantalizing sight. "You were good out there. Do you go dancing often?"

"No, I haven't been to a dance club since college. Back then, I would tear it up on a weekly basis." She laughed, pulling her hair up off her back.

"You should go to clubs more often. You're a natural." She could give me a private show anytime.

"That's what dance aerobics is for." Molly fanned her neck with a hand.

Her pull was too strong. I stepped closer, bracing one hand on the elevator wall behind her head. I tilted her chin to meet my gaze. "I want to join your gym." Be your personal trainer, and give you a workout. As she grabbed my shirt, Molly's smile was sly, although I could have sworn I heard a slight tremble when she inhaled.

"If you do, don't sign up for direct debit; they'll

lock you in for life." She pushed me away with a light shove.

I laughed; something about the moment and her delivery made me want to kiss her right then and there, even though she hadn't said anything sexy. I held off again. My reaction would have been too genuine and outside the terms of my contract. Despite being in Vegas with its motto, meaning no one cared what Molly and I did, I restrained myself.

The cab ride back to the hotel was longer than the ride there. Again, the driver took the side streets to avoid traffic on the strip. I didn't even have a chance to talk to Molly. The cabbie talked non-stop and monopolized the conversation. For some reason, Molly couldn't let him prattle on without engaging. This woman was sexy, hot, and genuine. A combination I didn't think existed anymore.

Ten minutes later, the driver stopped at our hotel.

I helped Molly out of the car, ogling her bare legs. I let my gaze linger longer than I should have. *Damn it!* I needed to squelch my desires, not fan the flames. I didn't trust myself to start a conversation. Instead, I kept quiet in the elevator. But Molly's pull was too strong, and I stole sidelong glances until arriving at the apartment. I unlocked the door and gestured for her to enter first.

She flicked off her heels and as she crossed to the window, she tossed her sweater on the couch.

I wandered over and stood behind Molly, longing to touch her skin. The proximity made my hunger almost impossible to resist; she was like a magnet. After a moment of debate, I gave in and brushed my fingers over her bare shoulder.

Molly's hand slapped against the window, and she bowed her head. Her breathing accelerated.

The primal response unlocked something within me. Grasping Molly's hips, I spun her around, my lips meeting the soft skin of her neck.

She gripped my biceps and gasped.

Her reaction scrambled my mind. For the first time in my career, I wasn't sure I could stop. The chemistry I felt for Molly was too much—I didn't have to fake or force anything. I wanted to devour her. Digging my fingers into the small of her back, I tasted my way up her neck and along her jaw.

She arched into me, cradling the back of my head.

Just before I got to Molly's mouth, I pulled back, my breathing heavy. My body told me to keep going, despite my conscience yelling my actions were unprofessional.

Her gaze fell to my lips.

I couldn't turn back. Cupping Molly's face, I leaned in and brushed my lips against hers. The kiss was tender and slow at first, but then I moved my mouth with increasing urgency.

She pulled me tighter, fingers entwined in my hair.

I tugged Molly's bottom lip with my teeth.

She moaned.

I let my lustful instincts take over. With one swift movement, I pinned Molly against the large window, crushing my body against hers. I deepened the kiss, my tongue tasting and teasing her.

She traced her fingers along my spine.

Molly's touch was a relief—a thirst I didn't know needed quenching—featherlight fingers full of desire.

Her thumb grazed along the crease of my hipbone.

The contact was too much. The voice in my head shouted *stop*. My carefully cultivated years of self-control crumbled. *What is it about this woman?*

Chapter 19

Molly

I closed my bedroom door and slumped against it, my throat thick and my stomach churning. What was I thinking? I know what I thought—I wanted to touch his skin, but doing so would have pushed the limits. Which was evident when he broke off the kiss and told me to turn in for the night before he did something he "shouldn't."

Shouldn't. That word was sexier than it should have been. Tracing my fingers along my kiss-swollen lips, I squeezed my eyes shut. But his kiss…. I replayed the moment in my head. I cradled my cheeks in my hands, nausea bringing sweat to my brow. My blatant desire for Jared was nothing short of unethical. Besides, everything he'd done, I'd paid for—an act for my benefit to show off moves he'd refined over his years at Plus One. Just because his body responded didn't mean anything. He was a man, after all, and the moment had been intense. My predicament was all my fault. Being attention-starved was no excuse for falling hook, line, and sinker for his moves.

Jerking my head up, I let my mouth fall open. "Oh no! No, no, no, no, no!" Would Jared consider my behavior a breach of contract or claim my lustful actions as grounds for canceling because he thinks I'm incapable of controlling myself? I covered my eyes with a hand. Explaining why I had to terminate the contract would make for an embarrassing conversation with Ms. Haversack.

But then again, *Jared* was the one who spun me around, pressing me against the window—*he* kissed *me* first. Just because I'd reciprocated didn't violate the terms of our agreement, right? The contract stated, *kissing and holding hands was permissible*. Jared and I agreed to act like a couple, and couples kissed. Wasn't that just considered "tasting the wine"?

Pushing away from the door, I paced the length of the giant windows, wringing my hands. I wasn't naive; I understood what I'd done to Jared out on the dance floor. And mission accomplished—Jared found me sexy. However, I shouldn't have gotten carried away and allowed myself to get so wound up. All it took was his fingers on my shoulder to lose my sense of control, which was absurd. I'd had guys turn me on before—plenty of times. But never like Jared had—never with such a slight touch.

My pounding head and weak knees told me the physical aspect of my fabricated arrangement wasn't the only reason I justified my actions. If my feelings had been purely sexual, I wouldn't be this upset. Perhaps I wasn't just attracted to Jared's looks. I tapped my lips with unfocused eyes, staring out over the strip. Letting my mind wander over the past few days, I cataloged my interactions with Jared.

First, I enjoyed talking to him, he made me laugh. Second, Jared appreciated my writing. He respected my craft—something no previous boyfriend, real or fake, had done. Lastly, he had gone along with my asinine fake-couple plan without batting an eye or making me feel like I was ridiculous. Because even Fin had given me a hard time about my choice of Plus One. Compile all those reasons, on top of how, when I stepped into the living room earlier tonight in my dress, the way Jared regarded me—I ran my hands over my hips—my whole body buzzed. No wonder I was confused. But any woman would have enjoyed his attention and relished the evidence of his desire. I was only human.

I hung my head. *Great.* I had a crush on a guy I'd hired as my fake boyfriend. Would it be too much to ask the floor to open and swallow me whole so I wouldn't have to face Jared again? But I couldn't be the first client to have done this.

With my hands behind my back, I struggled with my zipper, gritting my teeth. *Stupid dress.* I peeled the fabric from my skin and kicked the garment across the room before stomping into the bathroom. I scrubbed my face so hard, my skin was tender and raw. Flopping onto the bed, I hit something hard behind my ribs. I shifted, retrieving my phone. The screen displayed several missed texts from Fin.

—*Text me if you're still alive. Good luck with the research!* Winky face emoji—

My cousin was sweet with his well-wishes, but I wouldn't call what Jared and I were doing research at this point. Fin's following text was an hour after the first.

—*Hope you're having fun. Don't do anything I would do*—

My time with Jared was fun, until I had done something you would do. Fin's subsequent few texts were marked seconds apart.

—Wait, don't do anything I wouldn't do—

—Is that right? Is that how that phrase goes?—

—You get what I mean, Molly. Be good! And fill me in later! LOL! Devil emoji—

—Give me all the juicy details!—

I shook my head. I had no idea what was right anymore. As I texted back my cousin, my heart was heavy.

—Jared might cancel the contract—

Laying the phone on my chest, I pressed my palms to my eyes. As my phone buzzed, I jumped. I glanced at my screen, which brandished Fin's response.

—What did you do?—

Why was Fin awake at two a.m.? I really didn't care, but since he'd answered.... I shrugged and typed my response.

—I screwed up—

—TELL ME YOU DIDN'T SLEEP WITH HIM?—

—No, but I'd be lying if I didn't say how kissing him made me want to—

I pinched my eyes shut, my cheeks aflame. Fin would never let me hear the end of this.

—But you said kissing was fair game. Why would Jared cancel the contract? How did you screw up?—

—Because I pushed the boundaries, and he knows I would have gone farther had he not stopped me—

—Okay, Cuz, start from the beginning and tell me everything—

I spent the next hour tucked into my luxurious bedding, telling Fin what happened, including my feelings, however irrational or juvenile they were. His advice—don't sweat it. Fin reassured me Jared would be used to behavior like mine. I wasn't the first contract who'd wanted to throw the clause out the window and have sex. Fin's conclusion, of course, was not helpful. My crazy, jealous side didn't want to be just like one of the others. My heart was already convinced what Jared and I had was more than lust or a contract. I shouldn't care—didn't want to care—but the idiotic lingering hope he wanted me the same way wouldn't let up.

I put on my pajamas and wrapped my hair, repeating Fin's mantra, desperate to stop myself from making a mountain out of a molehill. What happened tonight had been contract-related, and the mutual physical attraction had been unintentional, and nothing more.

Then why did my heart ache?

****

The blaring chirp of my alarm penetrated my slumber at eight the next morning. With a half zombie-like movement, I slapped the off button. Even though I'd gone to sleep believing Fin's explanation about the make-out session last night, just recalling how Jared had to physically pry my hands off him made the prospect of facing him this morning feel like a walk of shame.

I rolled out of bed with a sigh and headed to the bathroom. Facing my bloodshot eyes and haggard face in the mirror, I squared my shoulders and mimicked a superhero pose—the confidence-boosting one—and filled my lungs. "You got this, Molly. You're a strong, independent woman and a phenomenal writer. The kiss happened, move on!"

Who was I kidding? My irritating, backstabbing subconscious brought every excruciating detail from last night to the forefront of my mind the moment I stepped into the shower. My muscles tensed. Should *I* end our contract before I made a bigger fool of myself today? Canceling wasn't the worst idea I'd had in the last twenty-four hours. The romance genre had made a fool of me. Fear was a more straightforward emotion to write about rather than anything dealing with matters of the heart. Because while they each incited the same thrilling physical reactions, the root causes were polar opposites of each other.

Slipping into jeans, a Bon Jovi concert tee, and my black canvas high-tops, I twisted around, scrutinizing myself in the mirror. At least my butt was on point. With a final once-over, I grabbed my phone and headed out to face the inevitable. As I rounded the corner, I stopped short.

Jared sat on the couch, reading the newspaper—a perk still offered at this expensive hotel—and drinking coffee.

I flitted my gaze to my handprint on the window, and my cheeks burned, kicking my heart into overdrive. "Hi." *Stupid shaky voice.*

Jared glanced up, a smile on his face. "Good morning, beautiful. Can I get you anything?" He folded the paper and set it on the coffee table, resting his elbows on his knees.

His deep-red T-shirt hugged his sculpted shoulders, and I let my gaze linger for just a fraction too long before shifting to his lips. When I could hear my pulse in my ears, I froze so my brain could catch up, and I blinked, breaking my stare.

Jared's eyebrows rose.

Had he asked me a question? "Um…?"

He stood and sauntered past. "I asked if you

wanted breakfast." The dining table hosted an array of pastries and baked goods spread across its polished surface. Jared gestured at the food. "I ordered a few things, but if you'd rather go out and get something, we can."

Spotting a chocolate Danish with my name on it, I strode to the nearest dining chair, imagining my superhero cape flying behind me. "This looks good. Do we have any orange juice?"

"Luckily, we do. I'll run grab it." Jared entered the butler's pantry and returned with a carafe and a glass. He poured some juice and handed me the drink. "Anything else?" The divot in his cheek deepened.

You served up on a platter. Shaking my head, I answered both his question and dispelled the appetizing image in my head before grabbing the pastry and sitting.

Jared took a seat opposite me.

The moment of truth had arrived; I was about to find out if he would discuss last night or ignore it.

"How are your notes coming along?" Jared pulled at the wrapper of his blueberry muffin.

Oh! He'd decided not to disturb the elephant in the room. *Fine by me*. "Good, good. Lots of stuff to write down. You've given me plenty of material." That was a bloody lie. I hadn't written a thing past the questions at The French Corner. Instead, I wasted last night talking to Fin, overthinking how today would go, and attempting to sort through my feelings. Real productive.

"Hmm. Like what?" Jared pulled off a chunk of muffin and popped the bite-sized piece into his mouth.

I picked at my napkin, scrambling for an answer. "Umm…The nightclub, *Les Mysteres des Reves*, the

Bellagio show, the Eiffel Tower." *Please drop the subject.*

The corner of Jared's mouth quirked up. "What about those things?"

Damn! He was onto me. "Well, um…let's see…they were fun…um…they were romantic…" I sounded like an idiot, but what could I say? I hadn't anticipated finding you so attractive I can't even think straight? How, after kissing, you can make my toes curl with just a smile? *No way!*

Jared chuckled softly. "I'm glad I'm helping." He stretched across the table and ran his fingers over my forearm.

His touch was like a burn, both hot and cold at the same time. While the contact sent shivers along my spine, I was also humbled with the reminder he played a part, just like I'd requested.

Chapter 20

Jared

Molly had no idea how badly her kiss had wrecked me last night—even I'd been surprised. Don't get me wrong; my reaction wasn't a bad thing. In fact, quite the opposite. The kiss was incredible, no, more than incredible—she'd blown my mind. But that was *precisely* the problem. The accompanying thoughts and emotions crowding my brain after entering my room made no sense.

The whole night had gone great. Sure, I hadn't expected such a strong physical attraction to Molly—or how she respected my opinions, treating me like an equal—but I thought I'd had my desire under control. That was, until her deft fingers grazed my hipbone. Molly's touch, even through my dress shirt, ignited something deep within me, driving me to the edge, and I had to end the moment before I lost control.

Almost all of the emotions that followed after the night ended and I locked myself in my bedroom were unidentifiable. Yet somehow, the most dominant of all the feelings, and the easiest for me to recognize, was the knowledge I was a fraud. That single emotion overshadowed any sense of contentment that had filled me earlier. But I couldn't deny that for all intents and purposes, Molly had every reason to believe I was a fake. However, the act of *pretending* to be a couple made me want to crawl out of my skin. Because the kiss was real; I was just me—Jared—and by letting her believe otherwise, I was wholly unworthy of her touch.

Since this charade began, Molly had been truthful and kind. Even when I'd suspected she might have lied, I'd been wrong. Until her, though, I'd only seen people try to fake those characteristics. They'd act that way because they needed something from me, not because they were authentic. But Molly was the opposite. She was strong, intelligent, and decisive—a combination of admirable qualities many women, like my mother, strived for but never achieved.

I was sure some shrink would tell me all these churning emotions must have stemmed from repressed feelings about my parents, my childhood, or my time at Plus One. But despite whatever I had going on, I didn't want those issues to interfere with my arrangement with Molly. I could figure out my problems on my own time.

"What's on the docket for today?" Molly studied her hands, her back straight.

Her stiff posture and averted gaze indicated she was self-conscious. I could relate. "Well, that depends."

She narrowed her eyes, her brow scrunched. "On what?"

Molly had no reason to be leery. I was confident in my plans. "How do you feel about axes?"

Her eyes widened, and the corners of her mouth tilted up. "Are we going axe throwing?"

The sparkle in her eyes warmed my chest. "That was the plan."

She pumped her fist. "Yes!"

I'd guessed Molly wasn't opposed to violent

weapons, considering she'd written plenty of thrillers, but watching her bounce in her chair like an impatient toddler was an unexpected bonus. "I take it from your reaction you've been before?" She gave an emphatic nod.

"At home, I have a fifteen-and-three-quarter inch SOG tactical tomahawk with a stainless-steel blade that I love," Molly said the last part with her hands against her chest, her eyes closed.

For a split second, even though I knew nothing about tomahawks, I was jealous of hers. "Well, I can't guarantee there will be a, what's it called, an SOG-something tomahawk at the range, but we should have a good time." But not so good I'll have to worry things will go too far. Axe throwing was a non-contact sport, after all.

She squeezed her hands into fists and squealed. "When do we leave?"

I laughed, my chest swelling. "It opens at ten." I motioned at her half-eaten Danish. "As soon as you're finished"—I grazed the back of her hand with my fingers, ignoring the tight feeling in my stomach—"we can go."

****

Molly fidgeted in her seat. "What's the address?" She craned her neck between the front seats to peer through the taxi's windshield.

Seeing the building was impossible from the car's current location; the range was still several miles away. "We'll be there soon." I smiled, squeezing her hand.

Molly met my gaze, then relaxed against my side.

I savored the warmth of her touch for the last few minutes of the ride.

The cab pulled into a large strip mall parking lot with oversized, tinted glass windows and a neon sign declaring the building as the throwing range.

Molly hopped out and waited on the sidewalk.

I swiped my card to pay the cabbie, then exited the vehicle and took her hand.

Molly pushed through the door. "This will be so much fun." She checked out the facility's main room, her smile widening.

Along the walls were displays featuring different hatchets and tomahawks and even a few larger, double-edged axes. A snack bar sat to my left. The floor had rows and rows of shelves with everything from play-on-words T-shirts to throwing knives, ninja stars, and targets.

Molly beelined over to the wall of tomahawks. "This one looks the most like mine; only this blade is black." She squinted at the weapons. "Why don't they display any polished or chrome options? Black is so boring."

Sidling next to Molly, I placed one hand on the small of her back, then stroked the blade of the nearest tomahawk with the other. "You think so?" I smiled with semi-closed eyes, laying on the charm. "I think black is sexy." *Like the lace of your dress last night.*

Molly flipped her hair over her shoulder. "The Jamaican half of me thanks you."

Shaking my head, I pulled up my scarred cheek in a smirk. "I see what you did there. Very clever." I found her quick wit charming.

She smiled with pursed lips, her hands tucked behind her back and rocked back and forth on her heels. "Ya, mon."

Molly's proximity sent a wave of desire through me once again. I took a step back. "I need to check in at the desk. Be right back." I wanted to give her a peck on the cheek but lacked the confidence in my self-control, thanks to the unfamiliar sensations floating around in my chest and midsection. Instead, I winked.

She bit her lip, the corners of her mouth twitching. Molly wandered the lobby, strolling down every aisle.

With my name in the queue, I followed Molly until the attendant called our turn.

A stout, short-haired woman with a sleeve tattoo explained the waiver and asked us to sign.

After running my company card, I took Molly's hand and followed the employee to a door off the main floor which served as a private ax-throwing area.

I stepped into the room I'd booked as part of the "Couples Therapy" package specifically chosen for Molly. Rough-hewn plank walls surrounded a long stall, with a chain-link fence just below the ceiling to protect the fluorescent lights and a waist-high block of wood at the entrance holding an assortment of axes in varying sizes. Even the far wooden wall sported a red-painted, heart-shaped target.

The burly woman outlined the axes and how to choose which ones would work best for different heights and weights, and after a brief tutorial on throwing techniques, she left.

Molly pulled a hairband off her wrist and deftly tied back her shiny, dark brown locks. She studied the array of weapons, reaching without hesitation for the first axe the attendant referred to as a one-and-a-half pound, eighteen-inch tomahawk with a three-and-a-half-inch, high carbon steel blade. "Can I go first?"

She was all business. I waved a hand toward the heart-shaped target and stood back to watch. While I'd only observed axe throwing, the mechanics seemed easy enough after the attendant's explanation. I was sure I could hold my own.

Molly stepped to the throwing line with a steady gait and a gleam in her eye.

My mouth went dry. I could tell from her radiating confidence, she would smoke me.

Chucking axes at a wooden slab should have been an unsexy tension reliever, but seeing Molly hold the tomahawk like an extension of her hand was anything but. She stood with her feet staggered shoulder-width apart, and her right arm cocked back like a pitcher poised to throw a fastball. Molly tightened her grip on the wooden handle and lined up her sight.

As I swept my gaze over Molly, I locked on her tight backside, the skinny jeans accentuating the lovely curve. Without warning, her tomahawk embedded in the heart with a thwack, and I caught my breath. Cheeks aflame, I dragged my gaze away from Molly to focus on the target. The blade was just within the outline of the heart.

Molly grabbed another axe, adjusted herself, and hurled a second one, burying it dangerously close to the center.

I gaped at the tomahawk lodged in the target, the air rushing out of my lungs. "What the…?" I couldn't even put my thoughts into words, but if I had to guess my emotions, they would be a mixture of pride, awe, and a hint of jealousy. I knew I was outmatched and would look like a clown in comparison.

Molly dusted off her hands, her smile wide.

I approached her side. “That”—I shook my head, my gaze focusing on the stone floor to hide my chagrin—“was incredible.”

Between her two throws, Molly had forged a line along the heart’s center. “Thanks.” She scrunched her nose. “For one of my books, I needed to know the mechanics of throwing an axe. So, I found a place and, as it turned out, I loved it.” She drew out the word *loved.*

“Which book?” I hadn’t seen the weapon in either of the two books I’d read so far; I wouldn’t have forgotten an axe murder. I couldn’t remember anything other than a few handguns and knives.

“*Picket Fences*. The manuscript was one of my first novels where a teacher stalked a student’s mother. She was a single mom, and the murderer cornered her in the garage—her son had a tomahawk for Ranger Scouts. Since I’d never thrown an axe or knew if killing an intruder with zero experience was even feasible, I figured I should experiment. Besides, a book always flows better if I understand the mechanics of the experiences firsthand. Kind of like how I’m gaining experience from you.” Molly ducked her head and strode toward the target to retrieve the axes.

Oh, I could give her experiences all right, but I was under contract.

Returning to the line, she placed the blades on the table. “Now, I’m part of a club, Axes in the Hole.” She rolled her eyes. “While the name sounds ridiculous, I’ve gotten to know some kind, strong women who’ve taught me everything I know.” Molly sidled out of the way.

I stepped to the block of axes, wishing I could have

had a few lessons from those ladies myself before I came here, but it was too late now. Taking one of the larger ones, I weighed the weapon in my grip. Not too heavy. I approached the line and staggered my feet like Molly and the employee had done. I raised the axe, pulling my arm back over my shoulder, aiming to target the heart's center, and let it fly. Luck wasn't with me because while the tomahawk hit inside the heart outline, it failed to lodge into the wood and fell like a discarded piece of trash to the concrete floor with a resounding clang. I closed my eyes and blew out my breath. *Might as well don a red nose and white makeup now.*

Molly's shoulders shook.

"Shut up." I smirked. "I'm just warming up." I cracked my knuckles and shook out my shoulders.

"Well, if warming up equates to a horrible stance, bad aim, and failing to nail the target—then yes, you're definitely warming up."

Hanging my head in mock shame, I couldn't keep the smile from my face. "Fine, I stink at this and have no idea what I'm doing." I peeked at Molly out of the corner of my eye. "Will you give me some pointers?" Raising my eyebrows, I hoped I came across as cute rather than vulnerable and inept.

Molly bit her lip again, and her eyes widened just a bit before she nodded and stepped forward.

Cute won out.

"You've got the basics right, so let's work on the details." Molly swallowed hard, straining the tendon in her neck. As she placed her hands on the waistline of my jeans, she squeezed her mouth shut.

Her grip shifted my hips until my feet were parallel to each other but still shoulder-width apart.

My skin burned where her fingers gripped my hipbones, and I fought hard to suppress the memories of last night.

"Since you're a newbie Jared, the most important thing to focus on"—she pointed at my forearm—"is keeping your wrist firm."

"My wrist firm? You mean I need to keep it locked?" I looked at the joint in question with my brows furrowed.

Molly nodded. "A floppy wrist will cause your axe to hit the target at an angle and fail to embed. You want the sides of the blade perpendicular to the wood."

I raised an appreciative eyebrow.

"Don't get too excited. Perpendicular is the only math term I know, and I only know it because we use it in conjunction with axe throwing." She bent and tapped the back of my left leg. "Bend your knee. You want to be loose and fluid in your movements." She stood and pulled my right arm back over my shoulder. "But don't forget to keep your wrist straight and"—she braced mine with her hand—"keep it pointed at the target."

Molly stood back, framing me with her pointer fingers and thumbs. Giving a curt nod, she stepped forward again and stood behind me, her left hand rested on my left shoulder, and her right hand supported my corresponding wrist.

I could feel her body pressed against my back, her warmth radiating through me. Again, the mixture of emotions I didn't quite understand churned inside my gut.

"Now, I want you to step into the throw, but keep your wrist in line with the target." Molly wrapped her fingers around my forearm, pushing my hand forward while simultaneously nudging her knee into the back of my left leg. She then took a slow step with me in a mock throw. "When you get to this point"—she pivoted around to my side and stopped my hand in the mid-swing position—"release the axe."

I nodded; she knew her stuff. This woman was full of surprises.

"Okay, you're ready. Step back behind the line and make your throw."

I mimed through the actions again in slow motion, then let the axe loose. The tomahawk didn't land in the heart but lodged secure and solid in the wood. That was something, at least.

Molly cheered and clapped.

I threw her a smile over my shoulder, my chest warming, before taking a second throw. This one didn't just stick but also landed on the right-side curve of the heart. My pulse thrummed, and I turned to face Molly.

She bounced on her toes, her fists raised in the air.

In two strides, I picked her up and spun her around.

Molly's arms encircled my neck.

I set her back down, her face mere inches from mine, hyper-aware of the lack of space between our bodies.

Molly's fingers curled into my neck and hair.

I could picture how the moment would go. All I had to do was lean in and kiss her, but my instincts would take over, and I wouldn't be able to stop.

Chapter 21

Molly

Jared met my gaze with wide, hungry, dilated pupils. The echoes of distant axes hitting their mark were the only sounds above my labored breathing. Irrational hope bubbled in my chest. *Is he going to kiss me?*

His intense stare softened after a moment, and Jared's lips pulled into his beautiful trademark smile, complete with sexy scar dimple.

I watched him curb the adrenaline from his successful throw, and a wave of disappointment ran through me, the fire extinguishing. I wasn't the only one restraining myself.

"Try not to embarrass me too bad." Jared released his arms, his voice rougher than usual.

I rocked back on my heels. "I think you already took care of that." Laughing, I stepped forward to face the throwing line and shook out my hands. I vibrated with pent-up adrenaline.

Jared rubbed the back of his neck. "Whatever."

Feeling emboldened, I shot him a wink before debating the larger hatchets with my heartbeat in overdrive. This time, just to show off, I grabbed the two-pound tomahawk and gave the weapon a cocky toss. "Wanna make this interesting?" With my tongue in my cheek, I smiled. I knew a bet would be unfair, but my competitive part couldn't help myself. I had this in the bag.

Jared smirked and crossed his arms. "What do you have in mind?"

His arrogant tone was endearing, and his stance emphasized his defined bicep muscles. "How about the loser tells the winner something about themself the other doesn't know? Something genuine—not on the books." Preferably some tidbit having to do with your feelings toward me.

Jared pursed his lips, then nodded. "Sounds like a deal."

Excitement sparked in my veins, and I clicked my neck to the left, then right in mock readiness. "You prepared to lose?"

Jared lifted his arms over his head, stretching out his triceps.

His shirt rode up just enough to reveal his super sexy hip *V*. The desire coursing through me almost knocked me off my feet.

He dropped his arms back to his sides. "I'm gonna love watching you eat those words."

I growled and snapped my teeth, wishing I could take a bite out of *him*.

Jared's eyes widened, his jaw slack.

A trill of excitement rippled along my skin. Unable to hold in my smug smile, I adjusted my grip on the axe and stepped to the line.

He schooled his features, leaving his cheek pulled up.

Jared's sexy smile rattled my brain. My first throw landed at the bottom of the heart. I drew my second axe, keeping my gaze away from Jared and hurled the tomahawk at the target. My throw hit just shy of dead center.

"Show-off." Jared squinted, and he sauntered over.

With two fingers, he gave me a gentle shove to the side and reached for the axes. His eyes blazed with mischief, and I stepped back to the wall, wishing he would pin me against the flat surface like he had last night. "You know, nobody likes a sore loser."

"We'll see who's the loser." Jared chose another nineteen-inch tomahawk and rotated his hand. "I'm a fast learner." He feigned a few throws, locking his wrist and stepping into his swing.

The fact Jared remembered everything I'd said was impressive. But he wouldn't win; he couldn't—I had over a year's worth of experience. Not to mention, I was in it to win.

Jared launched his axe, making the tendons in his arm ripple.

My stomach dropped, and I neglected to notice where his throw landed. Much to my surprise, his axe was stuck in the red. *Beginners luck.* I paid more attention to Jared's second throw, and when the tomahawk bounced off the middle of the heart, I pressed my lips into a hard line to hold back my smile.

As Jared turned to face me, he hung his head, his shoulders drooping.

I crossed my arms and raised a brow. "How does that crow taste?" Jared waved off my comment as if I hadn't just witnessed his demise.

"There's still twenty minutes left on the clock. I'm sure you'll be the one choking on feathers by the end."

"Uh-huh."

I bantered back and forth with Jared for the rest of our time at the throwing range, doing my best to one-up him. But in the end, as Jared's last axe fell to the ground, he couldn't deny I'd won.

He dragged a hand down his face and let out a slow breath, shooting daggers at the forlorn tomahawk.

Jared acted as if the axe had jumped from the target on purpose just to spite him. I strutted over to Jared, unable to help myself. "Can you smell that?"

He scanned the room, sniffing. "Stale beer, wood, and sweat?"

I shook my head, fighting to keep the smirk from my face. "No, the smell of victory."

"Ahh." He rolled his eyes and smiled. "Guess I need to come up with something to tell you."

"I'll give you a few minutes to think—make it juicy." As I let my imagination run wild, heat rushed to my cheeks.

After retrieving the axes and returning them to the block, Jared held the door.

I exited back into the lobby. "Eleven axes in the heart. That's a lot, right?" Gloating, I hip-checked him.

Jared stumbled to the side, laughing and fumbling, almost dropping his phone. "Hey, I'm requesting our rideshare." He secured the mobile with both hands.

I stopped at the desk, resting my elbow on the countertop, and cocked an eyebrow. "Who's the axe-throwing master?"

Jared slouched beside me, credit card in hand. "Are you really going to make me say it?"

I repressed my smile and nodded.

The bearded employee approached, and he asked for our room number.

"Four." Jared glanced at the man, before giving me a worshiping bow. "You are the axe master."

The grizzly guy behind the counter choked out a laugh. "You got schooled by a girl?" He made grabby motions with his hands. "Turn in your man card, dude." He set the point-of-sale terminal in front of Jared.

"Hey now—" Jared tapped his card and held up a hand.

My simmering rage for the chauvinistic employee couldn't be contained. "Excuse me, mullet man. Don't you go emasculating my date with a haircut like that. You have no idea what kind of man he is." I eyed the thirty-something, flannel-wearing man with a sneer. My pent-up aggression from one too many men doubting my abilities as a woman overtook my emotions. "You have no idea what this guy is capable of." I rested a hand on Jared's shoulder. "Have you ever base jumped off the Royal Gorge Suspension Bridge? Or free-climbed El Capitan?"

The guy resembled a deer in headlights. I snapped my fingers and shook my head, just like I'd seen my English-Jamaican aunties do when they'd put someone in their place. "I didn't think so."

Jared tugged my elbow. "Come on, tiger." He coughed to cover a laugh and ushered me toward the door. "He got your point." As Jared and I waited for the rideshare, his smile was glued to his face. "That. Was. Classic."

"Well, he had it coming. Doubting my abilities because I'm a woman, then putting you down?" I scowled at the building, fists clenching from the adrenaline still fresh in my veins. "You're more of a man than he'll ever be." I pulled out my phone. "I'm giving them a bad review. I don't even know how he still has a job with that mouth."

Jared placed a hand over my screen. "Thank you for defending my masculinity." He squeezed my wrist. "I've never had someone stand up for me like that. But I don't think we need to cost him his job."

The earnest sincerity in his gaze diffused my annoyance. I scowled and put my phone back in my pocket. "You're right."

Jared laced his fingers with mine. "By the way, how did you know I've base jumped in Colorado?"

My stomach dropped as heat flooded from my neck to my ears. I scrambled to think of a way to word my explanation and not sound like a stalker. "The Sky's the Limit website has loads of photos of you." That I'd studied way too long and often.

He squinted his eyes and shook his head.

Warmth drained from my fingers, leaving them cold. *Busted.* "I'm a writer, Jared. I research. It's what I do. You mentioned you worked there, so I checked out their website." He couldn't accuse me of being a creeper if I claimed my snooping was for the book, right?

"Well, I'm flattered. Thank you."

Was he blushing?

"And as for the bet…" Jared examined his hand in mine.

As I waited for him to fulfill his end of our bargain, I fought not to fidget.

Jared licked his lips.

I felt like a shaken pop can. *Ooh, here it comes!*

"Last night, I thoroughly enjoyed myself." He met my gaze from under his lashes. "You're a great kisser."

My insides combusted, and I let my jaw drop. Before I could unpack his words, I saw the rideshare pull up, and I slid into the back of the vehicle. My movements were stiff as though I was in shock. Was I supposed to continue our conversation now he and I were in the car, or was I supposed to act like his admission was no big deal? Maybe I could tell him I felt the same and go off the books, inquiring if he meant the compliment on a personal level?

"You're heading to Skewered, right?" The bald man with his thick gray mustache met Jared's gaze in the rearview mirror.

Jared turned to me with raised brows. "You still okay with kabobs?"

Unable to form a coherent sentence yet, I nodded.

Noting my confirmation, the driver pulled out of the lot, asking a million questions about axe throwing, which made further discussion on Jared's kiss comment impossible.

When Jared and I arrived at the storefront, the idea of mentioning how he liked my kissing had my shoulders in knots. While Jared purchased the chicken kabobs for lunch, he acted as though he hadn't just dropped his truth bomb at the range and continued the axe-throwing conversation from the rideshare.

Before long, I'd convinced myself I'd imagined his comment, but I hoped to jog his memory. "Maybe I should get a shirt that says *Axe Master*."

Jared rolled his eyes and took the steaming chicken from the doo-rag-wearing man behind the counter. "Please, you've only won once."

"Not true. I've whooped Fin, too." I elaborated on my victory over my cousin and the terms for whoever lost.

He barked a laugh. "You're telling me you'd have been okay with Fin drawing a mustache on you with permanent marker if you lost?" Jared passed me the first paper plate full of kabobs.

I inhaled the smoky, mesquite scent wafting from my chicken, and my mouth watered. "Who expected I would lose?"

"Clearly, Fin did." Jared took his own paper plate and thanked the server.

"Well, Fin's an idiot. He should have known better." I laughed to myself, knowing my cousin hadn't trusted me since then, and for good reason. I've tried to pull the wool over his eyes one too many times.

"True. After seeing what you can do, I'd never have agreed to that bet."

"Then why did you agree to my wager? You watched me warm up." *Did he want to lose?*

Jared handed me a napkin and ambled north along the strip. "Did Fin know you were an expert?"

"No." I ripped off a piece of chicken with my fingers, disappointed Jared hadn't picked up on where I wanted the conversation to go. "I never told Fin about the league. He assumed that was my first time going." I remembered how initially Fin was happy for me when I nailed my first throw. But the slow slip of his smile when I hit target after target was priceless.

"You sly little minx." Jared nudged me with his elbow. "You lied to your cousin?"

I swallowed my bite of chicken, almost choking on my unwarranted indignation. "No! I simply didn't feel the need to bring it up." I wiped my mouth with a napkin. "Lies of omission are commonly used plot devices in my suspense novels."

"Uh-huh. Sure." Jared shook his head. "You know they call that cheating, right?"

Fin would have agreed, but I didn't. "Um, no. It's called *winning*." Unlike what I had done with this conversation.

"And did he concede? Did Fin show you his text thread with his girlfriend since he lost?" Jared bit a chunk off his skewer.

"Let's just say he was red for the rest of the evening." I opened my mouth to slide another piece off the stick but had to swallow the rising bile at the memory of what Fin revealed.

"I want to be on your side, but I just feel so bad for your cousin."

"No, you should feel bad for me." I shook my head at a brunette extending a flyer. "I was the one who'd gotten an eyeful—they'd exchanged pictures." I shuddered, forcing myself to forget the images of places on my cousin I never wanted to see again.

Jared laughed, sidestepping a couple of showgirls posing for pictures. "Maybe you should have picked different terms, like when my friends and I make bets."

I give up. He's not mentioning the kiss. "What are your terms?" Images akin to the mindless daredevil reality show flashed through my mind. "Like whoever loses has to run down the street naked?"

Jared scrunched his face. "What, no! The loser has to compete in the Iceman Viking Challenge."

A light went on in my head. "Is that why you had your butt handed to you? You lost a bet?"

Jared stopped and pointed his kabob. "I said we don't talk about that race."

I kept walking, calling back over my shoulder, making an *L* with my index finger and thumb against my forehead. "Okay, loser."

As he caught up, the pounding of his steps increased. "I don't always lose." He wore a playful smile. "I would like to point out I've only ever done that race once."

"Yeah, but you didn't actually 'do it,' did you?" I bumped my shoulder against his bicep.

Jared clutched a fist over his heart. "Ouch. I can see why Fin doesn't trust you; you're mean." He stuck out his bottom lip.

I wanted to bite his playful pout—badly. I focused on the white tennis shoes of the woman in front of me. "You go on believing that, if it makes you feel better."

"Now I feel like we need to have another bet—one on an even playing field."

Please let me set the terms. Maybe then, I could get answers.

"How good are you at blackjack?" Jared bit into his second skewer.

Please no. "Never played." I avoided anything to do with math like the plague.

"Really?" Jared gawked, taking a bite of the seared meat. "You've never played blackjack?"

"Which part of 'I don't like math' don't you understand?" If he'd seen my report cards, he'd know better.

"But adding together two cards is simple." Jared veered onto the drive of our hotel.

I followed the half-moon sidewalk. "Yeah, but that kind of basic math still takes the fun out of the game." I didn't like to think while having fun.

He shook his head. "Okay, then, what game do you like to play?" Jared took our empty kabob sticks and plates and threw them into the trash can at the hotel entrance.

"Here, I'll show you." I grabbed Jared's hand, feeling like a kid at a carnival, and pulled him into the stale cigarette gambling area of the Euphoria Casino.

Rows of slot machines covered the busy ornate red carpet, their lights compensating for the lack of windows which, from what I'd seen so far, was a deliberate choice in all the casinos. I led Jared past various poker tables, a few crowded craps games, and the blackjack area until I spotted what I wanted. I waved a hand at the tables like a showroom model. "Roulette." I dragged out both syllables with sass and pulled him to the nearest game.

Jared had a bemused smile as he helped me into one of the cream leather seats before taking the chair beside me.

I purchased one hundred dollars' worth of chips from the bowtie-and-vest-wearing croupier and patted my small stack. "I'm doubling these bad boys."

Jared scoffed. "You know the odds, right?"

"Get stuffed. I'm gonna make you eat your words." Probably not, but I'd have fun anyway.

"I hope so." He leaned forward, examining the numbers on the felt. "What's your strategy?"

"Ha! I don't need one. Thank you. This game is simple." I grabbed a chip. "You pick a color, then a number, and then lay your bet on the square. If you want to get really fancy, you can lay the chip between squares to increase the odds of winning."

Jared burst out laughing. "But it also decreases

your payout."

I gave him a playful push, reveling in the hardness of his shoulder muscles. "Shut up with your logic." Despite his teasing, I found his brain a turn-on.

Jared pinched his lips together, and the corners of his mouth twitched. "So, any numbers in particular?"

I laid my first chip. "Fin's birthday."

"Naturally."

"One for the day I got my first book deal." I placed a bright green chip on number thirteen.

"Of course." He waved his hand in a flourish.

"Jon Bon Jovi's birthday."

"Who wouldn't bet on Jon?" Jared made devil horns with his fingers. "He's a rockstar."

I squinted. "If you plan on mocking me, then I won't tell you any more details about my numbers."

Jared's eyes crinkled at the sides.

He looked as though he wanted to laugh but found me endearing at the same time. Even though I had favorite numbers, I didn't have a real strategy, and I was rarely successful for any considerable amount of time. I'd already lost about half of my pile when a voluptuous Latina cocktail server in a black mini dress with a large peephole showing off her ample cleavage asked Jared if he'd like anything to drink.

To his credit, Jared kept his gaze on the woman's face before he turned and asked the same question.

The server's presence still took a hit on my self-esteem. I eyed her, fighting to keep my expression impassive. Even though I could have used a drink, I didn't want the brunette lingerie model returning to our table. "No, I'm okay. Thanks."

My bets disappeared fast, as if karma had it in for

me for my jealous thoughts about the cocktail staff, considering each one looked as gorgeous as the next. I counted my puny pile. Only eight more chips. "Okay, last bet." I pouted at the grid painted on the green felt. "Give me a number."

Jared raised each finger individually on his right hand and looked up. "Five."

His tone was confident, and I laid the chips on the red circle. "Why five?"

"It's the number of letters in your name." He ran the back of his fingers over my cheek.

Ignoring the electricity, I tilted my head to the side and raised an eyebrow. While what Jared said was super suave, I wasn't letting him have it. "Really? And you mocked *my* numbers?"

He exhaled a laugh, running a hand through his hair. "I was trying to be smooth."

"Lame, Jared. Lame." I shook my head, denying the truth, but made a mental note of the line for my manuscript. "Do you use that with all your clients? Because personally, I'd delete that line from your playbook."

He scoffed. "No, I don't say that to other clients."

Jared avoided my gaze. "You don't?" I had a hard time believing him.

His Adam's apple bobbed. "No"—he traced the seam of the maroon, vinyl, cushioned table edge with his thumb—"because none of them ever ask for my opinion."

My heart dropped like a lead balloon. My sarcastic attempt at being playful backfired. I couldn't believe anyone could treat Jared like he didn't matter. I watched a wall go up behind Jared's expression.

He kept his attention focused on the roulette wheel. His head jerked back. "You won."

I flitted my gaze to the table and widened my eyes at the clear dolly on top of my eight green chips. "Shut up. Shut up. No way!" I jumped out of my seat and threw myself into Jared's arms, unbalancing his chair. "I won!" Pulling back, I planted a kiss on his lips. The subtle curve of his full mouth against mine sent a ripple of desire from my head to my toes.

Jared froze for half a second before removing his mouth from mine and lowering me back onto my feet.

The hunger in his gaze was palpable. I fought the urge to lean in and kiss him again. *Control yourself, Molly. He's already pushed you away. Just because he said he liked the kiss last night doesn't mean he wants to do it again.* I focused on my stack of chips to staunch the fire in my loins. "Let's go cash in our winnings."

"Sure." Jared stood, running his hands down his thighs. "Good idea."

As I wound my way past more slot machines following the signs to the cashiers, I overthought the moment. Jared said he liked my kiss last night, yet my celebratory peck was the second time today he hadn't reciprocated my affection. Was his aloofness his way of making sure I didn't lose control? If it was, I didn't like it.

The Asian woman behind the counter with gray highlights framing her face passed me the stack of bills, then beckoned to the next customer.

I stared at the two hundred and eighty dollars in my hands and made an impulsive decision. "You should take half of this."

"What?" Jared held up his hands, taking a step

back. "No. Why?"

Splitting the bills, I pushed the money toward him. "Because your number won." *And I want you to see I'm capable of being levelheaded.*

Jared shook his head. "No way. I can't. Those are your winnings."

I could change his mind. "Okay." I shrugged. "Suit yourself." Folding the bills into fourths, I pulled out my shirt's collar and stuffed the money into my bra. I glanced at Jared.

He'd fixed his gaze on my chest and swallowed hard.

I quirked up my lips—just the reaction I'd hoped. "What? You said you didn't want your half."

Jared swiped a hand over his mouth. "I do now."

"Molly? Is that you?" A woman's voice sliced through the tension.

I jumped back, and a chill ran along my spine.

"Molly!" The soprano shrill called again.

NO! I whirled to see Evie Miller, my brother's blonde-bombshell, college ex-girlfriend heading my way. I felt my throat constrict. *Of all the people to run into, why her?* "Evie, hi." Her disgusting signature light-pink lipstick contrasted brightly against her store-bought tan.

She faux kissed me on both cheeks. "I thought that was you, Molly."

Evie's sickly-sweet floral perfume overpowered my nostrils. I watched her ogle Jared from head to toe as if he were prey.

"I was all prepared to throw you a pity party after your big breakup, but from the look of things, you've already moved on." She poked Jared in the chest with an index finger. "Is this your new beau?"

"Oh gosh, no!" I blurted. "He's not my boyfriend. Jared's just a companion I hired for research to help with my upcoming novel."

Jared stiffened.

My lungs felt tight. Why did I have to admit Jared's profession? I hated my big, stupid mouth. Evie would blow the situation way out of proportion.

She leered at Jared.

I was right. A heaviness filled my chest. *Here we go.*

Twirling blonde hair around her finger, she slinked closer.

Jared widened his stance, pulling back his shoulders. His hard gaze flashed in my direction before softening and focusing on Evie.

She ran her fingers down her neck, over her cleavage, and along her slinky, silver knit dress. "A companion? You mean, like an escort?"

The warmth from Jared's expression was gone. I crossed my arms, irritation sparking in my veins.

He flashed his dimple. "Similar. But the sex would cost you extra." He winked.

Evie giggled.

I stared at Jared, letting my jaw go slack. His words were sharp, like daggers stabbing me for revealing his occupation. "He's joking, Evie. Plus One doesn't allow that type of behavior." I kept the hostility out of my expression, but the anger seeped into my tone.

Jared sniffed, turning his full attention to Evie. His gaze followed her fingers along the plunging neckline of her dress. "Who said it would be on the books?"

He did not just say that. My stomach soured at his implication he'd have sex with her.

Evie belly laughed, putting a hand on Jared's arm and forcing her breasts against him.

Blood boiled in my veins watching her throw herself at Jared. First, Evie cheated on Mason and broke his heart, and now she wanted to get her hooks into Jared? *I don't think so.* She needed to leave. Now. "Don't you have somewhere you need to be, Evie?" I gritted my teeth.

She squeezed Jared's bicep.

He flexed.

Pain stabbed the back of my throat. Why was Jared playing along with Evie? Did he want to upset me?

Evie giggled a second time, pulling Jared in closer.

Relegated to the sidelines, I saw red. I grasped Evie's elbow, enunciating my words. "Shouldn't you be leaving?"

Evie's head whipped in my direction, and she narrowed her eyes. "Yes, fine." She wrenched her elbow away. "I was on my way to meet a friend for her bachelorette party." Evie pivoted to Jared and wrapped an arm around his neck, tracing the lines of his chest with the other hand. "Did you want to join us? I'm sure you'd be a welcome addition."

I gagged at her suggestive tone. "Sorry, Evie." I stared daggers at her makeup-caked face. "But Jared and I have plans." I cut him a glare, grasping his bicep. "Right?"

Evie pressed forward into Jared's chest again, jutting her bottom lip in a pout. "Well, that's a shame."

Her tone was almost juvenile. I had to swallow back my disgust. Her behavior was atrocious.

Jared unwrapped my hand from his arm. "If you give me your number, Evie, maybe we could get together another time. My contract with Molly ends on Thursday. If you're still here…"

Was he freaking kidding me? Red filled my vision. *What was his problem?*

Evie slipped her card into Jared's back pocket before slapping his rear.

He smiled.

Even though the emotion didn't touch his eyes, I could feel the walls closing in around me. My angry tears threatened to spill. I inhaled a deep breath to calm myself, but my chest was too tight, as if my lungs weren't working. These territorial feelings were out of character. At least they had been—until the fiasco with Enrique, but they were warranted then.

I was irrational, but because I'd picked Jared for my research, and he was here with me but flirting with that tramp, the same heart-aching feelings as when I'd learned of Enrique's cheating resurfaced. *What did* that *mean?*

"Bye, Molly," Evie trilled. "I *really* enjoyed running into you." She kissed a pointer finger and then touched Jared's lips. "And *you* call me about Thursday."

Over my dead body.

Chapter 22

Jared

Molly stalked toward the elevator.

Reluctantly, I followed. Sure, I acted like a jerk and had no doubt I'd gone too far by getting Evie's number. However, when Molly handled me like I was her possession, I felt my body go numb. Because after getting to know Molly over the past week and a half, I assumed she and I had developed a rapport and become friends. Then she went and told Evie I'm her companion and treated me like an object. With her one statement, Molly became like all my other previous clients, devalued me as a person, and sparked Evie's subsequent behavior.

I ground my teeth and balled my fists. Despite the reality of the situation, until Evie showed up, Molly'd made me feel like the boyfriend I pretended to be. So, why hadn't she said that? Masquerading as a couple was her idea. Evie assumed we were together, after all. Molly could have even said I was a work colleague. I'd have taken anything over the truth—to have Molly view me as something other than her little toy.

When the elevator opened, Molly and I entered, heading to separate corners, and faced away from each other. As the doors closed, I didn't know if ending up on the elevator alone with Molly was a blessing or a curse.

"Are you planning to call her?"

Molly's words came out in a hiss, and I shrugged. "Why not?" Like my private life was any of her business. I could do whatever the hell I wanted. "That's what companions do. Right?" My question was petty, but I was too angry to filter my words.

Her head jerked in my direction. "It sounds like you were more interested in what she could do for you *off* the books." Molly crossed her arms over her chest.

I matched her stance, watching her sneer in my peripheral. "You're right. I've been pretty pent-up lately. A date with Evie might be just what I need." *If only I could get* you *out of my head.* The doors pinged open.

"You're being a huge jerk." Molly marched toward the apartment.

She wasn't wrong, but I didn't care, and she wasn't being much better. I caught the door before it swung closed. "Hey, tonight's dinner reservation is at six thirty. Should I cancel or take Evie?" The quip was a low blow, but my emotions had taken over, and I wanted to hurt Molly like she'd hurt me.

Wheeling around, she jabbed a finger at my chest. "Oh no, you're not getting out of your contract that easily. That witch doesn't get to date you on *my time*. You're taking *me*. End of discussion." Molly spun on her heel and stomped away.

As her door clicked shut, I still fumed, but my anger didn't stop the shame from seeping in. I ran a hand through my hair and headed into my room with my tail between my legs.

****

The shower's hot water beat against my forehead, and I braced a hand against the tile. My emotions had gotten away from me—again—however, this time, in a bad way. But I'd enjoyed feeling respected rather than disregarded as a companion.

Whenever anyone found out I moonlighted for Plus One, their opinion of me changed entirely—I was either objectified or beneath them. Either way, they'd treat me like Evie had downstairs. People no longer viewed me as a person of substance, despite my math degree and ambitions. Molly's behavior had caught me off guard. I didn't expect she'd act like all the others. Although, she didn't deserve my snippy attitude. Molly hadn't hired me to be anything more than research. Assuming I was more wasn't her fault. But when Molly corrected Evie, admitting I wasn't her boyfriend, my heart sank like a rock. My reaction had me questioning myself. I didn't want to be Molly's boyfriend, did I? Well, I had fun pretending, at the very least. However, I wanted to be *something*. But I'd blown my chance by saying all those spiteful things in retaliation. *Way to go, Jared.*

Turning off the water, I toweled dry and threw on my black jeans, not bothering to button them up, and flopped into the overstuffed chair in the corner of my room.

A sharp knock sounded at my door. My heart kicked into overdrive. Had Molly come to cancel? I rose from the chair and strode to the door. Putting a hand on the cold metal of the doorknob, the length of my bare arm reminded me I was still shirtless. I ducked back into the closet, grabbing one of my light-blue dress shirts, and slid my arms through the sleeves, leaving it unbuttoned. I opened the door to find Molly wrapped in a white hotel robe, making my imagination run wild.

As she scanned my exposed torso, Molly's breath caught. She closed her eyes. "Never mind."

I had no idea what Molly had wanted, but her reaction to seeing me half-dressed was undeniable. Seeing her scuttle back to her room like a scared rabbit, I felt hope fill my chest. Molly had feelings for me. Maybe I could still fix the awkwardness between us, after all.

Chapter 23

Molly

Undoing the tie on my robe, I wafted the sides to fan my overheating body and paced the room. I just wanted to know what to wear to dinner tonight, and what had Jared done? Gone and opened the door half-naked. I couldn't stop staring and could've kicked myself for being so obvious. He probably had a good laugh at my immature reaction. Jared's washboard abs had scrubbed away all my rational thoughts leaving me tongue-tied and gawking like an idiot. His body was just as mesmerizing as his personality—at least, until Evie.

I took a seat on the edge of my bed. *How did today end up going so wrong? And why did I hurt so much?* Tears brimmed on my lashes. *Don't cry—your makeup is on point.* My plan had blown up in my face. At that moment, I'd rather have toothpicks shoved under my fingernails than go out to dinner with Jared, despite my impending deadline. I could only guess what kind of hurtful remarks he'd make at the restaurant.

Wanting to understand my conflicting feelings, I grabbed my notebook from my bag to outline the evening's course of events. Perhaps the exercise would help me decipher my emotions.

—Jared and I were having a moment after my big

win.

Yeah, we were.

—Evie showed up with her perfect, lingerie-model figure.

—Evie asked if Jared was my boyfriend.

Like my relationship was any of her business.

—I said Jared was research.

Damn it. Closing my eyes, I grimaced. I'd referred to Jared as an object—the exact thing he'd alluded to hating about his job. No wonder he'd been mad. I bit my thumbnail, rocking back and forth, needing to talk to someone before my anxiety developed into a full-blown panic attack. With a shaky hand, I reached for my phone on the nightstand.

—Fin, I need you to talk me down—

The tension in my shoulders loosened at seeing the dots appear on my screen.

—What's wrong?—

I recapped the confrontation with Evie—my idiotic comment, Jared's reaction, Evie's scandalous behavior, my fight with Jared, and Jared's magnificence at his bedroom door—barefoot, with partially done-up black jeans, an open shirt, and damp floppy hair.

—Wow, Molly. Did you really say Evie couldn't date him on your time?—

I hung my head.

—Yes—

—Ooh, harsh!—

—I know—

Knock it off, Fin. I felt bad enough. No need to pile on the guilt.

—Mol, you realize he's not planning on sleeping with Evie, right?—

Fin couldn't know what Jared would or wouldn't do.

—You weren't there. He was like a whole different person—

—Most likely, he was hurt by your reaction to the situation and acted out irrationally. He's only human, and you were insensitive—

Whose side was he on?

—That doesn't excuse his behavior, Fin—

— Give him a break, Molly. Why don't you just apologize?—

My pride prickled.

—Jared needs to apologize, too—

—I'm sure he will if you do—

Maybe.

—Still, he didn't have to take Evie's card—

—Well, Molly, sometimes when someone's falling in love and they're hurting, they do stupid things—

Warmth exploded in my chest, but I fought back my hope. *What did Fin mean?*

—You, of all people, should know that. Remember how stupid you were when you were with Enrique?—

I sucked in a sharp breath. Enrique didn't need to be part of this conversation.

—Wait. Forget about my ex. Do you really think Jared's falling in love—

—I didn't mean him. I meant you. You sound like you're falling for Jared—

Putting the phone down, my body went numb. Fin couldn't be right. Jared and I hadn't known each other long, and people usually didn't fall in love that fast. What was my cousin seeing that I didn't?

—You're full of it, Fin—

—Maybe I am, but answer me this—why are you bothered Jared's hurt? Why are YOU hurt? Would you be upset he'd flirted with some other girl, not Evie?—

I sighed, tapping my lips with a finger. Justifying my anger would be wrong now that I knew Jared had a right to be hurt. Even though what I'd said was the truth, and he was the one who'd been a douche, his actions were fair. My heart sunk like a lead balloon. Jared fighting back and Evie treating him like a piece of meat were my fault.

A shudder rippled through me. Just thinking about Evie with Jared made my skin crawl. She didn't deserve a guy like him. Plus, she had a reputation for cheating and narcissistic behavior. I was sure if Evie and Jared dated, she'd screw Jared over, just like she had with Mason. But if Evie did hurt Jared, then I'd always know I was to blame. I'd have been the one to have set that chain of events in motion. Focusing back on my screen, I fought the shame and denial still warring in my brain.

—I don't know why the situation irked me, Fin—

—Yes, you do. You're just not willing to admit your feelings yet—

My fake-date rendezvous was research. I wasn't supposed to develop any real feelings. Jared was acting unprofessional, and he broke character—kind of. Talking to Evie, he'd acted like an escort rather than a companion. But with me, he'd acted like a jealous boyfriend—not exactly the role I'd hired him for, but close enough. I was so confused.

—I need to get ready—

—Molly, be nice to Jared. You were mean, and he sounds like he's got it bad for you, too—

I couldn't keep my heart from soaring, wanting to

believe Fin's words, but they were clipped with doubt. I threw my phone on the bed. "Thanks for nothing, Fin." I stomped to the closet. "All you had to do was agree. I texted you for support, not perspective."

Even though I had no right to be, I was angry. I balled my hands into fists. The whole situation had gotten way out of control, and the tension between Jared and me was all my fault. Well, mostly my fault. He'd been irrational, too.

I yanked my black faux-leather pants and a backless halter top—which would pair nicely with Jared's dark jeans and button-up—off their hangers and threw them on. After jabbing in my silver, dangling earrings and shoving on a set of bangle bracelets, I spritzed my musky perfume on my neck, wrists, and ankles. Then I put on my heeled ankle boots and marched into the living room. "Ready when you are." My lingering anger flattened my tone.

Jared approached with slow, deliberate steps. "I… Uh… Yeah… Yeah, I'm ready. You look…"

His gaze embraced my curves, and Jared's dilated pupils looked ravenous. Combined with his fumbling words and slack jaw, Jared's body practically screamed he wanted me—at least physically. A sense of power pulsed through my veins, melting away all my defensiveness, replacing the emotion with something more primal. I was sure my face must have mirrored his own.

Jared had put on his suit jacket over the dark jeans and the same light-blue button-down shirt from earlier. The mere sight of him and the memory of what was underneath dropped my stomach through my pants. I could barely hold myself together.

I wasn't brave enough to speak in the elevator or as I waited next to him in line for a cab. But Jared couldn't seem to keep his gaze off me, and with each glance, I worked to gather my courage to apologize.

In the cramped space of the car, I sat as far as I could from Jared, staring out my window. Fin was right, the fight would be over if I just said I was sorry, but I didn't know where to start. The shame of how I treated Jared had my lips glued together. I feared he would never find forgiveness in his heart.

Jared helped me out of the cab upon our arrival, his gaze tracing the lines of my figure, his lips parting.

As I stepped onto the cement sidewalk beside him, I noticed his expression, and it ignited a budding hope for reconciliation like a firework within me.

"Have you ever been to a blackout restaurant?"

Jared's tone was measured, the spark in his eyes extinguished. His change in demeanor made me doubt what I'd seen just a moment ago. Wrinkling my nose, I kept my voice indifferent. "No, but is it one of those restaurants where you eat in the dark?" I was such a coward.

"Correct, the dining room is pitch-black. You can't see a thing. But customers say the deprivation enhances your other senses." He held the restaurant door open.

I swore I glimpsed a flash of wistfulness flit across Jared's face. Although, the expression happened so fast I wasn't even sure I'd seen it or if the reaction was just wishful thinking again.

Inside, a blonde, high-school-looking greeter had Jared and I sign a non-disclosure waiver. "Please leave your phones, purses, and anything else that will light up or glow in one of the lockers to your left."

I placed my things in the black metal box labeled *fifteen.*

Jared set his watch on top of his phone, closed the square door, and stuffed the key in his pocket.

A man wearing head-to-toe black, with a pair of military-looking night vision goggles, stepped to the greeter's desk. "I'm your server, Lamont. I will guide you to your seats. If you'll place hands on shoulders, you can follow me."

After stumbling behind Jared like a blind mouse through the restaurant, I fumbled into my chair.

Lamont explained the glasses and cutlery positions using the clock system, with the dinner plate being the timepiece's face.

A few moments of silence passed. I could only hear the other patrons clinking glasses and cutlery with murmured conversations, and I concluded Lamont must have left. Smoothing my napkin across my lap, I avoided the tension in the air.

"Why did you tell Evie I was your companion?" Jared's question tore through the air. "Why didn't you tell her I was your friend or colleague?"

Pain laced his tone, and I winced. Would he believe me if I told him the words just slipped out, and I didn't mean to insult him? *Probably not*. "Because I'm a horrible liar and you are a companion." I shifted in my chair.

"You're right. I am. But that's not what I want to be."

I furrowed my brow. "What do you mean?"

Jared was quiet for another heartbeat.

I gripped my fork. Now was my chance to grovel. I swallowed hard.

"Like I told you in the beginning, Molly. This job is simply a means to an end. Not a career." Glass clinked against something metal.

His words derailed my apology.

"I'm so close to buying out my boss, Chris."

Jared's admission was strained with desperation, making it sound like he didn't want to be a companion any more than I wanted him to be one. Was I his Hail Mary contract? "You're that close to buying Sky's the Limit? No way!" Warm embers ignited in my chest. "That's great news."

"Your contract takes months off my timeline."

Okay, I might not be his Hail Mary, but I at least gained him a lot of yardage.

"When I finally reach my goal, I can actually be the guy I am pretending to be, had we connected over the Internet—if this fake scenario were real. Recently, I've even thought of myself that way because you've treated me like a person with opinions and a brain. But then, hearing you refer to me as nothing but your companion today…just stung."

Our server returned, and he alerted Jared and I he was there with a clearing of his throat, then placed our meals on the table.

The knowledge of Jared's pain was like a specter haunting my thoughts, and I was grateful to have a moment to think before I responded. I fidgeted with my napkin. Letting the restaurant's intimate darkness fill me with the bravado I'd lacked in the car—the same kind chatting online provided—I allowed the pressure of my guilt to erupt like a volcano. "I can't apologize enough, Jared. I never meant to make you feel that way. My words were clumsy. I'm so sorry." I filled my lungs, finally able to breathe again. "I have no excuse for the way I treated you." Shaking my head, I wrung my hands. "I'm so used to talking about my research. I told Evie the truth. I didn't mean to objectify you. I don't think of you that way."

Silverware clanked against glass. "What do you think of me then?"

Jared's question was a low whisper, the earnestness making me cinch my shoulders. "I know you're too good for the likes of Evie." I inched a hand across the table, wanting to touch Jared so much I ached inside. "And I know I'd be hurt if you called her." My fingers met with soft fabric—his sleeve? I gave it a tug.

His hand found mine, gave a brief squeeze, then released.

A lump rose in my throat until the distinct sound of ripping paper emerged from Jared's side of the table.

"I never planned to."

His warm hand caressed mine on the table before opening my fingers and placing something in my palm. Pulling my fist to my chest, I used both hands to determine their contents—textured pieces of torn paper. My heart hammered against my ribs—Jared destroyed Evie's card.

Chapter 24

Jared

Oddly enough, despite the lack of sight and absence of sex, the vulnerability I experienced holding Molly's hand across the table was the single most intimate moment I'd ever had with a woman. Hearing her say she didn't want me to call Evie, I felt my heart soar. The blackout atmosphere of the restaurant aided in intensifying my desire and longing for Molly tenfold. I didn't know how to continue the conversation in the dark, with no body language or facial clues to guide me. I felt like I was in one of those dreams where you're naked in front of the class.

"On your plate at your four o'clock, what do you think that is?"

Adrenaline pulsed through my veins like a sugar rush. I was grateful Molly changed the subject, despite my lingering questions—why didn't she want me to call Evie, and was Molly jealous? But, because I wasn't sure of my own confused feelings over the situation, I grasped the olive branch with both hands. Picking at the bumpy, almost rubber-like cuisine on the lower right of my plate, I sniffed. "What is that?" I touched the bit of food at the end of my fork. "Feels like brains but smells garlicky." A peculiar, unappetizing, gelatinous sound emanated from Molly's direction.

"No, brains are squishier than this. Especially if they're fresh out of the body."

I chuckled to myself with a shudder. Of course, Molly would know that tidbit of information. "I'm confident you have an interesting story behind your comment, but I'm not sure I want to know while we're eating."

"Actually, I've sat in on an autopsy. Nothing as bad as you're probably thinking. But I won't describe the procedure since you've got such a weak stomach."

"Ha-ha. Nothing about me is weak." *Except my resolve toward you.*

Molly giggled.

I pursed my lips. If only I could show her. "But I appreciate you not describing it." I fumbled for my water. "Is watching an autopsy the scariest thing you've done in the name of research?"

"Well, not really. I've corresponded with a serial killer on death row, but that wasn't as scary as you'd think. I'd probably say…staying in the supposedly haunted, abandoned asylum was the worst."

I dropped my fork, letting my jaw go slack. "Hold on. I have so many questions. While *I* would never stay in an abandoned asylum, I get it. But you wrote to an actual serial killer?" I leaned forward and rested my forearms on the edge of the table. "Wouldn't you be scared he would track you down at your home and murder you if he escaped? Even though the odds of that are probably pretty slim. Still."

"It's not as slim as you think. Ted Bundy escaped police custody twice."

The smugness in her tone was evident. My friends said *I* was the adrenaline junkie? "Not helping your case, Molly." I grabbed my fork and resumed eating a slick leafy substance, tasting hints of balsamic vinegar.

"Don't worry. I used a P.O. Box and called the prison to ensure the killer was still incarcerated the day I collected my mail."

Swallowing my bite, I jabbed for another. "I'd say you were being very sensible"—I shook my head—"but I'd be lying. What was the haunted asylum like?" I chewed the leafy forkful.

Molly gave a hearty laugh. "I expected the place to be like this—dark with whispered conversations and noises I couldn't pinpoint. But the abandoned hospital was simply a rundown building with just enough furniture to make me feel worse for the previous occupants rather than scared of any looming ghosts trapped within its confines. However, knowing the archaic correctional methods used back then as I camped on a treatment room floor was enough to give me the willies."

As an image of some poor soul with pads on their temples strapped to a chair popped into my mind, I shivered at the ice running down my spine. "I bet. Are you saying, staying there wasn't helpful?" Reaching for my one o'clock, I bumped my water glass but caught it before it tipped over.

"Oh, no, it was. I nailed the location descriptions, furniture, and atmosphere. Plus, I get to impress people by saying I stayed there."

She wasn't wrong. I considered myself brave, but people who confronted the paranormal were on a whole other level.

Molly continued talking about other odd escapades she'd done in the name of research while she and I finished our dinner.

My respect for her increased with each tale, and I shook my head when she joked how, after she'd hired me alongside her thriller research, her browser history made her appear like a modern-day, gender-swapped Jack the Ripper.

"You know, because I used to research how to kill people, then I checked out escorts and companions?"

Despite her not seeing me, I shook my head and forced a laugh. "Yeah, I made the connection." The subtle reminder of my job pulled on the stitches of my wounded ego from earlier. Over the last few hours, I'd forgotten being with Molly was part of a contract. The run-in with Evie, the resulting standoff, and the intense conversation at the beginning of dinner had conjured genuine emotions. While they were foreign emotions, they were real. For me, at least. But after hearing Molly's wild tales, I better understood why she'd blurted she'd hired me for research when Evie asked. The outburst had nothing to do with whether Molly would consider me boyfriend material—which I doubt she did. Situations like my contract were just her normal—something she did for her books. I'd been an idiot to have believed otherwise.

Once I'd finished and squared away the bill, I escorted Molly out of the restaurant. After putting on my watch, I confirmed our rideshare.

Molly stood beside me on the sidewalk, squinting at the bright flashing lights and fiddling with her bangle bracelets. "That was fun. Thank you."

More like eye-opening. Without the darkness, I wouldn't have talked with such raw honesty. I was grateful we'd cleared the air. "You're welcome. Maybe you can use the experience in your book."

"Hmm, yeah." She skimmed a finger over her lips, turning to scan the front of the restaurant.

Seeing the wistful look in her eyes, I would have killed to know what she was thinking. Half of me wanted to go back inside and see what other truths the blackness might reveal. Instead, I double-checked the rideshare app. "We have six minutes." I returned my phone to my pocket. "We're looking for a matte-black hatchback." I ran a hand down Molly's arm, lacing my fingers through hers, ignoring the electricity sparking in my veins.

She looked at me and smiled.

Molly's countenance glowed brighter than the strip, making my heart pound, as if it was fighting to break out of my ribcage. I cleared my throat, forcing my emotions into submission, and kept my tone light. "We have two options for tonight."

Her forehead crinkled. "We do? I thought you had this down to a science?"

I struggled not to smooth away the lines on her brow. "Yes." I pinned my arms to my sides. "While planning this, I read about the Crime Scene Experience, but I worried solving a fake murder would fuel the wrong kind of creativity, so I also researched the LINQ Observation Wheel. The pods are essentially a club this time of night." Dancing with Molly would test the limits of my control again, but I would if that's what she chose.

"Is there even a choice?" Molly smacked my chest.

A shockwave rippled through me.

She clucked her tongue. "Duh, the Crime Scene Experience, of course."

My stomach twisted in a mixture of relief and disappointment. "And you're positive solving another fictional murder investigation won't set you back with your romance novel?"

"No way. Especially not with you there." Molly poked me in the chest.

My muscles tightened at her coy smile. "Okay, let's do it."

She did a happy wiggle with her hips.

My hungry gaze followed the gesture, and I forced it away from her lower half. *Keep it together.*

"Is the place far?" She made a cursory glance along Las Vegas Boulevard.

"Nope, less than a quarter of a mile. The building is just at the end of the strip." I took her hand and played with her bangles.

Until our rideshare arrived, Molly talked about some of her favorite episodes of The Experience's corresponding TV series.

Meanwhile, I strove to reconcile the feelings in my heart, my head, and my groin. When the hatchback pulled alongside the curb, I opened the door. After settling in my seat beside her, I instructed the driver. "The MGM, please."

I followed Molly as she entered the gift shop preceding The Experience. She checked out every hat, hoodie, T-shirt, and piece of memorabilia they offered, gushing over the signed photos of the actors. As I beheld Molly running around the store acting like a kid in a candy shop, I'd resigned myself that my feelings were one-sided. Because even though Molly explained her behavior and admitted she respected me, that didn't mean she and I were more than just a contract.

"You know what?" Molly stood beside me with her lips twisted to the side. "I don't think I want to carry a bag around while we crime solve. If I decide I want something, I'll make the purchase on the way out." She looped her arm through mine, squeezing my bicep.

I swallowed hard, hoping to erase the dryness in my throat. Then, with a nod, I led Molly to the desk at the rear of the store. I typed out our names on the kiosk screen, signing us in for The Experience.

A twenty-year-old guy with lots of black eyeliner called my name, then Molly's, and gave us a rundown on how to proceed, handed us papers, and told us to follow the red signs toward our crime scene.

Molly entered the room first.

I trailed behind, content to keep my physical and emotional distance so she could enjoy herself. I felt like a tourist in a foreign country, like my emotions were in another language and I couldn't efficiently navigate my surroundings. Ever since dinner, I'd been disoriented. My role as Molly's contract and my true feelings muddled together.

With a gleam in her eyes, Molly worried her lip and glanced over the entire scene—a staged living room arranged to appear as though a car had crashed through the wall and killed the homeowner, whose body lay under the front tire. After taking everything in, Molly threw back her shoulders and beelined over to something she'd spotted on the floor next to the dead dummy. Then, with detailed precision, she made her way around the car, even pushing onto her toes and squatting to see from every angle.

On the other hand, I wandered around the room without any real direction, kicking at the floor and internally cursing myself for developing feelings for Molly. Having no experience with investigations or these new emotions, I had no idea how to solve either problem. When a book with a bloody handprint just beyond the mannequin's extended arm caught my eye, I decided to at least pretend to inspect the room. I bent, reaching to examine the piece of evidence.

Molly slapped the back of my hand.

"Hey?" I scrunched my brow and stood.

"Sorry." Molly rubbed a thumb over my knuckles.

My skin tingled.

"This is a crime scene, Jared." She paused. "I know it's frustrating when you can't pursue what you want, especially when touching something might answer all your questions—a very inconvenient rule number one. But you'll get it."

The seductive lilt in her voice and the way she searched my face, as if trying to solve a jigsaw puzzle, gave me the impression she wasn't talking about the Crime Scene Experience. Was she referencing the constraints of our contract? "You're right." My tone was frail as my thoughts struggled like a fish swimming upstream. "But then, how do I proceed if there are things I'm not allowed to touch?"

"Well, remember, you can touch *some* things; you just can't touch *everything*." She eyed me and bit her bottom lip before glancing around the space. "Read the room, Jared. Get a feel for how things work." Molly's gaze landed back on mine with a slow blink.

My lungs constricted, making breathing difficult. Was she giving me the green light? Did she have real feelings for me, too?

Molly bit the end of her pen, her tongue running

along the cap.

I tilted my head to the side, my blood rushing south. The contemplative pose was very suggestive. Was she trying to be seductive? I was so confused; talk about mixed messages. I tightened my jaw. *Sandwiches.*

Stomping footfalls accompanied by raucous voices echoed from the hallway.

Molly's gaze returned to her paper.

I glanced over my shoulder to see a loud group of patrons follow the green arrows to an adjoining crime scene.

Molly cut me a glance, then continued examining every item in the second room, cataloging her findings.

She seemed oddly focused on taking notes, and my nerves coiled, ready to spring. I had no idea how to proceed. Again, I drifted behind her and pretended to search for clues.

When Molly arrived at the autopsy room, she approached the dummy lying on the examination table with a faraway look in her eye.

She hovered over the fake cadaver, rubbing the back of her neck with a frown. "I find it funny how something you know is fake can appear so real."

I stepped beside her and scrunched my brows together. Again, I had the distinct impression Molly wasn't talking about the investigation. "But can't a good detective tell what's real and what's not?" Surely, with all her research experience, she could discern my feelings were genuine.

Molly pursed her lips. "Sometimes even the best investigators can get confused."

That makes two of us.

While she finished collecting her clues, Molly

didn't say anything else.

She was just as precise and thorough here at the crime scene as she was when lodging her axe into the wooden heart target at the throwing range. I found her knowledge and expertise in such morbid pursuits intriguing. I'd reached the point where I could no longer deny my feelings. Watching Molly's confidence as she owned the room made me want to break my rules, say *to hell with the co*ntract, and explore a real relationship. I desired Molly in every way possible, because she was the opposite of everything I'd known and come to expect in a woman. The tight black leather pants on her backside weren't hurting either.

When I entered the debriefing room behind Molly at the end of our investigation, I could cut the tension with a knife. "You're really adept at noticing little details." I tapped Molly's paper, filled with her small but legible script, desperate to restore some normalcy between us.

"I can't believe you missed all those clues." Molly shook her head and met my gaze. "They were staring you right in the face."

Glancing toward the door leading back to the other rooms, I chose my words carefully in case her comment had a dual meaning. "Perhaps, but I'm not used to these kinds of scenarios. Maybe I'm denser than I thought." Considering how the night began, it progressed better than I'd envisioned. I was still unsure how to read Molly's emotions and figured I placed too much stock into her words during the investigation, so I kept my feelings to myself.

Molly decided not to purchase a souvenir at the end of The Experience but requested we stop somewhere for chocolate.

I obliged, and we visited a chocolatier on the strip just past two in the morning.

Heading along the crowded sidewalk toward the hotel, Molly studied one of the small pieces of candy-shelled chocolate pinched between her thumb and forefinger. "I remember when they used to have the tan-colored ones in the regular packages." She jabbed the side of my bag of candy, pointing out the color in question. "They used to be one of the standard six."

I pulled out a chocolate and threw it in my mouth, crunching on the shell. "When I was younger, I don't think I ever paid attention to the colors."

"No way! Really?" Her eyes were wide. "I loved these candies as a child, separating them into color piles before eating them. But peanut butter ones were more popular. You know, because of the movie where the little boy hid that alien in his closet?"

"Man, I haven't seen that movie in forever. It's such a classic." Heather and the oblivious mom in that film had a lot in common. "Too bad Hollywood doesn't make movies like that anymore. All the new releases are remakes. Nothing is original nowadays." I threw some more chocolate into my mouth. "How do you come up with your ideas for your books? Keeping the plots fresh?"

Molly flashed a smile, curling her shoulders and squinting. "I think of how I want to kill people who get on my nerves." She giggled.

I coughed, dislodging the candy from my throat. "You base the victims in your books off real people? Remind me not to get on your bad side."

She wobbled her head. "You've come close a few

times." As she chewed her chocolates, the corners of Molly's mouth curved up. "But seriously, in the book you're reading now, *Summer of Silence*, the woman who gets poisoned was one of my old schoolteachers who said I'd never amount to anything."

I stiffened my shoulders. "I don't remember telling you I was in the middle of reading *Summer of Silence*." Molly could only know that if she had snooped in my room. I raised my eyebrows, daring her to respond. She wouldn't meet my gaze.

"Um, I'm sure you did." Molly shoved another handful of candies into her mouth. "I'm positive. You mentioned it…"

Her chewing mumbled the rest of her words. *Liar*. But I should have expected her to check out my room. The question now was whether she'd snooped while I slept. I wiped a hand over my mouth, hoping she hadn't caught me snoring or drooling. "Okay, I'd argue my point, but I don't want this romance to become a tragic love story. I value my life."

Molly shook her head. "Don't worry. I need you too much."

My heartbeat stuttered. I cut her a glance.

Her gaze flashed to meet mine. "For the book. I need you to complete my manuscript." Molly flicked her head, letting a curtain of hair hide her face and motioned to the colorful chocolate drop in my hand. "I remember when they introduced the blue ones, too. That's what replaced the tan color I mentioned earlier."

Way to deflect. "You don't say?" I threw back a candy with a smile. In my experience, if someone was defensive about something, the conversation hit a little too close to home. Was that true for Molly? I hoped so.

"Yep, I'm a bottomless well of useless facts. But I'm guessing you don't care because you rarely eat candy. You couldn't if you wanted to keep *that* body." Her gaze lingered on my chest.

I took her rambling as a good sign. Fire erupted in my belly.

"What's your favorite color candy?" Molly dug into her bag of just reds.

Another deflection. I reached into my stash of mixed colors and pulled out another one. "Blue." I tossed the chocolate in the air and caught it in my mouth. Molly followed the motion with a greedy gaze before blinking rapidly and swallowing hard as if she was hungry and I was part of an all you could eat buffet.

"Figures. My brother and my dad love blue, too. Must be a guy thing."

"No, my dad's favorite color is yellow." I replaced my wistful smile with a frown, inspecting a coated chocolate of the same color. "He used to have a sports car in about this same shade."

"What happened to it?"

I waved a hand. "My mother got it in the divorce. I'm pretty sure she only demanded the car because he loved it, and he was the one who'd had the affair." I shrugged. *Served him right.*

Molly's shoulders slumped. "I'm sorry. I didn't mean to touch on unpleasant memories."

"Don't be. My parents were horrible together." I tilted my head to the side and pursed my lips, thinking through the years since their divorce. "They're horrible apart, too, actually." I still couldn't fathom how they'd gotten together in the first place.

She nodded. "Are your parents…" Molly shook her head. "Never mind."

I stopped. There wasn't any question I wouldn't answer—for Molly.

She hesitated beside me.

Trying to catch her gaze, I grasped her elbow. "No, what were you going to ask?"

Molly shook her head again and focused on the sidewalk. "Just forget it. The question sounded awful when I repeated it in my head."

I placed a hand on my chest. "I promise, you can say whatever you wanted to say. I won't be offended."

Molly squinted, peeking out of the corner of her eye. "You're sure?"

I crossed my heart. "Of course." When I realized I meant it, I was surprised.

"Okay, but remember you promised." She swirled the shelled chocolates around in her bag. "I wondered if your home life was the reason you didn't mind being the companion who's always making someone else jealous or being the rebound date?"

My friends asked me that question all the time. Sighing, I studied Molly's face, realizing she was right to an extent. However, my feelings about my job were complex. Instead of diving into my psyche, I recited my standard reply. "I'll admit, being a companion hasn't been very reassuring in the love department, but the job is not as cut-and-dry as you think."

"How so?" Molly threw back another handful of chocolates.

When I'd first joined Plus One, I asked Lucas the same question. He argued I wasn't being a douchebag for taking the job. I accepted his answer then because I needed the money, but after years of experience, I recognized the truth in what I was about to tell her. "Well, have you ever been on a double date as a fill-in? Or went to a bar after a breakup, hoping a guy would hit on you and boost your self-esteem?" A wave of jealousy washed over me at the thought. I held my smile in place.

Molly nodded, and as she continued strolling, she rubbed a finger over her lips. "Yeah, I guess I have."

I kept pace with her, wishing she'd never had to experience the pain of either situation. "There you go."

"But how could your parents' divorce and your time at Plus One not affect you?" She wiped the corners of her mouth. "You see only the downside of every relationship—all the bruised hearts and jaded women who want to get back at an ex-boyfriend or lover. Maybe you were able to ignore the effects at first"—she bumped her shoulder against my arm—"but you can't ignore them at this point. That must have taken a toll."

I kicked at a discarded beer can on the sidewalk. The hollow aluminum clanked and scratched across the cement. "Honestly, I've thought a lot about that lately. What if my normal isn't normal?" The idea left a sour taste in my mouth.

"What do you mean?"

I followed the progression of lights wave across the front of a casino, collecting my thoughts. "Well, being caught in the middle of all my parents' disputes and used as a pawn so whoever got custody could keep the bigger house definitely didn't make me want to rush off and get married. It wasn't until much later in life, when I met Rachael and Lorraine, that I understood people could disagree while still loving and respecting each other." I shrugged. "But even then, their relationship is unique." I had yet to see another couple like them.

"And they are…?" Her brows rose.

My conversation with Molly felt so natural, I'd forgotten she didn't know anyone from my real life. "Rachael is a fellow companion, and Lorraine is her wife. We're all good friends."

"That's great, but how does Rachael cope with being a companion? And her wife is okay with it?" She chewed on her chocolate with wide eyes.

I bit back a burst of laughter. "Her story is different than mine."

Molly scowled. "In what way?"

How did she not see my answer coming? "Because Rachael's a lesbian posing as a straight woman."

"Ohhhh." Molly nodded. "Yeah, that's not the same thing." She waved a hand. "Rachael's already sworn off guys, so she doesn't care if they're jerks." Molly cracked a small smile. "Now I understand why her wife isn't jealous—staying within the confines of her contract is easy."

I scoffed, shaking my bag to mix the candies. "It definitely is." Unlike how I've struggled not to break my contract these past two days.

Molly kept her gaze glued on the sidewalk. "But seriously, do you think your time at Plus One has affected your take on relationships and love? Like, when was the last time *you* were in a real relationship?"

I chewed on my bottom lip, wracking my brain. "I honestly can't remember. But I haven't had the time. Between both jobs, I'm pretty busy." Not to mention, I hadn't found a woman I wanted to date—until now.

"But what about at Sky's the Limit?" Molly spoke

fast, and she talked with her hands. "Loads of women must be falling all over you, being outdoorsy and all."

"Ha!" *If she only knew*. "Fake dating other women as a side job isn't the ladies' magnet you'd think it would be." Finding out about my job was always the deal breaker in my past relationships.

"I can imagine, but you said you were close to quitting. What about then?"

There it was—the question I hoped to avoid. But if I was honest, I'd focused so hard on my goal for the past few years, I hadn't considered my personal life after Plus One. At least, not until Molly. However, even though she flirted and her physical attraction to me was obvious, I doubted someone like her would ever be seriously interested in a guy like me. "Well, Molly"—I kept my focus on my candy because I didn't want to see the pity in her eyes—"let's say I buy the franchise and quit the companioning business. Where would I find someone who'd be interested in spending their life with damaged goods?"

Molly stopped short and grabbed my forearm. "I understand how you might not have faith in love because of your circumstances. But you can't possibly believe you're damaged goods."

Her gaze bored into mine. My emotions felt like they'd been thrown into a blender.

"Jared"—she squeezed my arm—"no one is so broken that they can't be fixed."

Molly's expression was unyielding, just like her tone—she still believed in the happy ever after. But considering what her ex-fiancé did, I simply couldn't fathom her faith. Regardless, she was wrong.

"For example, take the serial killer I mentioned

earlier. In his letters, he spoke about several women he'd been corresponding with who were interested in him romantically."

I locked my spine. "I'm sorry, what?"

"Oh yeah, I wasn't lying. Romances happen to almost all the inmates on death row." She shrugged, walking again.

I followed suit.

"Some of the prisoners even get married. I verified the information with the warden. So, believe me when I say—someone out there is perfect for you."

While I understood she meant to be encouraging, Molly's words were like a knife in my heart.

Chapter 25

Molly

Throwing back the down covers, I bolted upright, noticing I still wore my leather pants and backless halter. I swung my legs off the side of the bed and glanced at Las Vegas Boulevard in the dim light of dawn. The morning looked about as hazy as my brain felt. The last thing I remembered, I was on the couch waiting for Jared to bring me a hot chocolate so we could watch a movie. I must have fallen asleep before he returned, and he'd carried me into my bedroom. *Damn it!* Heat invaded my face, and I balled my hands into fists, both embarrassed I'd passed out and mad at myself for having wasted those moments.

By the time Jared and I arrived at our suite last night, I'd overanalyzed every conversation throughout the entire evening and questioned if Jared's comment about being damaged goods was, in fact, some sort of code asking about my feelings. When I received no response to my dual-meaning remarks at the Crime Scene Experience, I figured his obliviousness was because the spark I felt was most likely one-sided. But then he'd made the damaged goods comment, and I questioned everything all over again. I'd even devised a plan to mention our previous conversation before the movie, but I'd been too exhausted, and my tiredness had won out. Now morning had come, and the moment was lost.

Before heading into the bathroom, I peeled off my leather pants. Today would be my last day with Jared. As much as I wanted to enjoy these moments together, the chaos of my emotions and the ache of our looming separation weighed on me, which was stupid. I hadn't gone into this contract expecting I would develop real feelings for him—especially in such a short length of time. Back when I'd designed this asinine plan, I was naive in thinking I could walk away from any type of romance—that by pretending to be in a relationship, I would remain neutral and not get myself all wrapped up in the fantasy.

But the situation changed. Now, I'd gotten to know Jared, and I liked him—more than I expected or should. The problem was, aside from physical attraction, I still had no idea how he felt about me. Now, thanks to my body's need for sleep, I'd lost my opportunity.

Stepping into the shower, I hoped the hot water would clear my head. The whole predicament depressed me, because while my mind grasped the reality of the situation, my heart had a hard time getting on board—it wanted more. A real relationship with Jared wouldn't work, though; he was a companion. The idea of him continuing his services if he and I dated—no way. I was too jealous of a person to deal with Plus One.

The smell of my coconut body wash filled the tiled space but didn't comfort me. *Who am I kidding?* His job wasn't the problem. Jared planned on quitting and taking over Sky's the Limit in the near future, making the whole companioning business a non-issue. The dilemma arose from all the clients Jared accumulated in his ten years at Plus One. Ten years. How many women had come and gone and used him during the span of his career? I couldn't imagine he would respect me long-term knowing I was one of them. Sure, the situation wasn't the same, and I treated Jared with more respect than his other clients. But I still used his services to suit my own selfish purposes. Was I any different? Plus, I had no guarantee he wasn't just acting, and I didn't want to get hurt again.

I rinsed the suds from my body and let the water pressure beat against my back, hoping the heat would loosen my tense muscles. So much uncertainty because of a stupid book. "Ugh!" Shutting off the shower with more force than necessary, I yanked my towel from the hook, resigned to make the most of the time I had left with Jared.

****

For breakfast, Jared had chocolate chip scones waiting on the dining table. After helping me into my seat, he plucked one from the tray and sat. "How did you sleep? You conked out on me last night."

He regarded me like I was wrapped in *caution* tape. I swallowed the lump in my throat. "I know. I'm sorry. I thought I was wide awake, but I guess my body knew better." I picked at my scone, breaking off small bites. I'd ruined everything—I couldn't even taste the chocolate.

"No worries. I'm glad you're feeling refreshed."

Jared's smile seemed forced, and I wondered if he felt disappointed we'd missed out on the time together last night, too. Or maybe I was being delusional again.

He eyed my orange slingback flats and cringed. "I hope you take this for the suggestion it is, because those look beautiful on you, but you might want to wear some sneakers today."

I pouted, holding my right leg out, examining my footwear. "Why? Don't you like these?" As Jared's stare inched up my legs and over the rest of me, his left cheek pulled into what I'd decided was his signature sexy grin.

"Oh, I do."

My defensiveness melted away, and my heartbeat quickened.

"You look good in everything you wear, but I planned to show my Vegas virgin some of the other hotels this morning. I want her first time to be as comfortable as possible."

His words felt dangerous and a little illicit. I bit my lip, my imagination running wild with possibilities with Jared and my manuscript. "Any first with you is bound to be enjoyable." My insides blossomed—the banter was back.

He winked, his smirk growing more pronounced. "I've planned something that might get a little messy for later this afternoon"—he leaned forward and tugged on the hem of my cream blouse—"so you might want to change your top, too."

Jared's use of the word *messy,* combined with his smoldering gaze, sent my mind straight into the gutter, and I had to force myself to focus. Glancing over his magnificent form, I inspected his casual attire—gray sneakers, jeans, and a delicious tight black tee stretched and molded around the defined contours of his pectoral muscles. "How messy?"

He cocked his head and licked his lips. "Ruined for anything in the future?"

OMG. I focused on my outfit, cheeks aflame, and my insides rioted. "Good to know."

With Jared's inuendo branded into my brain, I dashed into my room and changed into a pair of camo trainers and a Duran Duran T-shirt I'd gotten from their concert a few years back when they played in Seattle. After tying the hem in a knot over the hip of my skinny jeans and regulating my breathing, I was ready to go.

Jared's stare could have incinerated my new outfit, and I had to turn away from his thirsty expression before I did something stupid. Instead, I wound my fingers through his, relishing in his warmth, before Jared led me out to wander the boulevard.

He had been right; comfy shoes were the smart option. I spent our morning marveling at the digital art columns of backlit silhouettes in the lobby of the Cosmo, taking selfies with the golden lion at the MGM, and strolling through the Egyptian aesthetic of the Luxor with Jared. By the time noon rolled around, he and I were near the south end of the strip. I had at least two blisters, so I voted to stop in New York-New York to rest and grab a bite to eat.

Jared and I sat in front of one of the Greenwich Village delis, finishing the subs we'd ordered. I marveled at the cement floors stamped to look like stone and brick walkways lining the old-school, faux-brick storefronts. Trying and failing not to fantasize about Jared and I being in his home state together, my writer brain craved details to round out my daydreams. "I'm curious, how does the casino rank in comparison to the real Greenwich Village?"

"I have to give props to the designers; they paid attention to detail. The only things missing are the trees and blue sky." Jared wiped his hands on his napkin. "For instance, look over there." He scooted closer and pointed to a maintenance hole in the floor. "See the steam?"

Nodding, I felt my heart lodge in my windpipe at Jared's proximity as I followed the billowing mist emanating from the circular cutout in the walkway with my gaze.

"That looks exactly like the maintenance holes in Manhattan."

"You're kidding? I assumed that was just for added effect in TV and movies." They were a standard in every crime series.

"Nope. The steam from the maintenance covers is real. Most of the downtown business district gets its heat and power from steam. The pipes run underneath the city, and well"—he shrugged, leaning back into his wrought iron chair, reestablishing the distance between us—"sometimes those pipes have leaks, and the steam escapes through the covers just like that."

"I'd like to see that in person." *With you.* "Every time I've been to New York for a writers' conference, I've not had the time to sightsee." I let my gaze drift back to the steam, picturing Jared riding his bike through the mist, his arms tensed and his legs pumping. The image punched the air out of my lungs, and I covered my sharp intake of breath with a cough.

"Well, if you ever come back, you'll always have a place to stay." Jared raised his glass in my direction before taking a swig. "I'll give you a tour of the city's best features." He bounced his eyebrows.

My muscles locked up. Did he mean what he said? Or was he still just being flirty? His invitation did sound like he wanted to see me after our contract ended. Although, the offer could have just been his charming demeanor mixed with one of those hollow invitations people make because they're being polite and know the plans won't happen. If Jared was serious, though, I vowed to make the trip a reality.

While I had my silent debate in my head, I watched him point out other architectural features, vaguely hearing his descriptions of the similarities between the hotel and his city. The way Jared's eyes lit up when he spoke about New York was akin to how he'd described me when I talked about Seattle or the Olympic National Park. I suppressed a sigh. Jared was simply doing his job and making small talk. I silently repeated the reminder like a prayer. Distance was yet another reason Jared and I could never work outside of this arrangement—we lived on opposite sides of the country and loved our respective homes. "It sounds like there's a lot I don't know about your home state."

"Yeah, when most people think of New York, they only think about Manhattan." Jared took a sip of his drink. "But the whole state is worth seeing, especially upstate. That's where all the mountain bike trails are." He flashed a sly smile.

At his mention of northern New York, a question popped into my head. "Speaking of upstate, does your dad know you work for Plus One?"

Chapter 26

Jared

Molly's question about my father turned my blood to ice. I set my glass on the deli's wrought iron table and wiped my mouth with a napkin.

"I'm sorry. What you share with your parents is none of my business."

She focused on her sandwich container and broke out in a self-deprecating smile, readjusting herself in her seat. The chaos of the casino blurred around me.

"My male main character won't be a companion, so I can't even say I'm asking for research." Molly shrugged. "I'm just curious. So, if you don't want to answer, you don't have to."

I stopped a drip of condensation from running down my glass, the cold numbing my finger. Normally, I dodged the subject of my father like a vampire avoiding the sun, but because Molly asked, I obliged. "It's fine. I don't mind. But my history with my father is a long story." I lifted my shoulder with a halfhearted laugh, realizing the truth of my situation. "Well, maybe the story's not long, just complicated." Molly's eyes sparkled.

"You know, twisted, complicated plots are kind of my thing."

Checking the time on my phone, I still had forty-five minutes until the next planned activity. "We have a little time." I took a deep breath, gathering my thoughts.

"So, do your parents know about Plus One?" Molly stared down, wiping the face of her watch with her thumb.

She appeared almost timid, like my answer might scare her. She had no idea the drama I was about to unleash. "Well, not all of them know." I wound and rewound the straw wrapper around my index finger. "My sister does."

"You told your sister?" The crease between her brows deepened. "You said you weren't close."

"We're not. And I didn't *tell* Willow." I ran a hand over my mouth. "One of her friends found my profile online." A stir of anxiety filled my stomach, recalling the email from Madame Erica with Courtney's profile attached. Seeing her image had triggered my gag reflex.

Molly's eyes widened, and she leaned back in her chair. "Please tell me you didn't go on a date with your sister's friend."

I grimaced. "Ew, no." A shiver ran down my spine at the mental image of taking out Willow's vapid friend. I shook away the thought. "But needless to say, when I declined her contract, she alerted Willow out of spite." I rolled my eyes. "Everything went downhill from there. The girl got her revenge, because my sister used the information as blackmail. Anytime Willow needed something from me, she threatened to tell our mother." If only the situation remained that simple.

"Nice." Molly sneered, then her face softened as she put a hand over her heart. "I couldn't imagine either of my siblings doing anything so vindictive. What a nightmare."

I shook my head, ignoring the heavy dose of shame weighing me down. "Well, it gets worse. Heather found out, too."

Molly's eyebrows shot to her hairline. "Did you refuse to do something, and Willow told her?"

"No. I wish. Willow wasn't the one who told our mother." I leaned forward and rested my elbows on the table, prickly heat creeping up my neck. "I ran into Heather while with a contract."

Molly's jaw dropped. "No. Way."

I gave her a tight-lipped smile and matched her cadence without enthusiasm. "Way."

A shaky laugh escaped Molly's lips, and she stretched across the table, grasping my forearm. "Oh, you can't stop there. I need details."

Heat radiated through my skin. If my situation wasn't so pathetic, I would be comforted by her tenderness. As I prepared to tell Molly about my dad's business partner's wife, Priscilla, I could only offer a half-hearted, playful smirk. "The client took me to her beach house in Malibu—a beautiful place with an open floor plan and panoramic patio doors that led onto a deck overlooking the ocean." I'd never forget Priscilla's house—the kind of place I'd like to own one day and the only bright spot in my story. "We'd just arrived and had headed out to have drinks on her balcony deck to unwind. She hired me because her husband constantly traveled for work, leaving her feeling neglected and unattractive. We'd been talking and drinking, and I'd begun"—I focused on the intricate pattern of the metal table, feeling the heat flood my face, and chose my words with care—"making my client feel better about herself."

Molly cocked an eyebrow. "Interesting choice of words…but go on."

I ran a hand through my hair. "Don't worry; everything was above board. My contract remained intact." For some reason, Molly knowing I hadn't violated any rules was important.

She ducked her head and averted her gaze. "Not my business."

If her skin weren't already so deep, I'd say she blushed. A good sign. Either Molly was embarrassed I clarified, or she was jealous. Preferably the latter. "Anyway"—I pushed on through my unease—"we didn't hear the neighbor's back door open. If we had, we would have gone inside. The client and I only broke apart when someone called my name."

Molly covered her face with her hands. "No."

I nodded. "You guessed it. My mother was on the neighboring deck. Her boyfriend at the time owned the house next door."

Molly dropped her hands, her gaze searching the table. "What are the chances?"

Her breathy voice told me she understood the horror of the situation. "Right?" I rubbed my palms down my thighs. "I should have bought a lottery ticket with those odds." My worst-case scenario come to life.

She bit her lip, repressing a smile. "So, what happened?"

I squinted. "Are you laughing at me?" I couldn't really blame her if she was. Looking back now, the irony wasn't lost on me.

Molly scoffed. "Yeah, the story is funny."

"Whatever." I gave the toe of her shoe a playful kick.

She smiled. "But in all seriousness, what did your mother do?"

"Heather outed me as her son and laid the guilt on my client by asking about her husband. The conversation was intense." I remembered watching the moment go sideways as if in slow motion. Heather's newfound knowledge was a guillotine she held over my head.

"Wait, did your mother *know* your client?"

"Yep." I popped the *p*.

"Then how did that client not know you were Heather's son when she hired you?"

It was a valid question. "Because my mother's friend hadn't seen me since I was eight when my parents split. I don't use my real name on my profile, and she didn't use hers, either." Learning Priscilla's true identity rioted my insides.

"So, I was right." She clenched a fist, her smile smug. "Jared's not your real name, then."

I could see the wheels turning in her head, but to Molly's credit, she never asked for my true identity.

"What happened next?"

I scratched the scruff on my chin, my other hand on my bouncing thigh. "Once my client made the connection that I was Heather's son, she basically choked on her own vomit—that was great for my self-esteem." I couldn't blame her, though. I'd wanted to hurl myself.

Molly cocked her head to the side. "Trust me; your self-esteem should be intact. The vomit was more likely due to her conscience over her marriage." She placed a hand on my fidgety knee.

I stilled the motion and watched her lace her

fingers into mine.

"She was an idiot. I would never be ashamed to be seen with you."

I hitched a breath, and my stomach flipped. Had Molly said the compliment to make me feel better, or had she meant more? I forced a smile. "Well, I figured as much when you chose me to be your Plus One."

Molly grinned, shoving my shoulder with her free hand, but I kept her other intertwined with mine. "Continue with your story. Your mother called you and the woman out; then what?"

As I prepared to admit something to Molly I'd never told anyone else, I felt my heart drumming a staccato rhythm in my chest. "Well, needless to say, the client canceled my contract, but Heather caught me before I headed home." I withdrew my hand from Molly's and rubbed the base of my skull. What I was about to say made touching her feel too vulnerable. "Heather said she wanted to make a deal. She'd keep my profession from my father if I agreed to pay for another round of wrinkle reduction and fillers."

Molly jerked forward, bracing her hand on the wrought iron table. "Your mother blackmailed you, too?"

I couldn't meet Molly's gaze, but I could hear the disgust in her voice.

"How could she do that to her own son?"

Shrugging, I studied a crack in the mortar between the bricks under my chair. I didn't have a good answer to Molly's question.

"I'm guessing you paid for her treatments?"

Nodding, I still avoided Molly's gaze. "But Heather didn't stop there." I clenched my hands into fists. “Next was a tummy tuck, then a facelift, a chemical peel, and bleaching.” I closed my eyes and released a slow breath through my nose, hoping to calm myself. “She’s been milking this for three years now. Feeding her and Willow money is part of why I still haven’t been able to buy the franchise.”

Molly rubbed her fingers over my knee. “I’m so sorry, Jared. I wish I knew what to say.”

I took her hand in both of mine, finally meeting her gaze. A lightness filled my chest now that I’d confessed my humiliating secret to someone. More than that, Molly sympathized. “There’s nothing to say. It is what it is. As soon as I have the money, I’ll quit. Then Heather won’t have any leverage.” My life would finally be my own—no more games.

“Well, if you don’t mind your dad finding out after the fact, would it be horrible if he knew about Plus One now? At least then, you could keep all your wages for yourself and quit sooner.”

If only. “Unfortunately, dealings with my father are not that simple.” I traced the lines on Molly’s palm with a finger. “Either way, my father would be embarrassed. But if I’d quit before he’d found out, then he could write off my being a companion as me being young and naive. At least, that’s what my father would say if his friends or co-workers found out.

“On the other hand, if he found out now, he would disown me and write me out of his will.” I met Molly’s gaze with a curled lip and made a halting gesture. “Not that I care about the money. I don’t. But”—I sighed, letting my shoulders relax—“despite our tenuous relationship, I don’t want to be completely cut out of his life. When I finally buy the adventure franchise, I want to look him in the eyes, knowing I'd achieved success by myself." I forced a smile. "Maybe then, my father would finally treat me like an adult. Who knows? He might even be proud."

Chapter 27

Molly

Jared continued tracing the creases in my palm, ignoring the line of people at the deli counter behind where I sat who could probably hear our conversation. If I hadn't felt so bad for Jared, the touch would've turned me on, but I didn't even know where to begin to try to comfort him. I still couldn't fathom how a mother could blackmail her son. The scenario hurt my heart worse than any of the betrayals I'd fabricated for my novels. I wanted to help Jared figure out some way to stop his mother and sister, but as good as I was at solving mysteries, his predicament had me stumped. "No wonder you call her Heather. She doesn't deserve the title of 'Mom.'" As soon as I'd said the words, I wanted to pinch them out of the air so they wouldn't reach his ears. I covered my mouth, horrified. "I'm so sorry. I've overstepped."

He pulled my hand away from my lips and laced his fingers with mine. "It's fine. You're not wrong." Jared scooted his chair a little closer, touching my knee. "I'm glad you're able to see my side."

Who wouldn't? "Still, though, I shouldn't have said it." As much as I appreciated him comforting me, I still regretted what I'd said.

Jared met my gaze, and his jaw muscle jumped.

"That's my fault for telling you something so personal."

How did he come to that conclusion? "No, don't blame yourself. I'm glad you did. Your actions say a lot about your character." I swallowed hesitantly, humbled that my initial assumption of a companion was so far off base from Jared's true nature. How he could still be open and vulnerable with examples like Willow and Heather shocked me. Jared had a big heart—caring about his family's opinion despite how they treated him.

"Thanks." His eyes widened, and he bolted upright. "But that can't go in your book."

I squeezed his hand. "Oh, no. I would never. When I said, 'your character,' I meant you—Jared—as a person." The last thing I wanted to do was betray his confidence. I'd leave that job to his family.

Pink dotted his cheeks, and I studied his face. Jared…He looked like a Jared. I went through my catalog of character names from my books—Jack, Michael, Elliott, Cole, Gaspard—tasting them on my tongue, but none fit as well as his pseudonym. I jabbed my straw into my plastic cup, ignoring the low squeak of the two rubbing together, and dug for the last sip of my water, wondering if I'd ever know his truth.

Jared's shoulders visibly relaxed. "I appreciate it." He collected the remnants of his lunch from the table. "Can I get that for you?" He indicated toward my plastic sandwich container.

"Yes, please." I stuffed my used napkins into the clear box and handed it to Jared.

As he strode away, I enjoyed the view and brainstormed what name fit this man with such a nice backside.

****

For the afternoon, Jared scheduled a wine and painting class, making sense of why he'd asked me to change my clothes earlier. In a small strip mall south of the Mandalay Bay sat a quaint little studio run by an adorable mom-and-pop couple. Both owners could have been straight out of the nineteen sixties. The wife, Amy, wore a crown of daisies in her long white hair. While her husband, Buddy, wore denim from head to toe.

Jared led me to a spot in the farthest corner of the room, away from the others.

"You should have everything you need at your stations," the wife bellowed, her husky voice carrying across the room. "Buddy and I will keep the wine flowing." She dragged out the *I* in *wine* and pointed at the two paintings hanging on the front, flat-white wall behind her. "This is your inspiration. Each of you will paint half of the sunset. Everyone on the left will paint this half, and everyone on the right will paint the other. Then together"—she shimmied her hips with her hands in the air—"you'll make a complete picture."

Jared shook his head, smiled, and pulled out my stool. "She's a character."

I giggled. The older woman was adorable. "I want to adopt her as my grandma." If I could stuff her in my pocket and keep her, I would.

Jared leaned down, inches from my face. "I have no doubt she'd love it."

His soft breath hit my ear, sending a wave of shivers through my torso. He seemed oblivious to my internal struggle with desire.

Jared took his place at his workstation. Opening the paint jars on the table between the canvases, his corded forearms flexed.

The scent of oily liquid wafted through the air. I drooled at the tantalizing sight of his muscles, and all my nerve endings hummed like live wires. He must have caught me staring, though, because he made a production of lifting the bottom of his shirt to wipe his brow, flexing his chiseled abs. I wanted to call him out for being obvious, but the effort of restraining myself took all my willpower.

"Want me to wet your canvas?" A hint of a smile tugged at the corners of Jared's lips.

My breath caught, and my stomach dropped to the floor. "Excuse me, what?"

Jared's dimple deepened. "Weren't you listening? We're supposed to prep our canvases with this." He held a jar of white gesso paint.

With flaming cheeks, I dipped my brush in the container and proceeded to wet my canvas with short choppy movements, blinking away my inappropriate fantasies.

Jared shook his head. He stepped behind me, pressing his chest against my back, and putting a hand around my waist. "No, like this." He guided my wrist, making long, broad strokes.

He was like a magnet, and my body leaned into him of its own accord.

As Amy made the rounds and approached our corner, she stopped beside my workstation. "Woo, feel the tension over here. Buddy"—she beckoned her husband with an arm—"bring over the wine."

I stepped to the side out of Jared's embrace, putting space between him and me.

The entire class turned in our direction.

I ducked behind my canvas, drawing my shoulders to my ears.

Jared stepped back to his canvas.

His charming, tilted grin told me he appreciated the attention, and his eyes flickered with what I assumed was amusement.

Buddy raced over with a goofy lope, holding the wine out, trying not to spill any, and filled our glasses.

"Drink 'em down, kids. There's more where that came from." Amy patted my shoulder. "I'd like to be a fly on the wall in y'all's room tonight." After giving an exaggerated wink, she ambled away to chat with another couple.

I gaped, my traitorous imagination feeding off Amy's words. Too bad Jared's Plus One restraints wouldn't let tonight be the show she expected. Those stupid rules were like rocks in my shoe, annoying me with every step of this contract.

Jared painted blue ocean stripes with his head down and tilted a fraction in my direction.

I could see him watching me out of the corner of his eye, his brow raised with what looked like a satisfied twist of his lips. Heat spread to more than just my face, and I wished I was telepathic. I dipped my brush, coating the bristles in a deep-orange paint. "Awkward."

Jared barked a one-syllable laugh. "Was she wrong?" His brush stroked the canvas, the tendons in his arms flexing again.

My lungs tightened, and I couldn't breathe enough air. What did Jared have planned for tonight? He was such a tease, because he knew as well as I did that I couldn't pursue what Amy suggested. I took a large gulp of my merlot, savoring the full-bodied, fruity flavor on my tongue, and recalled Jared's comparison of PDA to wine. How far could things go before Jared considered our actions as partaking of the last glass? My heart pinched; the line didn't matter. If I did give in to my carnal desires, I would only be hurting myself because doing so would be more than just physical—at least for me. I didn't want to be another notch on his bedpost. I wanted the dream I hoped to manifest in my manuscript—the happily ever after.

I felt an underlying current of melancholy weave from my brain to my chest, lodging cold and hard behind my sternum. Speaking my truth regarding my feelings had the potential of marring our last night together. Then again, saying nothing would be like a leaky faucet in the back of my head, dripping unresolved feelings that never turned off. I brought the goblet to my lips, hoping to drown my spiraling thoughts. "This wine's not bad." I held the glass toward the lights and swirled the deep-red liquid. "The flavor is sweet, not dry. I'm not too fond of dry wines. I wonder where they bought it." *Stop rambling!*

Jared glanced at the older couple dancing to the soft music playing from a wireless speaker at the front. "I'm guessing since they probably bought the bottles in bulk, they opted for quantity over quality, so—the Internet."

I feigned a laugh, setting my glass on the table and continuing with my painting, the warmth in my belly loosening my lungs. "Don't you be dissing online shopping. It's a lifesaver."

Jared made another stroke with his brush. "You mean with book sales?"

Oh yeah, that! "Well, I meant next-day delivery, but you're right; the Internet helps with book sales, too."

"Speaking of books." He added more yellow paint to his brush. "Do you think you can finish your manuscript in time?"

My stomach hardened, filling with dread. "Two months isn't very long, but I've met extreme deadlines before." Like when I wrote *Scattered Bones.* I based the book on a true story, and it required an interview with Vlad Petrov—AKA—The Bleacher. The serial killer was held in a maximum-security prison in Moscow with more red tape than I expected. After months of international negotiations, I finally got my chance, but the late date left me in a time crunch—just like my current manuscript. "Hopefully, I can do it again." I crossed my fingers for emphasis, but in reality, I had no choice.

Time with Jared was worth its weight in gold. He'd been everything a girl dreamed about and more. Too much more. But I was sure I could mold his moves into the perfect character. Even though our contract would end in my heartache, it wasn't his fault. Jared was only doing what I'd asked.

"We've had a productive time. Two months is plenty." Jared set his brush on the table and exchanged it for his wine, swinging the glass in a toast. "I believe in you, Molly. You've got this."

Bless him. Jared's confidence assuaged some of my niggling fears, and my eyes prickled.

He took a sip of his merlot. "What made you switch genres anyway?"

I sighed, knowing I'd kept the details of my

writer's block from him for too long. Jared deserved to know the truth. After all, he'd been extremely honest with me. As the start of a tension headache brewed, I pressed my fingers to my temples, rubbing in circular motions. "My ex-fiancé, Enrique." I shifted on my stool, giving up on my massage, grabbing my paint brush, and adding yellow to my canvas. "I was in love and assumed writing romance would be easy being so happy." Recalling my naiveté, I made a sassy eye roll. "I pitched the idea to Renee and landed a contract. But after everything that happened with Enrique"—heated anger from his betrayal surged through my veins—"I broke off the engagement." I dropped my head. "At first, I was lost but the empty feelings turned into anger, and writing about love wasn't helping."

Jared frowned. "Hence the writer's block."

I forced my lips into a tight smile. "You got it."

He nodded. "And that's when you hired me."

His words weren't a question. "I can't take the credit; Renee had the publisher breathing down her neck and threw the idea out there as a joke. I merely jumped on the suggestion, and…"—I softened my smile—"it's been the best decision I've ever made." I returned my focus to my painting, my heart thudding against my ribs, and I hoped he recognized the sincerity behind my words.

A vibration zinged up my right butt cheek, drawing my attention. I retrieved my phone from my back pocket and saw Enrique's name on the screen. A lump rose in my throat, and my breath whooshed from my lungs. Before I allowed myself to think about the implications, I hit *ignore* and put the device, screen down, on the table next to the paints. The vibrations stopped, but only momentarily. A second round of buzzes began, and I clutched my chair, willing my phone to stop.

Jared jutted his chin toward my mobile. "Aren't you going to answer?"

Concern was etched in his features, but Jared didn't understand. "No. The call's not important." As I stared at my device, I could feel the sweat trickling down my back with a hollowness in my stomach. For the life of me, I couldn't figure out what Enrique wanted or his reason for calling—not after a year apart.

Jared's brow furrowed.

My mobile went silent, and Jared and I stared at the shiny surface. I let my body sag. A final vibration sounded after another minute. Bile churned in my stomach. I had a voicemail. I swallowed hard. Did I even want to listen to the message? After almost gnawing a hole into my bottom lip and several not-so-subtle glances from Jared, I relented and reached for my phone. Keeping my gaze glued to the screen, I excused myself and sprinted to the bathroom, ignoring Jared's attempt to catch my attention.

I shut the restroom door and locked it behind me with trembling fingers. Bracing myself against the hard surface, I fumbled to retrieve the voicemail and stabbed the *Play* button, followed by hitting the speaker icon—hearing Enrique's voice close and in my ear would have felt too intimate.

"Molly, it's me."

My stomach rolled. Enrique's accented voice, so familiar yet unwelcome, sounded desperate.

"Please, hear me out. The baby's not mine. I took a paternity test and everything."

"Like it matters!" I screamed pointlessly at the voicemail. "You cheated on me!" Angry tears brimmed on my lashes. "The kid quite easily could have been yours!"

"I know the results don't change the fact I messed up"—his words flowed hard and fast now—"and you have every right to still be mad. But I know now Chantel was a huge mistake. Losing you has been the hardest thing I've ever had to endure."

"It couldn't have been that hard; you stayed with her for a year." I flared my nostrils.

"I can't apologize enough for what I did. But I still love you, Molly, and want to give us another chance. Please, please? At least think about it. That's all I'm asking. I'll wait."

The voicemail ended, and I switched off my phone. Silence echoed around the tiled walls. Taking loud, shallow breaths, I willed back the traitorous tears stinging my eyes. I felt a jolt of pain stab me from behind the ribs. Gritting my teeth, I was angry Enrique could still have such an effect on me. If he believed I would give him another chance, he was a fool. I tried to imagine how I would have felt if he had apologized sooner. A hollow void filled my chest. No. I would never forget what he did.

As I reflected on my time with Enrique, I'd believed I was happy. But when I ended things, I thought my world had imploded and I'd never know love again. However, over the last few days I'd shared with Jared, I'd noticed my mood was lighter than it'd ever been with Enrique. As if my mind cleared and I could finally see the whole picture, I perceived my relationship with my ex would have been subpar. I deserved more.

Picturing Jared, alone and dejected, painting in the other room, I mulled over what I wanted. Could Jared be that *more*? *If* what I experienced with Jared was real, then…maybe? All I knew for certain was when he kissed me, I felt heat all the way to my toes. I hadn't detected any pretense, and I doubted even Leonardo DiCaprio with all his acting accolades could have pulled off a fake kiss as good as that—it had to be real.

With suppressed delight, I felt goose bumps erupting along my skin. Jared had to like me. Why else would the fight about Evie—the anger between us—feel so real? Not to mention how my whole body smiled when I stared at Jared's exquisite face. Maybe I was delusional. Although I couldn't imagine looking at Jared and *not* wanting him. My hangup was whether or not I wanted to risk that kind of vulnerability again. Even though I was ninety-nine percent sure Jared felt *something,* too, my heart wasn't the only thing on the line. My career was, also.

Chapter 28

Jared

Molly hurried toward the bathroom.

I stared after her retreating figure. When she checked the number of the call, she turned white as a ghost. I couldn't imagine who would be calling to elicit that kind of reaction. Nerves clawed their way through my stomach. The fact Molly hadn't answered right away told me the call wasn't urgent. I swore the frown that settled on her forehead, and how she stared at her phone without seeing it, showed hints of fear. Who would scare Molly?

All the clues clicked into place, and a name popped into my head—Enrique. I slumped on my stool. What a sick twist of fate we'd been talking about him and he called. But why would Enrique contact Molly again now? Did she want him to? As if the wind was knocked out of me, I gasped for air. Staring at my half-painted sunset, I fidgeted in my seat, the colors blurring. I wanted to check on Molly, but I wasn't sure if I should. What if I was the last person she wanted to see right now? Suddenly, I was grateful I was sitting because I couldn't trust my legs to hold me.

An eternity passed before Molly returned. Her eyes were puffy, and as she smiled, her lips trembled, but she resumed painting as if the call never happened.

Emotion clogged my throat, and I had to clear it before I could speak. "Are you okay, Molly? Do you want to leave?" I rose from my seat, prepared to do whatever she wanted.

She reached out a hand. "No, I'll be okay. We can finish this."

Unconvinced, I sat.

Molly gestured to my canvas. "Your painting's very good, by the way."

She wasn't fooling me with her false bravado. The cheeriness in her smile didn't reach her eyes. Since she'd commented on my painting, Molly's behavior told me she didn't want to talk about her voicemail. Was her mind still on Enrique? An ache reverberated through my chest. I pushed aside the echo of déjà vu.

"I'm pretty sure I figured out why they serve endless glasses of wine." Molly waved her glass around the studio. "Because if you drink enough, you'll be convinced you're Bob Ross." She laughed.

Although her words sounded hollow, the small sparkle in her eyes seemed genuine.

"Buddy!" Molly snapped her fingers. "More wine, please." She held a hand to the side of her mouth. "I need some more inspiration."

The older man trotted over and filled Molly's glass.

I gulped my last swallow and extended my goblet for a refill, too—the nagging feeling of despair tugging at the edges of my mind.

Downing her wine, Molly stared at her canvas. "The painting's not getting any better."

I smirked, taking a large swallow. As the alcohol pumped through my veins, it took the edge off my concerns, and I realized something. Aside from her obvious crying, I had no reason to jump to conclusions. Molly's conversation could have been benign. Getting myself worked up when I didn't have all the facts would be stupid. Maybe the call wasn't even about her ex. The idea seemed plausible. My only option was to forget about the call and make the most of my last evening with Molly—to ensure she got the experience she paid for, despite my feelings, the phone call, or the inevitable outcome. Gripping my paintbrush, I leaned toward Molly's canvas, ignoring the emptiness in my chest. "Perhaps a little more orange right here." I globbed some bright paint onto her blue ocean as a highlight.

"Hey!" Molly shoved my shoulder.

Her bright tone bordered on hysteria. *Did I cross a line?*

"How would you like it if I painted on your canvas?" Molly clenched her jaw and drew a yellow stripe across my sunset with jerky movements.

My scalp prickled at my ruined scene. Was Molly mad or playing along? The weight in my stomach warned me I needed to lighten the mood. I narrowed my eyes but exaggerated my smile. Dipping my brush again, I mimicked the graffiti she'd done on mine onto hers.

Molly's jaw dropped. Scowling, she retaliated with another color.

The paint war continued until both canvases were a nasty shade of orangey-brown. Breathing hard with my paintbrush still in hand, I registered a moment passing before I realized the whole class gaped at Molly and me as if we'd murdered people instead of just our canvases.

Molly scanned the room, frozen like a statue.

Noting her expression, I erupted in a fit of laughter. Doubled over, I peeked again at Molly.

She clutched her stomach, fighting for breath between giggles.

Perhaps I didn't need to be concerned over the voicemail, after all.

Amy drifted toward our corner. "What's going on over here?" Her gaze bounced from our painting disasters to the inspiration at the front of the room, her mouth falling open. She polished off her wine. "Well"—Amy threw her hands in the air—"at least they match."

I locked my gaze with Molly's behind Amy's back and burst out laughing again.

Molly followed suit.

Using a fine-tipped brush, I signed my painting in red. "There." I handed the canvas to Molly. "You'd better hang onto that. My masterpiece will be worth a fortune someday."

She took the muddy-brown piece of art and smiled. "You know, artists usually only become famous after they're dead, but thank you."

The uninvited tension between Molly and me dissipated. I side-eyed her, getting back into the rhythm of bantering. "Are you threatening me?"

Molly put a hand on her left hip. "Let's just say you might want to go with your original email and sleep with one eye open."

I stifled the twitching corners of my mouth. "I like seeing you smiling again, Molly. But seriously, are you okay?" Seeing her upset threw off some sort of internal imbalance.

She took a deep, shuddering breath. "Yeah. I'm

fine." Molly stared at the floor. "The call was from Enrique, apologizing and asking for another chance."

The weight of her words sent a prickle up my scalp. *It was her ex.* I bit my cheek to keep my expression impassive.

"He caught me off guard, is all. The man deserves an Oscar for his acting abilities. He'd managed to convince me he had feelings that weren't there when we were together." She pursed her lips. "Heck, he could even give you a run for your money."

Pain pierced my heart—hard. All my doubts resurfaced. The void swallowing my insides from her comment crushed me like a boulder. I should have expected the disappointment. After all, someone like Molly doesn't fall in love with a guy like me.

Chapter 29

Molly

As Jared and I left the painting studio, my heart felt tender. While I tried to act all sunshine and rainbows with my chaotic feelings, I most likely came off more dazed and confused. I hardly remembered how Jared and I got back to the Euphoria to drop off our paintings. Jared had them sent to the suite by an accommodating concierge with a gap-toothed smile before he and I took the monorail to the Venetian.

The hotel's Grand Canal—a snaking channel of water wrapping around the second floor of the shopping promenade—held several Venice-style, black gondolas moored to a small dock where Jared checked in with a Venetian staff member. After nodding curtly at the hotel employee, Jared hopped up the stairs. Stopping a few steps below me, he extended a hand. "They're ready."

Jared's smile wavered for a fraction of a second before locking in place. My chest caved in. Something seemed off. In fact, as I thought back over the monorail ride, Jared had seemed tense since the gallery. Was he wary because of Enrique's call? If so, what did that mean?

As I followed Jared to the gondola, I felt a lurch wave through my stomach, and I focused on my feet, stepping into the boat.

Jared helped me get situated on the stiff, red velour bench before taking his seat.

The gondolier with his black beret, pushed away from the dock with the long red-and-white oar, rocking the boat and belting out his Italian serenade.

Jared pulled my right hand onto his lap.

His fingers trembled as they skimmed down my forearm and over my palm before lacing with mine. *Was he nervous?*

"Did you know"—Jared leaned closer—"the first public casino opened in Venice in the 1600s?"

His warm breath fanned against my ear. I fought the shiver wracking my spine. "I did *not* know that."

"Yep." He grazed the tip of his nose along my jawline. "It's almost poetic to have a Venetian hotel here in Las Vegas, right?"

"Hmm, true." My voice wavered with my desire. Perhaps the odd tension I felt on the monorail was simply *me* reacting to Enrique's surprise call and had nothing to do with Jared. *Stupid imagination.*

Jared rubbed circles on my arm with a finger as he nodded to one of the bridges passing overhead. "Venice also has over four hundred bridges." He raised my hand to his lips.

My stomach plummeted through the bottom of the boat. The longing in Jared's eyes was palpable, and his charisma was off the charts. *Yeah, the awkwardness is just me*. "Wow, that's a lot of bridges." I focused on the elaborate, Italian-gothic tracery overhead and the scent of chlorinated water as a distraction so I wouldn't implode. I could see at least five other bridges from where the boat floated, quite a few for such a small area.

"In Venice, cars are forbidden; foot traffic and boats are the only sources of transportation." Jared marched his fingers down my thigh. "They found a way to make the rules work in their favor."

His touch was like blistering embers. "Rules are stupid, anyway." I hoped he understood I wasn't referring to Venetian customs but rather my response was to what he *wasn't* saying.

The gondola headed toward the final bridge before returning to the dock.

Jared angled, taking my face in his hands. "According to Venetian custom, if a couple kisses under a bridge, they will remain in love forever." The shadow from the last plaster arch crept across his features.

My heart hammered in my chest. *Was that Jared's plan? Did he want to kiss me under the bridge? Did Jared intend to love me forever? Does he love me now? Did I want him to? Did I love him?*

I heard my phone buzz. Glancing at my cell in my lap, I saw a text from Enrique. *Not now!* My ex had terrible timing. I didn't care what Enrique wanted. I flipped the screen face down.

Jared's eyes tightened, and he exhaled through his nose.

Dammit! Trying to hide my phone now was a moot point—Jared had seen the message. The static in the air was like the silence before a storm. I waited, absorbed by the sight of Jared's lips, and held my breath, anxious to see what he would do. The boat was under the bridge, almost past it, and Jared was so close but still hadn't leaned in. Was he having second thoughts?

Stupid Enrique! The light from the painted sky overhead illuminated Jared's face. The boat was no longer under the bridge. The moment was gone, and he hadn't kissed me. I closed my eyes, my heart threatening to fracture.

As Jared's lips brushed mine, the warmth of his breath fanned against my mouth. His touch was light at first—once, twice, but the third time he met my mouth, I could feel his urgency. Liquid heat spread through my veins, and I grasped his shoulders, desperate to hold on to the fragile connection. I clung to Jared, my emotions teetering on the edge of a cliff, ready to fall.

But then the kiss shifted.

With his hands on my face, Jared withdrew, closing his mouth to my passion and placing soft, lingering pecks on my lips. The contact felt bittersweet. Longing and desperation clogged my throat. *Was this kiss a good-bye?*

Jared searched my features, a muscle tightening in his jaw.

My heart shattered. Enrique had ruined the moment again. Although this time, the devastation wasn't over him. It was because of him.

Chapter 30

Jared

I stroked Molly's cheek with a thumb, a burn like alcohol at the back of my throat. Even though kissing her under the bridge had been part of my plans right from the start, I'd chickened out. I wanted to kick myself for being so weak. But now I'd gotten to know Molly, my feelings were more complicated. When the moment came, and I saw Enrique's text on her screen, I couldn't convince myself to kiss her under the bridge. I wouldn't put Molly in that position when even *I* didn't know what was real anymore. The line between Molly and me and our fake identities had blurred too much. I was even more confused about where she stood. Sure, as I held her face, the yearning in her gaze was evident. But because of the voicemail from Molly's ex and what she'd said back at the art studio, I didn't know where she stood emotionally.

So, I waited.

After watching the light from the faux ceiling chase away the shadow of the bridge from Molly's features, I'd touched my lips to hers. I could feel the question in her touch and see the uncertainty in her expression. My heart splintered with the realization that while I'd known what I wanted, I was unsure if Molly's response was because she sought comfort in general or if she wanted comfort from *me*.

The gondola bumped into the dock.

I dropped my hands to lace my fingers with hers, my lungs paralyzed.

Molly and I disembarked and hiked up the flight of steps, following the signs toward the monorail. "Are you hungry?" I kept my tone light.

She curled into my bicep.

My chest ached, and my heart felt like it'd been knocked around like tumbleweed in a gust of wind. I'd gotten too involved, and now I didn't know how I would say good-bye tomorrow.

"I could eat." Molly's gaze wandered back to the dock.

Her blank expression confused me. Was she relieved or disappointed in the timing of the kiss? "If you're not hungry, then we can wander around awhile." I glanced at the shops. "Was there a store you'd like to visit?" Shopping lifted the spirits of most of my clients.

"No, I'm not in the mood."

Dammit! I had one job—romance Molly—and I failed miserably because I'd developed feelings. My disappointment stabbed me like a knife in the back.

Molly focused on her shoes. "Despite my comfy trainers, my feet could use a rest. Do you mind if we go back to the Euphoria and order room service? This is our last night together, and I'd rather not spend the evening in a busy restaurant, if that's okay."

She gave an unsteady sigh, leaning her head on my shoulder. The ache in my chest lightened just a bit. I didn't want to be around other people, either. "Room service it is."

****

The food arrived at our suite, and I tipped the attendant before taking my seat opposite Molly at the dining table.

She uncovered her plate. “Mmm. This burger smells delicious.” Molly grabbed the ketchup from the service cart and smacked the end of the bottle, the thick red liquid oozing onto her plate. “Hey, considering our time is coming to an end, would you mind if we talked shop?”

I popped a crispy fry into my mouth and let the salt dissolve on my tongue. “Of course, I’m happy to help in any way I can.” *Any way you need me.*

She removed the tomato from her bun.

As I did the same, I couldn’t help smiling.

“Well, I’ve chosen to write my book from a dual point of view. Since I’m not a guy, can I ask you a few questions so I can get a feel for how you think?”

She did not need to know my ungentlemanly-like fantasies I’d had about her—no way. But I’d give her whatever else she wanted. “Ask away.”

“On the first day, back on the monorail, I’d asked you how you’d become so good at romancing women, and you replied, ‘I’m gifted.’ What did you mean?”

I swallowed my bite of burger. Man, she must have thought I was pretentious. I definitely needed to clarify. “Please don’t hold that against me. What I should have said was romance is like a dance. While I might lead in the movements, I never take my focus off my partner. After our initial agreements with what will be okay, I use careful observation, like the expression in her eyes and how often she blinks, the way she flips her hair, or the movements of her lips, as clues to what my next turn should be and how my date wants to be touched.”

At least, that's how I interpreted things before my dumb heart got involved. Now, I didn't know how to proceed.

Molly swallowed hard.

My gut clenched. At least her reaction was something I could read. I jutted my chin at her throat. "Like that, right there. I said something that, what? Turned you on?" *Hopefully.*

She shifted in her chair, jabbing her fry into her ketchup. "What? Um… N…no, you just used a great description." Molly nibbled on the bit of potato. "Haven't you ever read a line so good you shivered?"

I had to admit some of her thrillers had given me chills. But I was pretty sure they weren't coming from the same place. "Fine, I'll let you have that one. Next."

Molly stared at her plate, and her complexion deepened. "Have you ever crossed the line with a client?"

"Never."

Molly's head jerked up, her gaze locking on mine.

Her reaction pierced my heart. *Is she pleased with my answer?* I had no idea. However, overstepping was grounds for dismissal. In reality, until Molly, I hadn't ever wanted to. Plenty of my previous clients were beautiful women who'd come on to me, but after a few condescending words from their mouths, the decision was easy. But with Molly…

"Okay…then how do you…"—she averted her gaze—"stop?"

I hoped her thoughts were on our first kiss just like mine were, so I was honest. "Sandwiches."

Molly bit her lip and smiled. "Good answer. Way to bring the safe word back around."

My chest warmed, and I squared my shoulders.

"Actually, I'd be fired if I crossed the line. But I would also need the woman's permission."

"Fair points." Molly nodded. "One more question, because this is a crucial plot point in a romance, and then I'll be done." She squinted. "How do men handle breakups?"

I scrunched my brows. "Are we talking about real life now or work?"

"Both." Molly laid her napkin beside her plate and leaned farther into her chair.

The back of my neck prickled. I wasn't sure where she intended to go with this, but the question had my nerves on edge. "Well, the work answer is easy. The relationships aren't genuine, and no actual feelings are involved; hence, nothing to get over." I took a sip of my wine, but the liquid tasted bitter from the lie that just rolled off my tongue. "As for my personal life, I haven't had any long-term girlfriends, so that answer isn't any different." I leaned forward and put my elbows on the table, but I couldn't meet her gaze, my vulnerability cinching my muscles. "As I said before, I haven't found many women who are eager to date a man who moonlights as a companion."

She touched my forearm. "They're missing out."

My world tilted. Molly had no idea how much her words meant.

****

Thirty minutes later, I put the room service cart in the hallway.

"Ugh, I ate far too much." Molly pulled on the waistband of her jeans. "Would you mind if I changed into pajamas? I want to be comfortable."

"Not at all. I'll do the same." A few minutes later, I

strolled out of my room in navy-blue lounge pants, still pulling my gray T-shirt over my head. "Are you sure you're okay staying in? It seems a little anti-climactic for your last night in Vegas. Especially because I'm sure you'll be locked in your apartment for the next two months writing."

Molly stood frozen in her doorway with her mouth agape.

I took her reaction as a good sign, but I didn't let it go to my head. Tonight would be hard enough with her looking irresistible in her light-blue, spaghetti-strap tank, and pants combo.

Shaking herself out of her trance, Molly strutted over to the couch and lay down, dramatically throwing the back of her hand against her forehead. "Oh, I don't know. Staying in this lavish apartment with my muse sounds like the perfect way to spend my last night in Vegas."

"Are you calling me a Greek god?" My words were backward. I was the one who wanted to worship her.

"Yes, Adonis." She smirked, raising an eyebrow. "I am."

Heat flared in my torso, but my lips were sewn shut. The compliment was the best I'd ever received.

"Oh my gosh! Jared Washington, you're blushing. I didn't think anything fazed you."

Rubbing the back of my neck, I dipped my chin. "Anywhoo…"—I let my gaze drift to the side—"can I ask a favor?"

"What did you have in mind?" She scooted to the corner and rested her head on the arm of the couch.

Ignoring the suggestive inflection in her tone, I jogged into my room, retrieving my copy of *Summer of*

Silence and a pen from my nightstand. I returned to the living room, my gaze dropping to Molly's lips. I wanted to taste them again. Swallowing to relieve the dryness in my throat, I handed her the items. "Will you sign this for Madame Erica?" I twisted, lifting Molly's legs, sitting, and resting her ankles on my thighs.

Molly autographed the book. "It's nice to know I have another fan." She placed the novel on the coffee table and curled an arm behind her head.

"Superfan. She worried I'd mess this up. She checked in constantly, making sure I'd contacted you and"—I made quotation marks with my hands—"gave you my full attention."

Molly leaned on her elbows. "Well, I'll be sure to let her know I'm completely satisfied with your service."

Desire saturated my veins. If only I could make her statement into reality. Something flickered across Molly's expression but disappeared too fast for me to register what it meant.

"When I get the website satisfaction survey, I'll obviously give you five stars. Will that help you achieve your goal to buy the franchise faster? Is there some sort of bonus for that?"

I scrubbed a hand over my face. The idea of Molly having to rate my service left a bad taste in my mouth, as if the action would relegate me to an object and not a man who cared deeply. But I knew that wasn't her intention. Besides, I couldn't deny the fee from Molly's contract was a massive step toward quitting Plus One and buying out Sky's the Limit—technically, we were both using each other. I had no right to feel defensive.

Shrugging, I took one of Molly's ankles into my

hands, rubbing my thumbs over the ball of her foot. "Um, the review system doesn't work that way. But a good rating will help me secure future contracts." The mention of other clients knocked the wind out of me. Anyone else after Molly felt wrong, and yet *I* brought up the subject of future clients in front of *her. What is wrong with me?*

Molly's eyes closed, and she laid her head down. "I'll be sure to get on that the moment I return to Seattle."

I'd swear her tone had a strained lilt, but the inflection was probably just wishful thinking. Digging my fingers into her heel, I could feel her muscles relax. A pleasure-filled sounding sigh escaped Molly's lips. Warm tingles waved through my body, and I froze.

Molly's head jerked up. "Don't stop. It feels good."

As I focused on the individual components of a club sandwich, I realized the sensation from having her legs resting on my thighs was too much. I needed to put space between her skin and my torso. "I'm glad you're enjoying yourself, but we should do this properly." I maneuvered from under Molly's legs, pushed the coffee table away, and knelt beside the couch.

She peeked out of the corner of her eye with a raised brow.

"To get a better angle," I lied, reaching for her foot once more. *Lettuce, mayo, pickles…*

Molly nodded and settled into the cushions. A smile ghosted on her lips.

She was onto me, but I continued rubbing her feet, staying away from her ticklish arches. After a few minutes, I switched legs and resumed the circular motions with my thumbs. Every touch on her skin was both agony and pleasure. “Molly, what’s been your favorite part of this week so far?”

“This.”

Her voice didn’t contain an ounce of hesitation. But Molly’s answer confused me, it had too many interpretations. “Are you talking about the massage?” I progressed to rubbing her hands.

Molly cracked an eye.

I wove our hands together before releasing them and giving each of her long, smooth fingers individual attention.

“No, the massage is just a godsend.” Molly smiled, wiggling her hips and shoulders, readjusting. “I meant this time with you. You’re easy to talk to, and I enjoy your company.”

My mouth felt like sandpaper. *She’s just being polite.*

“What about you, Jared? What’s been your favorite part?”

“Easy.” *All of it*. “The banter.” I switched arms and massaged my fingers into her left hand.

“Yeah, I’ve enjoyed it, too. In fact, I’ve enjoyed everything about this week…except when I put my foot in my mouth with Evie.” Molly frowned.

The remorse infused in her tone made me pause on her forearm, guilt weighing on my conscience. “Hey, didn’t we already establish *I* was overly sensitive?”

“No, you had every right to be upset. I should have been more respectful of your feelings.” She frowned.

My chest tightened at seeing the pinch of her brows. “Thank you.” I’d never had a woman respect my feelings the way Molly had.

“You’ve been so wonderful these past few days,

playing along with the whole charade, and going above and beyond." Molly kept her eyes closed. "I can't tell you how much that means."

Emotion saturated her words, but Molly had the situation all wrong—I hadn't been acting. Everything I'd done, I'd done because I wanted to for Molly's book—for her. While the contract began as help with her characters, it'd developed into more. I squeezed Molly's hand and suggested switching positions—I'd sit on the couch while she transitioned to the floor between my legs so I could work on her shoulders. I began massaging once Molly got comfortable again. "I wouldn't say I've been playing along this whole time."

Molly moaned beneath my touch.

I closed my eyes, the blood in my body heading south. Ignoring the sounds of her pleasure, I focused on regulating my breathing. "I've enjoyed my time with you. A lot. You've made my job easy." *Too easy.*

"That's kind of you to say." A moment of silence passed. The rise and fall of her shoulders quickened with each breath. "I have to be honest, I've never had this kind of connection with anybody before."

I froze. "Not even with Enrique?" I needed to know.

She gave a slight shake of her head, keeping her gaze forward. "Not even with him. My time with you has taught me I need to stop wallowing and start living again. To rethink what's important and what I want in my personal life."

The muscles in her shoulders tightened under my palms.

"I..."—Molly huffed—"I've been fighting my feelings because I'd orchestrated this whole situation.

We were supposed to be fictional"—she took a shaky breath—"but my feelings for you have become real."

As if my muscles had given out, I let my fingers slip from her back. I needed to look into her eyes and see if she meant what she said. "Molly?"

She twisted her head, her profile in shadow.

I tugged Molly's shoulder, coaxing her to face me.

She complied, kneeling and sitting back on her heels, and stared at the floor.

I caressed her cheek and waited for her to meet my gaze. Were those Molly's genuine feelings, or was I only hearing what I wanted? The twist of fate seemed almost too easy—that the whole arrangement, while fabricated, had transformed for both of us. Impossible, yet…

When she finally met my gaze, she had tears in her eyes. "I can't bear knowing I won't see you again after tomorrow." Her voice broke.

My head went fuzzy. Molly had developed feelings for me, too. An onslaught of emotions fought for my attention—relief, gratitude, excitement, desire—and something I hadn't experienced in a long time—hope. The magnitude of them combined and how much I needed this woman overwhelmed me. I slid my fingers into her hair and leaned in, brushing my trembling lips against hers.

Molly opened her mouth and fisted her hand into my shirt just over my stomach.

Heat washed over me like a tsunami. I deepened the kiss.

Her hands slid behind my back, and her fingers dug into my flesh through the thin fabric.

I pulled Molly forward between my legs. Exploring

her neck and jaw with my lips, I drank her in. I grasped her waist and clung biting her bottom lip with my teeth.

"Jared?"

My name sounded like a sin, and my resolve was ready to break. Breathing heavily, I leaned back to search Molly's expression. As if I'd been stranded in the desert and she was an oasis, my entire body craved every inch of this woman. But my next move would shape both of our futures. *Could I do this? Should I?*

Molly traced the scar on my left cheek with her thumb before running her fingers over my lips, her eyes half-closed. "Please?"

The raspiness of her voice incinerated the last of my resolve.

I was all in.

Chapter 31

Molly

As Jared stroked my jaw with hungry fingers, he smoldered, perched on the edge of the couch. Every nerve in my body was hyperaware and raw everywhere he touched.

His hand traveled down my neck, arm, and around my hips until he scooped me off the floor and onto his lap.

I straddled Jared's thighs, the heat from his legs igniting my desire. The lights and shadows from the street below danced across his beautiful face.

Jared gripped the nape of my neck, bringing my mouth to his.

He devoured my lips. Pushing him against the back of the couch, I deepened the kiss and pressed into him.

Jared's hands tightened on my hips.

A deep hunger within me yearned for more. I sucked on his bottom lip and pulled back.

Jared's head reared up; his gaze locked on my mouth.

He wanted more, and I rewarded him with a sly smile, skimming a finger down his neck and around the collar of his shirt.

Jared growled and roughly flipped me onto my back, laying my body on the stiff cushions. He climbed over me. His weight sank onto my hips.

I released a shaky breath, relishing the pressure pinning me to the sofa.

His cheek pulled in a primal grin before leaning down, his tongue teasing my mouth. Jared's fingers curled around my thigh, pulling my leg against his side. His teeth grazed my ear.

Jared's ragged breaths sent shivers trailing along my skin.

He rocked his hips.

Excitement rippled through my core. Desperate to get closer, I grasped his shirt, pulling at the fabric. "Oh, Enrique."

Jared froze. He caught my wrist and pulled back, eyes squinting. "What did you say?"

I gaped at the brittle tone in Jared's voice. *What* did *I say?*

"Did you just call me Enrique?"

My breath felt trapped in my lungs. *No, I would never. I didn't.* Paralyzed with fear, I silently replayed the last few minutes. I widened my eyes, horror washing over me, and my stomach rolled. I relinquished Jared's shirt.

He released my hand. With slow movements, Jared peeled himself away and slumped on the edge of the sofa, closing his eyes.

I broke out in a cold sweat, though my insides boiled. "Jared, I…I'm sorry…it was a mistake…his name just slipped out. It didn't…I wasn't…" I wiped my clammy palms down my thighs. "I said Enrique, because he'd called earlier… I…" I would never have intentionally called Jared by my ex's name. Enrique's phone call must have rattled me more than I'd realized, and he was the last person I wanted to think about at that moment. *What had I done?* "I'm so sorry, I—"

"No…"—Jared shook his head—"just stop." He shoved a hand through his hair.

Pain laced his tone, and my chin trembled. "But—"

"This was exactly what I was afraid of." He exhaled sharply. Jared's elbows rested on his knees, and his gaze focused on his hands. "My brain warned me, but I didn't want to listen."

His words had my mind reeling. I had no idea what Jared meant. I sat straight, crossing my legs under me. I'd beg; he was worth it. "Listen to what? Jared, I can't apologize enough. I know you're not him, and I don't want you to be." I splayed a hand over my heart. "I'd only said his name because of earlier, back at the painting thing, I…" I scrambled, grasping at words to string together into an explanation he would accept.

Jared stood, facing the wall of windows with his arms crossed over his chest, his shoulders rising and falling with each breath. "Just stop." He bowed his head. "This was a mistake."

His whispered words sent a numbness through my body. "What? No!" Hadn't I made my feelings clear? I wanted Jared. He wanted me.

"Come on, Molly." As he faced me, he dropped his hands to his sides. "I'm nothing more than an expensive rebound. You've just bought into the illusion." He rolled his head back. "Again, I'm just a tool to get over an ex."

I gaped at Jared's rigid silhouette against the light from the windows. He was wrong. What he and I had wasn't just a fantasy, and he wasn't a rebound. I loved the way *he* made me laugh—the way *he* made me feel alive. Since initiating this whole thing with Jared, I couldn't deny my feelings had been all about *him*. Before I could speak, I met his gaze, and saw his eyes brimming with tears.

"Just because I played a different role with you than with my other clients didn't change the fact, you'd still given me a role." Jared clenched his jaw. "This has happened before, the infatuation with the illusion. Only this time, the joke is on me"—he thumped a fist against his chest—"and I'm mad at myself for letting it happen." The cords in his neck tensed. "I'm not one of your characters, Molly. I'm a real person."

I stood and reached out, desperate for him to understand. "I know. I know you are. I'm sorry—"

Jared backed away. "So. Am. I." He stalked toward his bedroom, without even a backward glance before slamming the door.

Chapter 32

Jared

Shoving the door, I stumbled, my knees buckling, and I collapsed on my bed. I rolled onto my back. The door clicked shut, and I flinched. I blinked away the moisture in my eyes and rubbed at my aching heart—a hurt worse than anything I'd ever imagined. On top of that, I was mad. Not at Molly, but at myself. I'd been so gullible—convinced Molly wanted *me* when only a few hours ago, she'd been upset about the phone call with her ex. I should have listened to my gut—she wasn't over him. I fisted my hair, angry I'd bought into the fantasy just as many of my past clients had, which only added a layer of guilt to my building mountain of self-loathing.

I was such an idiot. My insides had the same cold feeling they had after I'd watched my favorite Bruce Willis movie—the gut-punching moment when he revealed himself as a ghost at the end. I wanted to kick myself for not recognizing the clues all along, considering I'd witnessed his character get killed in the opening scene.

My opening scene was to be the muse for Molly's upcoming novel because she'd gotten writer's block over her breakup with her fiancé. The fact I was hurt, and she'd used me to get over him—that was on me.

****

A couple of hours passed before the adrenaline left my body. My limbs weighed a thousand pounds, but I had a flight to catch in a few hours. After what happened, I didn't want to face Molly again. The confrontation would be too painful and humiliating. Sitting and wallowing at the airport alone was a better option. I wanted to hide because Molly was privy to details about me and my family previously only Rachael knew. Pulling the pillow over my head, I hoped to assuage my naked feelings. Tonight, I'd been reckless. I opened my heart and allowed my desires to be validated and seen, overrunning my common sense. Now, I would pay for my mistake.

Pushing past the lethargy, I stood and robotically collected my things. As I tucked the Income Axes Range's business card into the pocket of my carry-on, I tried not to think of the irony of their logo—a picture of an axe lodged into a wooden heart target. I averted my gaze from the mess of paint scribbled on Molly's canvas aptly describing my mood. And, when I slid the *Les Mysteres des Reves*' program into the top pocket of my case, I couldn't keep my subconscious mind from connecting the plot to Molly—my dream and my passion. I blinked away the stinging in my eyes. But when I logged onto the Plus One site to record the details of our contract and mark the job complete, I paused.

Would keeping Molly's money be ethical?

The situation was a moral dilemma. Because, at least in my case, my time with Molly hadn't been an act. Despite my aching heart and wounded ego, I hoped Molly had enough material to mold into a character. My gut told me I should return Molly's money, even though I'd technically fulfilled my contract. However, if I refunded my fees, I'd be stuck at Plus One for the entire year.

I closed my eyes. My father's condescending voice bellowed in my head, "Take the money. Feelings should never get in the way of a business transaction. Emotional interference is unprofessional."

Bile rose in my throat, and I scrubbed a hand over my face. With a heavy heart, I marked the contract complete, knowing, for once, my father would be proud.

Chapter 33

Molly

I sat hugging my knees to my chest, back against the headboard, staring out the window in my Euphoria room at nothing in particular. The flashing lights from the strip lit the dark walls. My eyes had already dried up—itchy, dusty, salt flats devoid of moisture. I'd messed up. Of all the things to have said to Jared, why did my brain have to revert to *Enrique*? I was finally over my ex, but then he called out of nowhere and ruined everything—again. Knowing my subconscious mind had dragged up Enrique's name at such an intimate moment, I was surprised I hadn't ground my teeth into dust. Because I wasn't kissing my cheater ex or even the idea of Jared, just Jared—I loved *him*.

Bracing my hands on the mattress by my sides, I felt my heart skip a beat.

I loved Jared.

Spots crowded the edges of my vision. I thumped my head back against the wall again and again. *You. Are. So. Stupid, Molly.* My thoughts were like molasses, slogging through ways to improve my situation but I had nothing. Even though I'd explained myself to Jared earlier, he hadn't listened. Then again, if I'd heard him call me by another woman's name, I wasn't sure I'd have listened right then, either. Although I wanted to fix this, now wasn't the time. The pain I'd caused him was too fresh, and I didn't think Jared would even answer his door if I knocked. My last-ditch effort would be to catch him in the morning before his flight and apologize again. Maybe, perhaps after some sleep, he'd be willing to hear me out.

****

I woke with my head aching and my eyes still puffy from the tears. The night had been rough. By the time I'd cried myself to sleep, only a couple of hours remained before my alarm sounded. Looking in the mirror, I cringed at my crow's nest hair and bloodshot eyes. I tamed my locks into a messy bun and dabbed on some concealer. The makeup did little to help hide the fact I'd been crying, but perhaps my disheveled appearance would help my case.

After throwing on jeans and a T-shirt, I padded across the living room. A piercing silence permeated the apartment, and I scanned the space for any evidence Jared had come out of his room. But everything appeared just as it had the night before—wine glasses still on the coffee table, lights dimmed, cushions scattered—nothing had changed.

Smoothing my shirt, I took a deep, cleansing breath and knocked on his door with a shaky hand. "Jared?" I waited for a few seconds before knocking again. "You awake?" I put an ear to his door—silence. I glanced at the time on my phone. Nine zero eight a.m. He had to be out of bed by now. His flight would be leaving in a couple of hours. I worried my lip, debating on whether I should open the door. *What if entering his room makes the situation worse?* I released the handle and waited. At nine thirteen a.m., I knocked again—still nothing.

He couldn't be that sound of a sleeper. My intuition flickered. With each passing minute, the weight on my chest grew heavier. I was desperate to confess my love to Jared. He had to have all the facts before he made any final decisions.

Feeling my heart beating in my throat, I threw caution to the wind. Bracing a hand against the door, I cracked it open. "Hello?" I peeked inside, straining to hear any sounds—running water, shuffling feet, rustling sheets, but was met with only silence and darkness. As I stepped across the threshold, I felt my skin prickle. In the dim light from around the drawn curtains, everything appeared too neat—even the covers on the bed were straightened. I tiptoed to the closet and peeked inside. The hangers were bare.

Like a stab in the heart, the realization forced all the air from my lungs. I curled my shoulders, wrapping my arms around my torso, and crouched to the floor in a ball. I couldn't hold myself together—to keep my form while the pieces of evidence stared me in the face—Jared was gone.

Tears streamed down my cheeks, and my shoulders shuddered from the sobs. I didn't realize I could hurt this much. My lungs were so tight, I wasn't sure I'd ever breathe again. I let the cold wood of the floor press against my sodden cheek. Losing Enrique didn't come close to this level of pain.

****

I took a rideshare home from the Seattle airport instead of the initial plan of letting Fin pick me up. Comfort wasn't something I deserved right now—I'd done this to myself, and I needed to own my mistake. However, I should have known Fin wouldn't believe me when I told him I was fine. As my cousin and best friend, he understood me better than anyone, so it made sense that as I exited the elevator to my apartment, I found him waiting with a bottle of wine and a box of tissues. My whole body shook with the strength of my tears.

He took me in his arms. "Shhh, it's okay. It's okay." Fin rubbed my back. "Let's get you inside, and you can tell me all about it."

I recapped what happened the night before while Fin sat beside me on my gray sectional, and I cried another round of fresh tears on his shoulder.

"Enrique, huh?" He sucked in a breath through his teeth. "Yikes, you haven't mentioned his name in a while."

"I know." I erupted in tears again.

Fin cringed.

"I was such an idiot."

"Yeah, you were." He handed me another tissue. "But I already knew that."

I sat straight and blew my nose, then scowled. "Get stuffed."

Fin pursed his lips and waved a hand. "What made you think of Enrique after all this time, anyway?"

I was unable to sniff through my blocked nose. "Pfft. It wasn't like I always think about my ex. He only popped into my mind because he'd called and texted me yesterday afternoon."

Fin scoffed. "Information that would have been helpful five minutes ago." He rolled his eyes. "What did the baby daddy have to say?"

I sighed, pulling apart the sodden tissue in my hands. "That he's not the baby's daddy. He made a mistake and wants me back. Blah, blah."

Fin's eyes widened. "Ooh, scandal! Teach him to keep his pants on." He put a hand on my knee. "Wait. You don't want him back, do you?" Fin pinned me with a stare.

I shook my head. "Ew, no way. Absolutely not!"

"Phew." He mimed a wipe of his brow. "Thank goodness. That could have gone either way."

"What? Hell no!" I blew my nose. "Not a chance. Hearing from Enrique was a shock, for sure. But at that moment, thinking of him with someone else no longer hurt my heart I was finally *me* again." With a fist on my chest, I sighed. "I no longer loved him." Grabbing my phone, I pulled up my messages. "In fact, I'll take care of Enrique right now." Tapping on his thread, I blocked his number and deleted Enrique as a contact. I placed my phone beside me.

Fin leaned back and put his feet on my rustic wood coffee table with a *thunk*. "What are you gonna do about Jared now?"

I exhaled, my lips vibrating. "What can I do? I've already apologized, and he wasn't having it."

"That's it?" Fin's brows drew together, his lip curling. "You apologized the one time?"

Covering my face with my hands, I deflated. I couldn't even count knocking on Jared's door earlier this morning since he'd already left for the airport. I was pathetic.

Fin perched on the edge of the couch, his lips in a hard line and his brow furrowed. "Okay, here's what you need to do." He stretched across me, grabbed my phone, and slapped it into my palm. "Text him, tell him you're sorry again. See if he'd be willing to talk. I'd even pitch in for a plane ticket, if you want to fly out there."

Bless him. Fin was such a sweetheart. However, I didn't share in his hope. I stared at the smooth, dark screen of my phone. "But what if Jared doesn't answer?"

Fin shrugged. "Then you know where you stand, and at least you can say you tried."

I opened my messages. A ZipCash alert flashed across my screen.

—Payment from Rachael V.—

Who was Rachael V.? Clicking on the app, I widened my eyes. My current balance was the exact amount of my Plus One contract. The accompanying message made my body go numb.

—Refund from Jared—AKA Enrique—

Chapter 34

Jared

The *whoosh* from the sent transaction reverberated through my ears. My stomach barrel rolled. "Why did you write *that* as the message?" As I stood behind Rachael sitting on my couch, I couldn't keep my blood from boiling. I should have never asked her to return Molly's money via her ZipCash account. Letting Molly know my personal contact details would've been better than this.

"What?" Rachael glared with a cock of her lip. "She had it coming after what she did. Not to mention, you used your savings to cover Erica's cut."

Shaking my head at her resentful tone, I paced my small apartment. I should have asked Lorraine to come over, too. She was the more level-headed one in their relationship and could have kept Rachael in check. "Regardless, I wish you wouldn't have done that."

"You wouldn't have done the same for me?" She crossed her arms and glared. "Where's your friendship solidarity, Jared? If somebody hurts you, then they hurt both of us."

I stopped pacing, guilt replacing my anger. "I appreciate that, but I don't want you to hate Molly. *I* don't."

"Sorry."

The sarcasm lacing Rachael's apology made it hard to trust her sincerity. Gripping the back of the couch, I registered the scratch of the frayed seams on my palms. I needed to make my friend understand my goal wasn't to hurt Molly or even make her feel guilty. I just wanted to return the money.

"If you're so upset, why didn't you use your Plus One phone?" Rachael shrugged.

"You know why." I ran a hand through my hair. "Because Erica would have known."

Rachael settled into the couch. "Then deal with it."

I didn't have a choice. Knowing I had strong feelings for Molly when I took her payment made me nauseous. Only my father was cold and heartless enough to believe business trumped love. Despite my father's abundant success and current marital status, I didn't buy he was truly happy and at peace with himself. At least now, my conscience would be clear. "Regardless, you shouldn't have sent that message. Because it doesn't matter whether Molly is over Enrique or not. I don't want her to think *I'm* mad."

Rachael scoffed. "I would be if I were you."

"I'm not mad at *her*. It's just…" I couldn't think of the right words. "I should have seen this coming. I'm really just mad at myself. It's my fault I believed what we had was more." I gripped my shoulders and hung my head back.

"If it's anyone's fault, it's hers." Rachael pulled one of the navy-blue throw pillows onto her lap. "Maybe if Molly were a good enough writer, she wouldn't have needed to hire you in the first place."

"She's an excellent writer, Rachael." Molly wasn't to blame, despite my being miserable, and I had to clarify. "I shouldn't have let my guard down and put myself in that compromising of a situation."

Rachael pursed her lips. "Well, she practically threw herself at you."

And I caught her with arms wide open. "You're forgetting I'm the one who initiated the massage."

"Typical woman, thinking a massage always leads to sex."

I shook my head. "Pretty sure that saying only applies to men."

She tsked. "Tell that to Lorraine."

Rachael was close enough to be my sister. The thought of her and Lorraine's love life was the last thing I wanted to envision. "I didn't want to know that." I side-eyed her. "But it doesn't matter. The point is, I have feelings for Molly, and I didn't stop myself."

"Well, if she couldn't see what she had in you, she's missing out." Rachael peeled herself from the couch and hugged me.

I returned the embrace. Needing the comfort more than I'd realized, I held on a few moments longer.

Eventually, she released her arms and stepped back. "Don't worry about the money. You'll make it back in no time, and all this will be a distant memory." Rachel fluttered her hand away from her forehead.

The stale air from her movement wafted across my face. I doubted that. Molly would always be at the forefront of my mind and in my heart. Knowing my feelings, the idea of dating other women, even if the circumstances were fake, felt wrong. I let my arms fall limply to my sides, a hollow sensation in my chest. Staying on at Plus One was no longer an option. "About my savings." I tensed my shoulders, and I chose my words carefully. "I have another favor to ask you, and you'd probably better get Lorraine on the phone, too." I wasn't taking any more chances.

Rachael's brow furrowed. "Why?"

When I'd left Molly, I felt like my heart imploded—pieces of me were scattered, most of which remained behind in Las Vegas. I intended to fill the gap by pushing forward with my investment plan. But I didn't have the capital and in no way could I remain a companion. "I'm quitting Plus One."

Rachael scratched her cheek with a frown. "But what about the franchise? Don't you still need the money?"

Leaning on the back of the couch, it groaned under my weight. "That's where I'm hoping you and Lorraine can help."

I'd done some research on my flight from Las Vegas to New York. I couldn't acquire a large enough loan by myself to purchase Sky's the Limit. Not to mention, I didn't have collateral, and I wouldn't anytime soon working solely as an adventure guide. I'd still need the Plus One income. Unfortunately, I now understood the crushing ache of being on the other end of a broken heart—just like most of my clients. Now, even though my plan depended on the money, I couldn't in good conscience, stay on with Madame Erica and capitalize on their situations.

Every avenue I'd considered to accomplish my goal crashed into a dead end. My only viable path—asking Lorraine and Rachael to co-sign on a loan. Requesting Lorraine to use her trust fund inheritance as collateral sent a prickle along my scalp. However, to sweeten the deal, my proposal would include letting the women be part owners in the franchise. I hoped they'd agree because the scenario was the best I could think of satisfying all my criteria.

Rachael called Lorraine and put her on speaker while I outlined my idea. Hearing the women agree, I breathed a sigh of relief, feeling almost giddy. The three of us set a time to meet at the bank later in the week. The last thing left was to turn in my notice to Madame Erica.

"Wow." Rachael ended the call with Lorraine and squinted. "Who are you? Quitting Plus One for a woman and giving back the fee. The Jared I used to know never let his contracts get under his skin. Money was all that mattered."

I shoved my hands in my pockets, my chest aching. "You're right. But that was the old me, and I'd never met someone like Molly." My life was so shallow before. Now, it would never be the same.

Rachael gathered her purse off the hook on my brick wall and headed to the door. "She's really done a number on you, hasn't she?"

"You have no idea."

Chapter 35

Molly

As I stared at Jared's blue eyes mocking me from the corner of my laptop screen, I sipped my hot cocoa with a heavy heart. Fin had called me a masochist for keeping a picture of Jared open while I wrote, but I was an author, and he was my muse, and that's just what we writers did for inspiration. Or at least, that's what I kept telling myself. Two sharp knocks reverberated on my front door.

Fin barreled into my apartment, juggling three paper grocery bags. "I brought food. I hope you like TV dinners because I can't make your chicken curry from scratch."

Leave it to Fin to buy me my favorite meal as a microwave dinner. Piercing beeps sounded from the kitchen followed by an electronic whirr.

"Please tell me you've showered since the last time I was here."

I sniffed my armpit. Only a slight musty funk, not too ripe; perhaps he wouldn't notice. "Of course."

Fin rounded the corner and skidded to a halt. "Liar. You're in the same gross clothes from yesterday. Did you even sleep last night?"

Not a wink. I kept typing and ignored him.

Fin swung my chair around, crouching to my eye

level. "Molly, you can't keep working like this."

Exhaling through my nose, I wished he would shut up, but I reminded myself he was here because he loved me. "Do you understand the time crunch I'm on, Fin?"

"I do, and you've been close to a deadline before. But I've never seen you like this."

He gestured at my overall appearance—a ratty T-shirt, stained from the meal Fin brought me yesterday, gray sweatpants, fluffy socks, and leather sandals. Pursing my lips, I feigned ignorance at the same outfit I'd had on for the past three days. "Like what?" I was well aware of what he referred to—my girly, post-breakup behavior. The one thing missing was a tub of ice cream—only because Fin had failed to buy me some.

"You're barely eating, and your sleep schedule is all messed up." He pointed over my shoulder at my laptop. "And you're not helping yourself by having his picture taunting you on your screen."

I scowled. "I told you—"

He held a palm toward my face and turned his head. "I know, he's your muse, yadda, yadda. But having his face on your laptop is *not* helping."

I don't know why I assumed I could fool Fin; he understood me better than anyone. But admitting the truth would have been more brutal than facing a bear. A lie lingered on the tip of my tongue, but as tears sprang to my eyes, all my pent-up emotions came to a head and the dam burst. "You're right. I don't know what I'm doing anymore. I'd believed writing about Jared would help me cope, but if anything, I feel worse." I wiped the moisture from my nose with my sleeve. "He's in my every thought. He's in my dreams. And no matter what

I do, the pain won't go away." I'd even made irrational bargains—if I finished seven chapters, I would allow myself to stalk Jared online for the umpteenth time. Unfortunately, the strategy was less productive than I'd hoped.

Fin took me into his arms and stroked my hair.

I bawled into his chest—again, flinching when his fingers got caught in my matted curls.

"It's okay, Molly." He yanked his hand free.

I massaged my scalp from the missing hairs.

"This will get easier."

"Will it?" I sniffled, wiping the evidence of my sobs from his hoodie.

"Of course. If the pain remained, the world would be a miserable place. Everyone would be wandering around brokenhearted. You got over Enrique, and you'll get over Jared, too."

I ripped myself from Fin's arms, indignation flooding my veins. "But this breakup is not the same. Unlike Enrique, Jared was a good person. He read my books, listened when I talked, and even studied my Bookstablogger enough to buy me my favorite hot cocoa." I ticked off Jared's qualities on my fingers before throwing my hands up with a whiny sigh. "Jared was different."

Fin arched an eyebrow. "You don't think all that was because of the contract?"

The accusation in his tone ruffled my feathers. While his words could have been the case, I refused to believe everything Jared did was a lie. Even now, with my shattered heart. "Let's say you're right, Fin. Then why would he put that much consideration into a contract if he wasn't a good person?" I crossed my arms.

"I don't mean to rain on your parade, cuz, but he could just be really good at his job."

My insides shook with irritation. "Well, if you're so smart, explain why Jared refunded my money." *Ha! Got him!*

Fin's brow furrowed. "Fine. I can't. But either way, I'm sorry you're having to go through this again."

I shook my head, letting my shoulders sag. "Don't be. I'm glad I hired Jared."

Fin's head reared back, and his eyes widened.

"I know. I sound neurotic. But it's true. I've learned some valuable lessons from all of this." I swiped a tear from my cheek, wiping it on my sweatpants. "I was young and naive when I accepted Enrique's proposal. A marriage to him would have been mediocre at best. I didn't know who I was or what I wanted back then. But thanks to my experience with Jared, I now know I will never allow myself to settle." Not that I believed I would ever find anyone quite like Jared again.

Fin squeezed my hand. "Well, now the bar is set. You have a goal."

I let my gaze drift to the screen and fought the fresh tears blurring my vision. "But how do you get better than him?" I gestured toward Jared's image, my lower lip shook, and I hated the waver in my voice. *How am I not stronger than this?*

Fin patted my leg. "Maybe you don't." He jutted his chin at my mobile. "Have you tried getting in touch with him again? Vegas was a month ago; maybe he'd listen now."

"I texted him just last week"—*and every day*

since—"but he never responded. I tried emailing, too"—*multiple times and from different email addresses*—"but they bounced back as undeliverable. Not to mention, when I logged onto the Plus One website"—*two minutes before you arrived*—"Jared appeared to be booked out indefinitely. He doesn't even have a day off for the rest of the year." I flopped back against my office chair, grabbing the box of tissues.

"Are you sure he still works there?"

I hadn't even considered that idea. "What else would he be doing? He still needs the cash to buy his franchise—especially after returning my money."

Fin shrugged. "I don't know. It just seems sketchy he suddenly doesn't have *any* openings."

The booked schedule was probably because he was gorgeous—making him in high demand. Besides, if Jared had quit, why would his profile still be on the Plus One site? Either way, I couldn't figure out another explanation to save my life.

A beep sounded from the microwave in the other room, reminding me my dinner was ready, and the scent of curry lingered in the air.

"You're a tough lass. We'll get through this together." He stood and pulled me to my feet with a grunt. "Let's go eat." Fin draped his arm around my shoulders, sniffed, then winced. "And after that, I'm throwing you in the shower."

I forced a half-smile. Little did he know I didn't have time for self-care. With only twenty thousand words on the page, I was down to the wire.

Chapter 36

Jared

"What the hell is this?" As Erica stared at my letter of resignation, she dropped her wide smile. "I'm not happy, Jared." She shoved the paper in my direction. "You are my number one companion."

The despondency in Madame Erica's voice cut me to the core. Though I respected her, I couldn't stay. "You're just sour it didn't work between us." I winked and pushed the letter back, maintaining a lighthearted appearance despite the heaviness shadowing my heart.

"Don't try to flirt, Jared. That only works when you're earning me money."

Her beady eyes narrowed. I sighed and sat back in the cold, red-leather club chair and glanced out the windows behind her desk for the last time, avoiding her stare. "I'm one of a hundred employees you have on your books. You're overreacting."

She leaned across her laminate wood desk and jabbed a hot-pink acrylic talon. "When has that phrase *ever* gone well for a man?"

I held up my hands. "You're right. I'm sorry." My apology was sincere. "I didn't set this appointment to upset you." Angering Erica was the last thing I wanted. "I stopped in to say good-bye and sign my exit paperwork in person because, after ten years, I owed it to my Madame." She'd been good to me.

Erica's face flushed.

I let my shoulders sag. I would miss riling her up.

Erica brushed her dark brown bangs out of her face, wafting her heavy floral perfume into the already saturated air. After a moment, she rolled her eyes. "At least, I won't have to hear you call me that anymore."

The hint of a smile on her lips betrayed her words. Deep down, I knew she liked the title. She would miss me, too.

Erica opened one of her desk drawers and retrieved some documents. "Whatever. Let's get this over with." She pushed a pen in my direction along with the exit interview forms. "Sign and turn in your phone."

Grabbing the pen, I glanced over the paperwork. I couldn't believe I was about to end this chapter of my life with one stroke of my wrist. My time at Plus One had taught me many things from my clients—red flags come in all shapes and sizes. I'd also gained perspective on unhealthy relationships and how *not* to treat a woman. I was sure all my accumulated knowledge was what helped me recognize I was in love with Molly. While the realization didn't change my situation, I'd like to think my time at Plus One made me a better man. Pursing my lips, I signed my name, then stood.

Erica collected the papers. "Your profile will come down at the end of the month when the website refreshes. Until then, I will block out your calendar."

"Thanks." I pulled my copy of *Summer of Silence* from my satchel. The book was heavy in my hands. Closing my eyes, I took a deep breath. I'd already made the decision to part with the novel. But before I handed the hardback to Erica, I gave in to the irresistible urge to fan through the book one last time. Stopping at Molly's photo on the jacket fold, I paused. Memories thrashed around my head, and I closed my eyes. With a deep exhale, I flicked the cover closed and extended the novel to Erica. "I brought you something."

She took the book with indifference until she spotted Molly's name on the cover, her eyes going wide. Then, gripping the spine with white knuckles, she flipped the book open. Erica gawked, her whole demeanor brightening when her gaze landed on Molly's autograph. Snapping the book closed, she rearranged her face into a scowl. "Don't think this means I forgive you."

Heading toward the door, I took in Erica's office one last time and cocked a half-smile at the suggestive Georgia O'Keeffe print on her wall. Stopping at the edge of the dense, jazzy red-and-gray rug, I glanced over my shoulder, pointing at my face. "Hey, my eyes are up here."

I closed the door on Erica's eye roll, Plus One, Molly, and the last decade of my life. From here on out, my future was Sky's The Limit.

Chapter 37

Molly

"I'm sorry, Molly. My assistant was an idiot. I don't know why Brian assumed leaking your nom de plume would help him get ahead in the publishing industry, but rest assured, I've fired him."

Renee had been apologizing on the phone all morning, ever since the alias I'd used as a pen name for my romance due to come out in nine months had gone viral on the Internet only a month after I'd turned in my manuscript. "You didn't need to fire him." My heart broke for the man who'd lost his job because of me.

"Yeah, I did. And I'd do it again in a heartbeat. I can't have someone I don't trust working in this office. What if Brian stole a manuscript next time and tried to pass it off as his own? No, I did the right thing. This industry is hard enough without someone stabbing you in the back."

Sighing, I rubbed my forehead. "You're right." I was gutted, regardless.

"Of course, I'm right. You've spent too many years building your career for some idiot to bring you down. Doing this interview is the way to go—get ahead of the rumors instead of having to play catch-up on damage control." Papers rustled from the other end of the conversation. "When you hear from the interviewer, tell them you chose the name Ruby Moss because you were challenging yourself through your change in genre, and the nom-de plume would help you reach out to a different fanbase."

Her words were verbatim from the email she'd sent earlier. I chewed on the inside of my cheek, placing a hand on the window in front of my desk. The cold from the glass radiated through my palm. What Renee said made sense—a justification I'd known other writers used. However, she and I both knew the excuse wasn't the truth.

When I'd handed in my completed manuscript three months ago, two days before the deadline, I was a mess—Fin was ready to stage an intervention. As a compromise, he and I had come up with a plan—distance myself from the book by using an alias. Renee was confused by my proposal until she read the draft. For all intents and purposes, the novel was a tell-all about my feelings for Jared—my raw emotions bled onto the page and the dream I'd envisioned of what Jared and I could have been if things had worked. The book would feel like having my heart on display labeled with my name.

Although five months had passed since Las Vegas, I still wasn't sleeping well—even when I had gone to bed utterly exhausted. I couldn't get Jared out of my thoughts. Everything reminded me of him and our time together—Fin's Bob Ross shirt, my tomahawk, Italian food, and even reruns of my favorite crime shows. I lived and breathed Jared's memory. Now, thanks to Renee's assistant, my anonymity was off the table, my heart was on the chopping block, and I'd have to face the music. "Sounds good, Renee. I'll take your advice.

Thanks for defending me and scheduling this interview. I know the leak wasn't your fault."

"You're not just my client, Molly; I'd like to think we've become friends."

The sincere inflection of Renee's soft, gravelly voice was like a warm hug.

"I've got your back."

"Thanks. I appreciate it." Wholeheartedly. "Take care." Ending the call, I glanced around at the sad mess I called my home. I'd really let myself go. Grabbing some gloves, a sponge, and some disinfectant, I vowed to scrub my condo from top to bottom while I waited to hear from the magazine. Despite Renee's continuous reassurance, my stomach was still in knots. I feared the repercussions of my predicament. I was confident Jared would hear about the leak. After all, the hashtags #MollyCovington, #RubyMoss, and #nomdeplume were trending on the Bird app. With every wadded-up tissue I collected, I told myself when the book was published, Jared wouldn't read it. But as I tied the trash bag full of microwave dinner containers and take-out boxes, I'd overthought the situation and convinced myself he would.

After washing my hands, I sat at my computer, rubbing my temples. I had no choice but to take every precaution I could to make the manuscript sound like a work of fiction—throw Jared off the trail. He couldn't know I'd been wallowing for the last five months. The first step in hiding my true feelings would be nailing this interview.

Not wanting my answers to sound awkward, I pulled out my trusty notebook, scribbled out Renee's excuse, and repeated the words into the bathroom mirror several times, hoping to make the response sound natural. It didn't. So, I continued the mantra and went about cleaning, hoping, at some point, I'd convince even myself. As I stepped out of my sparkling, lemony-fresh shower reciting the hundredth mantra repetition, I heard my phone buzz. My heart seized at the unknown number. Throwing my sponge in the sink, I grabbed my notebook. With my phone and excuse in hand, I perched on the edge of my bed and ran a finger over the slider. "Hello? This is Molly Covington."

"Hi, Molly. This is Sandra Crandall from *Cultured Women* magazine."

Her articulate soprano voice had a business edge, and I sat straighter.

"Is now a good time for the interview?"

My stomach somersaulted. "As good a time as any."

With any luck, Sandra would stick to the leaked information and not fish for more details about my main character, Sam—the alias I'd kept for Jared. Because if she dug too deep, then I was sure my true feelings would betray me.

Chapter 38

Jared

Entering the midtown bar, Sip, I sniffed and the smell of stale beer and dressed-up greasy food assaulted my senses. I scanned the crowd of hipsters and middle-aged executives, until I spotted Lorraine's white-blonde hair sitting beside Rachael's brown locks at a high table in the middle of the upscale establishment.

Rachael waved me over.

I wound through the metal pipe pillars and low-hanging Edison lights.

"Hey, hotshot. How's it going?" Lorraine pushed me a beer.

I perched on the industrial barstool and grabbed the bottle. "Great." I plastered on a huge smile. "The new adventure excursions are a hit. Business is booming." I wasn't lying.

Rachael and Lorraine saluted me with their drinks. The jukebox in the corner fired up.

"I've just hired three more guides and added seven more bikes to our rental inventory." I shouted over the music. "I'm even considering expanding and opening a second store location."

Since acquiring Sky's the Limit, I'd been working overtime to reinvent the adventure brand and increase the activities the company offered to keep my mind occupied and away from thoughts of Molly. Things at the store were going better than I'd ever imagined, but my success somehow still wasn't enough and hadn't filled the hollow in my chest. "Unfortunately, the few places I've checked as new storefronts haven't felt right, you know?" I curled my fingers over my stomach for emphasis and took a swig of my beer, letting the bubbles settle on my tongue.

Rachael rolled her bottle between her hands. "So, is owning Sky's the Limit everything you dreamed?"

My lungs tightened, and I nodded. "Yeah, for sure." While technically my dream had come true, I didn't feel the sense of fulfillment I'd expected. I rubbed absently at the ache in my chest. Was I unsettled because I still owed on my loan? Maybe, down the road, once I'd paid the debt off and bought out the women's shares, I'd feel different—satisfied and whole again.

Rachael shared a look with her wife and grabbed a magazine from her bag. "Good, I was hoping you'd say that because I read this." She flicked to a dog-eared page and pushed the article across the table.

As I held the glossy magazine, I became wary at the edge in Rachael's tone. I read the headline, *Molly Covington, AKA Ruby Moss, talks about her debut romance novel*, next to a recent picture. I skimmed the article with my heart lodged in my throat. The entire piece discussed why Molly chose a pseudonym and a question-and-answer section between her and the interviewer. Halfway through the page, Rachael had highlighted a particular passage. My vision blurred, and I blinked to clear my eyes.

Interviewer: The chemistry between your two main

characters, Jade and Sam, is intense. I can't believe that you, a single woman, could have conjured all that passion from your imagination. Are you sure you didn't have a muse?

Molly: No comment.

Interviewer: Ooh, I hit a nerve. Is this book more of an autobiography? Is the title Men in Books Aren't Better *because you have a muse better than Sam in real life?*

Molly: It's none of your business, and no, he's no longer in my life.

Interviewer: I sense some regret. Do you wish things had gone differently?

Molly: I'm sorry. This is still a sensitive topic. I'd rather not continue this discussion. Can we move on, please?

Blood thrummed in my veins. Molly sounded defensive in the article. *What did that mean?* I checked the date of the interview. April fifteenth—just two weeks ago. I took in shallow breaths, and the room's sounds faded like cotton filling my ears. Locked in a loop, my brain scrambled to decipher what Molly had said and put the pieces together in a way that made sense. Swaying, I leaned onto the table, grappling to catch my breath.

Rachael grabbed my bicep. "Whoa there, Jared. Calm down."

I nodded, panting hard. Counting each inhale, I focused on my breathing. Like increasing the volume on a stereo, the music and surrounding conversations once again filled the room. I took a drink of my beer. Wiping the condensation on my jeans, I focused on the label. I'd come to a conclusion, and I had to force the words through my lips. "Molly. Loved. Me?"

"No. Molly *still* loves you." Lorraine tilted her head and smirked.

I furrowed my brow. Wrestling with the hope filling my chest, I met her gaze. "How do you know?"

Lorraine tapped on the highlighted passage again. "Because she says the topic is still sensitive."

Molly's words had me glued to the page. "But what if you're wrong, and that's not what she meant?"

Both women shook their heads.

"You don't speak woman." Lorraine laughed. "I promise. She's not over you."

"Agreed." Rachael patted my arm. "I was wrong to dismiss your relationship before. You keep saying you're happy, but we know"—she smiled at her wife—"you've been miserable ever since Las Vegas. This"—Rachael stabbed her finger on the glossy article, crinkling the paper—"is your chance. What are you gonna do about it, lover boy?"

I gripped my beer with both hands. "What can I do? I don't have access to Molly's personal information anymore. Erica revoked my privileges the moment I quit Plus One." I swept my gaze over the table as if it would magically contain an answer.

"True." Rachael frowned, shifting on her barstool. "Even though I still work there, I can't get her details. That would be illegal. Do you have any ideas, babe?"

Rachael's words had a conspiratorial tone with a hopeful edge that threatened to pull me under.

Lorraine grabbed the magazine again and flipped through the pages; the corners of her mouth lifted.

My intuition prickled.

"You know, the article says she'll be on a panel at

the annual writers' conference at the Harbor Regency tomorrow." Lorraine traced the lip of her martini glass with a manicured finger. "But I'm sure Jared's not interested in going since he's not a writer."

She flicked drops of gin at my gaping mouth. I wiped the liquor off my face. Was Lorraine suggesting I crash the writer's convention? Did I have to be a writer to get in? I rubbed my forehead, as if my heart were screaming the answer at my brain but had to wait for my thoughts to catch up.

It doesn't matter! Go!

My mouth dried, and I downed another swallow of beer. "Which Harbor Regency?"

Lorraine broke out with a huge grin. "Jersey City, just across the Hudson."

Chapter 39

Molly

Mother's ranch-style home stood dwarfed by the Sitka, elm, and spruce trees towering over its roof like giants in the backyard. I smiled and exited the car. Growing up with the forest as my playground brought back some of my happiest memories—zipping through the trunks, swinging from branches, making forts from the brush as if I didn't have a care in the world. Too bad the heady earthy aroma couldn't replace my worries now. I opened the oversized oak front door. "Hello?"

My mum bustled around the corner from the kitchen wearing leopard print flats and gray cotton capris, with a matching cardigan under her Elvis apron. The outfit was too dressy for a casual family dinner, and her wide smile screamed she was up to something.

"Hey up, me duck." She dropped her arms and skidded to a stop on the hardwood floor. Grimacing, she took hold of my elbow and rushed me into her bedroom.

Where was the usual hug that always accompanied her typical British greeting? She treated me like I was two years old. Almost tripping on the seafoam-green rug with its curled-up edges, I rounded on her. "Oh, Mum, what's going on?" I pried my arm from her grip.

She pushed the rug with her toe and forced the

door closed, her brow fierce. "What are you wearing?"

I balked at her harsh, but whispered, tone and glanced over my outfit. "My tracksuit and trainers. Why? What's wrong with it?"

"You couldn't have worn something nicer?"

I squinted. *She* was *up to something*. "You told me I was having dinner with you and Fin, so why would I dress up? And why are we whispering?" I had no idea what she'd planned for tonight, but considering her outfit—not to mention I could smell her powdery, floral perfume—and her reaction to mine, it had to be pretty significant.

My mum pinched her lips together, wringing her hands.

Here we go.

"Well, I"—she averted her gaze—"invited Camille and her son, Jensen, for dinner, too."

"Mum, no." Now I sounded like the two-year-old she'd acted like when she'd dragged me into the bedroom. "Please tell me you didn't plan this as a blind date." I was not in the mood. Especially to be set up with my mum's best friend's kid. "This was supposed to be a quiet dinner, just the three of us, before I left for my writing conference tomorrow."

"It still is, but Jensen's a huge fan. Since he was visiting his mum, the polite thing was to ask them to join us."

"Mum." I dragged out the single syllable. Setups were terrible enough, but a fan, too? I would never live up to his expectations.

"He's easy on the eyes."

Her words came out in a singsong tone. *Ugh.* My mum's idea of easy on the eyes was Ed Sheeran. "This isn't the right time."

"Now, sweetie"—she gently squeezed my left shoulder—"I've read the interview."

Her patronizing tone grated my nerves. I hung my head, as if it wasn't bad enough I screwed up the interview and the magazine revealed details I didn't want out in the world, now my mum had made my personal life her business as well.

"Clearly, Las Vegas was more than research."

"Mum—"

"Now, I know you still don't want to talk about what happened"—she held a halting hand—"but months have passed. You need to get yourself back out there."

I stomped my foot, but the dense pile of the carpet swallowed the sound. My mother's meddling was exactly what I was afraid of. "Sheesh!"

"Look, I'm not asking you to marry the man. Just give him a shot. He's a million times better than Enrique, and he's here because he wants to be, not because you paid him."

Ouch! I winced. *Is she really throwing that in my face?*

"Sorry to be the voice of reason, but you know I'm right." She lifted my chin with her finger. "Humor me, please?"

I rolled my eyes, giving up. When she'd made up her mind, fighting with her was pointless. "Fine. Where's your makeup?" After applying some mascara and blush and doing the quickest curl job ever, I returned to the living room which hadn't changed in years. The back window still had the same checkered-print curtains from my childhood, and the cream couch had seen better days. "Hello?" I called again as if I'd just arrived for the first time.

"We're in the kitchen." My mum's voice echoed from the far side of the room.

I marched in to find Fin in his skinny black jeans and pastel tie-dyed T-shirt, leaning against the granite countertop island, chatting with my mother and her best friend as if he didn't know what my mum had done.

"Hi, Camille." I kissed the tall blonde woman on her gorgeous high cheekbones. She was striking, per usual, in a drapey purple blouse, skinny jeans, and black ankle boots.

"Sorry about this, hon." She shot a glare and a smile at my mum. "I told her to warn you."

"Personally"—Fin hip-checked me into the newly refinished cream cabinets—"I'm glad Auntie Gillian didn't." He put his lips to my ear. "Nice outfit, by the way."

I rubbed the spot on my hip that hit the counter. "Shut your pie hole, Fin." I kept my voice low. "If I'd known Camille's son would be here, I wouldn't have invited *you*." I shoved his head away.

Fin clapped his hands and rubbed them together. "This is gonna be awesome!" He sang the last word.

My mum swatted Fin on the arm. "Stop." She nodded toward the back door and squeezed my wrist. "Jensen's out at the grill. He's an excellent chef."

How hard is grilling hamburgers? I glanced out the back window. While I could only see his back, I admired Jensen's tight physique wrapped in slim-cut jeans and a grey-blue button-down stretched over muscular-looking, broad shoulders. I had to give it to my mum; from where I stood, Jensen was a far cry from

Prince Harry. He did appear easy on the eyes.

"Here." My mum shoved a plate of assorted cheese slices into my hands with a wide-eyed smile. "These are for the burgers." She made a shooing motion toward the back door. "Go."

Fin stifled a laugh. "Yeah, Molly. Go." He shoved my back, pushing me forward.

I scowled over my shoulder. "Traitor." He would pay for his actions.

Fin inclined his head with a smirk.

I paused just outside the back door and took a deep breath, using the familiar rich, crisp scent of the forest to calm my nerves. *Remember, this isn't Jensen's fault.* "I've got some cheese." I twisted my lips together. "Oh my gosh, that sounded so cheesy." I wobbled my head, averting my gaze. "Pun intended."

Jensen turned, his smile lighting up his whole face. He grabbed a towel hanging on the back of one of the mixed-matched patio chairs. As he sauntered through the pergola covering most of the rectangular pavement patio, he wiped his hands on the cloth, then threw it to rest on his shoulder. "Hi, I'm Jensen." He took the plate.

A tight, Van Halen T-shirt hugged Jensen's pecs from under his open button-down. I ignored the swoop in my belly. "Molly." His teeth gleamed in the fading sunshine. Jensen was even more impressive from the front, with his choppy, gelled, brown hair and soft crinkles around his eyes formed by a beautiful smile with light scruff.

Jensen ducked his head. "I know this sounds creepy, but I'm totally fanboying right now."

My ears warmed. He was a straight shooter. Maybe

dinner wouldn't be quite as awkward as I'd imagined. "Thank you. I always love meeting a fan."

He set the plate beside the grill. "Do you say that to everyone, or are you being genuine?"

Closing the distance, I stood beside him. I did say that to everyone, but I was surprised to find this time, I meant it. "Both." I shrugged.

Jensen nodded, pink patches creeping up his neck. "Honesty. I like it." He placed slices of cheese over the sizzling patties, sending the scent of charred meat through the air. He bowed his head, speaking from the corner of his mouth. "Don't look now, but our mothers are watching from the kitchen window."

Of course, they are. "What do you think they're talking about?" I leaned in, whispering conspiratorially. I was pretty sure I didn't want to know.

"They're probably wondering if you will say *yes* to being my plus one at a work event this Friday?"

Heat swirled from my cheeks to my temples. Why did he have to use *those* words? His comment reminded me of Jared, and if I weren't still smarting over Las Vegas, I might have been intrigued by Jensen's offer. Searching his hazel-green eyes, I decided Jensen did seem like a nice guy and maybe my mum was right. Months had passed since my contract with Jared; perhaps now was the time to move on. "Can I think about it?"

Jensen sucked in a breath; his brow pinched. "Ooh, crash and burn."

"No, really." I held up my palms. "It's not you."

He rolled his eyes.

I couldn't blame Jensen for his reaction. "No, seriously. I've just gotten out of a relationship." *If I could even call what we had that.* I offered him an encouraging smile and squeezed his forearm. "You were actually quite smooth."

Jensen exaggerated wiping his brow. "Good, because I'd been rehearsing that line all day." He collected the burgers off the grill.

I followed him inside.

Over dinner, Jensen shared facts about the numerous book launches he'd attended. "A few years ago, when I attended the release for your book *Burned*"—Jensen dumped more potato salad onto his plate—"they had a trivia contest, asking questions about *Summer of Silence.* The employee had one of the facts wrong. He said the curtains in your main character's room were blue. Can you believe it?" Jensen met each of our eyes, his brows raised.

Fin returned Jensen's stare with an exaggerated nod, clearly egging him on.

"I mean"—Jensen scoffed—"everyone knows they were a yellow lace."

"Duh!" Fin smirked and rolled his eyes. "It's the same color of the underside of Molly's bra." He swooped his fingers under his pecs for emphasis.

"Fin!" Camille, my mum, and I protested in unison.

He held up his hands. "Hey, Jensen was talking about trivia, and I figured he'd like to hear some of my fun facts, too."

Jensen ducked his head, struggling to hide his laughter.

I scowled. "Don't encourage my cousin, or he'll never stop."

****

After finishing our coffees, Camille and Jensen

said their good-byes to my mum.

Fin cleared the farmhouse table.

I escorted Jensen and his mother to the door where I gave Camille a hug.

"Good luck at the conference." Camille's gaze darted between her son and me, then she scuttled along the flagstone path, her boots crunching against the gravel driveway where she parked her car.

Jensen paused under the overhang, breathing in, and inflating his chest. "I had a great time."

I stifled a laugh; he was so obvious. "Are you peacocking?"

"Is it working?" Jensen flashed me a grin before his chest deflated again. "Never mind, if you're asking, it's not." His cheeks flushed. "Please don't hold that against me."

I laid a hand over my chest; he tried so hard. "Never."

"Thank you."

He was so endearing, if only my heart were in a better place.

Jensen pulled a business card from his wallet. "Let me know what you decide about Friday. If I don't hear from you by midweek"—he lifted a shoulder—"I'll assume you had a better offer."

Leaving the option to call in my hands was a bold move. Jensen was kind of growing on me if I was honest with myself. I glanced at the card, rubbing a thumb over the raised font of his details. "You're a *doctor*?"

He focused on his feet, scuffing the walkway with his toe. "Pediatric specialist."

"Of course, you are." Despite being overly zealous

of my books, Jensen was too good to be true—a little too perfect. "And I bet you work at the soup kitchen on the weekends and adopt rescue dogs, too."

He smiled, rubbing the back of his neck. "I don't volunteer *every* weekend. Sometimes, I'm on call."

"Seriously?" He had to be joking.

Jensen shook his head with a laugh. "No, but if doing so will make you say *yes* to Friday, I'll sign up." He kissed my cheek.

His scruff tickled.

"Think about it."

The guy had game. I tucked the card into my tracksuit pocket and half-smiled. He was persistent if nothing else.

Jensen strode toward his car, walking backward and waving. He tripped over an uneven paver, shouting, "Mulligan," then continued walking, attention now on his feet.

Waving, I laughed at his do-over golf reference and headed inside where I knew Fin and my mother were waiting to pounce.

"So, I was right, wasn't I?" My mum looped her arm through mine and steered me to the couch.

She flashed a coy smile, and I sank into the deep cushions beside her.

Fin sat across from my mum in the oversized tan leather chair.

"Yes, Mum. He was very nice." The fact she was right chafed my behind.

"And he knows more about your books than you do." Fin made a flourish with a hand.

"Will you attend his awards ceremony with him on Friday?" Mum clasped her hands against her chest.

I gaped at my pleading mum. "Awards ceremony?" She lit up like the Fourth of July.

"Yes." She spoke with her hands. "He's receiving recognition as one of the top ten pediatricians in the greater Seattle area."

Wow. She boasted more than Camille did. Jensen's success had no bounds.

"Did you agree to be his date?" My mum pinched my leg.

I rubbed my stinging thigh. Her interest made me even more suspicious. "How did you know he'd asked me to accompany him on Friday?"

Fin rested his chin on his fist, batting his eyes, attention focused on my mum.

He appeared so eager; I was surprised he hadn't busted out some popcorn while he enjoyed the show.

"You left the door open, honey." My mum gestured toward the entrance. "You can't fault me if voices carry throughout the house."

Fin put a hand on the side of his mouth and leaned toward my mum. "It helps when you're standing behind it, right, Auntie Gillian?"

Mum swatted at my cousin. "Pfft, Fin. Stop."

His shoulders shook, but he didn't say anything more.

Mum glowered, arms extended and palms up. "Well?"

I didn't want to tell her, but I was sure Camille would fill her in later anyway. "I told him I'd think about it."

She covered her mouth, giggling. "Good. But don't make him wait too long. Jensen's a catch." Mum patted my knee, then squeezed. "And being a pediatrician could be handy for any future kids."

I rolled my eyes. "I'm not dignifying that with a response." Knowing my mum, she'd probably picked my wedding venue already.

"Eh, I don't know, cuz, your biological clock only has a few hours left. If I were you, I'd get on that."

I grabbed a throw pillow and hurled it at Fin. Like I needed him to remind me.

He caught the cushion with a grin.

Mum shook her head and headed to the kitchen.

I glared at Fin. "Why are you my favorite cousin again?"

He whipped his hair off his face. "Because I'm awesome."

"Whatever." He was, but I would never give him the satisfaction of saying it out loud. "Seriously, Fin, what should I do about Jensen?"

His eyes softened. "I think you should call him. You deserve to be happy."

I knew what Fin meant, but I wouldn't be unless I was with Jared. Standing, I rounded the glass coffee table, pulling Fin into my arms. "Thanks, cuz." His unconditional love had my heart threatening to burst.

He squeezed me tight. "Just remember, his name is Jensen. Not Enrique."

I shoved him away from me. "Really, Fin?"

"What?" He shrugged, wide-eyed. "Too soon?"

The whole drive back home, I considered Jensen's offer to be his plus one. The words seemed rather ironic. Although I knew he checked all the right boxes for the perfect guy on paper, I didn't know if I could go out with Jensen. I wasn't over Jared. But I had to stop thinking like that. I mean, what was I waiting for? I'd blown my chance with Jared, and he'd made his feelings perfectly clear with that ZipCash message. I had to move on. First, though, I needed to take Fin's advice.

After returning to my apartment, I bolted straight to my laptop and found the picture of Jared I'd downloaded when I'd first chosen him to be my companion. I studied his beautiful face one last time, pushing past the sting of tears and committing the blue of his eyes and the dimple in his cheek to memory. Holding my breath, I hit *Delete*. I did the same thing with the photos on my phone, check marking the images I'd saved from his profile, but I paused at the one of Jared and me, cheek to cheek on the Eiffel Tower. A warm tear hit the back of my hand. I gritted my teeth. *Stop crying!* Swiping at my cheek, I tapped the trashcan icon and hit *Confirm*.

I marched back into my bedroom and yanked the bag I'd used in Las Vegas from the corner of my closet. Other than retrieving my toiletries, I hadn't touched my case in the months since I'd been home. I rifled through the clothes and retrieved Jared's muddy-brown canvas. Placing the ruined masterpiece in a trash bag, I dropped it by the front door. Next, I headed into my office and located my notebook—the one I'd used for notes on the trip. It, too, had to go. Ironically, although I hadn't cataloged a whole lot about my time with Jared, when I'd written my manuscript, I hadn't needed to refer to any of the pages. Rereading my notes wasn't necessary when I could easily recall everything with perfect clarity anytime I wanted—if I believed I could handle the pain. I opened the cover. Averting my gaze, I ripped the pages out, one by one, tearing each into smaller pieces. They sat like a pile of confetti on my floor—a pitiful celebration of my attempt to move forward. Scooping the mess into the trash, I dusted my hands together. I was done with Jared.

I pulled Jensen's card from my pocket and stared at his number. "What do I do about you?" Theoretically, he had no outward faults. He was handsome, stable, intelligent, smooth, and funny. But his exemplary credentials weren't the problem—Jensen was too good to be a rebound. However, I had to start somewhere. I made my decision. Before the time got too late and I could talk myself out of my decision, I dialed his number.

"This is Dr. Edwards."

"Hi…uh…Jensen. Um…it's me, Molly. Molly Covington." I smacked my forehead with my palm. Hopefully he didn't hear the thwack. *Real smooth, Molly. Real smooth.*

He laughed. "Yeah, I remember who you are. You're the girl with the cheese, right?"

"Right." Thank goodness, he had a good sense of humor. "So, I considered what you said."

"Um-hmm?"

Here goes nothing. "Friday sounds great."

Chapter 40

Jared

I didn't even wait for Lorraine to come to a stop before I leaped from the car, shouting a hasty "Thank you" over my shoulder and flew up the wide concrete steps into the Harbor Regency. Barreling through the door, I was hit by a wall of heat. I skidded to a stop and surveyed the scene.

The hotel's entrance hall was off-white, with commercial tan-and-blue-speckled carpet. Cascading staircases ran along the side walls which were made of windows. A few people milled about. I scanned their faces. Molly wasn't anywhere in sight. Fifty feet from where I stood was a long row of folding tables blocking access to a hall labeled *Ballrooms*. I approached the end table where a middle-aged man in a green velour sports jacket covering a wizard fandom T-shirt lorded over a stack of papers labeled *V-Z*.

"May I help you?"

My stomach bottomed out. "I'm here to see Molly Covington."

He eyed me with a sneer from head to toe.

I pulled at the collar of my jacket, self-conscious about my choice of clothing. I should have worn something from a book fandom.

"So is everyone." He slow-blinked. "Do you have a

ticket?"

His question and condescending tone brought me up short. "No, I don't." I scoured the table, desperate to spot a roll of tickets. "Where can I purchase one?"

The guy huffed. "We're sold out."

"Do you have scalpers at these types of things?"

His head drew back, and he grimaced.

"You know, people who've bought tickets and are selling them outside the venue for profit?" I twisted my head, scanning the sidewalk in front of the doors for people milling about, flicking tickets in their hands.

"No, that kind of thing doesn't happen here, sir."

The wizard man's nasal voice could have passed for parseltongue. I pulled out my wallet and a couple of twenty-dollar bills. "Does this work as a ticket?"

He scowled. "Sir, entrance into the conference for today is three hundred and fifty dollars."

I gaped. The man acted as if my lack of a ticket was somehow a personal offense. "Per person?" I paid less for floor seats at Madison Square Garden.

"No, that price is just for you." He sighed, with an eyeroll. "Of course, it's per person."

I gritted my teeth, my shoulders getting tenser by the minute. "Do you take cards, or do you have an ATM on the premises?" Again, I scanned the lobby. The space held nothing but tables with books and a soda machine in the hall to the left with the restrooms.

Yanking on the lapels of his jacket, the guy puffed out his chest. "We. Are. Sold. Out. If you do not leave, then I will call security."

The man was as stuffy as the air in the building.

"Jared?"

I searched over the wizard guy's shoulder from the

direction where someone called my name. There stood a twenty-something man with a red elastic headband holding back his long, brown, scraggly hair, wearing skinny jeans, a One Direction T-shirt, and, thankfully, a nametag on his hot-pink lanyard. "Fin! Aw, man, I'm so glad to see you."

Molly's cousin approached the table with a smile and shook his head. He placed a hand on my shoulder and squeezed. "Long time no see, Jared."

I winced under his grip. "Yeah, too long." As I pleaded with my eyes for Molly's cousin to have pity on me, I felt sweat trickling down my back.

Fin spied the forty dollars in my grip that I'd failed to use as a bribe. Shaking my hand, he palmed the money. "I'm so glad you showed up—*finally*."

His inflection screamed he believed I should have come for Molly months ago. Fin was right; I should have.

He flashed a challenging stare and leaned toward the guy behind the table. "Sorry about the confusion, Dennis. He's part of Molly Covington's team."

The convention worker's face pinched, but he waved me past the line of tables without a second glance.

I felt like I could finally breathe as I followed Fin under the north staircase behind a sponsor display.

He spun on his heel. "What are you doing here, man?"

The sweat on my back froze. "Please, Fin, I need to talk to Molly."

"Dude, I get you didn't like Molly calling you by the wrong name. But you had your chance. These last six months have been rough." Fin's last word came out in a deep vibrato. "She's only just finding the courage to move forward." He threw up his hands. "I can't let you barge into her conference and undo all her hard work."

I clenched my fists, grinding my teeth. He had to—I just needed to convince him. "I get it, Fin. I really do, and thank you for being her support." I swallowed hard and wiped my damp palms on my jeans. "But I love her, too. And shouldn't *she* be the one to decide if I stay?" I hoped my sincerity showed in my expression.

As he crossed his arms and tapped his foot, a muscle in Fin's jaw twitched.

"Please? Let her decide?" I could beg—Molly was worth it.

He tied his hair into a man bun with the red headband. "You're right. You're right."

"I am?" I let out a breath, feeling the tension leave my shoulders. "Great! Where can I find her?" I was amped like a sprinter at the starting line.

"*Ballroom E.*" He slapped my shoulder.

I winced at his force.

"If this backfires, I had nothing to do with it." Fin mimed washing his hands.

"Sure." I scanned the line of rooms, impatient.

"Good luck, man."

"Thanks!" I called back, darting toward the ballrooms. But when I reached the end of the long, carpeted hall, I hadn't seen a *Ballroom E. Damn!* Her room must be on the second floor. *Thanks for the heads-up, Fin.* Instead of heading to the main staircases in the lobby, I slammed through the metal door marked *Stairs* meant for emergency exits. I vaulted up the musty steps two at a time and yanked the second-floor entrance open. A large, gold *E* sat above the white double doors just off to my right. *Jackpot!* I smoothed my hair and straightened my jacket. Opening the door, I pushed slowly, striving to make as little noise as possible. I had no idea what would lie on the other side. My heart stuttered.

Molly stood on the platform, looking magnificent in a black pencil skirt and plum blouse. The contrast with her beautiful, light-brown skin was sexy as hell. She had a microphone in her hand, but when her gaze locked with mine, she froze.

The large, well-lit room with a tall, coffered ceiling and colorful, ornate carpet lay between me and the stage. Rows upon rows of occupied chairs split the room in half, and everyone in them turned to see what took Molly's focus away from her presentation.

Murmurs erupted around the room.

I gathered all my control not to run onto the stage and take Molly in my arms, but I'd already made a scene, so I stood by the door.

"Jared?" Molly's voice strained around my name as it echoed through the mic for everyone to hear.

My stomach knotted, and I raised a hand in a tentative wave.

"You shouldn't be here." Molly's smile wavered with her voice, her attention glued to where I stood.

My face went cold. I deserved whatever insults she wanted to throw. *Take it like a man, Jared. Take it like a man.*

Chapter 41

Molly

As I called Jared out, I could hear my heartbeat in my ears, and my lungs constricted. *What is he doing here?* I'd conceded I'd never see him again. The implications of his unexpected appearance splintered my heart. I distanced my mouth from the microphone so the audience wouldn't hear my ragged breathing.

A fellow author crept forward and covered my microphone with an age-spotted hand. "What's going on, Molly? Do I need to call security?"

Albert's rusty, whispered words sucked me back into the moment. The distraction allowed me to tear my focus from Jared's face to his. "What?"

"Do I need to have security escort that gentleman out?" The bespectacled author nodded toward Jared.

Panic seized my chest. "No!" The word came out too loud.

The audience grew restless.

Jared had to stay because I wanted answers. No, I *needed* answers. But I was in the middle of my presentation. These people had paid a lot of money to be here, and storming off the stage to sort out my private life wouldn't be fair.

"Molly?" My co-panelist nudged my arm.

The tweed of his jacket scratched my elbow. I

glanced again at Jared. Waiting wasn't one of my strong suits, but making everyone happy in my current situation seemed impossible. Unless… "I'm so sorry, Albert. Where are my manners?" I faced the love of my life, swallowing my nerves. "Jared, would you like to come and assist me with my presentation?" I flung out an arm and beckoned him with a wave. "We were just discussing inspiration and muses." As if being on stage was the last thing he wanted to do in the world, Jared fastened the button on his sports coat.

Coming from the back of the room, he strode toward the small stage, focusing anywhere but on me.

Damn, he looked good in his jeans-and-black-blazer combo. Every movement Jared made was familiar—awakening the pieces of my heart that had gone dormant since the day he left our Vegas hotel room. My emotions betrayed me, and hope ignited in my chest. Yesterday, I was determined to move on, but now everything I'd wished for over the last six months strolled down the aisle.

Jared hopped up the two steps onto the raised platform. Taking my hand, he leaned close.

I inhaled a whiff of his woody, citrus scent, and my stomach clenched. The dark cloud over my head dispersed just being near him again. My brain and heart were at war, sending a jumble of emotions to pulse through my veins—heartache, hope, anger, love, and fear.

"Molly, can we go somewhere and talk?" Jared's lips brushed my ear.

I fought the shivers wracking my spine. Mustering every ounce of courage I had, I deftly pushed him away and covered the microphone. "Help me with this, and

I'll talk anywhere you want." Thankfully, my voice hadn't wavered.

Jared swallowed hard and nodded.

A warmth filled my chest seeing he appeared nervous, too. "Can someone get Jared a mic—?"

"Got it!" As Fin sprinted toward the stage, his voice rang across the room. Nabbing a microphone from one of the other panel members, Fin passed it to Jared with a wink. He leaped back onto the floor, then flashed his VIP badge at a gangly guy in khakis and navy polo on the front row.

Rising from the seat, the guy marched to find an empty spot in the back with a scowl.

I smiled at Fin. *Thank goodness he's here.*

He took the man's seat and shot me finger guns.

Giving my cousin a nod, I squared my shoulders and faced the crowd. "I'm sorry for the disruption, folks. Let me introduce you to Jared Washington."

A few members of the crowd clapped.

Jared held up a halting hand.

The room fell silent.

"Actually"—he paused—"my real name is *Evan* Jared Washington." He dipped his chin and glanced from under his lashes.

Oh my gosh! I knew Jared hadn't been using his real name, but I also didn't think he would be this honest—especially in front of an audience. "Okay, this is Evan." I presented him again with a wave of a hand.

He shook his head. "I prefer Jared, but I didn't want any more misunderstandings between us." He met my gaze.

My heart stopped. What was Jared implying? Had I misunderstood his feelings? Had he misunderstood mine? I had no idea, but I *could* find out by working my questions into an impromptu interview. "Okay then, moving on." I addressed the crowd. "I'm sure many of you read the interview I gave for my upcoming book, *Men in Books Aren't Better*, and well, I did have a muse." My heart contracted, and I gestured in Jared's direction. "This is him."

A buzz rippled through the crowd.

The side of Jared's mouth pulled up, showing off his dimple.

My body double-crossed me with a wave of desire. "Jared, why don't you tell them how that came to be?"

"Of course." He moistened his lips. "I met Molly when I used to work as a companion at Plus One."

My breath caught, and my hands trembled, shaking the microphone.

"You wrote saying you wanted to hire me as research for your romance novel."

I wasn't sure I'd heard him right. Reaching out, I placed a hand on his arm. "You no longer work as a companion?"

Jared shook his head. "No, I don't. You were my last contract. I now own the Manhattan location of the Sky's the Limit adventure franchise."

You did it! Jared had achieved his goal. My megawatt smile upon learning *I* was his last client could have powered the Las Vegas strip. What I interpreted as unfiltered amusement crossed Jared's expression, and I pinched my forearm to control my elation.

"But to continue with your original question, you'd asked me to pretend we were a couple who'd met online and were preparing to meet in person for the first time." Jared stared out over the audience. "From Miss

Covington's first email, I knew this"—he motioned between himself and me with a thumb—"would be fun."

Quiet chuckles echoed from the audience.

My core heated. "Are you saying, Jared, that our time together differed from your previous contracts?" *Please let me be right.*

He flashed his dimple again. "Yes, very. You were the first client who treated me like I was a real person whose opinions and viewpoints mattered."

My throat tightened, and I faced the onlookers. "I remembered the first time he'd shared that information; I was heartbroken." I placed a hand on my chest, feeling the staccato rhythm of my heart.

"It was hard to admit."

Jared's gaze bored into mine as if peering into my soul, incinerating my insides, and muddling my brain.

He turned to face the audience. "Until recently, because of everything I'd been through, I'd become pretty cynical. Being a part of and witnessing so many bad relationships can wear on you after a while." He rubbed the back of his neck and glanced in my direction before returning his attention to the crowd. "But my views have changed, and now, I believe relationships can be partnerships. That as a couple, two people can make each other better. Love is possible."

Was Jared serious? Had his view on love and relationships changed? Was that why he was here—to tell me he wanted to be with me? I swallowed the lump in my throat. "You do?" My words came out strangled.

Jared's gaze focused on mine as he stood with his left hand in his pocket. "Yes. Very much so." He took a step.

Now, he was only a couple of feet away, and my fragile heart thumped a jagged beat. I had to fight back the hope threatening to fill my chest. "Then"—my voice would have been inaudible if I hadn't held a microphone—"how would you handle a client who'd fallen in love with you?" I bit my lip and waited, concentrating on keeping my unsteady knees from giving out.

Just like he had back in Las Vegas, Jared withdrew his hand from his pocket and tugged on my chin, freeing my mouth. "If I had a client I cared about fall in love with me, I would mess it up completely by saying all the wrong things and misinterpreting the situation. I would let my fears override my desires, and I would push away the one woman who'd truly seen me for who I was." He caressed my cheek. "I'd break her heart—along with my own—because of my stupid pride and misguided beliefs. I'd spend months agonizing over how much I missed her and craved to have her back in my life while suffering through the delusion and torture of thinking she'd never loved me." He swallowed. "Then, when I'd learned I'd been wrong and she might still have feelings, I'd make a fool of myself, barge into her presentation, and throw myself at her mercy." The muscles in Jared's neck strained. "I'd be willing to beg if she would just give me one more chance to show her how much I love her. Because I didn't want to go one more day—no, not one more minute—without her in my life."

I was a puddle. In front of everyone, Jared just admitted he loved me, he was sorry, and he wanted me in his life. Struggling to see him past my tears, I held back from throwing myself into his arms. I needed to be sure I wasn't just getting caught up in the moment. After all, hadn't I agreed to go out with Jensen yesterday? "What would you want her to do?"

Jared brushed the moisture from my cheek with a thumb. "I would hope, more than anything, she'd forgive me and allow me the opportunity never to hurt her again."

I clutched his hand and held it to my face. Blinking away my tears, I searched Jared's eyes. His speech was beautiful, and in my heart, I yearned to believe every word.

A crease formed between Jared's brows.

Pinning my other arm to my side, I fought the urge to smooth the wrinkle away. I would *not* allow myself to touch his beautiful face—not yet—not until I'd thought through all the implications. I examined my mess of feelings. Could I do this? Would a relationship with Jared work? Searching within myself, I pictured what walking away would look like. A pain so deep I almost doubled over pierced me right through. I couldn't say no—my heart had already decided. "I think she'd give you that chance"—the microphone struggled to catch my whisper—"because there was nothing to forgive."

"Kiss him!"

"Kiss him!"

"Kiss him!"

Fin threw his voice and yelled in different octaves.

The rest of the crowd joined his chant.

As I peered at Jared, I laughed through my tears, tingling from head to toe.

He stepped forward until less than an inch away. “Well, we don’t want to disappoint your fans, do we?”

Hell no!

Chapter 42

Jared

My rom-com moment with Molly concluded her presentation, leaving my chest tight. Interrupting and making a fool of myself on stage wasn't my intention. But I'd refused to pass on the opportunity to win Molly back—no way, hence my public declaration. However, now Molly's lecture was over, and she and I were standing just outside room *E*, everyone wanted my attention to rehash what had happened.

The crowd, primarily other romance writers, had loved how the interview unfolded and dubbed me the new Hugh Grant. Molly, however, wasn't thrilled about all my new, adoring fans and hung on my arm anytime anyone approached—even glaring at the last retreating figure who'd kept her hand on my bicep during our entire conversation. I didn't mind her jealousy, though, and I couldn't stop smiling.

"Did she have to touch you while giving you that compliment?"

Even Molly's scowl was adorable.

"I mean, come on, whatever happened to personal space? Or boundaries?" She mimed a box around herself.

"Are you saying you don't like people invading your personal space?" I trailed my fingers up her left arm and along the part of her exposed collarbone peeking out from under her blouse's wide neckline. Desire surged in my veins. "Am I too close?" I nudged the small of her back with a thumb, pressing our torsos together, my mood as bright as the fluorescent lights overhead.

Molly's breath caught. Her gaze focused on my mouth.

She couldn't disguise the longing in her eyes. Her expression warmed my insides.

"Invade all you want. I surrender. In fact"—she wound her arms around my neck—"I would say you're not close enough."

Her words were breathy against my lips. I leaned in, savoring the soft feel of her mouth against mine, and deepened the kiss.

Molly tore away with a gasp, covering her mouth with a hand. "Oh my gosh, I have a date this Friday."

I reeled back on my heels, going cold. "I'm sorry, what?"

She shook her head and pinched her eyes shut. "Friday. I'm supposed to have a date."

I let my jaw drop, unable to process her words.

"Yesterday, before all this"—Molly indicated me and the ballroom—"my mother set me up with this guy, Jensen."

My throat dried. I took another step back. "I'm sorry. I…" My cheeks burned, and I couldn't even meet Molly's gaze. "I just assumed after reading the interview in the magazine that…" *That what? I could just step back into Molly's life?* Sure, she'd said she'd forgiven me back on stage, but mercy didn't mean she'd take me back. Or that she'd waited. I was too late.

Someone else had come into her life. *I am such an idiot.*

Molly put a hand over my mouth. "Stop." She rubbed my cheek, tracing my scar with a thumb. "It's fine. I'll cancel."

I pulled my brows together. "If—" I took a deep breath, steeling my heart. "If you've moved on, I'd understand."

She marched her fingers up my chest. "While I appreciate the sentiment, my heart's stuck on you." Molly stood on tiptoes and gave me a quick kiss. "You're cute when you're jealous."

I grinned, her comment echoing my thoughts from a moment ago. Focusing on Molly through my lashes, I drank in her radiant smile, knowing I'd put it there and branded it into my brain. I wanted to make my relationship with her official—sooner rather than later. "Sorry, I want to be the bigger man." I took Molly's face in my hands. "But the mental image of you with someone else kills me. I'd be willing to step aside, if that's what you wanted." I struggled to get the words out, but I meant them. "Your happiness is what's most important." *Although I'd want to kill him.*

Molly pulled me close. "*You* make me happy."

I kissed her again. After savoring the moment, I reluctantly broke away and rested my forehead against hers. "Now what?"

"Well"—she took my hands and held them against her heart—"I should probably call and cancel Friday. I was supposed to be his plus one at an awards ceremony." Molly's lips screwed to the side. "I feel awful canceling last minute."

I raised my eyebrows. "You were supposed to be

his plus one?"

Molly nodded with a smirk.

Laughter burst from my chest at the irony. "I'm sure I could help you find him a replacement." *It will be my pleasure*. "Do you want me to call Erica?"

"Oh! Brilliant—just not, Rachael." She held her hands palms out. "Not because I have anything against her, but I'd rather have someone a little more removed from our situation."

I nodded. "No problem." Considering Molly's only interaction with my friend had been negative, I didn't blame her. I jutted my chin toward the stairwell. "Why don't you call your Mr. Friday and tell him we'll have someone lined up?" *And that you're off limits*. "Then, later tonight, you can help me choose his perfect date."

"Sounds like fun." As she pulled out her phone and stepped away, Molly smiled, then turned toward the stairs.

Fin strutted out of the ballroom. He held the door for a petite blonde in rolled skinny jeans and a navy blazer, juggling a laptop. He leaned in close, his lips at her ear, moving in a hum of murmured conversation. When Fin's gaze met mine, he broke away. "I'll text you later." He wiggled his phone with a wink. "We can pick up where we left off."

The blonde giggled, practically floating toward the main staircase at the front of the building.

Fin stopped beside me and tilted his head in Molly's direction. "What's going on over there?"

I didn't want to tell him, but I couldn't avoid it. Squinting out the bright sunlit windows, I heaved out a breath. "She's canceling her date for Friday."

"Oh yeah! Jensen." Fin rocked on his heels with

his hands in his pockets and stared at Molly's back. "The pediatrician. He's a great guy. A fan, too. The kind of guy who could give my cousin a secure future and treat her how she deserves. While your little show back there on stage was commendable"—he thumbed over his shoulder—"I still have to ask, can you be that guy, Jared?"

Straightening to my full height, I squared my shoulders. I couldn't blame Fin for his defensiveness. Being Molly's best friend and her cousin, I was sure he was privy to all the gory details of what had happened back in Las Vegas. "That's my goal, Fin. I wouldn't have come here if those weren't my intentions. Molly deserves to be happy, and I want to spend the rest of my life ensuring she is." The thought made my heart soar.

Fin peeked from the corner of his eye. "The rest of your life, huh?"

I faced him head-on. "Every damn day."

Chapter 43

Molly

I stood at the top of the stairs overlooking the convention center lobby and tapped on Jensen's number. He answered on the second ring.

"This is Dr. Edwards?"

"Hey, Jensen. It's me, Molly." I chewed on my thumbnail. I could hear the crackle of his smile through the phone. *Why did he have to sound so excited?*

"I know it's you; I've already added you to my contacts."

The knife in my back twisted, but I reminded myself I wasn't just canceling. I'd called with a plan. "About Friday…"

"Ugh. I know what you're about to say."

"No, no, no." I held a halting hand, even though he couldn't see. "It's not what you think."

"You're coming on Friday?"

"Well, no—"

"So, I was right?"

"Also, no." I shifted my weight from one foot to the other. *I feel like such a jerk. He'll probably never buy another one of my books.*

"What are you saying, Molly? I'm so confused right now."

I took a deep breath. "I'm unable to make our date

on Friday, but"—I drew out the word—"I have a proposition." I noticed Jared talking to my cousin and smiled.

"I have no idea where this is going."

Jensen's chuckle sounded forced, but I persevered. "I have a friend—"

"Oh no, not a friend blind date."

"Not exactly." I shook my hair behind my shoulder. "At least, not how you're thinking." I leaned against the smooth, plaster wall. "As I was saying, I know a friend. He works—or, I guess, he used to work—for a company called Plus One." Heat flared through my veins and my stomach somersaulted. "They specialize in providing dates, or companions, for important events."

"You want to set me up with a prostitute?"

I knew that's where his head would go—that's where mine went when I started this endeavor—but I couldn't think of a better way to explain Plus One's services. "No, the company's not like that. They provide *companions*."

"Molly, I'm not desperate; I know what the word companion means. That's worse than a pity date."

Irritation laced his tone, sending another wave of guilt through my insides. "I'm not pitying you, and she wouldn't be a sex worker. She'd simply be someone to make sure you wouldn't attend an award event—where you're one of the main nominations—alone."

"Thanks, but no thanks. I'd rather go stag."

"Come on, Jensen." I hated how whiny my voice sounded. "We both know that's not an option. If you don't find someone to take my place on Friday, you can't deny our mothers will."

"I know some women I can ask."

Putting a hand on my hip, I huffed. "Yeah, and with this late notice, the women will know they weren't your first choice."

"Fine." Jensen sighed. "You've got a point there."

Hope bloomed inside my chest. "Plus One is a respectable company, and all the companions are gorgeous. They have a no-sex policy and a non-disclosure policy." My words came out rushed. "Your date would dote all over you, act adoring yet professional, and look beautiful on your arm. Please don't say no; I feel awful about canceling. It would be my treat." I waited for an answer but was met with silence. "You'd never have to see her again, and no one would be the wiser." I hoped I sounded convincing.

"You're positive our mothers wouldn't find out?"

"Not if *you* don't tell them." A considerable pause silenced the line.

"Fine. What do you need from me?"

Jared broke away from Fin and sauntered in my direction.

A smile spread across my face, and I shot Jared a thumbs-up. "Just text me where you'd like to meet her."

Epilogue

Molly—one year later

Standing on the coastline, Jared looked unfairly sexy in his wetsuit, life vest, and helmet. Even the oar in his hand did a number on my insides. "I promise, babe, in the fifteen years I've kayaked on the President Channel, I've yet to see a shark." I beckoned him with a wave. "You'd have a better chance of getting attacked by an orca."

Jared smirked and took a step back from the water. "You're not helping your case, Molly."

I cut through the waves as I paddled closer to the shore, cool drips of water falling into my lap. "Would tying our kayaks together make you feel better?"

"So, we can both die?" His eyebrows shot to his hairline.

Panic laced his tone, and I couldn't help the laugh that escaped my lips. How could someone so strong and adventurous in every other aspect of his life be so scared of such a low probability? "Come on, Jared. You're the one who wanted to try this. Jack's getting burnt out."

The Sky's the Limit Seattle location had taken off over the past year. Jared commuted back and forth from New York for the first couple of months after the West Coast franchise opened until he found someone he trusted to manage his East Coast store. Having Jared relocate to Seattle, I felt like a weight had lifted from my shoulders. The long-distance thing had been hard.

Now, Jared had his hands full out here on the West Coast. His kayaking tours around Orca's Island had become one of the company's most popular excursions. So far, Jared only had one employee who could teach kayaking, Jack, and he was overworked. I'd offered to help by leading a few tours myself, but sweetly, Jared refused. He didn't want to take away from my writing time.

"You're right." Jared's shoulders dropped.

Like a skittish cat, he placed one foot on his kayak and steadied the boat. "There you go, you got it." I hoped I sounded encouraging rather than patronizing.

He pulled in his second leg and sat with lightning speed. Jared threw out his hands, steadying his kayak.

Once the wobbling subsided, he paddled across the waves in my direction like a kid on a bike for the first time. Seeing him close enough, I grabbed his boat. "That wasn't so bad, was it?"

Jared glared, gripping my seat with white knuckles, and growled.

A zing ran along my spine, and I tied his boat to the side of mine in tandem. "Here, just close your eyes and feel the waves. I'll keep you steady."

Through gritted teeth, Jared did as I instructed.

I stifled a laugh. "Relax and trust me."

"If you weren't the breadwinner, maybe I would ask you to quit your day job so I could hire you." He squinted from the corner of his eye. "You're good."

"The water is soothing, right?" A warm gust of wind tickled the stray hairs around my face.

He scoffed. "I wouldn't go that far."

"Whatever, you love it." I pushed his shoulder.

His panicked widened eyes flashed to the knotted rope between the kayaks.

But his boat wasn't going anywhere. I steadied him. "Are you ready to venture farther out?"

"Because I love you and trust you, I'll say *yes*."

Those words still sent butterflies to my stomach, despite the year we'd been together. I couldn't imagine my life without him anymore.

Jared took a few minutes to coordinate his paddling with mine, but after a while, he appeared to get the hang of kayaking. The two of us headed out to sea.

I kept our conversations to a minimum because of the look of concentration on Jared's face, which gave me time to reflect on how much my career path had changed. The switch in genre had gone well, aided, I had no doubt, by Jared's appearance at the conference in New York. Interviewers were fascinated by our real-life love story compared to my novel because men in books *weren't* better than Jared. I had the real deal. Thanks to him, I had plenty of material to draw from for my latest manuscript. I paralleled the shores of Orca's Island beside Jared, and I couldn't keep the pride off my face.

"What are you smiling about?" Jared rested his oar on his lap, staring at my lips.

"You."

"If I didn't think it would cause me to fall out of this kayak, I'd kiss you right now." His cheek pulled in a half-grin, showing off his dimple.

He was so damn sexy. "Maybe we should head back to shore so you can make that happen." I raised my eyebrows in a silent question and gripped my paddle, eager to thrust it into the water.

Jared held out a hand. “Hold on.” He undid the pocket on the front of his lifejacket, pulling out a small, black velvet box.

My chest tightened, and tears stung my eyes. *Is that what I think it is?*

“Now, this isn’t the actual ring, Molly—the real one is back at the cabin. I had enough sense not to bring an expensive piece of jewelry when I was still so unsteady on the water. But I knew if I found the courage to get out here, I had to seize the opportunity. I’ve wanted to do this for weeks.” With shaky movements, Jared opened the box and met my gaze. “I want to be your plus one forever.” He cleared the roughness from his throat. “Molly, will you marry me?”

I stared at the gunmetal-gray silicone ring, my heart overflowing with love. “Yes. Yes, I will.”

A word about the authors…

We're a co-writing team of best friends who share imaginary worlds. Lisa-Marie Potter (BIPOC) is a mom of four who grew up in Nottingham, England, and now resides in Alaska with her husband and golden retriever. Amanda Nelson grew up in Maryland and moved to Arizona, where she attended college and currently lives with her husband and four kids. Both women are members of the Author's Guild, belong to a Manuscript Academy Podcast featured writing and critique group, and have a Twitter following of over 12,000. Each of their other social media platforms, Instagram and TikTok. have a combined following of over 1,700. They attend writing conferences, Manuscript Academy classes, and are beta reading ninjas. They also review books on their blog, hike the Olympic National Park, and fight over the same fictional crushes. NelsonPotter.com

Thank you for purchasing
this publication of The Wild Rose Press, Inc.

For questions or more information
contact us at
info@thewildrosepress.com.

The Wild Rose Press, Inc.
www.thewildrosepress.com

Printed in the USA
CPSIA information can be obtained
at www.ICGtesting.com
CBHW070844300924
15131CB00001B/7

9 781509 258789